DEMON WRATH

Two points of orange glared like coals from the darkness; starlight traced a hooded figure with folded, six-fingered hands. Jaric hissed through his teeth. Even as he grabbed for his dagger he knew that defense was futile. The creature confronting him was Llondian, demon and enemy of mankind.

It regarded the human boy with no flicker of emotion, pupils slitted against irises of burning gold. *'Keeper of the Keys, you may not pass; nor will your bond to Anskiere be completed until you accept the heritage of the Firelord who fathered you.'*

"No," said Jaric. "I must pass. There is no other choice for me." Sweating with fear, the boy raised his blade . . .

KEEPER OF THE KEYS

Praise for Book One of the Cycle of Fire— STORMWARDEN . . .

"Outstanding . . . an excellent and absorbing tale."

—*Andre Norton*

"There's high magic here and, more importantly, real people and fine writing."

—*Lynn Abbey*

"A great natural storyteller!"

—*L. Sprague de Camp*

JANNY WURTS

KEEPER OF THE KEYS

BOOK TWO OF THE CYCLE OF FIRE

ACE BOOKS, NEW YORK

This book is an Ace
original edition, and
has never been previously
published.

KEEPER OF THE KEYS

An Ace Book / published by arrangement with
the author

PRINTING HISTORY
Ace edition / August 1988

ISBN: 0-441-43275-1

Ace Books are published by The Berkley Publishing Group,
200 Madison Avenue, New York, New York 10016.
The name "Ace" and the "A"
logo are trademarks belonging to
Charter Communications, Inc.
PRINTED IN THE UNITED STATES OF AMERICA

10 9 8 7 6 5 4 3 2 1

Acknowledgments

Special thanks to:
My youngest sister, for proofing,
and two extraordinary friends,
an author from the West Coast and a sailor from the East,
for support and suggestions respectively.
Lastly, to the friend no longer living,
who reviewed the preliminary draft.

to Shadowfane

Northsea

Wrecker's Bay

Clover's Warren

Felwaithe

Kierkforest

Murieton

Canyon Lake

Riftwater

Kisburn

Eastplain

Royal Palace

Cliffhaven

Mainstrait

Elrinfaer Tower

Merk's Point

Terin Sea

Elrinfaer

Telshire

Cael's Falls

Mhored Kara

Deshforest

KEEPER OF THE KEYS

Prologue

Chilly wind slapped the swells into whitecaps off the west shores of Elrinfaer, where, a lone fleck of color under frowning cliffs, a fishing sloop spread tanbark sails beneath the leaden gray of the overcast. She was an aged craft, patched and stained with the wear of her labors, but now her nets hung slack. Her occupants, two brothers, leaned idle on the landward rail. Grizzled and gray and dour, they squinted shoreward at a dark bundle of cloth sprawled on the sand above the tide mark.

The younger one spat into the sea. "It's a boy, that. Flotsam don't wear boots, not that I ever saw."

"You say?" The sibling grunted in disgust. "Only last week, you missed the buoy marking the headland. Near to run us aground for that, and now you claim you got eyesight!" Still, intrigued, he did not order the boat put about. "If that draggle o' cloth is human, I'll give a week's coppers, and buy you a beer a night."

"Ye'll lose, then." The younger brother laughed, and sprang to haul in the sheets. Dearly loving a wager, he braced himself against the shuddering heave of the boat as wind-tossed canvas thundered taut. "If he's drowned, I get his rings."

The elder brother caught the worn tiller. "We'll see." And he turned the sloop, which reeked of cod, and sent her dashing in a heel for the beach head.

Lashed ashore by a rampaging flood of surf, the craft's sturdy timbers grated and grounded against sand. The elder brother leaped the thwart, his callused, twine-scarred hands braced to steady the prow. The younger brother vaulted after and, kicking sand from his wet boots, stumped up the beach to determine the winner of the bet.

He bent over the dark lump by the tide line, sending gulls flapping seaward. Tentatively he touched, then drew back.

1

Impatient, the brother by the boat bellowed after him. "Well? Who's doing the buying this week?"

The answer came back, subdued against the boom and echo of breakers under the cliffs. "It is a boy." The younger fisherman paused, and slowly stood straight on the shore. "A sick one."

The elder brother cursed, the exhilaration of the wager abruptly gone sour. Now out of decency they must take on a passenger; sick, even dying, the wretch would need food and water, and the sloop's hold was not yet full enough to pay even the cost of reprovisioning. "Better bring him in," he shouted. "And the beer copper goes for his bread."

The younger of the two fishermen shrugged philosophically, then lifted the limp body from the sand. His find proved to be slight, black-haired, and dressed in the remains of fine clothing. The eyes opened in delirium were blue, and the hands ravaged by what looked like burns.

"He probably eats like a flea," the younger brother muttered as he arrived, breathless, and deposited his burden in the sloop's bow. "Weighs little enough."

But the elder brother remained unsympathetic. He jerked his head, anxious now to be away from shores that were deserted, ruins of the once fortunate kingdom of Elrinfaer.

"And anyway, you have the sporting instincts of a grandmother," groused the younger. He set his shoulder to the sloop and shoved her ungainly prow seaward. As she slipped, grating, into deeper waters, the boy in the bow groaned in the throes of fever.

"Would you have left him, then?" accused the younger, bothered at last by his brother's silence. When he received no answer, he shrugged; the castaway wore court clothes, badly torn, but the dirt on the tunic was fresh. Perhaps he would have wealthy relatives who would reward his rescuers for his safe return.

Betrayal

By evening, they gathered in the great hall on Cliffhaven, a rough-mannered crowd of sea captains, sailhands, and men at arms. All were exiles, lawfully condemned as thieves or murderers by the Free Isles' Alliance or the outlying kingdoms; except one, a slight, black-haired girl, almost lost in the brocade chair where she sat with her feet tucked up. Her arms were sunburned and briar-scratched, her nose peeling; but the robes she wore had the pearly sheen of a dreamweaver trained by the Vaere. For that reason, the bearded captain who wended through the press of beer-drinking companions approached with guarded respect.

Jostled by celebrants, sailors with silver-hooped earlobes, and officers still wearing mail, he gained the relative peace of the corner. There the captain set his tankard aside. He had been assigned the task of ensuring the enchantress's comfort, and at present the girl wore a troubled frown. He had to yell over the noise; immediately he regretted that his shout sounded gruffer than he wished. "Taen Dreamweaver?"

At her name she looked around, pale eyes enormous under the shadow of her brows. Her age was eighteen, but seemed less. "Jaric isn't here."

"No? Are you certain?" Surprised the boy should be gone, the captain stroked the knife at his belt out of habit. He echoed the girl's concern as he scanned the crowd in search of the sole surviving heir of the sorcerer Ivain Firelord.

The victory celebration had been organized hard on the heels of war. The timbers of the main door still slanted, singed and blackened and half-torn from their hinges by a barrage of enemy sorcery. The crannies between revelers were stacked with broken furnishings, upholstery bristling with arrows. Men could not yet be spared from the labor of repairing defense works to clear the hall of wreckage, and the Kielmark, who ruled this den of renegades, was never a man to pause for

3

niceties. Abetted by Taen Dreamweaver's talents, his garrison had just repulsed attack by an armada that included demons. By his orders, the survivors would have their chance to release their aftermath of tension, and to mourn the loss of dead comrades; but only tonight. Tomorrow captains, crews, and men at arms must be fit once more for duty.

The atmosphere was predictably boisterous, with arguments and slangs and bouts of arm-wrestling compounding into a crescendo of noise. Meticulously patient, the captain sorted through the motley press of renegades, all armed, some bandaged, and most laughing and expansive with drink. Yet from one end of the hall to the other, where the bodies of senseless sailors snored off their excesses in a heap, his efforts yielded no glimpse of the tousled blond head of Jaric.

Nearby, someone banged the pommel of his knife on a tabletop, denouncing the careless pitch of a cluster of singers. The captain winced, unsure whether dreamweavers cared for obscenities. He glanced back to the girl and found her worried gaze still upon him. "You searched?" he asked, referring to her Vaere-trained powers, which could trace the mind and memories of any man she chose with little more effort than thought.

"No." As if the question were painful to her, Taen knotted nervous fingers in her lap. "I don't have to. Jaric has gone to the ice cliffs."

The captain sucked in his breath. "Kielmark'll be stark tied. Better tell him now." Purposefully he recovered his tankard, his intent to steer toward the end of the room where the revelers pressed thickest, and the great booming laughter of the Sovereign Lord of Cliffhaven wafted over the lesser din of the crowd.

"Corley, no," said Taen, unexpectedly calling the captain by name. But if her powers of cognition were uncanny, the hand she laid on his arm to restrain was human, and sorrowfully thin. "I'll find Jaric, trust me. Don't risk what we both know will happen if the Kielmark discovers him gone."

"Kordane's Fires!" swore the captain. But she spoke sense, this enchantress with the eyes of a child. The Lord of Cliffhaven maintained sovereignty over the criminals who served him through wily cunning and a distrust that brooked no exceptions. Though only a boy, as Firelord's heir Jaric aroused the Kielmark's suspicion in dangerous measure, for even the finest fleets and fortifications in Keithland were useless against he potential of a sorcerer's power. Corley looked at the Dreamweaver, assessing, and saw by the set of her jaw that she would stop him reporting if he insisted; Vaerish sorceries made her capable. Defeated, he tipped his head heavenward, his words almost too soft to be heard above the noise. "Girl, on my life and manhood, I didn't hear you say that."

He glanced back to find the enchantress already going, her silver-gray robe an oddity amid leather leggings, studded baldrics, and the plainer linens of the sailhands. Corley watched, unsettled, as she crossed the crowded hall. The most hard-bitten fighters in Keithland parted readily to let her by, some drunk and argumentative, but all saluting her passage with a sincerity rarely seen on their scarred and sea-tanned faces. The Kielmark had made no secret of the facts: without the Dreamweaver's help, Cliffhaven would have fallen to King Kisburn's army, and his demons sworn as allies would have spared no lives in their quest of vengeance against humanity.

Taen slipped between the bronzed bulk of a quartermaster and a sailor with missing teeth. Both raised their tankards in her honor, and as she vanished into the hallway, Corley silently longed to be elsewhere. The situation was a right mess; the Dreamweaver had defied her Vaerish masters to stay and defend Cliffhaven. No mortal understood the extent of her peril by doing so, but the Kielmark had sworn to remedy the lapse with all speed and set her on a southbound ship no later than dawn next day. Added to that, Jaric's hasty departure was the height of bad timing. Angry now that the boy could not at least have asked for escort, Corley's fist tightened upon his tankard. To leave the King of Pirates ignorant when two under his protection presently traipsed through the wilds of his domain in the dead of night bordered upon an act of insanity. Corley had served on Cliffhaven long enough to learn what his life was worth; he took a hefty swallow of beer, and decided precipitously not to honor the Dreamweaver's request.

But even as he strode forward to inform his master of the girl's departure, her dream-touch cut his mind. *'Don't!'*

Corley froze between steps and cursed. She watched, then, with the unknowable talents of her kind; her sending carried awareness that she would stop him by force if she must. Having no wish to test himself against sorcery, the captain sat carefully in the brocade chair left empty by her departure. He laughed, very quietly and not without humor. Then, much against his careful nature, he lifted his tankard and quaffed the

contents to the dregs. If the Dreamweaver chose to follow the
son of Ivain Firelord to the ice cliffs that imprisoned the
Stormwarden of Elrinfaer, at least one captain in Cliffhaven's
great hall decided he wanted no part of the matter. With luck
and a little time, he could arrange to be drunk to the edge of
prostration when the Sovereign Lord of Cliffhaven discovered
both enchantress and sorcerer's heir gone from his party without leave.

Outside, a damp salt wind scoured the bailey. Clouds hazed
the moon's setting crescent, and gusts off the harbor blew
sharp with the scent of impending rain. Taen paused in the
archway, blinking while her eyes adjusted from the candle-
brilliance of indoors to the dimmer flicker of torchlight.
Canny enough to be silent, she stifled the flapping hem of her
robe with her hands, and looked carefully for the sentry; rev-
elry on Cliffhaven could never be expected to slacken the
diligence of the Kielmark's patrols. Yet no man waited, spear
in hand, to challenge the girl in the bailey. Empty cobbles
shone wet in the dew, and the ring which normally tethered
the saddled horse lay flat, a steely disc of reflection.

At that, Taen caught her breath. She bent her Dreamweaver's awareness to the stables, and immediately encountered activity. Already guessing the reason, she narrowed
focus, and found the sentry questioning the horse-boy. Between them they would not take long to sort out the fact that
someone not under orders had removed the horse kept saddled
and bridled in the bailey for the Kielmark's emergency use at
any hour of the day or night.

Jaric, thought Taen; she muttered an epithet learned from
the fishwives of Imrill Kand that would have reddened even
the sophisticated ears of Corley, then stepped swiftly out into
the wind. She must hurry before the sentry carried word to the
Kielmark. Pounding, breathless, through the passage to the
horse yard, Taen engaged the talents only recently mastered
under the Vaere. The minds she sought to influence were less
informed, and therefore harder to convince than that of Captain Corley. The bailey sentry was an old hand, well familiar
with the Kielmark's temper; and the horse-boy was native to
Cliffhaven. All through childhood he had seen men hung out
of hand for disobeying orders. Beside that sure punishment, to
him a dreamweaver's sorcery seemed the lesser risk.

Taen crossed abruptly from shadow into torchlight, making

both sentry and horse-boy start. Neither truly saw her for what she was, a small, disheveled girl with trouble marking frown lines on her face. Their eyes took in the silver gray of her robes, and stopped, wary.

"Enchantress," murmured the horse-boy. "Kor's grace, don't bewitch us."

Taen paused, swallowed, and wondered if anyone would ever treat her normally again. "Ivainson Jaric is the key to Keithland's survival." She shifted her regard to the sentry, standing sweating in the light of the stable lanterns with his hands locked around his spear. "The Kielmark and the Firelord's heir must not meet at this time. The boy is distressed, enough to make him careless. He would cross your master, and certainly get himself killed. But if you loan me a mount, I can stop that, and ensure you won't suffer any consequences."

Neither the sentry nor the horse-boy was moved by the promise. The Kielmark's discipline was legend on land and sea, and no man who gainsaid him survived. A tense moment passed, the gusty dark laced through with the distant beat of the sea. Taen gripped her whipping robes, and strove to maintain patience. She would not use compulsion on these two, not unless she was desperate. But when the sentry whirled with a look of stark fear and bolted, she was unequivocally cornered. Her powers answered, reliably, and blanketed the running man's awareness. Between one stride and the next, he pitched forward, to land in a sprawl across the midden.

The horse-boy gasped.

"He's unharmed!" Taen said, and though her skills were still raw and new, she managed to translate awareness of just how unharmed directly into the boy's shocked mind. "Saddle me a mount," she added gently. "And please do believe me when I tell you I can manage the Kielmark's rages."

The horse-boy regarded her skeptically, as if he noticed for the first time that she was not so very much older than he; yet her powers had deceived demons. With a shrug and a shake of his head he turned to do her bidding. Only his attitude of nonchalance was spoiled by the fact that his knees shook.

Taen leaned back against the timbered half door of a stall. Relieved she had not needed to engage her dream-sense a third time, and taxed more than she cared to admit from swaying the sensibilities of Corley, she tried to stop worrying. Around her rose the black granite walls of the stoutest bulwarks in Keithland; surely for a short time more she would be safe.

Tomorrow would see her on a ship bound for the Isle of the Vaere, only five days past the date imposed by the fey master who had trained her. Even if demons knew of her existence, they could hardly act so swiftly.

In the dark at her back, a horse snorted. Taen started forward, and barely managed not to cry out as a warm muzzle bumped amiably against her arm. She backed away, just as the horse-boy reappeared with not one but two mounts on a leading rein. The smaller he handed wordlessly to Taen; the other rolled eyes showing nasty rings of white. War-trained, it sidled as the boy tugged its headstall and expertly directed it through the passage, to the tether ring in the bailey. Taen sensed his preoccupied thought. Granting an enchantress a mount was perhaps excusable, but if the Kielmark chanced to ask for the saddled horse and found no animal ready, his great sword would answer the offense before he spent breath with questions.

Taen faced the blaze-faced mare she was to ride, and preoccupation with the horse-boy's problems faded before immediate troubles of her own. She was brought up among fisherfolk—the largest animals raised on her home isle were goats. Riding even the gentlest mounts invariably gave her the shakes.

She was still staring at the stirrup when the horse-boy returned. "Here," he offered gruffly. Before she could protest, he caught her around the waist and tossed her slight body into the saddle. "Go before the sentry wakens." And he punctuated the advice with a clap of the mare's hindquarters. The animal leaped into a trot, stirrups jarring painfully against Taen's ankles. Skewed sideways, she grabbed mane with both hands, and barely caught the boy's parting shout.

"If you're still here when that sentry recovers, he'll be honor-bound to put a spear through your back."

Jolted, gasping, through the gates into wind-tossed dark, Taen made a sound halfway between a sob and a laugh. Once she centered herself precariously within the saddle, spears became the least of her concerns; the Kielmark's rages and the ferocious loyalty of his men at least were predictably certain. The reactions of Ivainson Jaric were not. Wistfully Taen wished the advice of her mentor on the Isle of the Vaere; for Jaric rode now to return the Keys to Elrinfaer to the Stormwarden, Anskiere, believing that once his errand was accomplished, his bond to the sorcerer would be ended. What he did not know, and what Taen had no gentle way of telling him, was that Anskiere now was sealed beyond reach within his wards beneath the ice cliffs. Without the presence of a firelord's skills, the Keys could not be returned to their rightful master. They could only be guarded, and perilously at that, for the demons would again seek control of the Keys they had narrowly been thwarted from gaining. Worse, if Kor's Accursed ever guessed the fact that Ivain Firelord had left a living heir, Jaric would become the prey in a ruthless hunt for survival, since his latent potential for sorcery might come to threaten their plots against humanity.

Taen gripped the reins. In an agony of fear and courage, she kicked her mount into a canter, and sent it clattering through the gates. Torchlight and the inner fortress fell behind. The mare slid, scrambling, down the broad stone stair which cut through a slope of thorn and olive trees. Below lay the town, a sprinkling of lights between the dark bulk of the warehouses. The harbor beyond was a scattered patchwork of silver and black shadows, the moored brigantines of the Kielmark's corsairs. Yet Taen did not head downward to the townside gate. Instead she tugged the mare to the right, through the northern portal that led to the ridge road.

The sentries let her pass with alacrity, since Jaric had passed that way earlier. The mare's gaits proved gentle on level ground, and since she showed no untrustworthy tendency to drag on the bit and run, Taen gradually relaxed. Her feet found the stirrups, and the rhythmic ring of hooves eased her mind enough to free her dream-sense. A nagging jab slapped her intuition in the night-dark lane before the outer gate.

She hauled the mare clumsily to a halt, at last giving way to irritation; a check on affairs back at the great hall revealed the Kielmark in a seething temper, bellowing orders to men at arms who scattered running to seek weapons, helms, and horses. Never doubting that Jaric and she were the cause, Taen narrowed her focus and sought the single white-hot thread of consciousness that mattered.

Thought answered her probe, sharp as a whipcrack. *'Enchantress! Meddler! What have you done this time? Where is Jaric?'* Dangerously unstable at the best of times, the Kielmark's mind now blazed with raw fury. Taen encompassed the essence, though it burned cruelly. Sweating with the effort of her talents, she bent impatience into calm, deflected violence into confusion, and madness into a hole wide enough to send coherent communication.

'*Call off your men at arms. I will look after Jaric.*' She sorted the spikes and angles of the Lord of Cliffhaven's thoughts, and observed that he already guessed the boy had gone to seek Anskiere. The ravening desire to deploy an armed patrol still overruled any attempt to instill temperance. Sad, now, Taen countered with the one fact that might restrain him. '*Let the boy be. He won't find what he most wishes to obtain.*'

Surprise answered, followed by calculation, followed by some keenly intuitive guesswork. '*The Stormwarden is helpless, then?*'

Taen sighed in the windy darkness. Mad, but wily as an old wolf, the Kielmark made few mistakes when it came to assessing Keithland's weaknesses. As his thoughts shifted rapidly futureward, to planning and intricate countermeasures, the Dreamweaver released the contact. She urged the mare on into the scrub pines on the heights, certain now that the men who ran to fetch swords would be called back to their beer. The Kielmark would allow her to seek Ivainson Jaric without interference, and since the ways of enchantresses could be expected to foul even the most carefully laid network of patrols, probably the sentry would get by with a tongue-lashing.

Yet barely a mile farther on, with the trees tossing around her and the first raindrops spattering in the dust, Taen heard a drum roll of hoofbeats bearing down from behind. Not a patrol; the men who kept watch on the island's outposts never reported alone, and a relief watch would number five. Annoyed now, and chilled by the wet, the enchantress reined up and waited as the rider overtook her. Expertly slowed from a gallop, his horse clattered to a stop. Sparks shot from the concussion of steel shoes on stone, and Taen's mare sidled.

She controlled it, mostly by accident. Her reins tangled uselessly with her fingers, and her legs swung, clumsily inept. Still, she managed to keep her seat, even when the man she recognized as the sentry from the bailey jostled his mount against hers and tossed the heavy folds of a cloak into her hands.

"Kielmark's compliments," he shouted breathlessly. Then he grinned. "Said his patrols could see you weren't ambushed, but damned if he'd have you perish of cold."

Taen grinned back, recognizing Corley's deft manipulation

behind the gesture. Then, as she flung the wool over her shoulders, her hand caught on the huge ruby which adorned the brooch at the collar. The most feared and powerful man in Keithland had sent her his personal cloak, and not as an afterthought. In sparing his fortress from Kor's Accursed, Taen Dreamweaver had earned something more complex than the Kielmark's gratitude. She strove to wring comfort from that fact. Ahead of her, the troubled heir of Ivain Firelord had a decision to make that would affect the continuance of humanity; and behind, painfully abandoned at Elrinfaer, was the brother she had lost to the demons.

For Marlson Emien, hope no longer existed. Collected from the sands of Elrinfaer by the unsuspecting charity of two fishermen, he lay limp beneath a shelter jury-rigged from tarpaulins as the first fall of rain pattered over the sloop. The brothers who took him in had treated his palms, unaware that his burns were a caustic reaction to bare-flesh contact with a solution of demon-controlled Sathid crystal. Neither did they guess that his fever was no illness but the effects of transition as the entities he harbored melded and established mastery over his mind. Irrevocably possessed by Kor's Accursed, Emien did not hear the foaming rush of the sea, nor the thump and rattle of planking as the sloop tossed, spume-drenched, on her heading. Cold did not touch him, even when run-off from the tarps leaked down his shoulders and back. His opened eyes stayed blind as marbles, his limbs still. Only his mind knew agony. As the Sathid coursed through his body, his awareness twisted in a pocket of nightmare, utterly powerless to win free.

The sister who sorrowed at Cliffhaven would never have recognized him now. Demon thought-forms overran his humanity and alien desires ravaged his spirit. Emien had known hatred; but never in life had he experienced the depth and intensity of spite which racked him as his new overlords raged over the loss of the Keys to Elrinfaer. A decade of intricate plotting had failed them, and once more their hope of exterminating humanity had been thwarted. Only one part of the grand design remained to be salvaged: a new pawn had been gained to replace Merya Tathagres. As the Sathid entity assimilated Emien's personality, the demons explored their find.

Voices rustled in the boy's mind, dry and numerous as dead leaves whirled by wind. The words were in no human tongue,

and the speakers far distant, conferring in a place beyond the
north borders of Keithland. Yet through the bridge of the
Sathid-link they were a part of Emien, and Emien a part of
them. Comprehension required no translation.

'Who, tell me, who is he?'

Another voice answered, gruffer, and curt with authority.
'Man-child, forsaken-one. Called Marlson Emien, but ours
now, destined to become the bane-of-his-kind.'

'Knowledge, fast-tell-me, what memories does he possess?'

Demon thought-probes jabbed into Emien's mind. He
moaned faintly under the tarp, powerless to hinder as demons
rummaged ruthlessly through his being. Most of his past experience they discarded as meaningless, but not all; where his
new masters had interest, they poked and pricked and prodded, pitilessly sorting out what information they wished. They
examined his childhood, the poverty and the shortcomings and
the discontent he had known as a fisherman's son on Imrill
Kand. No nuance escaped scrutiny. Demons knew the rough
wooden loft where he had shivered in the misery of his nightmares, and the quiet, careworn widow who had raised him.
They knew the peat smoke and tide wrack, and the sour smells
of nets drying through twilights smothered in fog; and not
least they knew Taen, the sister who had collected shells on
the beaches, and run dancing through wildflowers with the
goats on the tor until the day the accident had left her lamed.
When at the last she had found her cure, her family lost her;
for the Stormwarden, Anskiere, had stolen her loyalty and
sent her for training to the Isle of the Vaere.

Here the demon probe paused, sharpened to cutting interest. Emien flinched. Unnoticed by his fisherman benefactors,
he quivered and sweated in the sloop's damp bow, while the
enemies of humankind pursued details of the sister's existence
more thoroughly. The voices reached a fever pitch of excitement in the dark.

'Behold, this-proof, another Vaere-trained enchantress
walks Keithland, to our sorrow.'

The probe twisted, gouged deeper, and exposed Taen's
presence in the battle that had prevented Cliffhaven's conquest. 'Vaere-trained, yes, most certainly Dreamweaver
gifted.' Now the grip in Emien's mind tightened and focused
with cruel clarity upon the sister as he had seen her last,
standing windblown upon the heights by Elrinfaer Tower. She

clung, trembling, in the embrace of Ivainson Jaric, the Keys to Elrinfaer gripped in her whitened fingers. Her shift was torn, and her skin spangled with salt from an ocean crossing. The pallor of her face accentuated her exhaustion, and her black hair tumbled in tangles over shoulders grown gaunt with stress. Yet where human vision ended, the enhanced perception of demons gleaned more: a halo of greenish light shimmered around Taen's form, tangible effects of the Sathid-enhanced powers she had challenged and mastered. The voices whispered over this, and refined their scrutiny until patterns became visible in the aura, and abruptly their concern dissolved. The demons' murmured commentary transformed to ridicule that sang and echoed through Emien's being.

'She is undone, this Dreamweaver trained by the Vaere. Too soon sent to defend: see! The aura is distressed. Her crystals are yet immature, and imminently dangerous.' An interval followed, dense with murmurs of agreement. 'The compact need not fear Marlsdaughter Taen, Emien-sister. Doom stalks her, even-as-we-speak. The Sathid she mastered to gain her powers shall soon seek replication, and the changes effected upon her body will assuredly kill her.'

Chilled, and now utterly still upon the rain-sleek planking of the sloop, the conscious spark that remained of Marlson Emien pleaded inwardly for explanation. The voices quieted, considered, and with a bitter flash of malice granted his request.

Their answer came shaped in dream-image. Emien observed a sorcerer who had served as Grand Conjurer to the Kings of Felwaithe seven generations in the past. Yet demon recall spanned centuries; the memory was replicated with a clarity faithfully sharp. During a time of war, a devastating assault by demons had brought this man to attempt an unsupervised bonding with a Sathid crystal. The sorcerer had survived to win mastery, only to perish afterward, as the entity he harbored cycled to reproduce itself. Granted vision by demons, Emien saw the man writhe in torment, his sickbed the flinty, lichen-crusted stone that comprised the fells beyond Keithland. He quivered and sweated, all control of his sorcerer's powers overturned by the nightmare throes of delirium. Even as Emien watched, the man's flesh became suffused and discolored, muscles tortured into knots of tension and agony. Then, in the hours before daylight faded, his shivering ceased. The congested purple of his bruises opened into ugly weeping sores. Sickened, gasping in the throes of his own horror, Emien saw shards of crystal erupt through the dying sorcerer's flesh. The man screamed. His piteous cries were swallowed without echo by the empty fells, as bit by bit his vitals were lacerated from within by knives of glittering mineral.

In the end, only crystal remained, a jagged-edged remainder of what once had been human. Agony seemed inscribed in the very form, here the suggestion of clenched hands, and there the contorted arch of the back. *Taen would die so.* She carried within her the seeds of a crystalline entity that should have been safely separated from her flesh before it acquired full maturity. Yet the Vaere had dismissed her prematurely, or so Emien believed, that she could counteract the plot of the demons who threatened Cliffhaven. Ultimately, the Stormwarden who lured her away had betrayed her. For that, the voices in the shadows agreed that Anskiere of Elrinfaer should be made to suffer payment.

The assurance had a calming effect. Emien no longer tossed in discomfort as his overlords resumed their analysis of his mind. Instead he subsided into feverish sleep, the whispers and the voices a litany against a background of dreams while the probe of Kor's Accursed turned from remembrance of Taen Dreamweaver to focus next on the boy who comforted her.

He was blond, salt-stained as she, and as confused. His shirt and tunic had torn on the briar; the limbs beneath were well muscled and tanned from long days at a sailboat's helm. Yet for all his wiry strength, this boy carried himself diffidently. He had thrown down the sword he had used to win the Keys to Elrinfaer, but his hands shook through the moment of his victory, and his sun-bleached hair blew back to reveal tear-streaked cheeks.

'*Who?*' demanded the voices. The touch of demons prodded and tore at Emien's memory until the slight, untrained heir of Ivain Firelord was identified.

Silence resulted then, stillness that hinted of rage and resentment. Vaere-trained sorcerers were ever a threat to demons, but, among them, Anskiere and Ivain Firelord had caused the fiercest damage. The former was prisoner, trapped by his own wards in the ice cliffs. But the revelation that Ivain had left an heir with talent and potential to match his skills caused consternation and anger and a raw desire to destroy.

'*The boy must be hunted down,*' fretted the first voice.

'*Killed,*' chimed in a second.

'*Destroyed, most-utterly,*' wailed a third, and the howl of multiple companions made Emien's mind ring with hate. He lay twitching in reaction, even as his demon overlords instructed the Sathid which directed his fate. '*Call in the captured pawn. Compel him, the moment the sickness of bonding relents enough to permit him to act. Let the man-child steal the boat from his fisherman benefactors and sail north to Shadowfane. Scait Demon-Lord must sample his mind and memories. Then shall the hatred of Marlson Emien be granted training and weapons; and Ivainson Jaric, Firelord's heir, shall be hunted down and slain.*'

⟨⟩ II ⟨⟩

Keeper of the Keys

Jagged, icy rocks tore Jaric's hands as he climbed. In darkness the escarpments beneath the ice cliffs were steeper and more perilous than he recalled, despite the storm which had harried him the first time he made the ascent. A wave thundered over the reef below. Spray sheeted his back and subsided with a hiss into the sea. The soaked wool of his tunic clung to muscles which quivered with fatigue, yet he groped for a fresh hold and clawed upward. One shin banged painfully into granite before his boot found purchase; pebbles skittered under his sole, the rattle of their fall swallowed by seething surf below.

The Firelord's heir winced and clung gasping to an outcrop. Neither danger nor discomfort could deter him. Until the stormfalcon's feather and the Keys to Elrinfaer were returned to the Stormwarden who was their rightful guardian, no portion of Ivainson Jaric's life could be called his own.

The boy shook sun-bleached hair from his eyes and reached for another hold. Scant yards above, he saw a rim etched faintly against the night sky: a ledge cut across the rock face. He jammed his foot in a cleft, thrust higher, and fumbled with scraped hands until he found a fingerhold overhead. A breath of cold washed over him. Jaric shivered in the darkness and transferred his weight. Inured to the pain of stressed tendons, he wrenched his body upward and hooked his forearm over the ledge. Above loomed the ice cliffs where abided the Stormwarden, Anskiere.

Although elsewhere spring thrust wildflowers through the thornbrakes of Cliffhaven, here ice glistened silver by starlight, towering cascades arrested in mid-fall by the relentless grip of winter. The view could dizzy the senses with its splendor, leave a man stupid and staring with awe until the cold stiffened his limbs. Jaric clenched his jaw and kept his eyes on the rock face. Although the cliffs had frozen barely a year

16

past, sailors' tales already made a myth of them, fancifully describing galleries filled with riches, and jeweled chambers where Anskiere worked his spells in solitude. In fact, the glassy ramparts shaped a prison more secure than any dungeon fashioned by man. Here the granite was smooth, as if the escarpment itself was hostile to human presence. Jaric found neither crevice nor outcrop sufficient to bear his weight.

Aching with fatigue, he hitched his body closer to the stone. Defeat never entered his mind. Too many times the debt inherited from his father had ripped his life into loss and hardship; with the promised release from that bond waiting only yards above his head, Jaric ran his hands over rock and hooked a sloping edge. The hold was inadequate for the move he intended. Yet a fall onto the reefs below was less risk than guarding the Keys through the night. Demonkind had plotted and killed to acquire the powers Elrinfaer Tower safeguarded. Only a fool would believe they would not try again. Jaric set his weight on the toe left wedged in the crevice, tensed his fingers, and thrust.

He caught the ledge under both elbows as his feet kicked out into air. His body struck the lip of the outcrop, jouncing the breath from his lungs. For a moment Jaric teetered, muscles straining. Then his left hand began to slip. Gravel turned under his palm. Desperate, he hiked his shoulders and lost a torturous inch. A breaker hissed hungrily across the reefs; Jaric shut his eyes and tasted sweat. He twisted sideways and raised his knee, sensed rather than felt a bulge in the stone beneath his body. Trusting friction and luck, he hitched himself up and grabbed left-handed. His wrist slapped the ledge. Two fingers hooked in a fissure and thwarted gravity for one precarious minute.

Jaric caught his breath with a painful gasp. He knotted tortured muscles and dragged himself higher. Chest, waist, hips, he gained the ledge by slow inches. At last he heaved his torso over the edge of the rock. There he collapsed, exhausted, and for an interval hung with both feet dangling above the sea. Had the cold been less cruel he might have rested until his lungs stopped aching. But air currents off the ice cliffs bit through his sodden clothes and quickly set him shivering. Jaric rolled, brought his knee up, and flopped onto his side, panting like a beached fish.

Securely on the ledge at last, the boy fumbled with chilled hands for the leather bag strung on a thong around his neck.

The hard corners of basalt inside dug into his palms, assurance the Keys to Elrinfaer Tower's great wards and Anskiere's stormfalcon feather remained with him still. Comforted by the belief that his responsibility to the Stormwarden would shortly be discharged, Jaric looked up, and only that moment discovered he was not alone.

Not a yard from his position, two points of orange glared like coals from the darkness; starlight traced a hooded figure with folded, six-fingered hands. Jaric hissed through his teeth. His shoulder banged painfully into rock as he sat up. Even as he grabbed for his dagger he knew that defense was futile. The creature confronting him was Llondian, demon and enemy of mankind.

'*No.*' The Llondel spoke no word, but its thought-image struck Jaric's awareness like a hammerblow. '*I am here for Anskiere.*'

Cornered against empty sky, Jaric felt a mental tug, and images followed, of sea winds and salt wrack which threaded the demon's pattern for the Stormwarden's name. Speech was alien to Llondian kind; they communicated with thought impressed directly onto the mind, and when they chose, no mortal could inhibit their sending. Neither could man attack Llondel with impunity. Yet Jaric saw no choice. His freedom, and the survival of all Keithland, would be threatened should the Keys to Elrinfaer fall into demon hands.

That Anskiere might have Llondian allies was surely impossible; unwilling to challenge the demon's falsehood, Jaric phrased his reply like a peacemaker caught in a hostile court. "Then for the sake of the Stormwarden, let me pass."

The Llondel did not move. It regarded the human boy with no flicker of emotion, pupils slitted against irises of burning gold. '*Keeper of the Keys, you may not pass; nor will your bond to Anskiere be completed until you accept the heritage of the Firelord who fathered you.*'

Jaric flinched, haunted with dread, for the Cycle of Fire brought madness along with mastery of a sorcerer's powers. Not even demons could make him forsake his humanity and request such training from the Vaere.

"No," said Jaric. Guile would not avail him. Already the demon knew he possessed the Keys; certainly it would strike to kill. "I must pass. There is no other choice for me." Sweating with fear, the boy raised his blade.

The Llondel hissed warning. Its eyes darkened to sultry

red, and seamed, six-fingered hands clicked against rock as it stiffened.

'No harm to you, Firelord's son,' the demon sent; but its image became that of a human body spared a fall on the reefs. The meaning was murder withheld.

Jaric struck with the full strength of his arm. The demon retaliated before the weapon cut. Images sheared like lightning through its victim's mind, upending all sense of existence. Jaric's blade clanged harmlessly into stone, scattering sparks across the outcrop as he fell limp at the demon's knees.

Imprisoned by Llondian imaging, the boy heard nothing, felt nothing beyond the sting of steel piercing his shoulder. Plunged through transition and darkness, he emerged, staggering to his feet, in another place, a closed chamber where torchlight glimmered off strangely carved walls. A slight, pale boy struggled in his arms. He held the human close, though it pained him, and with a horrid shock of surprise, Jaric realized that *the boy was himself.* In the dream he was *other;* his hands, the same hands which gripped the human child, were gray-skinned, six-fingered, and spurred. In one shattering instant, Jaric recognized the moment: through enemy eyes he shared the agony of the wound the Earl of Morbrith had dealt a Llondian in the sanctuary tower last summerfair. The knife thrust had been intended for the heir of Ivain, but a Llondel demon had died instead.

Jaric had no chance to unravel ironies. The dream-image rippled like windblown tapestry. Torch flame spat and flared in the wall sconce, then transformed to a Llondian's glowing eyes. *'One of us perished, Firelord's heir, that you might survive to develop your talents.'*

The implication was damning in its simplicity. Jaric resisted, desperate. "Why?" His shout echoed in darkness. "Since when have demons concerned themselves with the affairs of men, except to bring discord and suffering?"

But exactly as before, the Llondelei smothered protest in dreams. Jaric felt himself hurled back to an earlier day when he had scaled the ledges of Cliffhaven to answer the geas set upon him by Anskiere. Soaked and shivering and trapped in the past, he saw rain clouds cleft by new sunlight. Amid sudden, miraculous calm, while storm-whipped seas tumbled raggedly over the rocks, he heard once again the command Anskiere had shaped on the wind.

"You will recover the Keys to Elrinfaer and hold them safe

until they can be returned." But here Llondian influence twisted Jaric's memory, crushing his spirit with an overwhelming burden of guilt. The human boy had been negligent in his judgment; the Keys to Elrinfaer were endangered still, and Anskiere's request neglected.

The accusation shocked like a death wound. In hurt and pride and raging anger, Jaric protested innocence. He had recovered the Keys in good faith, left his home, renounced friends, even abandoned principles he held dear to complete his bond to the Stormwarden. The Llondel alone prevented his return to Anskiere. The injustice of his quandary whipped Jaric to blind and murderous frenzy. For an instant the demon could not counter the scope of his response. Its hold slipped, and dream-images fled like shadows before fire.

Jaric roused to cold and darkness and the sour smell of the sea. Sprawled on the ledge at the Llondel's feet, he stirred skinned knuckles. The knife was gone from his hand. He groped after it, brushed a fold of gray cloth, and instantly recalled the ice cliffs and his interrupted purpose. A lump pressed against his chest, proof that the pouch which held the Keys to Elrinfaer remained tucked inside his tunic; still he was defenseless. The demon could steal from him whenever it pleased, and its dispassionate stare made him feel like a mouse teased by a cat.

Jaric dragged himself to his knees. Before he reached his feet, the Llondel touched his mind again. It grasped the fact that he attributed its interference to cruelty, and the shallowness of his reasoning roused it to rage.

'Mortal fool,' it sent. *'Ignorant child. Do you not know what the wards over Elrinfaer Tower defend?'*

"No!" Pressured beyond caution, Jaric shouted his defiance. "How should I? All my life I was a scribe keeping records in a backlands keep. Did you think I asked to be involved in the affairs of sorcerers?"

'You are what you must become,' the Llondel returned equitably and, with pitiless force, overturned his senses.

Jaric staggered back, blinded by a cruel flash of light. Etched against the night he saw the falcon and triple circle that symbolized the Stormwarden's mastery. The vision had no sooner faded when a second image ripped into Jaric's mind, edged with a clarity that cut to the heart. The Llondel showed him the ice cliffs, but changed in a manner no mortal could perceive. Cascades rose in frozen rungs above the rocky reefs of Cliffhaven. Their majesty stung Jaric to tears, for here stood a monument to inexpressible sorrow. The expanded perception of the demon revealed a corona of light like lacework across the sky; here shone the wards themselves laid bare, patterns of force which bound the weather to eternal frost. Although understanding of the structure lay beyond the grasp of an untrained mind, Jaric perceived that the Sorcerer had borrowed energy from his own being to balance the existence of his creation. Sadness echoed like a song's edge. Before the boy could contemplate whose grief made him weep, the spell unraveled into night. But darkness offered no reprieve. Jaric plunged into silence and cold without end.

Frost shackled his limbs. His heart slowed until the bindings of his spirit loosened and his body lay a hairsbreadth from death; yet the existence Jaric shared was another's. Through the guidance of the Llondel, he experienced the fate of the Stormwarden of Elrinfaer whose powers had provoked such hatred among men. Anskiere lay suspended in stasis deep beneath the cliffs, his limbs enshrouded in ice. Though his flesh was imprisoned and helpless, his mind roved a landscape of dreams. Through the window of the sorcerer's memories, Jaric encountered strife and sacrifice, and a tragic understanding of the Firelord who had fathered him. . . .

Ivain had not always been mad. At one with a younger Stormwarden, Jaric knew the twilight dimness of an enchanted grove. For Anskiere, the place held memories within memories. Once a Prince of Elrinfaer, he had waited in the selfsame place and renounced his royal heritage for the powers of wave and weather. Now he sought the Vaere to answer a demand of his own, for a grievance weighed upon his heart. The Stormwarden called repeatedly, but the fey being who trained him to mastery did not appear.

In frustration, Anskiere shouted, his voice an echo among the cedars. "In the name of Kordane's mercy, what have your gifts brought Ivain? Of us both, he was the better man. Did you mean to break his mind? Answer!"

The Stormwarden held his breath and listened, but nothing moved in the grove. No shimmer of air disturbed the silvery gloom. The cedars brooded in breezeless stillness. Anskiere clenched his fists. "I spoke with the seeress at Cael's Falls. She said each time Ivain summons fire, the flame that he masters consumes his living flesh. He does not burn, she said,

nor does he consciously suffer agony, not since the Cycle of
Fire seared his soul to a cinder. He has no nerves left to feel.
Did you know that the torment would steal his humanity from
him? He once was the gentlest of men. Now he is spiteful and
cruel, and cursed by his own kind."

But the Vaere did not answer. Heartbroken by that silence,
Anskiere left the grove. Through the trials to come he never
ceased mourning the ruin of the minstrel's son who had been
his dearest friend. Although the Vaere never accounted for
Ivain's broken mind, years and experience tempered Anskiere's sorrow. As he wielded his powers to hold Keithland
secure, he found enemies more ruthless by far than any Vaere.
The deadly wiles of demonkind eventually made Anskiere understand that mankind's chances of survival were slight without the defense of a firelord's skills. Twisted as Ivain became,
the Stormwarden never forgot compassion for his friend, even
on the day the two sorcerers battled the most terrible demons
ever to threaten mankind.

The Llondel's imaging replicated Anskiere's recollection of
that betrayal; the circumstances were not at all as common
men believed. The surviving Mharg-demon was ancient, broken in mind and body from Kordane's Fires; his wings were
too scarred to fly, and his breath barely sufficient to wither the
lichens he devoured for sustenance. Yet he had life and hatred
enough to fertilize one last, lost clutch of eggs, forgotten since
the Great Fall until demons recovered it from the sea bottom.
The Mharg-male buried his brood in the heart of Keithland
before he died. In time, they hatched and flew over the Tors of
Elshend, to wreak final vengeance upon mankind. In the
towns, the priests prayed for Kordane's mercy. Had their faith
been the land's sole defense, all Keithland would have been
laid waste. But the Vaere sent Stormwarden and Firelord
against the Mharg-hatchlings. No archive at Landfast held
record of the conflict; the priesthood dared not credit sorcerers, lest the faithful cease to supply the temple coffers with
their silver.

Slogging through reeds in the lowlands west of Telshire,
Anskiere wasted no thought on the priests' petty pride. But
Ivain cursed long and vehemently, his resentment sharpened
by the suck and spatter of mud beneath his boots.

"Prostrated themselves so zealously for Kordane's mercy
they bruised their kneecaps on the prayer carpets. And Great
Fall, the hangovers from the rites! You know they sucked the

temple wine stores down to the lees?" Ivain tossed back red
hair and regarded Anskiere with dark, unreadable eyes; eyes
whose set and color were the same stamp as Jaric's, but old in
a manner no mortal could comprehend. "If a song of blessing
for our efforts strains their sotted throats overmuch, may they
slip while pissing and drown in their jakes."

Ivain kicked a clod of grass. A marsh thrush started up
with a whir of barred wings. Its cry rang over deserted fields,
for the folk of Tor Elshend had fled the peril of the Mharg-
spawn. No one remained to tend the hearth fires in the cottages. Ivain swore as if the emptied landscape could respond
to the vicious anger in his heart.

"It's you, I think, who overindulged in drink last night,"
Anskiere said mildly.

Ivain laughed, a wild sound that frightened the marsh
thrush's mate from her nest in a nearby bush. She took wing
after the male, a scrap of brown and white against the overcast
sky. Ivain flicked his fingers. The bird burst into flame, transformed by his malice to a conflagration of feather and bone.

Anskiere flinched as the pitiful handful of cinders tumbled
over and over in the air and crashed with a hiss in a reed bed.
"That was ill done. Her fledglings will now die also."

Ivain shrugged without remorse. "All Keithland might perish as easily. Have you forgotten? The priests have, and how
convenient it is for them! We who are their true defense
against demons are feared, spit on, outcast, and unsung."

The cries of the marsh thrush's mate filled a comfortless
interval of silence. Anskiere had no word to speak in behalf of
Kordane's sacred brotherhood. Ivain's accusation was true,
but much of the people's ill will toward sorcerers stemmed
from his own spiteful nature. Anskiere could not share the
Firelord's bitterness. What man could sow fields and raise
children, knowing his family lay continually in peril? Kordane's priesthood offered faith, cloaked in illusions of tradi-
tion and security. Would a sorcerer be resented any less if men
understood the truth, that they were helpless as ants before the
threat of demons? Anskiere thought not. But Ivain continued
to taunt his complacency as they hiked to the site where the
Mharglings had broken nest.

"We could show them, smash one of their pompous little
towns to wreckage." Ivain flicked a tick from the ragged edge
of his cuff and laughed again. "You haven't the stomach for
that, though, if you'd mourn the charred corpse of a thrush.

Had the bird been a child, would you weep, or would you puke? Perhaps you'd discover a way to manage both at once."

Anskiere clenched his jaw. Unwilling to yield to anger, he regarded the fresh fronds of the willows, so like the palace grounds of his boyhood. Tor Elshend lay on the southern borders of Elrinfaer, and the stream-laced meadows and forested hills prompted remembrance of his royal sister and the times they had gathered wildflowers and herbs for the healer's cupboards. Now, in the boots of a Vaere-trained sorcerer, he did not leap the hummocks or pause to skip stones in the pools. Foxglove and faerylace crumpled under his step, and no memory could ease his longing for the Ivain who had first met the Vaere, a ready smile and a whistle on his lips.

But presently even nature offered no distraction from the Firelord's soured spirit; the wind brought a taint of rotted earth and the hills rose scabbed like old wounds between areas of new growth. Abruptly Ivain ceased carping. Shaken by the ruin of the tor's bright beauty, he walked at the Stormwarden's side and spoke no more of birds or vengeance. The grasses turned sere and brown underfoot. As the sorcerers neared their destination, the hillsides stank and oozed, and their feet slogged through a gelid slime of dead plants. No living thing remained of the forest or the wildlife which once had inhabited Tor Elshend. The Mharglings were not far distant.

Suddenly a hiss cut the morning stillness. Tension raised sweat on Anskiere's neck. Though the air was mild with spring, he felt chill down to his bones. Ahead, where maples had once lifted full crowns to the sunlight, he saw branches stripped like the beams of a burned croft. A scaled head arose above them, patterned iridescently emerald, turquoise, and gold. The creature's snout was flat, slitted with four sets of nostrils; centered within a maze of scarlet stripes, its single eye glared, black as a bead, and intelligent.

"By the Vaere," said Anskiere. In size alone the demon was daunting. "We'll be lucky to finish this alive."

Ivain shrugged. Sarcasm sharpened his reply. "Does it matter? Never doubt, the Vaere has chosen our successors already."

The Mhargling spotted their approach. It opened toothless jaws and hissed warning, membranes glistening through the fumes which issued from its throat. If its bite was harmless to man, the vapors were not. Ribbed rows of ducts emitted caustic digestive gases, and the breath of the Mharg-spawn rotted forests, fish, and animals into slime with killing speed. The creatures lapped the remains to feed. In a season they could ravage every living acre of Keithland, and afterward neither soil nor ocean would support any life.

Anskiere licked dry lips. "Are you ready?"

Ivain replied with an obscenity. Without warning he ripped a fireball out of empty sky and dropped it in the Mharglings' midst.

Four heads snapped erect, warbling screams of fury over the crackle of flame. Membranous wings thundered on the air as the Mharg-spawn took flight, talons unsheathed for battle. Enraged and deadly and fully sixty spans long, they wheeled and dove at their attackers. Though nettled by Ivain's precipitous action, Anskiere was not caught off guard. He raised his hands with speed and wove a whirlwind in the demons' midst. Squalling surprise, the Mharglings tumbled, tangled, and pinwheeled earthward in a knot of threshing wings. They struck amid a blinding explosion of flame.

A gust of heated air stung Anskiere's face. He blinked away tears from the blast. Outlined in glare, the first wings arose, stretched upward, and beat strongly amid the fumes. The fact the Vaere had warned that victory would be difficult made the moment no easier to accept. Wings cracked as the Mharglings scuttled clear of the smoke. They took flight, utterly without scathe, except for scales which glinted a hot reddish yellow where the flames had touched them.

At once Anskiere knew he must merge minds with Ivain. Their skills must answer as one to counter the Mharglings' deadly speed. Fire daunted the creatures not at all; the air currents already cooled their heated scales. The Stormwarden buffeted them with gusts, yet they stayed separate from each other, knifing through turbulence like quarrels shot from a crossbow. *Tire them,* he decided, confident Ivain would catch his thought. *Wear them out and try to survive, and when they weaken, seal them living in a tomb of rock.*

But when Anskiere extended his awareness to mesh with the Firelord's mind, his linking thought touched emptiness. Mharg-wings flogged the air with the sound of storm surf battering sand. The creatures spiraled upward with a rattle of scales, and yellow fumes billowed from their mouths. Anskiere turned, fearful the silence in his mind meant he would find his companion injured.

Yet the Firelord stood unharmed, with his thumbs hooked

negligently through his belt. His chin lifted as Anskiere faced him.

"We should teach those priests a lesson," Ivain said. A mocking smile spread over his lips. "The event would be sporting, don't you think? A Mhargling against a prayer?"

Flicked by a monstrous shadow, Anskiere whirled. His cloak snapped like a flag as he raised a gust to drive off the poisonous fumes. Still his eyes stung and watered, and the blown ends of his hair turned from silver to black. "That's madness!" he shouted, for a moment unwilling to face the Firelord behind him. "You'll kill us all, and for what? Simple jealousy?"

Ivain's eyes narrowed. "Not of the priests' popularity. Kordane's faithful are insects, to a man. Should we prevent demons from swatting them?"

Anskiere jerked and spun around. For an instant Stormwarden and Firelord regarded each other, one with outrage, the other with naked enmity. Then the Mharglings screamed and stooped for the kill; Anskiere experienced a tangible dissolution of resistance as Ivain relented. The sorcerers' powers merged.

Power coursed through Anskiere's body with the inexorable force of the tides; nerve, sinew, and bone sang with stresses never meant for mortal endurance. Yet the Stormwarden held firm. He joined with Ivain and fought the Mharg with the combined masteries of earth and fire, water and wind. The battle spanned hours, or maybe days, without surcease.

Anskiere called up tempests, and rain fell. Lightning slashed the sky, striking sword-metal highlights on scaled hides. Still the Mharg flew. The temperature plunged, and hail rattled into the ground. Battered by ice, the Mharg howled but did not land. Ivain split the earth. Lava spurted from the rift, red as an opened artery. The Mharglings yowled, enraged. They shot straight up. Anskiere belted them with a downdraft, without success. The Mharg-spawn hissed and wheeled northward, over the hills of Elrinfaer. Through a murky rain of ash, forests withered. Pine trees crumpled like sodden silk, and the wind reeked of death.

Racked by exhaustion and inflamed nerves, Anskiere pursued. His eyes became blinded by tears, that the land he was once to rule should suffer such ruin as this. Tired feet stumbled over blackened earth, and his robe clung to shoulders which steamed with sweat. Caustic slush blackened his boots where the Mharg had passed. The leather softened and dissolved and the slime burned his bare soles. Beaten by sleet and wind, the Stormwarden paused to wrap his blistered feet in his cloak. A Mhargling hissed down out of the dark. In an instant the ground became an inferno as Ivain chiseled an outcrop into lava and drove it off. Still the demons flew. The Vaere had warned that their strength arose from a world never inhabited by men. Tortured by fatigue, Anskiere wondered whether the creatures would settle at all.

"If they land just once, we have them." Ivain's face glistened with rain and sweat. Mharg-breath had long since singed his cloak to rags. "Did you notice? They don't care for molten rock."

Anskiere grunted assent, his throat too raw for speech. With a shiver of foreboding, he raised his eyes skyward once more. Repeatedly the Mharg-demons retreated to the north; if they were not brought to ground very soon, their rampaging would destroy the orchards which were the pride and the wealth of Elrinfaer. And close by lay villages and farmsteads he was bound by birthright to protect.

Aching, the Stormwarden rose to his feet. As he raised his powers to renew the fight, Ivain regarded him with curious malice. But the dream which unfolded through Llondian influence was nothing more than a memory. No warning could alter the past.

Sudden fire flared. The earth spewed forth dust to clog the Mharglings' lungs, and the Firelord's face became veiled by grit. Powers burned through Anskiere's hands, vast and wild as a cataclysm. He needed every scrap of concentration to manage them. No resource remained to examine Ivain's vagaries, and of necessity his peril went unnoticed. Storms shook the ground. A forest burned, branches seared to skeletons against a wall of glare. Still the Mharg flew; but at long last they showed signs of flagging. More often they glided, as if resting tired wings, and their attacks became sporadic, even sluggish compared to their earlier efforts.

Dawn broke. Dust drifted in the air. The sun glowed sullen orange above fields scorched to stubble. Anskiere pounded the air with gusts, and the Mharglings cut and wove in maddened circles to stay airborne.

"Open a shaft. They're slowing." The Stormwarden shaped his request to the Firelord in a croaking whisper, unable to manage more. His skin was patched with abrasions. Sparks had scored holes in his clothes, but his eyes were alight with the triumph of victory.

Ivain faced him over the gutted remains of an oak, hair streaked with grime. "Do that yourself." A smile brightened his smudged face. "It's not my kingdom at stake."

Anskiere stared, speechless with shock. At first he refused to believe Ivain's words were not simply another malicious taunt. But the face confronting him was that of a madman. Overhead the Mharglings screamed, banked, and shot off to the north. Torn between rebuke and compassion, the Stormwarden searched for means to restore Ivain's lost reason and stave off the destruction of Elrinfaer.

"Your countryfolk deserve the lesson." Ivain spat on the broken soil. "They should never have refused me hospitality last solstice."

"Vaere witness, you wrong them," Anskiere managed, his voice mangled with pain.

Ivain perched insouciantly on the fallen oak, his hands lax at his sides. With terrible finality, Anskiere felt the presence of the Firelord dissolve within his mind. Grief caught him like a blow. Separate and alone, Anskiere turned quickly lest the Firelord laugh at his sorrow. Elrinfaer still lay dearest to his heart; the Mharg-spawn would make a desert of the land, farms and cities and wilderness, and all his Stormwarden's powers could not prevent them. . . .

Bound into sympathy by the Llondel's link, Jaric screamed over and over in anguish. Never in life had he known such suffering as the Stormwarden experienced at Ivain's betrayal.

There seemed no end to such agony of spirit. From the depths of trance, the Firelord's son flung a desperate appeal to the entity which imprisoned his will. "Free me!" Jaric's cry battered like a moth against lantern glass, seeking light though it killed him. For an instant, he thought he glimpsed stars and the crashing of waves smoking over the reefs of Cliffhaven. His throat was lacerated from screaming, and his lips stung with the taste of tears. He rolled, gasping from the cold, and saw two eyes glaring down at him with baleful and inhuman indifference.

"Let me go." Jaric shivered. Lashed raw inside by the demands of forces he had no schooling to understand, and terrified of that legacy as never before, he was aware Anskiere's struggle to save Elrinfaer was doomed; whatever powers the Stormwarden summoned, their fury was surely more than a boy's untrained mind could support. "Do you wish my death?"

'*No*,' sent the Llondel.

It flicked gray fingers, and Jaric tumbled back into darkness. Through Anskiere's eyes, he watched Elrinfaer die, slowly, inexorably, like embers beaten to ash by rain.

⌒⌒ III ⌒⌒

Warning

No longer could Anskiere influence the direction of the demons' flight. Without Ivain's command of fire, the Mharg drove across inhabited lands unhindered. Their wake became a wasteland of towns filled with smeared corpses and rotting bones. The Stormwarden stumbled over broken ground where only minutes earlier a flock of sheep had grazed, guarded by a dog and a boy with a reed pipe. Livestock, grass, and child were now dead, reduced to unrecognizable masses of slime by the Mharg. Bereft of alternatives, the former Prince of Elrinfaer tried desperate measures to preserve his land from ruin.

Anskiere called down the cold. Power answered, streamed like water over a rockfall from his raised fists. The temperature fell, and fell again. Spring transformed to winter; in the space of a single breath, the heartland of Elrinfaer silvered under a spiked mantle of frost. Cattle stampeded in the pastures. Inside town walls, parents hustled children from the dooryards and slammed their shutters in fear. Anskiere shouted again, and the skies darkened. Rain fell in white torrents and froze to a glaze of ice. Apple blossoms wore hardened fists of glass; animals fled for shelter only to stiffen like statues in their tracks. Field hands died at the sowing, and women washing on the riverbanks cried in terror, their wrists trapped fast in black ice. Grim as death itself, Anskiere tightened the bindings of cold over Elrinfaer; crops might fail and people perish, but an armor of ice might possibly shield the land from the total devastation of the Mharg-breath. Seeds would survive the cataclysm, and some of the plants, and surely the majority of the people, enough to rebuild their losses after the crisis passed.

But the tactic failed. Mharglings swept from the sky and attacked an isolated homestead. Their poison reduced the ice to hissing steam and razed everything beneath to stinking slush. Anskiere wept. All his Stormwarden's powers could spare neither land nor people. Nearly broken by defeat, he splashed through a pool of filth. His foot snagged on metal, a gate hinge cast loose when the wooden post which supported it dissolved into soup. The sorcerer stumbled, caught himself short of a fall, and continued, trying not to think of the dead who had raised that fence for their cattle. Inflexibly schooled by the Vaere, a part of his mind still sorted options. His final resource, and Keithland's sole hope, rested in the sea. If the Mharg flew over ocean, one chance remained that Anskiere might trap them through water.

The western coastline lay over mountains, weather-stripped rocks with snowbound passes where roads stayed treacherous even through high summer; to the east, fifty leagues of farmland sprawled toward a shore settled by fisherfolk. Anskiere rubbed the blistered skin of his brow. The Mharg flew where they would; he could do little but follow and ply the winds, try to keep them airborne as much as possible.

The trials which followed melted one into another; Anskiere's days became a misery of existence between terrible events of loss. Storm force resonated through his body. The terrible ebb and flux of power heated nerve and sinew and spirit to pitiless agony, burning away his identity until he could no longer separate which pain was his, and which his kingdom's. Days melted endlessly into dark and time itself lost meaning. Still the Mharg flew. Events became jumbled; scenes lapped together like patchwork, each one a vignette of tragedy.

A city fell and a sister died, the same a young prince had promised to defend when he left seeking the mysteries of the Vaere. Her image haunted his memory, girlish fingers clenched around a scepter she had never wanted, and her fears checked by nothing but royal pride. She had been born with the sight. Now Anskiere wondered whether she had known she would die while he slept. The first night he succumbed to exhaustion, the Mharg had veered east and brought death to the fair court of Elrinfaer. Anskiere clenched his fists and the sky spat lightning. Flash after jagging flash split the dark as he stumbled through courtyards littered with bones. In grief the sorcerer summoned storms to cleanse the streets; his tears became the drum roll of rain.

Summer came, and dust blew over wasted acres. Anskiere climbed a rock face, barefoot, his fingers lacerated from gripping cruel stone. The Mharg circled lazily on an air current, jewel-bright against the zenith. But so long had Anskiere been immersed in storm-weaving, his eyes saw no sky but patterns of tangled light that mapped the force lines by which he read the winds. And his weather alone kept the enemies airborne, harried them westward over the peaks to the sea.

He knew hunger then; days of snow and sun glare and gale-driven ice. Some nights he was too tired to deflect the temperature enough to keep warm. Clothed in little but rags, he rested, shivering on bare rock. The Mharg roosted on the peaks and preened like painted gargoyles. The voracious demand of their appetites would drive them to the air before long. Anskiere forced himself to his feet. Solitary under glittering pinpoints of stars, he traversed a slope of moraine. Pebbles scattered dangerously under his feet, and the air rose cold off the snowfields. Under the cliffs where the demons slept, the Stormwarden raised a fist and summoned his powers. Wind arose, howling over the rocks, and slapped the demons from their perches. They launched with a screeling wail and turned downward toward the sea. Anskiere pursued. His memory of that night's run blended indistinguishably into the tormented days which followed. Storm-torn, savaged by the forces he shaped with his mind, he existed only as a tool for his craft. For a time he lost all awareness of self, his mind blistered beyond mortal recognition by too much power.

Later, bone-thin, the Stormwarden huddled on a beach, his head cradled on crossed wrists. Waves thundered over rock bare inches from his body. Matted hair clung to wet skin, and he breathed in sobs, too spent to move. Sixty yards offshore, a waterspout raged, battered by a screaming howl of elements. In its heart, the Mharglings lay trapped at last, but a week passed before Anskiere recovered enough presence to balance the forces which held them. The months of his labors had taxed him. He could not weave the energy strong enough to perpetuate itself. Daily he had to strengthen his handiwork, and he dared never leave the site.

Anskiere scavenged the beaches. Filthy as a shipwreck victim, he ate raw fish. Dragging the waterspout and the Mharg it confined up the coast, he at last reached a derelict light station on Elrinfaer's northwest shore. The keeper dwelling there was senile, a hermit who had neglected to tend his lamps for half a score of years. Clicking, muttering, and running his tongue over toothless gums, the man still had wits enough to listen when Anskiere asked him to brick every window in the tower with stones. The lightkeeper scratched his groin and spat. But he helped until the task was finished. The moment the last chink was sealed, Anskiere summoned his powers. He heated the air to a blinding inferno. Reft of Ivain's talents, he drove himself until, at the uttermost edge of life, the stones of the tower melted and fused, leaving no break in the walls. The new-made prison rose sheer and black from the cliff, and there Anskiere confined the Mharg. They would fly no more. In time, only eggs might survive, but the sorcerer cleansed the place with wind, leaving no moisture within to trigger a second hatching. The Stormwarden sealed the entrance, rested, then plied his mastery once again. When he finished, the Tower of Elrinfaer held secure under the strongest wards ever forged by a weathermage.

He wept at the end. Battered, ragged, and blistered from his labors, he sat on the cliff's edge while the waves creamed over the beaches and the gulls squabbled over flotsam in the tide wrack. In fingers that shook he turned a small basalt block which had once been a trinket of the lightkeeper's. The facets flashed over and over and over. Absorbed by the play of the light, Anskiere never heard the footsteps of the visitor who approached. Nor did he guess he was no longer alone until a familiar, sardonic voice called out to him.

"You did admirably." Ivain paused, thoughtfully tossing pebbles from hand to hand. His hair gleamed copper-bright in late sunlight. "Wrecked yourself, truly, and for what? The survivors will say you caused the devastation. Their priests will curse your name in song, and children learn to fear you."

Anskiere rose, clumsy with exhaustion. "There were no survivors. That's why the Mharg sought the sea. *Nothing else remained for them to spoil.*" He paused to control an anger he lacked the strength to express. "You're lucky the destruction didn't spread beyond Elrinfaer."

"Why?" Ivain's hands stopped in the air, and the stones fell rattling to the ground. "I'm tired of working for the Vaere."

Before Anskiere could respond, the ground parted. The sorcerer who was both Firelord and Earthmaster vanished beneath the soil, his laughter ringing like curses upon the air.

"I'll find you," whispered the Stormwarden. "When I do, I will bind you with a geas so potent you'll *never* forsake your kind again."

So began the hunt for Ivain which culminated at Northsea; forced at bay against the ocean, the Firelord crouched at the

Stormwarden's feet. There, under duress, Ivain completed the
bindings, stabilizing the enchantments which prisoned the
Mharg-demons. The powers of his Earthmastery impressed
the Keys to the wards into the cube of basalt that once had
served as the lightkeeper's door stop. After, Anskiere had pronounced his sentence upon the Firelord who had deserted him
at Elrinfaer, the bitter effects of which were to pass through
the next generation, to Jaric.

That instant, the dream shattered. Flung precipitously out
of the Stormwarden's memory, the son of Ivain tumbled
through blackness. Sound, sight, all sensations were lost to
him. The Llondel withheld any guidance. Abandoned to some
nightmare pocket between his own existence and the sorcerer's past, Jaric cried aloud. He struggled to reorient, half-
deranged by panic.

That moment a voice boomed out of the dark. *"Name
yourself, trespasser! What brings you to intrude upon the
Stormwarden of Elrinfaer?"*

No longer able to distinguish where dream-image ended
and reality began, Jaric felt his awareness netted by a will like
steel shackles. Power tore through him, ruthless and sure,
stripping him to his innermost self. Threatened by total anni-
hilation, he abandoned resistance. The touch softened and
abruptly released. Light flared and dimmed. Thrown to his
knees, Jaric opened his eyes to the sight of a carved stone
fireplace, and a room that disoriented him utterly. No trace
remained of ice cliffs, rain, or the chill of the windy night. His
hands dug into the pile of a richly patterned carpet, and the
clothing on his back was dry.

"Ivainson Jaric," said a voice at his back, gently, but terrible with command.

The boy rose. Bewildered and shaken, he faced the
speaker, and for the first time beheld Anskiere of Elrinfaer.
The Stormwarden waited before a faded square of tapestry.
His robes fell from straight shoulders, the velvet creaseless
and blue as the skies of summer. Firelight played over silver
hair, jutting brows, and a face creased deeply by weather and
hardship.

"You sought me," the Stormwarden said.

Jaric blinked. "Where am I? How did I get here?" He
raised a hand to his tunic, groped, and found the Keys to
Elrinfaer missing. Panic shook him. "The Llondian!"

"Sent you to me," Anskiere finished quickly. "This

chamber is an illusion, no more and no less than a thought within my mind. And the Llondelei are not your enemy."

Jaric reddened. "They are demons."

"All races of Kor's Accursed are not alike. Some would consummate their hatred against man to the detriment of the rest. If the Mharg fly again, the Llondelei would perish." Anskiere watched with understanding as Jaric absorbed this revelation. "Where the Keys are concerned, the Llondel is your ally."

Jaric met the sorcerer's eyes, found them deep as the horizon at the sea's edge. He wanted to feel anger, but could not. Once he had believed that Anskiere had cursed the Firelord in vengeance for past wrongs. Now he knew differently. The geas delivered at Northsea had been created solely against need, that the betrayal which ruined Elrinfaer should never again be repeated.

Anskiere spoke into the silence. "When I sent my summons, I already knew Ivain was dead."

The statement held multiple meanings. Jaric felt his throat constrict. Ivain dead meant his heir must answer, perhaps repeat the tragedy engendered by the Cycle of Fire; this Anskiere had known. Even as he called, the grief of that decision had stamped irrevocable sorrow on his heart. The Stormwarden saw, down to the least ramification, exactly what consequences he had set upon the untrained shoulders of the boy from Morbrith Keep.

"If you have questions, ask them now. I will answer as best I can. This may be the last time we communicate." Anskiere clarified with unemotional calm. "In sending you to me, the Llondel has shortened the span of my endurance. She took a risk that won't be repeated."

"She?" Jaric looked up, astonished. He had never thought of demons being female.

Anskiere returned a half smile. "They are not human, Jaric, but in some things the Llondelei are as mortal as you or I."

Mortal; Jaric flinched to hear such an admission from a sorcerer whose deeds had bent the very course of history. Yet the discovery should not have surprised him; the Stormwarden was not all-powerful. Prisoner himself, Anskiere dared not unbind the ice without a Firelord's skills; to loose those wards would release the frostwargs, demons themselves, and nearly as deadly as the Mharg. Jaric felt the blood go cold in his veins. How long could the Stormwarden survive in stasis beneath the ice, if no candidate mastered the Cycle of Fire?

Although Jaric lacked courage to voice his question, Anskiere answered directly. "My days will number less than the span of your own life."

The fire abruptly felt too warm at Jaric's back. He sweated, resisting an urge to step forward. "What of the frostwargs? If you die, will they escape?"

"Not immediately." As if sensing Jaric's discomfort, the Stormwarden turned and stared at the tapestry, which depicted a seascape in bleached blues and greens. The sorcerer qualified in a voice as worn as the thread. "The wards would deteriorate slowly. If electrical storms stay few and mild, the bindings might hold for a century and a half."

"The Vaere would send your successor," said Jaric.

"They might." Anskiere did not add that talent was rare; even the most gifted often failed to endure through the trials of a sorcerer's training. But his silence on the subject spoke volumes, and Jaric found none of the reassurance he sought. Every exchange with the sorcerer led him closer to the Cycle of Fire, until acceptance of the torment which had destroyed his father seemed inevitable as death.

"No." Anskiere whirled from the tapestry. He lifted eyes passionless as ice water and added, "The decision to undertake the Cycle of Fire can never be forced on a man. I charged you with one trial only: recover the Keys to Elrinfaer and hold them safe until they can be returned."

Jaric shrank from the sorcerer's gaze. Naked before perception which pierced through denial, and unraveled his dread of Ivain's mad fate to reveal the inner core of his shortcomings, for the first time he fully understood the burden set upon him. Memory replicated the conflict at Northsea and the doom Anskiere pronounced upon Ivain. "*. . . And should you die, my will shall pass to your eldest son, and to his son's sons after him, until the debt is paid.*"

As if cut by the lash of a whip, Jaric paled. His hands knotted beneath the cuffs of his tunic. "Can you not relieve me of the Keys?"

Anskiere replied with surprising gentleness. "Only if I am freed, son of Ivain. Until that day, you, or your children after you, must protect the Keys from demons."

"I have no such powers of defense!" Too late Jaric wished the words unsaid.

Anskiere smiled, implacable. "You have the potential."

"No!" Jaric abandoned restraint. Cornered by the Storm-warden's presence, and inwardly seared by the shared recall inflicted by the Llondel's thought-image, he spilled the horrors which had festered in his mind since the moment he discovered his parentage. "Who am I to assume those powers? Kordane's Fires, sorcerer, how many people did my father harm before he ran a knife through his heart?" Once started, Jaric could not stop. His voice thickened. "You, *Stormwarden,* with all your wisdom and compassion, *how many died at Tierl Enneth?*"

The accusation died into silence. Jaric stood with his chin lifted; he could not regret his defiance. The reproach was surely just. All Keithland remembered the wave which had roared in from the sea and despoiled the shores of Tierl Enneth. Four thousand people had died, each one under the Stormwarden's sworn protection.

Anskiere bent his head, vitality and strength drained from him until suddenly he seemed an old man. "I'll explain, Firelord's heir, though I've told none before but the Vaere. I pray you have wisdom enough to understand." He lifted tired eyes. "The demons found a way to twist the human mind and seize control. A terrible thing, for those they choose to corrupt are the talented. One called Tathagres came to me asking for apprenticeship. She proved to be the demon's own, and she discharged the powers of my staff one day while my back was turned. Such a simple betrayal I never thought to guard against. The staff was protected; to this moment I don't know how she manipulated the defense wards and lived. But her meddling raised the seas and destroyed Tierl Enneth. The act was done to discredit me."

Jaric let his hand fall, shaken to discover sweat on his palms. "Tathagres is dead."

The sorcerer responded fast as a slap. "Did her secrets perish with her?"

"Perhaps." But Jaric did not finish the thought, that more likely the witch had bequeathed her corruption to another. Drawn as an overpitched harpstring, he closed his eyes, wishing darkness could obliterate the destiny his inheritance laid before him. The sorcerer held no answer but the Cycle of Fire to his quandary; and that fate Jaric was determined to avoid, lest power beget more wrongs for demons to exploit. Since the Llondel had emphasized the perils of mankind's survival, Jaric

dreaded to be the one to upset the final balance and consign
his own kind to extinction. With a curse of agonized denial,
he wished himself elsewhere.

The carpet buckled without warning underfoot. Pitched off
balance, Jaric fell but struck no floor. The room dissolved into
air around him. Light melted into blackness, and the Stormwarden's final words scraped like the whisper of a ghost in a
void.

"Demons will seek the Keys, Ivainson Jaric. Guard them
well. Make what choices you must with boldness and courage.
My hope and my blessing go with you, however you fare."

Jaric strove to respond, but words stuck in his throat. Over
and over he tumbled, buffeted by powers beyond mortal control. When his voice broke free at last, he screamed with pain
and fear. The sound stung him awake. Roused to cold and
sharp rocks and the booming roar of breakers, Jaric opened his
eyes on the northern shore of Cliffhaven. Clouds had blanketed the stars. The ice cliffs towered upward, shadowed
white buttresses against the stygian dark of the sky. Shoreline,
reefs, and rocks blended beneath, stark as a drawing in mono-
chrome, except for two points of orange. The Llondel watched
still from the ledge, her cloak tucked over crossed legs and her
eyes emotionless sparks beneath her hood.

Jaric shifted and sat up. He set his back against granite and
cautiously studied the Llondel, but found no visual clue to
confirm her sex. Uncertainty followed; what if Anskiere's
words had been a dream, or, worse yet, an illusion designed
by the Llondel to blunt his sense of caution? Undermined by
mistrust, Jaric groped inside his tunic. Only when his fingers
located Anskiere's basalt block did suspicion leave him. If the
Llondel had not stolen the Keys by now, chances were her
intentions meant otherwise.

As if his thought cued movement, the demon blinked. Gray
cloth sighed in the dark as she leaned intently forward. *'Firelord's heir and Keeper of the Keys, you have spoken with
Anskiere. What now will you do?'*

The thought-image rang dissonant with threat. Jaric swallowed and found his throat dry. He was not out of danger yet.
Carefully as he sifted answers, in the end only truth would
suffice before the demon's empathic perception. Braced by
bravado he never knew he possessed, Jaric attempted an answer. "I will safeguard the Keys as best I am able. But I will
accept neither training nor power from the Vaere."

The Llondel hissed.

Jaric recoiled into rock. His next words came barbed with bitterness. "Did you know my father?" Desperate to be understood, he sent pictures flicking one after another through his mind; the Llondel would read them, he knew. Jaric showed the Firelord whose cruelty had so vividly marked the memories of man. Told in taprooms and singer's lament, and written in legal records, Ivain's capricious temper had inflicted destruction upon every corner of Keithland; burned hostels, slagged fields, and even the blistered hands of a stableboy too slow to bridle his horse.

Jaric finished, but the Llondel sat still as carved stone, eyes like candles under the shadow of her hood.

Uncertain what might move a demon to empathy, Jaric tried again. "Even when matched with noble intentions, the powers of the Vaere have brought grief to my kind." Once more the boy chose images, showed the grief which haunted Tierl Enneth after the discharge of Anskiere's staff let in the sea. "No matter how wise the sorcerer, power on that scale is too easily misused. I cannot." Jaric paused, swallowed, and doggedly resumed. "I won't be responsible for that kind of risk."

The Llondel hissed and surged into a crouch.

"No!" Jaric slammed both fists into his calf. "Wait and listen! There must be alternatives. *Won't you understand? Sorcery brings nothing but ruin.* If I must, I'll find another way to preserve my kind and return the Keys to Anskiere!"

A charged moment passed. Then the Llondel settled back with a ripple of robes. She extended an arm and with ritual deliberation scraped her spur along the stone between Jaric's knees. The sound raised hair on the boy's neck. Though the gesture was not customary among humankind, its meaning was unmistakable.

'I warn,' the Llondel sent. *'You are marked by the Vaere, and your path will be noted.'*

Chilled to the marrow, Jaric caught his breath, for the Llondian showed him an image of himself ringed by a triple band of fire. The pattern was all too similar to the seal on the Keys which symbolized Anskiere's mastery. The Llondel implied danger; she cautioned that the Firelord's heir would be not merely noticed, but *hunted.* The vision held warnings within warnings; Jaric's potential as a sorcerer posed threat to the demon compact at Shadowfane. His reluctance to develop

those talents yielded no safety at all, for since he lacked the
defenses of a Firelord's training, enemies might defeat him
without risk.

But danger alone could not shake Jaric's resolve. Brutal-
ized by memory of Anskiere of Elrinfaer's mastery, the undis-
ciplined mind of the boy could not fathom the weather sorcery
which had scoured the depths of his awareness. He knew only
that resonance of such power caused pain; the pitiless and
terrible self-command required to bend raw force into control
daunted comprehension. No margin existed for doubts.
Trapped by the realities of his own inadequacy, the heir of
Ivain met the Llondel's silence with denial.

For an interval, man and demon sat locked in stubborn
conflict. Then the Llondel whistled through the crescent slits
of her nostrils.

'*A true son of your father*,' she sent. Sharpened with Llondian frustration, the comparison wounded.

Jaric recoiled. "No!" He spoke out in rising anger. "I'll
have no part of Ivain's cruelty! By the Great Fall, even Anskiere said he couldn't force me to try the Cycle of Fire."

The Llondel trilled a mournful seventh. For a space her
eyes burned with an almost human sadness. '*Firelord's heir,
Keeper of the Keys*.' She wrought image with the subtlety of a
master musician, blending sight, sound, and ancestral memory
into a wail of inflexible destiny. The illusion echoed through
Jaric, choked his spirit with grief. '*Go as you will, son of
Ivain. But take heed. O little brother of your race, take heed*.'
And his sight of the Llondel's face rippled deftly into dream.

Blanketed by a touch like fog, Jaric slipped into the pattern
of her imaging. His awareness of ice cliffs and rock shifted,
transformed to the wallowing toss of a boat on the open
ocean. Barely larger than a dory, the craft carried patched
sails, a gaff rig, and piled nets which reeked of fish. Through
Llondian perception Jaric understood he viewed the present;
this boat sailed *now* off the western shores of Elrinfaer. Two
brothers in oilskins hauled twine over the gunwale. Unaware
of observation, they worked in silence, lit by a storm lantern
lashed to a ring in the sternpost. Salt-streaked glass threw
starred patterns which swung with each roll of the boat, and in
fitful intervals of shadow and light, Jaric noticed someone else
sprawled on the floorboards in the bow.

Sweating in the throes of fever, the third man lay half-cov-
ered by a rough wool cloak. The arm flung over his face was

streaked with dirt and sand, and clothed in ragged linen. Jaric
saw glints of goldwork on the cuff. With a twist of dread he
recognized the pattern of the weave. He examined the man
more closely, saw fingers scabbed with blisters and seal-black
hair caught in tangles beneath. Without looking further, Jaric
knew. Here lay Taen Dreamweaver's brother, Emien, whom
Jaric had forced to yield the Keys to Elrinfaer over the bared
point of a sword scarcely three days past. The fishermen must
have found him wandering the beaches and taken him on
board. The sight of Emien's suffering should have inspired
pity; instead, Jaric felt dread, as if something had gone irrevocably amiss.

From the depths of the Llondel's dream, he called out.
"Why? What harm can Emien do? His mistress, Tathagres, is
dead, murdered by his own hand on the shores of Elrinfaer. It
was she, not Emien, who conjured through the powers of
demons."

The Llondel responded with images. Jaric watched the
fishing vessel blur, then shift in some subtle manner, as if a
veil suddenly fell away. With eerie clarity, the scene that followed recorded what would happen in a time yet to come.
Jaric saw Emien shed his wool covering, rise, and take an
unsteady step. His eyes glistened with fever and his arm trembled as he grasped the gunwale to steady himself against the
heel of the boat over the waves. The sullen set of the sick
boy's features unsettled Jaric with foreboding; though Emien
walked with the abandon of a sleepwalker, he acted for a
purpose beyond the vague stirrings of delirium.

The boat wallowed over a crest and the lantern tossed.
Shadows wheeled, pooling and receding over faded planking
as the stern settled deeply into the trough. Twine chafed
against the thwart, dragged seaward by the relentless pull of
the water. The nearer fisherman swore irritably. His sea boots
stamped against floorboards as he set his weight to his work;
had he looked up, he would have seen Emien leave the bow.
But, absorbed by their labor, neither brother noticed the fugi-
tive they had rescued from Elrinfaer bend and search out the
flensing knife stowed in the forward sail locker.

Only Jaric watched as quivering, blistered fingers tightened
over the steel. Then the air surrounding Emien's body rippled,
as if wind stirred curtains of light made visible. The boy's
form shimmered with a glow similar to the aura which had
surrounded the Stormwarden of Elrinfaer when Jaric had ob-

served through the Llondel's perception. Yet, although related to power, this configuration was *other,* evil in itself. Plainly Taen's brother had inherited Tathagres' affinity for demon possession.

Jaric shouted, but in the half-world of the Llondel's dream, his voice made no sound. Reminded that he experienced nothing more than a prescient image, he watched helplessly as Emien wrenched the knife from the wood. The reddish aura flickered, strengthened, became a hard-edged veil of force. Infused by a rush of demon strength, Emien lunged and sank his blade in the back of the nearest fisherman. Hands slackened on the nets. Twine grated over wood, reclaimed by the sea, and the man slumped against the gunwale with a gurgling cry. Blood snaked across his oilskins, black in the lanternlight. With a yell of outrage and surprise, his brother spun around. He glimpsed a fevered face, tangled hair blown back from a demented smile. Then Emien's knife found his chest. The fisherman toppled backward into the silvery mass of his catch.

The boat rocked, unbalanced by the sharp shift of weight. Amid a hellish whirl of shadows, Emien cast the net free. Weights rattled and splashed into the sea. The man's dying struggles sank slowly beneath the waves as, heartlessly practical, Emien kicked the second corpse overboard. He moved aft and took the tiller. The fishing boat ducked, swung, and jibed. Canvas banged taut with a clattering crash of blocks, and the compass needle steadied on a northerly heading.

Guided by Llondian prescience, Jaric peered futureward through a stormy crossing that ended far north on the shores of Felwaithe. There the beloved black-haired brother of Taen Dreamweaver debarked, met at last by the masters who had chosen him for service. Haggard after his weeks upon the sea, Emien stumbled across the sand, to be caught by the waiting hands of demons.

Jaric whispered denial, in vain. Powerless to influence the course of events, he watched Kor's Accursed lift Emien onto a litter and bear him off to the northeast. The image rippled, changed. Jaric saw beyond the borders of Keithland to a vista of windswept rock. There the land lay barren, unchanged as the desolation before the Great Fall; nothing lived but the sparse growth of lichens. Outlined by empty sky, demon masters bore Emien up the slope of a jagged crag. A fortress reared from the summit, all gray angles and spindled tiers of towers. Overwhelmed by despair, Jaric beheld the keep and knew, though never in life had he gone there. Legend named that castle Shadowfane, prison of the damned and the stronghold of demon might. If Emien ever emerged, his purpose would be the ruin of his own kind.

⌒⌒ IV ⌒⌒

King of Pirates

Jaric awoke to a fine, soaking rain. Water dripped from his hair, spilled coldly through his fingers, and trickled across the rock beneath. The Llondian's dream left him desolate; trouble would come from Shadowfane, trouble such as Keithland had never known. His own responsibility could no longer be denied. Once he might have prevented the murder of the fishermen, even spared Emien the damnation of Shadowfane's dark halls. Huddled in the misty darkness of the ledge, Jaric wished he could forget the moment the Keys had been reclaimed on the shores of Elrinfaer; then he had held Emien at bay beneath the naked point of a sword, yet not struck home. Unmanned by the sister's grief and his own reluctance to kill, he had hesitated. Jaric bit his lip. No good would come from that moment of mercy. In letting Emien escape he had only left the demons another tool to work evil upon Keithland.

Slowly, stiffly, Jaric sat up. No orange eyes glared at him through the darkness. The ledge was deserted, empty rock silvered by a patina of water. The Llondel demon had gone. Free to leave, Jaric knew an instant of sharp distrust. Only when he ascertained that the Keys to Elrinfaer and the storm-falcon's feather remained safe beneath his tunic did he relax enough to assess his position. Drawn by a faint gleam, he discovered his knife on the stone, its handle neatly turned toward him. Nearby lay a second object.

Jaric leaned forward. Pebbles grated beneath his thigh as he transferred his weight and cautiously touched the dagger. No Llondian appeared to prevent him. Jaric closed his fingers over the hilt with a grateful sense of relief. He sheathed the weapon swiftly. The other item waited, forbidding and pale as bone in the dark. Jaric preferred to go without touching it; but his mistake with Emien at Elrinfaer had taught him never to leave an unknown peril at his back.

Jaric explored the object with tentative fingers. The surface felt strangely warm, as if it had recently lain close to living flesh. Carved of wood, and chased with fine whorls of inlaid shell, the thing was recognizable as a flute. Twelve holes pierced its shaft, spaced for alien fingers. Prompted by intuition not entirely his own, Jaric understood that the instrument had been left for him to use at need. If he sounded the highest note of the scale, he could summon Llondelei aid.

Alarmed by the perception, Jaric flinched. Only demon imaging could prompt an explanation of the gift. No doubt the creature lurked nearby, out of sight, yet watching still. Made cautious by fear, Jaric hesitated. No man dared trust a demon, and possession of any Llondian artifact could bring a charge of heresy within the civilized borders of Keithland. Harmless or not, the demon's gift must be refused.

Jaric returned the instrument to the niche and rose. Poisoned by mistrust, he suspected the dreams. His recent exchange with Anskiere's consciousness might all have been an illusion wrought by Llondian imaging. Possibly the creature had sought to relax his guard, undermine the tenets of his own kind, and, as with Emien, bring about his downfall. Though soaked to the skin and aching with stiffened muscles, Jaric flattened himself against the escarpment. He resumed his climb to the ice cliffs with driven determination.

Though the worst of the ascent lay behind, rain-slicked rocks made treacherous footing. Cold had slowed his reflexes, and a misstep could tumble him over the brink, send him crashing down jagged granite to drown, broken, amid the savage maelstrom of breakers and reefs. Jaric inched forward. The smell of seaweed soured his lungs as he breathed. The ledge sloped upward, to widen gradually into an outthrust shelf of rock. Anskiere's prison arose beyond, white ramparts dirtied by drifting fog.

Jaric felt dwarfed to insignificance in that place. Surf reared up, crested, smashed into foam against the ice; the cliffs amplified the hiss of falling spray until it sounded immediately underfoot. Wind sighed over the crags, driving rain that trickled coldly down Jaric's collar. When he had received Anskiere's summons before, the Stormwarden had called to him in words shaped of wind. Jaric had listened against a silence so complete even the sea seemed muted. But this time the elements reflected only the random patterns of storm and tide. No breeze, no word, and no welcome awaited the boy who carried the Keys to Elrinfaer.

Chilled and disheartened, Jaric braced his back against the rock face. "Anskiere!"

His shout reverberated across the chasm, lost amid drumming waves. Jaric lacked the heart to try a second time. No spoken word could reach the Stormwarden of Elrinfaer, and with a heavy sense of foreboding the boy suspected the Llondel's vision might be accurate. *Keeper of the Keys* the demon had named him; the title left him bitter. Nothing in life had prepared him for such responsibility. Since the day Anskiere's geas overtook him, he had acted without thought or strategy, forced to complete the sorcerer's bidding within a framework not of his shaping. Now, chilled by the discomforts of rain and fog, Jaric fought to choose for himself. He would seek his own course instead of answering power with like power; rather than attempt the Cycle of Fire with its ruinous train of consequences, he would search until he found some other solution. Surely somewhere in Keithland an alternative existed to answer the threat of the demons.

More alone than he had ever been before, Jaric laced icy fingers over his face. He knew the perils. Each hour that passed lent the demons of Shadowfane time to design against him; more than his own peace might shatter before he finished. One day Taen Dreamweaver would learn of her brother's alliance with the enemy; her Vaere-trained talents made discovery inevitable, for no mortal on Keithland could hide truth from her dream-sense. Despite her exceptional courage, the grief of Emien's defection might break her. Of all risks, that one galled Jaric most sorely. If he ever completed his search, he swore as Firelord's heir he would shelter her.

Dawn broke dingy and gray through the drizzle which fell over Cliffhaven. Half-buried in the oiled-wool cloak lent by the Kielmark, Taen Dreamweaver perched on a rock above the tide mark, waiting. Jaric would return shortly. She knew without extending her powers; since the Vaere had employed her talents to lure Jaric into the bindings of Anskiere's curse against Ivain, the Dreamweaver perhaps understood the Firelord's heir better than he knew himself. Yet the effects of that betrayal had scarred the boy, and bitterness and distrust still shadowed their friendship. With Jaric, Taen dared not delve deeply. He knew her touch, and far too much of Keithland's safety lay balanced in his hands for her to risk any chance of upset. She sat patiently through rain and the lingering shadow of night until Jaric chose to come down.

Daylight brightened the sky above the ice cliffs. Gulls banked and swooped on the air, scavenging morsels the tide had left amid rain-blurred profiles of rock. Taen peeled wet hair off her cheek and tugged her maroon hood forward to shield her face from the wind. The smell of soaked wool mingled with tide wrack and damp. She barely noticed her cold feet. Brushed inwardly by a change subtle as shifting current, she smiled for the first time in days; for, on a ledge above her vantage point, Jaric rose and finally began his descent. He weathered his disappointment well, thought Taen. She sighed with relief. A touch of color returned to her cheeks, and she lifted blue eyes to the cliffs where Jaric would soon reappear. Although the Vaere had rebuked Taen often for her impetuous nature, she could not help but hope. Both Anskiere's deliverance and Keithland's future depended on Ivainson's mastery of the Cycle of Fire.

The darkest hours of night had passed more easily than those last minutes while Jaric descended the ice cliffs. Taen rose as he leaped the last yard to the strand. He stumbled on landing, muscles stiffened from chill. Light hair tumbled down over his eyes in the rain. Even from a distance Taen could see that he shivered.

"Jaric!" Breaking waves drowned her call. Irritated, the Dreamweaver raised her voice again. "Jaric!"

He stopped and looked up, brown eyes wide with surprise. Pleased he had not detected her surveillance through the night, Taen muffled a grin behind one wool-draped wrist and ran to meet him.

She arrived breathless at his side and, tilting her face up to look at him, saw exhaustion stamped across his features. "You've got fish-brains between your ears." Her hands seemed childishly small as she worked loose the brooch which pinned her cloak. The moment the fastening freed, she flicked the wool open and bundled Jaric inside; the Kielmark's garment was generous enough to accommodate both of them.

"I'm soaked!" he protested.

"Fish-brains!" The word transformed to a gasp as the seal-wetness of him penetrated the dry layers of Taen's shift. "No you don't," she added as Jaric tried to draw away. "You'll hate it more if I have to feed you broth in bed."

He did not smile, which was unlike him. Instead he

glanced at the big, square-cut ruby which adorned the cloak pin. Taen felt him tense.

"That's the Kielmark's," Jaric said sharply. "He knows you're here?"

"Fish-brains is too generous," Taen replied. Warned by her dream-sense that contact with her body was adding to Jaric's uneasiness, she loosened the cloak slightly. "When his Lordship the King of Pirates noticed you'd left his banquet without permission, he shouted like a madman and told half his captains to arm themselves directly and look for you. I offered to come in their place. I told him I already knew where to find you." Jaric would know her words were understatement. The Sovereign Lord of Cliffhaven was about as easy to influence as a rabid wolf, particularly concerning strangers who trespassed on his island domain.

Yet Jaric did not probe beneath her light humor. In tight-lipped silence he lifted the brooch from her hand, then rammed the pin violently through the collar of the cloak. When he spoke, he answered the question she dared not voice; and the real reason behind the Kielmark's short-tempered concern: would he accept his heritage as Ivain Firelord's heir, or would he abandon the Stormwarden to the ice and leave Keithland in jeopardy?

"I'm going to the libraries at Landfast." Jaric paused, expecting rebuttal. Taen held her breath, waited with patience like sword steel until he resumed. "If there is a way for me to avoid repeating the sorrows my father loosed upon men, I will find it without mastering the Cycle of Fire."

He took a sudden step forward. Taen stumbled against him as the cloak between them snapped taut. Reminded of her presence, Jaric flung an arm about her shoulders to steady her. "I'm sorry, little witch." He phrased the nickname with affection. "But I'm weary of the ways of sorcerers."

Argument would not move him. Taen suspected he kept something from her, but the resistant set of his jaw warned against using dreamweaver's skill to probe deeper. If she attempted to tamper with his decision, she would strike where he was guarded, so deeply did he resent the fact that he was puppet to a sorcerer's geas. Worn by more than her nightlong vigil, Taen dragged her feet through the sand.

Jaric's fingers tightened against her sleeve. He freed his other hand and gently tucked an ink-black strand of her hair back under the hood. "Shall we return this cloak to the Kielmark before he sends one of his bloodthirsty captains to collect it?"

Taen nodded, resigned. She would have to trust him. The struggle to recover the Keys to Elrinfaer had opened new depths in Jaric; his decision to research at Landfast did not entirely disown responsibility. Still, the choice brought little reassurance. If Ivainson found no alternate answer, if Keithland's threat became imminent, with the Cycle of Fire the only choice left to ensure mankind's survival, Taen foresaw an unpleasant consequence: the Vaere might command her to betray him, just as she had done once before.

The weather grew worse as the day progressed. By the time Jaric caught and bridled his horse, rain battered the earth in white sheets. Leaving the cloak to Taen, he helped her into her saddle, then swung astride his own mount. Bent against a whipping north wind, he reined around toward the main fortress of Cliffhaven. Taen endured the ride, uncharacteristically silent as the horses carried them inland. The terrain sloped upward. Dune grass gave way to thornbrakes, and rocks thrust through mossy tufts of ground cover. The hills beyond lifted into serried ranks of mountains, and cedar-crowned summits reared above valleys choked with fog. The air warmed as the ice cliffs fell behind. The horses scattered droplets from sweetfern and wildflowers, and splashed through streams in the fells. One league from the beach, the two riders broke through to the cliff road where the horses made better speed. Hooves clattered over a beaten track shored up with stone, built to allow fast passage for the Kielmark's patrols. Well before midday, Jaric and the Dreamweaver pulled their steaming mounts to a walk beneath the flint-black walls of the harbor fort.

Jaric led toward the town side entrance, a cramped archway which pierced the fortifications between the matching black turrets of the gate towers. Rain glistened over rounded, weather-scarred stone. Beyond the crenellations loomed the angled roofs of artisans' alley, shops and forges jammed like blocks against the steep pitch of the slope.

Jaric drew rein before the wall. As Taen stopped her horse beside him, he shook the water from his hair and inclined his head toward the town. "You go in. I'm going on to the harbor."

A sudden clang of metal from the gatehouse obscured

Taen's protest. Both riders started in surprise as a siege shutter crashed back.

A bearded guardsman leaned out. "You'll both come in," he shouted. "Kielmark's orders. He sent me along to escort you."

Jaric's mouth flinched into a line. He touched heels to his mount. Hooves banged on wet cobbles as his horse sidled around to face Taen. "You didn't," he accused.

Taen shook her head, at first unable to speak over the din as the guardsman wrestled the siege shutter closed. "I told the Kielmark I would find you, no more. He summons us through no act of mine."

The officer reappeared in the shadow beneath the archway. "Hurry along!" His shout sounded surly. "The watch already sent word of your return, and the Kielmark waits."

Jaric did not obey. His brown eyes remained intently fixed upon Taen, and his heels made no move in the stirrups. The Dreamweaver shifted uncomfortably in the saddle. Her fingers clamped on the reins until her horse shook its neck in protest. To defy the command would be madness; the Kielmark was ruthlessly swift to punish inefficiency, and the rogues who served him often killed rather than provoke his anger. The officer strode impatiently from the archway. Raindrops caught like jewels in his mail as he closed his hand over his sword hilt. Even then Taen dared engage no dreamweaver's power to search Jaric's reason for delay. If Ivainson were ever to trust her again, her word alone must suffice.

The officer hissed through his teeth. "Have you both gone *crazy?*" He spoke out in genuine dismay, and with a start of relief Taen recognized his voice.

"Corley?" She twisted in the saddle to be certain. Rain had darkened the man's beard to burnt chestnut; a mouth customarily crooked with laughter now bent into a grim scowl of annoyance. No ordinary officer of the watch, Deison Corley was the Kielmark's most trusted senior captain. His presence could not be ignored.

"Jaric," Taen pleaded. "Will you come?"

The boy accepted the fact that he was beaten with open reluctance. A shiver whipped his frame as he reined his horse toward the gatehouse. Taen's animal needed no incentive to follow. Corley saw his charges turn, and ran to escape the downpour before his last dry patch of clothing became sodden. He preceded them under the arch, his surcoat mottled with damp across broad shoulders.

"Kor!" The captain's clipped north-shore accent lifted over the confined echo of hooves. "I should have the both of you back to polish gear after this. Two things the Kielmark hates alike, and that's rust on his ships or his officers' swords."

Taen grinned beneath her dripping hood. The complaint was all bluff and banter; Corley, she knew, kept whetstone and rag in his pockets. During idle moments he maintained the disconcerting habit of sharpening his knives one after another in succession. Once, during a lengthy council of war, Taen had counted nine separate blades on his person; barracks rumor claimed there were more.

Hunched against the weather, Corley glanced over his shoulder at Jaric. "Well," he said to the stiff-faced boy. "Ride at my back, mad as all that, and I'd sure feel less nervous if you'd swear."

The quip raised no response. The storm met them with a white wall of water on the far side of the archway, and Jaric rode in bitter silence. Battered by wind and discomfort, the party passed through narrow, switchback streets to the Kielmark's inner stronghold. Jaric stumbled badly when he dismounted. Only then did Taen realize his behavior stemmed partly from chill. Exhausted after his nightlong vigil on the ice cliffs, the boy was numbed to the point where mind and muscle would barely respond. Taen called upon her powers as Dreamweaver and touched Corley's mind with concern.

The captain's eyebrows rose. He flashed Jaric a startled glance and bellowed irritably for the horse-boy.

But the child on duty ran from the stables already. He caught the reins Corley flung with deft efficiency, relieved Taen of her mare, and jerked his head at Jaric's gray. "Let that one go. He's battle-trained to stand."

"On, then." Corley caught Jaric's arm in a firm grip and steadied the boy's first steps. Bent against the downpour, Taen followed the two of them across the rain-sleek slate of the bailey.

"Kor *damn* the weather!" Corley stepped through the vaulted arches from the dooryard. "Made just to please the ducks."

Blotting his face on his surcoat, he marked puddled footsteps the length of the hallway beyond. Taen shed her cloak as she walked, and nearly repeated Corley's oath as a thick lock

of hair snagged on the Kielmark's ruby pin. She worried at the
tangle with her head tilted sideways, out of habit veering toward the entrance to the main hall.

"No, Lady," said Corley without turning around. Cued to
the Dreamweaver's change in direction by the sound of her
footsteps, he added more kindly, "The Kielmark waits in his
private study."

Taen yanked her hair free of the brooch and irritably hurried to catch up while the captain steered Jaric up a short flight
of steps. She followed the length of a corridor floored with
gold-veined marble. The ironbound door at the end lay ajar,
firelight shining through the crack.

Corley shouldered the panel open without knocking. "I
have the both of them, Lord, sopped as fishes, but secure."

The door swung wide, revealing a patterned expanse of
carpet, carved chairs, and tables untidily sprawled with charts.
Flame-light glanced over gilt carving and curled parchment,
and cast crawling shadows across walls lined with books. No
method attended their shelving; Cliffhaven castle held priceless treasure, plundered and gathered as tribute from ships
which hailed from the farthest corners of Keithland. But the
owner cared nothing for neatness. A pearl and lacquer side
table supported a box of rusty horseshoes, and a smiling marble cherub danced with the Kielmark's buckler and great
sword slung across its wings.

A man muscled to match that weapon rose from behind the
charts. Candles flickered in the draft from the door, spattering
light over eyes pale and restless as a wolf's. Beneath wavy
black hair, the Sovereign Ruler of Cliffhaven wore an expression ominous as thunderheads. "You're late," he opened
sharply. "The watch reported twenty minutes ago." Rubies
sparkled in the torque at his throat as he moved around the
table.

Corley offered no excuse, but turned and gently latched the
door. Long years in the Kielmark's service had taught him
when to keep silent. Left facing Jaric, the Lord of Cliffhaven
treated the boy to a glance of rapacious intensity. Then he
crossed the chamber in three fluid strides.

"Young fool." The Kielmark caught Jaric's shoulder, spun
him deftly into a chair, and bellowed for a servant to bring
mulled wine. Then he gestured for Taen and Corley to be
seated.

"Don't mind the wet clothes," he barked as Taen hesitated.

"There are plenty more pretty chairs in the warehouses by the dockside."

Taen sat, wincing with the abused brocade. As the candle flames steadied and brightened, she noticed that the Kielmark's leather tunic was creased and soiled with ship's tar; his nails were rimmed with dirt, and his hair lay in soggy curls against his neck. No doubt he had come directly from the wharf, where his men shortened docklines against the rising wind.

Restless as live coals, the Kielmark paced before the hearth. Although his face lay in shadow, his displeasure could be felt the breadth of the room. He stopped without warning and spoke. "Kor's Fires, boy, the Dreamweaver told us you wouldn't raise Anskiere. Did you have to stay out sulking all night?"

Jaric stiffened, and Taen stifled a cry behind her knuckles.

Before she could speak, the Kielmark rounded on her, eyes slitted with keen speculation. "Ah, so you didn't tell him."

Taen shook her head, annoyed to see her efforts wasted. As Jaric turned resentful eyes toward her, she tried desperately to mend the damage caused by the Kielmark's thoughtlessness. "You wouldn't have listened, Jaric. No matter what anyone said, you would have gone to the ice cliffs to see for yourself."

Yet Jaric misinterpreted. His grip tightened on the arms of his chair until the fingers stood white against the wood. Fair, wind-tangled hair dripped water down the line of a jaw just starting to show a beard. Barely eighteen, he was ill prepared to contend with the fate Ivain Firelord had bequeathed him. Caught by a moment of pity, Taen reached out with her powers, and brushed lightly through the surface of his mind in an instinctive desire to reassure.

Jaric felt her touch and flinched. Cut by his mistrust, and unpleasantly aware of how closely the Kielmark followed the exchange, Taen tried again. Her tone turned sharper than she intended. "Jaric, I needed no Vaerish sorceries to see your desire to be released from Anskiere's geas."

That moment the latch clicked. The Kielmark spun on light feet as the door opened and a grizzled servant entered with a tray. Wary of his master's mood, the man moved with maximum speed and no noise. He rested his burden by the box of horseshoes. The scent of spices and hot spirits filled the room as he began to pour from a cut-crystal carafe.

The Kielmark caught up the first tankard the instant it was full and personally handed the steaming drink to Jaric. "You're numbed witless from the cold, boy. A girl-child could knock you down with a rag doll."

Jaric lifted the tankard to his lips. He managed a shaky swallow, and a thin flush of color suffused his cheeks. The Kielmark folded his arms; as if softened by a woman's touch, his stance relaxed, and Taen sensed the tension leave him. Corley released a pent-up breath, pulled a knife from his boot, and with soft, rhythmic strokes scraped the blade across the whetstone in his other hand. As if the habit signaled safety, the servant resumed his duties.

"Now," said the Kielmark. Parchment crackled as he braced his weight against the chart table and swept a glance around the chamber. "Here is what I propose."

But his tone of voice suggested outright command. As Taen accepted mulled wine from the servant, she understood no debate would be tolerated. Corley knew also. His steel sang crisply under the pressure of his hands, and his deep, cinnamon eyes stayed shadowed under his lashes.

"My brigantine *Moonless* is provisioned and a full crew stands anchor watch." The Kielmark hooked his thumbs in his belt. "When the tide turns, she'll sail and take you both to the Isle of the Vaere under my flag."

Jaric perched his tankard between his knees. His cheeks flushed red in the firelight as he looked up. "No."

Corley's whetstone bit into steel with a clear and savage ring, and the servant fled from the chamber. Taen felt a stab of dread. Fearfully she watched the Kielmark's sword arm bunch until the muscles strained the stitches of his cuff.

"Boy, I didn't hear you say that."

"You will." Jaric lifted his chin with unprecedented composure. "My boat *Callinde* was a loan. She must be returned to a fisherman in Mearren Ard."

Deliberate as a cat, the Kielmark straightened. Corley's fingers froze on his knife, and the whetstone's whispered stroke went silent. Taen's skin prickled with alarm. With the sensitivity of her dream-sense upset by an overpowering threat of violence, she saw Jaric must desist, or risk destruction. She acted without thought, and initiated the rapport shared through the dangerous recovery of the Keys to Elrinfaer. For she knew the single fact which could forestall his headlong course and protect him from the Kielmark's wrath. Given no time to soften fact, Taen balanced her gift, bent Jaric's mind to a place leagues distant, and forced him to see.

Under her influence, the chamber rippled, transformed, became a misty shore haunted by the dissonant cries of gulls. In the smoke-dimmed interior of a shack which reeked of fish, a girl wept over the body of an elderly man. Closed in death, his eyes no longer shone with the piercing clarity of a sailor; work-crippled hands lay slack against mottled, silver-tipped furs costly enough to clothe a prince.

Through the rapport of the dream-link, Taen felt the echo of Jaric's shock as he recognized the girl and her uncle. His grief cut like a cry through darkness, for the man, Mathieson Keldric, had once answered a boy's desperate need and traded his only treasure for a cloak of ice otter fur he had not wanted. Repaired and seaworthy, *Callinde* had sailed; Jaric had been spared, but the loss of a beloved boat had broken the old man's heart.

The link shattered, dissolved into firelight and book-smell as Jaric wrenched free. "Kordane's Blessed Fires!" He turned tortured eyes to Taen, and she read there a desperation beyond her ability to fathom. "You might have spared me that!"

She stared at the carpet, her toes jabbed angrily into patterned wool. Tears stung her lashes. She held them back, determined Jaric should not see. Spare him she could not; had he persisted in sailing for Mearren Ard, the Kielmark would have lost his temper, and in the unpredictable reaction which followed, the Firelord's sole heir might easily have been killed.

"So," the Kielmark concluded. Muscle rippled under his tunic as he braced one arm against the mantel. "You'll not be sailing to return your craft to a corpse."

Jaric sat spear-straight in his chair. Steam drifted from his tankard, wound lazy ribbons through the air before him. "Neither will I sail for the Isle of the Vaere. I'm going to Landfast to study the libraries instead."

Corley stopped breathing. The Kielmark released a great, rowdy laugh, but the sound held menace like barbs wrapped in velvet. "I'd kill you," he said simply.

"I'd let you." Jaric's hands remained motionless in his lap. He held the Kielmark's furious gaze and his voice continued, passionless as ice water through the charged atmosphere of the room. "Better I died, I think, than accept the madness, the recklessness, and the cruelty of my father's heritage."

The Kielmark's brows knotted. His eyes narrowed in surprise and he glanced swiftly at Taen.

The enchantress nodded, dream-sent a spurious message much as she had when in the heat of the battle she had helped defend Cliffhaven against the demons. *'He means it, Lord. Jaric has been pressured as much as a man can be, and still believe in himself. Remember and be cautious. He faced down the Stormwarden before you, and lost.'*

The Kielmark stretched like a dog kicked out of sleep. He ran thick fingers through his hair and suddenly grinned. "You're a bold one, I'll give you that," he said to Jaric. "And more like Ivain than you'd know, there's fact if ever you discover manhood enough to face it." His manner changed, abruptly turned to challenge. "Why Landfast?"

Jaric drew a shaky breath and spoke over the careful scrape of Corley's knife. "I intend to find an alternative answer to sorcery."

"Ah." The Kielmark pushed off from the mantel, began restlessly pacing the rug. "Then you'll sail there on *Moonless,* and Corley will captain."

Jaric made a slight sound. Before Taen could gather a shred of power in defense, the Kielmark plucked the sword from the cherub's back. Steel sang from his sheath with killing speed. In one spinning instant, the bare blade lay poised against Jaric's neck. Corley froze in place. Taen felt her hands break into sweat. With painstaking control she balanced her awareness, knowing all the while her powers were useless. Whether or not she stunned the Kielmark unconscious, the sword lay too close for safety. If the hand that held the weapon loosened, the weight of the blade alone would cut the flesh beneath.

The Kielmark spoke into sudden stillness, his voice barely audible over the snap of the fire in the grate. "You'll listen, Firelord's heir." His fist tightened; steel pressed against Jaric's skin, drawing a thin bead of blood. "One hundred and eighty-four of *my best men* lie dead because of the Keys to Elrinfaer. I'll not repeat the experience, not for pride or any man's protest. Where you go, the Keys go. Demons and trouble will follow like sharks on a gaffed fish. You know this."

The Kielmark's wrists flexed, and the sword lifted so abruptly the edge sang through the air. "You may have your time at Landfast. But only if you and that Dreamweaver board *Moonless* at once. There's a man waiting at the docks with a longboat. If you wish, your sloop *Callinde* may go along in tow, but you'll sail *nowhere* without my escort. Am I clear?"

Jaric swallowed, nodded, and touched a finger to the tiny drop of blood on his neck. Beside the Kielmark's great bulk, he seemed slight to the point of fragility. His brown eyes turned poignant with uncertainty, as if he doubted his choice. Yet at length he stirred and stood.

"So," said the Kielmark. He sounded strangely tired. "You're dismissed."

Like a warning, Corley's whetstone and knife stayed silent. Taen set her tankard down. Her hands shook and she dreaded the act of standing. Sapped by a sudden, fervent desire to be safely back on the Isle of the Vaere, she shut her eyes to regain her composure. A touch smoothed the hair against her shoulder. Taen looked, found Jaric before her with one hand extended. He half lifted her to her feet. Through his wiry strength, she felt the tremors which shook him; but whether he shivered from cold or the aftermath of fear she could not tell.

"Corley, I want a word with you." The Lord of Cliffhaven rested his sword point downward against the carpet. He stared through the rain-washed glass of the casement, and did not move until Dreamweaver and Firelord's heir had departed.

⟬ V ⟭

Crossing

The latch clicked shut, and the sound of footsteps dwindled down the passage beyond the Kielmark's study. The Lord of Cliffhaven sheathed the sword he had turned upon Jaric and carefully lowered his muscled bulk into the nearest chair. Light from the candelabra fell full across his face, illuminating abrasions and bruises left over from his ruse to defeat Kisburn's army. Four days with too little rest had not encouraged healing. Deison Corley studied the Kielmark's pose with perception well honed by familiarity, and at once understood what the effort with the sword had cost. The captain bent with all the tact he possessed and sheathed his dagger in his boot. Then, absorbed by the movement of his hands, he straightened, flicked his wrist, and caught the slender blade which slithered from his sleeve. With what seemed limitless patience, he set steel against whetstone and began rhythmically to hone the point.

"That boy is a brash one," the Kielmark said presently.

Corley scraped his blade across stone and grimaced. "Got a will like one of Tierk's new anchor chains. And the girl's no different. Ever wonder how old she was when the Vaere took her for training?"

"Taen?" The Kielmark rested his chin on his fist. "She told me once." His voice resumed quietly over the whispered ring of the dagger. "The last memory she had before her passage into mastery was that of a ten-year-old girl."

Corley's hands faltered, stopped. "Kor's Fires!" But blasphemy was inadequate; with an incredulity that prickled the hairs on his neck, the captain recalled Taen's part in the recent battle against Kisburn's army. She might wear the body of a grown woman, but in years and worldly experience, she was poignantly, vulnerably young. "Did you know her age before you asked her to dream-weave those defenses?"

"No," said the Kielmark abruptly. With Corley he made no

effort to school his manner. "Count on this, though. The Vaere themselves are desperate. Jaric is their final hope for Anskiere."

Steel sheared ringingly across whetstone. Corley remained silent, aware as no stranger could be that orders were forthcoming.

The Kielmark straightened without warning. "You will sail *Moonless* to Landfast. Place Jaric in the hands of Kor's priests, for trouble will nest with him like swarming wasps and he mustn't be caught defenseless in the countryside. I want the Dreamweaver clear of danger. She broke her oath with the Vaere to remain here and save Cliffhaven. Guard her life as you would my own, and return her to the Isle of the Vaere."

Corley set his whetstone on his knee and laid the little knife aside. He knew the Lord of Cliffhaven well enough to expect more instructions.

The Kielmark rose. Propped by one arm against the edge of the table, he fished beneath horseshoes and with a clanking jangle of metal, retrieved a leather sack. This he tossed to his captain. Corley stretched and fielded the object without upsetting knife and whetstone. Coins chimed as he thrust the bag beneath his tunic.

Across the room the King of Pirates stared at sky through the casement. "Someone well versed in arms made sure that Jaric carries a very fine sword. Corley, you must see he finishes learning how to use it. Instruct him during the crossing to Landfast. When you make port, use the gold to hire the city's most skillful weapons master. He will pose as a tutor, but actually serve Jaric as bodyguard. The boy is not to know. Let him believe his teacher saw talent, and chose as a gift to develop it."

Cued by a shift in his master's stance, Corley slipped his whetstone in his pocket. He sheathed the knife with an almost imperceptible movement and stood, awaiting the Kielmark's final instructions.

"Make a safe passage, old friend." The King of Pirates clapped Corley's shoulder in a rare gesture of concern. "I'd trust this task to no other."

"Fires." Corley rolled his eyes at the ceiling, a devilish grin on his lips. "You would've, and for a song, too, if Selk's old hag of a wife hadn't tripped on that hen and done herself in with a pothook. One yell from her, even demons'd flee.

Any kid old enough to eat meat would've taken to weapons in self-defense."

The Kielmark rewarded him with a genuine shout of laughter. "Get out," he said, gasping. "Warp *Moonless* out of the harbor, or I swear I'll attach Selk's wife's maiden sister to your pay share!"

Corley laid his hand on the latch. "Don't. She's community property. We're saving her for the light tower in case the fog bells ever crack." And he spun through the door before the Kielmark's quick mind could find a rejoinder.

The rain abated, but wind arose to replace it, whining through the stays and rattling *Callinde*'s mast and yard with the abandon of a madman drumming sticks. Docklines creaked against the bollards as Jaric stepped aboard. Bundled in a cloak of green, hand-spun wool, he knelt on the floorboards and set both hands against the sternpost. The wood was checked and gray; the marks of the tools which shaped it had long since worn away, battered out by a generation of weather. The fingers which had done the carving now lay cold, forever stilled.

Jaric bent his head, vision marred by wet lashes. "I'm sorry," he said, as if the old boat could hear in place of the crippled fisherman Taen's dream-image had revealed in death. "I never intended to keep her."

A gust slammed the dock and *Callinde* rolled, lines groaning with strain. Jaric sank down beneath the lee of the thwart. He stared at palms scabbed over with blisters from the steering oar, record of his storm-ridden crossing from Mearren Ard. He drew breath into his lungs, and felt trapped, felt selfish to be alive after the sacrifices others had made to see him safely to this moment. Once he had excused himself on the grounds of the Stormwarden's cruelty; but since the Llondel's intervention, that defense no longer sheltered. Anskiere's decision to call the heir of Ivain into service had been founded on nothing but compassion and desperate need.

Jaric clenched fingers into fists. A solution must lie at Landfast; he had to search, and quickly, before the demons completed their work with Emien and struck again. If he refused the Cycle of Fire without finding an alternative to defend the Keys to Elrinfaer, then, in accepting *Callinde* to complete Anskiere's summons, Jaric saw that his actions had murdered the fisherman, Mathieson Keldric, as surely as if he had knifed the old man directly. Tears were useless. Grief would mend nothing. The niece who had woven the cloak on Jaric's back would mourn, and marry, and eventually forgive the ruin he had caused. But rocked by the lift of the swell under *Callinde*'s keel, the boy understood he could never make peace with Mathieson's memory until he had accomplished the legacy of Ivain.

A shout rang out from the shore. *Moonless*'s boatswain waited with a line and a longboat to warp *Callinde* from the wharf. Jaric rose and made his way forward, running a hand along the thwart for balance. Worn, net-scarred planking contrasted with the sharper edges of new timber; though built to an ancient design, the craft was sound and well tested by the sea. Still Jaric fretted, checking the tension on the rigging and fussing to be sure each halyard was cleated. Once she was under tow, no one would be aboard to ensure *Callinde*'s safety.

Boots clumped on the dock. "Tide's turnin' lad. Corley's crackin' his knuckles on the quarterdeck, an' it's the crew who'll suffer if he heats up."

Jaric nodded. Wind fanned pale hair across the collar of his cloak as he bent to secure a locker. But the gear inside had shifted somehow and pressed the cover askew. The latch would not quite close. "I'll be a minute."

"Going t'fasten lines, then," said the boatswain. *Callinde* rocked under his weight as he stepped aboard.

Jaric opened the locker, reached to reorganize the contents, and instantly froze. *The ash flute he remembered from the ledge on the ice cliffs lay crosswise on top of the spare headsail.* But in the main harbor under the vigilant eyes of the Kielmark's sentries, how had a Llondian demon managed to leave it and go unobserved? Jaric drew a quick breath. Forward, the boatswain leaned over the bow threading towline. While the seaman's back was turned, the boy grabbed the demon's offering and flung it over the rail. Delicate wood struck the sea with a splash, and its silver and shell decoration sank swiftly out of sight.

Jaric banged the locker closed. Mathieson's death left his confidence shaken; more than ever, he wished no help from demons. Caught by a queer surge of anger, the boy rammed the latch home and hastened to assist the boatswain.

* * *

Moonless sailed from Cliffhaven under full canvas and a sky scattered across with shredded drifts of storm cloud. Fair weather would bring a drop in wind; driving his command on a beam reach, Corley ordered the staysails set. As the boatswain bellowed instructions to the crew, the captain left his place by the wheel and paused at the stern rail, absorbed by the bobbing prow of *Callinde*.

Cautious of his mood, the quartermaster steered as if mesmerized by the compass. Canvas cracked overhead. *Moonless* shivered, heeled, and gathered speed as the staysails bellied taut. She sailed without incident through sunset into night, but Corley remained on deck. The Kielmark's order was simplicity itself. Why, then, could he not shake the feeling that trouble brewed like a storm front just beyond view over the horizon?

Yet at first the captain's apprehension seemed entirely unfounded; *Moonless* made swift and easy passage across the Corine Sea, her crew in good spirits, and her two passengers apparently secure. If Taen worried over her disobedience of the Vaere's directive, she appeared not to fret. Mornings she could be found clinging to the netting under the bowsprit, hair blowing in the breeze, and her laughing face drenched in spray. Mealtimes she teased the cook in the galley, and the off-watch crew corrupted her sense of fair play by teaching her to cheat at cards. The first mate especially liked to bait her until she blushed. He did so without fear of retaliation, until one night all on shipboard were disturbed by his yells of angry outrage. Taen was found by the scuttlebutt, crumpled helplessly with laughter. Under the amazed stares of the deckhands she admitted to filling the mate's berth with live fish. Called in to mediate, Corley belatedly recalled that the Dreamweaver had been raised on Imrill Kand, where bait and hooks were the staples of survival. Thereafter, he assigned her the task of filling the dinner pot with her talents, though the card games continued, with stakes of dried beans used for winnings.

Jaric smiled over Taen's popularity with the deckhands, but he did not join her antics. Corley's promise to the Kielmark kept the boy busy with sword and dagger, through exhausting hours of practice. A week passed, then two days more. His hands blistered, grew new layers of callus, and Corley's exacting instruction turned briskly unforgiving. Jaric sweated, striving to master his footwork while the captain hammered blow after blow against his guard. The sun shone hot on the deck, striking blinding reflections from the swells. Squinting against glare, neither tutor nor student noticed that Taen did not sit by the stern scupper with her lines, as she usually did in the morning. The quartermaster and the mate were aware; but with *Moonless* lying twenty-eight leagues from port, neither one thought to interrupt their duties to inquire why.

Taen lay in the heat of the stern cabin, hands pressed tight to her face. Above decks, she could hear the clang of swordplay, and Corley's voice exhorting Jaric to mind his guard. The drill had begun at daybreak, and near noon showed no sign of ending, though *Moonless*'s master estimated landfall by sundown.

"Watch it!" Steel chimed and stilled. "Your feint was too wide." Feet thumped planking. "Go again, Jaric, *move.*"

The din resumed. Taen flinched and buried her ears in blankets. No matter how inclement the weather, Jaric's practice kept schedule. Ofttimes Corley drove the boy to exhaustion, yet Taen never heard a complaint. Ivainson did his best to learn. White-faced and determined, he persisted, though the roll of *Moonless* marred his control time and again; Corley battered him dizzy with ripostes and cursed him often for clumsiness. This morning, with the voyage all but over, the captain insisted on exchanging practice weapons for rapiers.

Metal scraped and parted. "Better," gasped Corley. A dagger clanged a cross guard, and something bumped the deck. "*Damn* you, boy, I said watch that footwork!"

The Dreamweaver *felt* rather than heard Jaric rise and lift his sword arm. A rapid exchange followed, the ring of tempered blades repeated over and over until Taen felt battered by the continuous onslaught of sound. Buried beneath the sea-dampened weight of her blankets, she sought the calm taught by the Vaere, that inflexible inner stillness she perfected to bring her Dreamweaver's talents into focus. Yet, oddly, the discipline of her craft served only to increase her disorientation. Swept by a rush of heat, Taen felt her ears ring as if with fever. The clash of swordplay thinned, suddenly faint as the jangle of the wind charms which hung from the eaves of the house where she had spent her childhood. Sifted through a febrile mesh of memory, the present slipped away. Corley's curses whirled like leaves into darkness.

Taen struggled to orient her dream-sense, separate vision from presence, and restore awareness of her cabin on board the brigantine. Control eluded her. Too late Taen recognized something amiss. Images swirled through her mind, fragmented glimpses of other people's lives drawn from the island of Innishari to the south. The bell of steel deepened in Taen's ears, gradually acquired the slower rhythm of a blacksmith's hammer. Heat burned her face, traced ruddy lines through a beard, *not her own;* yet even as she wrestled to regain her own identity, she felt the ache of sweating fingers clenched on iron tongs and turning a glowing horseshoe upon an anvil. The Dreamweaver snapped the link with a touch sharpened by fear. Yet as the smith's awareness faded, her perception did not return to normal. Tools transformed in her grasp, became the worn wood of a broom handle. Coal-fire cooled into the packed earth of a door stoop where a farm wife shooed six bedraggled hens from a measure of dried corn. The chickens took flight, squawking, and the air turned sickeningly around them. Taen blinked, whirled into the dusty, cluttered confines of a shop where a weaver wound gray wool on his shuttlecock. Desperate now, she banished the dream, firmly bent her mind away from the town and back to the clean, open sea.

Salt air slapped her face like wet cloth. Gasping, Taen centered her awareness, and immediately saw she had failed. *Moonless* plied westward, amid the archipelagoes of the Free Isles' Alliance. There the sun shone fair at the zenith and the islets scattered near Landfast notched the horizon. In place of this, her dream-sense had spilled her into a place of storm-tossed whitecaps and stark, pewter-gray swells which matched no sea where the brigantine sailed. Terrified, Taen tapped her reserves. Power flared and sparked, but would not answer; the image escaped her control like water through a sieve. Sliding downward into panic, Taen beheld an object awash on the breast of the swell. She thought it was a snarled length of fishing net negligently abandoned to the tide; until she noticed the catch which dragged between the painted markings of the floats. Showing through the twine were fingers, a jacket of rent oilskin, and boots.

Certain the corpse was a vision from her own past, Taen shouted, "Father!"

Yet, tossed over a crest, the body turned; foam subsided to reveal hair that was not black but fair, and trailed like weed across the swollen features of a stranger. Taen shuddered. Too shaken to struggle, she abandoned her mind to the vision. Mist drifted like gauze over the water, shrouding the net's grisly burden. Even as the fog thickened, Taen caught the glint of a knife sunk in the breast of the dead man's jacket. Before she could ponder the significance of the murdered fisherman the sight melted into featureless white, then gray; light drained out of the day, and night fell unbroken by lantern or star. Sound arose through that unnatural dark like bubbles from the depths of a well. Taen heard a door slam faintly, and footsteps. Someone's hand touched her shoulder; the blackness around her crackled. A sheet of fire shot across Taen's mind, blinding orange-gold and white with a heat which did not burn. Strangely, she felt none of the terror which had infused her earlier dreams. A human presence lay behind this conflagration; someone restless, intense, whose touch was nearly as familiar to her as that of the brother she had lost.

Taen started violently and woke, jarring her cheek against the bulkhead. "Jaric!"

"Are you all right, little witch?" His voice was filled with concern, and very close by.

Taen blinked, realized how severely she trembled. Not trusting her voice, she did not speak as Jaric drew her gently into the light which filtered through the salt-stained panes of the stern window. Disoriented and inexplicably cold, Taen looked up, met eyes whose brown lay shadowed under brows hooked into a frown. The ties of Jaric's shirt swung unlaced at his throat; his skin glistened, finely sheened with sweat, and his nostrils flared slightly, as if he was winded from recent exertion; normal enough if he had just left practice with Corley. But Taen sensed a detail out of harmony in the instant she touched his mind.

"I was on the way to fetch the ship's healer when I heard you cry out," said Ivainson. "Are you ill?"

There *was* something; his voice confirmed the fact. "No," said Taen. Brought fully and sharply awake, she shoved a hand into the crumpled blankets of the berth and sat up. "I had a nightmare, no more." She studied Jaric intently, but found nothing. Afraid he would leave before she could trace her suspicion, she qualified quickly to delay him. "I dreamed I saw a murdered fisherman floating in the waves."

Jaric stepped back, his expression abruptly guarded. But Taen noticed nothing beyond the crimson-splashed knuckles of the hand held pressed against his side. Her breath caught in her throat. "You're hurt!"

Jaric shrugged in immediate reassurance. "Only a little.

Corley cursed me well for carelessness, and rightly. The mistake was mine."

His voice held jarring relief. Startled, Taen looked back to Jaric's face. Diverted by concern for his cut hand, she took a moment to recall the words she had used at need, which, surprisingly, had distressed him. Then she wondered why mention of a dead fisherman should prove so alarming. Jaric's stance suggested reluctance; he would refuse answer if she asked. Taen considered using her dream-sense. But that instant the lookout called from the masthead. *Moonless* crossed the perimeters of the Landfast defenses, the net of energies woven by the initiates of Kordane's brotherhood to ward against entrance by demons. Taen sensed the barrier as a prickle of cold force. For an instant she shivered, gripped by a power that ruthlessly tested her humanity; then the moment passed. Sunlight through the stern windows rinsed away the discomfort.

Jaric seized the interruption, backing hastily toward the companionway. "Have you ever seen the towers of Landfast?"

"No." Infected by his excitement, Taen kicked bare feet free of her blankets. "I'll meet you on deck, but only after you've shown the healer that cut."

"Shrew," said Jaric. He grinned amiably. "Would you throw something at me if I refused?"

Taen brandished a fist. Jaric ducked in mock fright through the companionway and left her. As the door banged closed the Dreamweaver sighed, her pretense at levity abandoned. A force beyond her understanding or control had inflicted visions upon her; the event was no slight matter. She had disobeyed the directive of the Vaere, and if this was the first sign of the consequences, no strategy of the Kielmark's could aid her. Against mishaps by sorcery, all of Corley's skill with weapons and seamanship could offer no safety at all. Taen slipped unsteadily from her berth. Much as she valued her freedom, now, her return to the Isle of the Vaere could not happen quickly enough.

To Jaric, standing wind-whipped by *Moonless*'s rail, the towers of Landfast thrust like fat spearmen ranked against serried banks of cloud. Although he had never beheld the Free Isles before, the city which governed the Alliance had fascinated him ever since his apprenticeship as copyist in a backlands keep. Here lay the heart of human endeavor. Scholars claimed that the Landfast archives preserved even the mysteries of Kordane's Blessed Fires. Maintained by Kor's Grand High Grace and a staff of priests and initiates, the libraries contained the histories of all mankind, preserved since the Great Fall.

Familiar with the landmarks through a painting which had hung in Morbrith's copy chamber, Jaric touched Taen's arm and pointed out several slender, silver-domed spires which soared skyward from the central cluster of buildings. "There, do you see? Those are the sanctuary towers of Kordane's shrine, where seventeen masters guard forbidden texts. The archivist who taught me said no woven cloth, nor any item which will sustain flame, is permitted in that place, and that the inner-circle brotherhood undertake a vow of isolation. They enter, never to leave."

Jaric fell silent, his face animated with wistful excitement. To a boy whose childhood had been limited to books and writing, Landfast held wonder and the promise of dreams. In bright sunlight, amid the bustle of sailhands and shouted commands, he could for a time forget the terrible burden which compelled him to visit these shores.

The wind freshened, then shifted northeast. Driven on a broad reach, *Moonless* shuddered under tautly curved canvas. She rounded the headland with her bowsprit and star-crowned figurehead glistening through flying sheets of spray; then, ducking like a haughty maiden, she jibed and bore down upon the light beacons marking the jetties which flanked the harbor entrance. Landfast lifted ahead like a jeweled diadem set on a sea-beaten headland of sandstone. Black against tawny bluffs, wharves, shops, warehouses, and fish shacks cluttered the shoreline beneath; and shadowed by the painted towers, the docks at the bay side teemed with boats of scattered shape and description, some inhabited, others packed to the thwarts with vendors and wares.

Corley called orders from the quarterdeck. Jaric roused from his reverie. He shed his shirt and passed it to Taen. Then he set his bandaged hand on the ratlines and swung himself up to join the topmen who clambered aloft to shorten sail. The cut on the back of his wrist did little to blunt his dexterity, and work on the main royal yard granted him a splendid view of the city, with its narrow twisting lanes, bronze statuary, and tiled courtyards.

Corley left the quarterdeck, and the mate called commands in his place.

Flying the scarlet and silver wolf which blazoned the Kielmark's standard, *Moonless* backed sail. She dropped anchor inside the barrier islet of Little Dagley with the enviable precision that earmarked every vessel in Cliffhaven's fleet. A crowd of frowning men clustered on the harbormaster's dock to watch. But no lighter launched to claim anchorage fees. Hated, respected, feared, and left strictly alone, the Kielmark's vessels plied every port in Keithland exempt from tolls or tariffs. Though merchants and officials complained waspishly, they voiced their bitterness out of earshot. To arouse Cliffhaven's ill will brought ruin to trade, since any shipping bound for eastern kingdoms must run the narrows of Mainstrait; there the King of Pirates imposed an inflexible demand of tribute in exchange for amnesty from his fleet of corsairs.

Last to descend from the rigging, Jaric found that the boatswain and second watch had already launched a longboat. Corley stood with knuckles buried in his beard, briskly selecting his oarsmen. Clad unfamiliarly in dress colors, he wore bracelets on both arms and a maroon doublet with the Kielmark's badge of rank embroidered in gold on his right shoulder. But genteel trappings could not blunt his dangerous air of command; fine cloth and hose only emphasized weapons whose hilts bore no ornamentation but the oiled sheen of purpose. As Jaric swung from ratlines to deck, the captain called out to him.

"Fetch your things, boy. Shore party's nearly ready, and I've no mind to linger in this port."

Jaric pushed past the crewmen, heading for the companionway and his cabin. As he rounded the mainmast, he caught sight of a figure huddled in shadow beyond. Taen sat on a bight of rope, hair tumbled like ink over slim shoulders, and her face hidden behind clenched and bloodless fingers. That, and an impression of unbreathing stillness about her person, roused Jaric to sharp anxiety.

He hurried to her side. "Taen?"

She started slightly and looked up. Blue eyes remained unfocused in her elfin face and her skin was chalk-pale. Her hands trembled; the instant she noticed, she hid them in the crumpled cloth of her shift. "I left your shirt on your berth. Better go there and gather your things. Corley's irritable."

When Jaric hesitated, she forced a smile. "I'm going to miss you, that's all."

Something very different troubled her. Only once before had she sounded this strained, and that the time her brother had done murder. But having had his innermost will overturned and bound to a sorcerer's service, Jaric was wary of involving himself in the particulars of Vaerish mysteries. He shrugged away concern with a forced grin. "Miss me? Not likely, but when you leave, certain sailors on this vessel are going to be left at a loss. What do you suppose they'll make of the beans they've hoarded as winnings?" He paused and touched her thin shoulder. "You'll be safe on the Isle of the Vaere."

Taen looked up, too quickly. At once Jaric knew he had been careless, that his distress over Emien's fate lay too near the surface of his thoughts. He ducked behind the blocks of the main halyard, and left before Taen's intuitive powers could probe his distress. In haste, he caught his heel in the line left flaked on the deck.

"Clumsy!" Taen called as he stumbled. "Watch out! You'll break your silly nose."

Jaric hurried on without rejoinder; and because for the second time that day her Dreamweaver's powers would not answer will or reason, Taen never guessed his silence was involuntary. Wrenched by the innocence in her upturned face, and the trembling fingers she had stilled with the same courage she had used to engineer Cliffhaven's defense, Jaric watched ocean, pinrail, and shrouds shatter through a lens of unexpected tears. He feared for Taen. He never realized how much until now. Her fragility never seemed so poignant, for once her brother reached Shadowfane, her presence would be known to the enemy. Landfast's great libraries must contain an alternative to the Cycle of Fire; if not, there would be no haven. Kor's Accursed would not rest until they had destroyed the Dreamweaver who had wrested away their conquest at Cliffhaven.

Taen was gone from the deck by the time Jaric returned. He carried sword, dagger, penknife, and a spare shirt bundled in the green folds of his cloak; heavy on the thong at his neck hung the Keys to Elrinfaer and the stormfalcon's feather. Looking for the Dreamweaver's dark head among the crewmen, Jaric found the longboat already laden and waiting. He cursed Corley's efficiency as the boatswain caught his elbow and impatiently steered him to the rail. "Get aboard, boy."

Reluctant to leave without saying farewell, Jaric grabbed the beaded wood and resisted. "Have you seen Taen?"

The boatswain shook his head, copper earrings swinging. "Cap'n's temper's up," he warned. "Don't try him when he's hurrying." And he pushed Jaric firmly toward the battens.

Callused hands tugged Jaric's bundle free, tossed it carelessly down to the oarsmen in the longboat. Hustled from *Moonless*'s decks, Jaric descended into shadow and stumbled awkwardly into the rocking longboat below. The instant his feet touched floorboards, Corley ordered the craft cast off. Oar shafts bit into the sea. The strong backs of six crack seamen bent to their stroke, and Jaric half tumbled into the last empty seat.

His bundled weapons landed in his lap, thrown without gentleness by Corley. "Put on your sword belt, boy. I didn't blister your hands at practice these days only to see you robbed in the streets because you kept your steel swaddled in wool. Hereafter you'll *never* walk strange shores without arms, understand?"

Jaric bit his lip against anger. He rose, braced his knee against the aft oar bench, and buckled on sword and dagger while frantically searching the faces at *Moonless*'s rails. The officers had already begun to disperse the crew; Taen was not among them. Wedged uncomfortably between the bony frame of the ship's purser and an empty water cask, Jaric watched *Moonless* shrink astern as the pull of the oarsmen drove the longboat toward the main wharf at Landfast. The creak of leathers in the rowlocks and the rhythmic splash of the looms replaced conversation for what seemed a very long time.

"Boy?" said a voice over the rumble as the rowers shipped oars.

Jaric lifted his eyes from *Moonless*'s tracery of masts and saw the purser regarding him, hooked features keen with interest. "I'll tell the lass you looked for her."

Jaric considered the man's hooded eyes, then the clever fingers laced in his lap, their precise, waiting stillness seldom found in honest trade; rumor held that the purser had courted women and stolen their jewels before he took sanctuary on Cliffhaven. "Thank you," Jaric said, and left the issue there. He did not trust the man enough to add that Taen acted oddly, and might need help. On that matter the boy resolved to speak directly to Corley.

The longboat drifted to the wharf, caught and steadied against the swell by her forward oarsmen. Jaric rose at once. But blocked by men lifting casks, and buffeted in the swirling commotion of the landing, the boy took several minutes to reach the piling and pull himself onto the damp boards of the dock. He looked, but could not locate Corley's maroon tunic in the bustle. Though he called, his shout became lost amid the clatter of hooves and iron-rimmed cartwheels as two wagons passed on the street; whips cracked, and drovers yelled for clearance with deafening persistence.

"Cap'n's gone, boy," said the nearest of *Moonless*'s seamen through the tumult. He paused to tie a red scarf above his creased eyes. "In a hurry he was, to finish his business ashore." Misinterpreting Jaric's concern, he added, "Not to worry, then, he left instructions fer yer *Callinde*. She's to be towed in an' given free dockage, same's if she were one o' the Kielmark's own. Harbormaster'll tell you where. If he cusses, spit on his rugs and ignore it."

Jaric turned away from the seaman's grin. Bitterly concerned, he realized he would have to catch Corley in the streets. Not an instant remained for talk. Leaving the seaman, the boy dodged *Moonless*'s rolling water casks and ran. The wharf was a maze of activity. Forced to twist and duck through stacks of baled cargo and drying fish nets, and jostled by brawny, half-naked longshoremen, Jaric raced headlong for the town.

ᠵᠦ VI ᠵᠦ

Landfast

Crooked, narrow, and jammed with carts and stalls, the streets of Landfast were a difficult place to locate a man in haste to finish an unknown errand. After running down three dead ends and tripping twice over the same grape seller's basket, Jaric abandoned his search for Corley. Frustrated, sweating, he braced his arm against the sun-warm bricks of a hostel to catch his breath.

The press of commerce swirled around him, overlaid by the spiel of a woman selling cakes for coppers. Two straining mules and a wagon laden with beer casks rumbled by. The spinning hubs of the wheels narrowly missed Jaric's hip. When he made no effort to step clear, the drover cursed and brandished a whip; but Jaric's sword and dagger, and the scowl beneath his tangled hair, made the man continue without further argument. The boy himself remained unaware that his appearance had intimidated a stranger twice his age and weight. A flock of geese flapped around his boots, arched necks lifted away from a girl with a stick who prodded them to market. She smiled invitation at him, her small feet dancing beneath lifted skirts.

Yet Jaric shrank and turned his face away. Even now he could not forget the teasing he had received from the serving wenches at Morbrith. The teeming streets, and the racket with attendant strange smells and bustle, made Landfast a world removed from Seitforest, where he had wintered. The beginnings of self-reliance he had learned in the trapper's trade became displaced by uncertainty; even his feats of seamanship lost significance, until every recent accomplishment seemed delusion wrought of dreams. With the dust of the city in his nostrils, the resolve made in the open air of the ice cliffs now seemed vain folly. How inadequate were his hopes to safeguard the Keys to Elrinfaer, far less protect Taen Dreamweaver from the brother she had lost to Shadowfane.

Jaric straightened, and pushed off from the wall before the tremble in his gut became an outright urge to run. His last and most sensible option was to write a note addressing his concern for Taen's welfare and trust the crew of the longboat to deliver it to Corley. Ink and paper could be found with the archivists, where Jaric intended to apply for work to earn bread and board. Although his plan now seemed futile, to do nothing invited despair. Resigned, the heir of Ivain Firelord tucked his bandaged wrist under his sleeve, and hastened to overtake the cake seller.

She accepted his copper with a quizzical expression. Then, with her trays balanced against a packing crate, she raised a plump hand and tucked her hair in her cap while Jaric asked directions.

"You'll want the residence of the Grand First Archivist, then." Belatedly discovering her fingers were still sticky with sugar, the woman abandoned vanity and let her arm fall. "Go up the east stair, boy. Pass two courtyards, and you'll find the door between the checkered towers beyond Lionsgate."

Jaric phrased his thanks with court courtesy. He moved to depart but the passage of mounted couriers in plumed helmets forced him to leap back, or be trampled. Raised in an earl's household, he instinctively shielded the woman from the horses' streaming trappings.

"You have the manners, then." The cake seller studied him curiously. She looked beyond scuffed boots and uncut hair, and either his slenderness or his uncertainty aroused her sympathy. "Have a cake, boy. And I won't keep your copper."

Jaric shook his head with startling vehemence. Painfully he had discovered that motherly behavior was inspired only by the helpless. Ignoring the cake in the woman's outstretched hand, he shoved his way back into the press. Nothing in Landfast could bring him to turn back, even when a pony shied back in its traces, showering straw on the cobbles and earning blasphemies from an oat farmer's wife.

Inland from the harbor the crush of traffic became less frantic. Warehouses and seaport trade gave way to guildhalls and houses. The streets rose steeply, cleft by switchback turns and a chaotic crisscross of alleys. Jaric found his way with difficulty, for the thoroughfares here were jammed with people and beggars on foot. A few lanes were sparsely traveled, like the street of cloth weavers with its clatter of looms and the heated reek of dye pots. Jaric spotted Lionsgate long before he climbed the east stair. Supported by pillared arches, cats carved of amber marble reared above the tilted slates of the rooftops. Jaric squeezed past a trio of quarreling merchants and stopped, his purpose obscured by awe.

To one side, between the shaded façade of two buildings, he saw a circular plaza of sand-colored marble. Grilled gates closed off the access, and neither people nor carts passed through. Deserted in sunlight, patterned stone inlay described the four points of the compass, and the center bore the stars and fire-burst symbol of Kordane's Brotherhood. Jaric turned toward the place, impelled by curiosity. But at the end of the access lane, a voice called out in challenge.

"Halt, boy! None may pass this way."

Jaric started back, even as a sentry stepped smartly from the shadows by the gate and lowered an enameled ceremonial spear. His helm was plumed and decorated also, but the facings were steel; and his weapon was tempered and honed to a killing point. Aware of the boy's confusion, and the plain sailor's linen that clothed him, the guardsman eased his stance. "You'd be new to Landfast, then, boy?"

Jaric nodded. "I'm trying to get to Lionsgate."

The sentry gestured down a side street. "That way, boy." Then, seeing Jaric's eyes still fixed on the forbidden plaza, he lowered his weapon and leaned on the shaft. "No man goes there but priests initiated to the mysteries. Yonder's the entrance to the sanctuary towers of Landfast."

"There?" Skepticism colored Jaric's tone as he regarded the polished paving. No door was visible.

"The stair leads underground, and the locking mechanism that hides the entrance is a secret kept by the Inner Echelon." Suddenly out of patience, the sentry seated his spear butt with a clang against the cobbles. "Now get along, boy. Regulations forbid me to jabber with passersby, and the captain of Kordane's guard has a mean way with slackers."

Reminded that his own errand would fare poorly by delay, Jaric hurried on down the side street. Houses with jutting balconies shut out the light. The air beneath was sea-damp, and smelled faintly of garbage. Town sweepers did not pass here to clear the gutters, and apparently the resident tenants were too lazy to tidy their door walks themselves. Since their shutters were latched closed in full daylight, Jaric wondered whether this was an alley of brothels. Ahead lay an intersection, and beyond, a small square, the final ascent to Lionsgate. The staircase to the arch was all but empty, since commerce slowed in late afternoon. Anxious to speak with the Grand First Archivist before the libraries closed at eventide, Jaric tackled the steps at a run. Near the top, panting, he spotted the twin towers the cake seller had described, their bases faced with bands of checkered agate. The doorway framed between bore a device of scrolls and crossed swords, symbolic of knowledge's double-edged legacy.

Jaric leaped the last triplet of stairs and hurried headlong through the arch. The shadows slanted steeply toward sunset. The longboat must not leave the quay without his message to Corley.

The entrance to the scribes' hall stood open in the heat. The tiled foyer within proved invitingly cool, and musty with the smells of ink and old parchment. A clerk in brown robes rose from an ambry as Jaric entered. He banged the doors closed with ill-concealed annoyance, and stared at the boy who confronted him, a hand-woven cloak of green wadded under an arm tanned as a sailor's.

The clerk sniffed, unimpressed. "Are you lost?"

Jaric shook his head once, sharply. "I've come to ask for work."

The clerk twitched his lips. "We don't hire swordsmen."

"I'm not a swordsman." Jaric stepped forward, desperate to save time.

"Fisherman, then," said the clerk. He gestured, openly vexed. "Get back to your nets. You're too old for apprenticeship."

Jaric stiffened. His eyes narrowed. "Are you deaf? I said work, not apprenticeship. I know my craft."

The clerk's brows lifted. He glanced again at the sword, noticed heavy calluses on the boy's hands, and took a step back. Muttering for his visitor to wait, he walked precipitously toward the stair. Jaric paced back and forth before the ambry through what seemed an unreasonable span of time.

At length the clerk reappeared. He leaned over the balustrade, an overweening sneer on his lips. "The master in residence will see you. Mercy on you if your claims were boasting. The man dislikes nuisance, and the Grand Magistrate's his drinking crony."

Too annoyed to react to threats, Jaric bounded up the stair, unbuckling his sword belt as he went. He followed the clerk down a carpeted hallway, past door after door which opened upon rooms of books. His escort showed him into a chamber, rich rugs slashed with sunlight which spilled through lancet windows. Jaric paused past the threshold, momentarily dazzled.

The clerk poked sharply at his elbow, "Are you an oaf? Bow before your betters, boy."

Jaric ignored the prompt. Squinting, he took a step toward the broad desk with its stooped, white-bearded occupant. Then, suddenly timid, he stopped. The towering shelves of books, the ink-smell, and the still air wakened unwanted memories of his childhood at Morbrith. Once the silence of the copy chamber had been his only refuge from the cruel jibes of his peers.

"You come from the Kielmark's brigantine?" rasped the elderly man at the desk. His spectacles glinted white, unfathomable as the eyes of dead insects.

"Yes, Eminence." Jaric lifted his burden, carefully laid weapons and cloak on the marquetry table near his elbow. "But I'm not in Cliffhaven's service."

"That I know." The master in residence raised a crabbed hand and beckoned the boy closer to his chair. "Pirates have small use for written words."

Jaric stifled an unwise urge to contradict. Plain in his thoughts lay the Kielmark's personal study, walls lined floor to ceiling with volumes any prince might treasure. The books had not been for show, he knew; once in curiosity he had pulled one down and found it clean of dust.

The elderly scribe leaned forward. "You're very quiet, boy."

"Oh, he talks, all right," offered the clerk from the doorway. "The question is, can he write?"

"That's quite enough!" The old man stood. A collar ornate with embroidery and pearls dragged at the cords of his neck. "You have work to do, yes? Well then, leave me to mine!"

After a venomous glance at Jaric, the clerk spun and departed. As his steps faded away down the hallway, the master in residence returned his scrutiny to the applicant standing by his chair. One hand was bandaged; the other bore marks from the sword and the sea. And gold hair fell untrimmed over the muscled leanness one saw in the shoulders of the young who trained for posts in the Governor's guard. Still, this boy had features too sensitive for a fighter; and his manner, a queer mix of diffidence and impatience, harbored no arrogance at all.

The master in residence sighed and sat. The faintest of smiles crinkled his cheeks as he pulled off his spectacles, rubbed eyes of clearest gray, and said, "Are you perchance in some difficulty?"

Jaric drew a troubled breath. "I need work, as a scribe or a copyist. I can also tally accounts. Only, if you'll have me, I would beg use of a pen and an hour's leave to deliver a note to a friend."

"Well then." The master pulled open a drawer. Blue-veined fingers dipped within and emerged with a square of parchment. He thumped the sheet on the boards before Jaric and gestured impatiently at the quill which rested in the inkwell by his wrist. "Write your letter first, boy."

Jaric bowed his head. "Master, you are generous."

His voice had steadied. The accent at last was plain, of north-shore origin, but cultured. This boy had not learned his speech or his manners in the farmsteads. His scarred fingers gripped the pen with recognizable expertise, and as line after line of even, cleanly phrased script flowed beneath his hand, the master ceased to watch.

"What are you called, boy?"

Jaric's writing did not falter. He answered with the surname given him by the Smith's Guild of Morbrith, for everywhere Ivain's name was remembered with vicious hatred. "Kerainson Jaric, Eminence."

"Then, young Kerainson, have you quarters?"

Jaric signed his missive and reached instinctively for the sand tray. He dried the excess ink quickly and well, blurring no letters in the process. "I have a boat."

The master in residence grunted. "Open to the sky, no doubt. Well, it isn't raining. Tomorrow is soon enough to arrange your bed and board."

Jaric raised uncertain brown eyes. With his letter clutched to his chest, he waited, afraid to speak.

"Well, get along, boy." The master in residence restored his spectacles to the grooved skin of his nose. "Deliver your note, but get back here sober by sunrise. I've three keeps full of books to be copied, and never enough hands for the pens."

Jaric barely waited to voice his respects before bolting for the door. Running by the time he crossed the threshold, he forgot to pick up the sword and dagger left on the table by the entry. Hall, stairs, and landing passed by in a blur of haste, and as he crossed the foyer he answered the clerk's sour query with breathless words.

"I'm hired."

Afternoon had all but fled. Landfast's towers framed a sky blending toward the fallow gold of sunset. Surely *Moonless*'s longboat had departed by now; Jaric raced for the stair and cannoned squarely into a man coming in from the outside. Fingers clamped like trap jaws on the boy's wrist. A neatly delivered push spun him off balance, and he crashed, sprawling into the stone pillars of the railing.

"Why the haste?" said a voice, consonants clipped with annoyance. "Are you a thief?"

Jaric shook the hair from his eyes and looked up at a lanky man with a seal-brown mustache. His body was clothed in russet trimmed in black, and sinewy wrists lay crossed at his waist, hands lightly gripping the hilts of a jeweled sword and dagger.

"Your pardon, master." Belatedly remembering his abandoned weapons, Jaric's fingers tightened. The letter in his hand crumpled slightly. "I am much in haste." He pushed himself away from the pillar and attempted to walk past.

The man moved like a fox. Steel sang from his scabbards. Blades flashed blue in the sunlight and fenced the boy on the stair. "I *said*, are you a thief?"

White, angry, and desperate, Jaric stared at the weapons angled at his chest. "I haven't stolen anything! Ask the clerk, and then let me pass."

The points remained so steady they might have been nailed in place. "You aren't very convincing, ship-monkey. The clerk could be your accomplice."

Jaric gasped, shocked. He jerked a glance at his antagonist, and saw him smile, teeth glinting through his mustache; but the eyes above were cold blue, and the brows questioning, as if the exchange were deliberately meant to provoke.

"Why insult me?" said Jaric. "I've neither sword nor dagger, and wish no quarrel with you."

The stranger laughed. "No sword and no dagger? Then certainly I'll skewer you where you stand."

"Oh no," a voice broke in from behind. "You won't bloody this stairway with fighting."

Jaric whirled, just as a robed figure emerged from the hallway. Clutched awkwardly in his arms were two familiar weapons bundled in a salt-stained green cloak. With a grimace of distaste, the clerk unloaded his burden next to Jaric. The metal on the scabbard guards grated, dissonant as a knife on a whetstone, as the cloth settled against the stair.

"Take your dueling elsewhere." The clerk set his hand on the chased brass doorkknob and gave a mighty pull. "That's an order from the master in residence." He ended with a smirk as the panel began to swing.

The door crashed closed. Jaric swallowed and spun to face his tormentor. "Be reasonable. There's no purpose in fighting over accidental clumsiness on my part."

"Except, dear boy, that I want to." Scarred from years of sparring, the man's hands stirred impatiently. "Carry on."

Jaric straightened, ash-pale. "I won't."

"Ah," said the man. "But I think you will." Again he moved, so fast his blades sparked like fire in the sun.

Jaric felt air whicker past his knuckles. The letter in his hand parted, sliced cleanly in two. The severed portion drifted, turning over and over, and settled across the cloak with Taen's name and his own signature slashed cruelly in half. For a stunned second, Jaric forgot to breathe. Then he bent and recovered his steel. In anger he drew and attacked.

Blade met blade with a furious clang of sound. From the first moment Jaric had no doubt he faced a master swordsman. The stranger's parry met him, lightly, easily, and the riposte followed in a smoky blaze of light. Jaric caught the stroke on his cross guard. The force rattled his teeth. Too furious to care, he beat, feinted, lunged, and gained two steps on the stair.

"Oh, very nice." The man smiled, foxlike, through a crossed barrier of blades. He disengaged and struck.

Jaric's foot slapped the edge of the step. Forced to parry high, he twisted. His opponent's dagger darted out of nowhere, cleanly eluding his guard. The boy felt a tug. A breath of cold kissed his sweating skin. He lifted his arm to cover and saw his sleeve was slit. But the touch might as easily have gone home to maim muscle and sinew.

Forced back a pace, Jaric riposted. "You're toying with me." His blade struck a guard implacable as stone.

"Perhaps." The man in russet caught his sword in a bind and twisted. "But it's a game you must win, yes?"

Tendons tightened in Jaric's wrist. Feeling his fingers shift on the sword grip, he responded as Corley had taught, and escaped getting disarmed. His heel bashed hard against a riser. Belatedly he discovered he had lost a step.

"Tell me," drawled the man. "Is the note for a lady?"

Busy defending himself, Jaric said nothing. Cut, parry, riposte, the steel whistled and clashed until his ears rang with sound. The continuous jar of impact stung his hands. At some point, unnoticed, he received a nick on his thumb. Blood laced his wrist, and sweat ran stinging under the bandage from his morning's mishap.

Then, with the rail pressed to his side, and the breath burning in his throat, Jaric saw an opening. His sword thrust shot under defending block, and opened a line of red on the stranger's collarbone.

The man collected himself instantly. He leaped backward. His feet landed lightly on the cobbles at the foot of the stair, yet he cast down his weapons. Steel chimed deafeningly on stone. Poised to follow through, Jaric checked his rush. Hair slicked damp to his forehead, he waited, panting, while the man pulled a cloth from his sleeve and delicately dabbed his cut.

"What, no shout of victory?" The man's hands stilled and he looked up.

Jaric did not voice the obvious, that anytime previously the stranger could have sliced him to ribbons. In a few breathless minutes, the boy had perceived how pitifully inadequate were his skills; a fortnight of Corley's training had barely sketched the rudiments of technique. But this time the man refused to break the silence. Jaric shivered, set his sword point against the stone, and asked the only question that mattered. "Why attack me?"

The man kicked his dagger aside and mounted the steps. "For devilment, I suppose." His breath betrayed no sign of exertion.

Jaric gritted his teeth. "Then devil and demons take you. *I couldn't spare the time!*"

He turned on his heel, retrieved his buckler and cloak. The slashed letter fluttered under his feet as he sheathed his weapons with short, angry jerks. A hand touched his elbow. Jaric recovered his torn note and whirled, his face a mask of fury.

But the stranger laughed no longer. His brows knitted with contrition and he said, "I'll make it up to you."

"I doubt it." Jaric pushed past. "You've no idea what you've done."

"No." The man shrugged and fell into step beside him. "But you're not without talent, you know. I could instruct you, as compensation. The next time someone sought to delay you, your lady need not be kept waiting."

Jaric stopped. A bitter laugh escaped his throat. He regarded the swordsman, who held his bloody handkerchief pressed beneath his collar, and whose light eyes remained shrewdly intent. The boy's features twisted, assumed a look wholly Ivain's. "That won't mend it," he said.

But by his tone, the swordsman understood that Corley's protégé saw the sense in accepting. Not without friendliness he offered, "My name is Brith. If you come to the practice yard by the city guard's quarters, we can start tomorrow."

"I'll consider it." Jaric was curt. *"Now let me go!"*

Sunset silhouetted the humped profile of Little Dagley Islet and the waters of Landfast harbor deepened slowly to indigo. Loud in the evening quiet, the last wagons rumbled away from the dockside. Brith crouched in the dooryard of a spice shop and watched the boy, Jaric, who lingered alone by the wharf. Sea wind tossed the hair from his face, revealing a glint of unshed tears; while, beyond the beacon towers of the inlet, a brigantine flying Cliffhaven's colors shook out her stunsails and scudded south for the Isle of the Vaere.

Brith swore softly. He tossed his stained handkerchief in the gutter, and wondered again why the Kielmark's foremost captain should concern himself with a boy who hated fighting. The swordmaster shrugged and, feeling the laces of his collar fret against his cut, cursed again. The pay was generous, but the idea he might spend the night skulking like a dog in an alley had never entered his mind when he accepted responsibility for Jaric. On the verge of rising to coax his charge to consider retiring to the comfort in an alehouse, Brith froze.

Jaric spun abruptly and threw something, his arm a blur of force. The watching swordsman ducked hastily as the object struck the boards above his head. It bounced once, and rolled to a stop against the instep of his boot. Brith retrieved what proved to be a letter, crushed and wadded into an unreadable pulp. Cautiously the swordsman looked up and found Jaric on the move once more. Stealthy as a cat, he followed.

His charge strode to the dockmaster's shed and pounded on

the panels until the door opened. The official inside thrust forth an angry face and swore until his lungs emptied of air. Although no money changed hands, he finished with directions. Jaric left without thanks. He interrogated a beggar and a street urchin for knowledge of landmarks and, poorer by two coppers, eventually found his way to a slip where a fishing boat of ancient design creaked against her lines.

Brith tensed. If the boy tried to cast off and chase the brigantine, the swordsman did not fancy the prospect of stopping him; but Corley's orders had been explicitly clear: Jaric was to be trained for the sword, and under no circumstances should he leave the shores of Landfast. But the boy apparently realized his *Callinde* could never match *Moonless*'s speed under full canvas. He made no effort to sail, but tossed his weapons, unoiled, into a locker, and sprawled prone beneath his cloak. Brith guarded and listened, and at length settled resignedly against a damp pile of fish net. If the boy wept, no sound betrayed him. Perhaps in the end he slept, for nothing moved on board *Callinde* until dawn silvered the horizon to the east.

Wrapped in the fog by daybreak, *Moonless* shuddered over a swell. Canvas rippled aloft and fell taut with a coarse smack. Shirtless, and clad hastily in hose and boots, Corley arrived on the quarterdeck. He squinted at the compass without pausing to consult the officer on watch.

The quartermaster blinked moisture from his lashes. "Wind's changing."

"I know." Corley gazed over the rails. Beyond the curve of the swell, the air lay dense and dead, horizon buried in mist. "Stuns'ls will have to come down. We're in for a blow, I can feel it." Deftly he skirted the wheel and shouted orders to the boatswain.

Moonless came alive as men leaped for the rigging. Corley watched, unsettled and critical. When his cabin steward appeared at his elbow with a shirt, he accepted the garment with a preoccupied frown.

"Where's the Dreamweaver?" He dragged the laces tight at his throat and adjusted his cuffs, eyes fixed intently on the activities aloft.

Sensitive to the captain's mood, the steward replied concisely. "The girl's asleep, Captain. She's been very quiet."

Too quiet, Corley suspected, but did not voice his thought.

His stillness prompted the steward to qualify. "I'd guess she misses the boy. Any man with eyes might notice that she and Jaric were close."

"Enough," snapped Corley. He raked tangled chestnut hair with his fingers and finished with a gesture of dismissal. "I'll be down to look in on her shortly."

Taen might pine for Jaric; but the captain had not missed the fact that she had failed to come on deck to bid her companion farewell. Since leaving Landfast, she had made herself scarce, behavior markedly changed from her earlier habit of riding the bowsprit with her hair flying in the wind. The fighting spirit observed during the defense of Cliffhaven could not be reconciled with a girl who suddenly languished in emotional sentimentality. But with storms pending, and canvas being shortened aloft, no captain worth the Kielmark's pay would be caught below decks. Taen's vagaries would have to wait.

Corley checked the weather gauge and frowned again at the compass. Lines squealed in the blocks overhead as the crew shortened sail. Mist trailed through the yards, shredded to scarves by gusts. The waters heaved gray and leaden beneath, fretted by the faintest whisper of disturbed air. The wind had definitely shifted. Since speed had dictated a westerly course through the narrow channel that separated Landfast from Innishari, *Moonless* had only a scant margin of sea room. Should the weather deteriorate before midday, she would have to put about. The Kielmark's captain paced anxiously. Conditions would inevitably get worse. He had been too many years at sea to misread the signs. If, as he suspected, some difficulty beset Taen Dreamweaver, he had but one desire, and that to make landfall at the Isle of the Vaere as swiftly as ship and sinew could manage.

Watery sunlight struck through the fog as day progressed, striking highlights against the waves. Yet the brightness proved short-lived. Hounded by rising wind, storm clouds rolled in from the south, darkening the mist to sickly green. Stripped of flying jibs and topsails, *Moonless* reeled close-hauled, thudded by swells which struck with the might of siege engines. Spray dashed the quarterdeck.

Sodden, Corley shook water from his hair and shouted commands to the boatswain. "Reef the main! And send the slowest man below to batten hatches."

While the crew swarmed aloft, the captain flung away from

the rail and nearly belted into the steward, who brought him a cloak of oiled wool.

Corley accepted the garment with a bitten word of thanks. "How's the Dreamweaver?"

The steward seemed taken aback. "Sir, I don't know."

"Why not?" With his brooch poised to stab cloth, Corley phrased his next words with warning care. "I thought I told you to look in on her?"

"Your pardon, sir." A gust forced the servant to raise his voice. "You said you'd see Taen yourself."

Corley rammed the pin into place and twitched the cloak over his shoulders. "Damn the weather," he replied. "I did say that. Check her for me and report back, could you?"

"Aye, sir, at once." The steward left.

Corley hastened to the binnacle, glared at the compass, and swore afresh. "Kor's Fires, the wind's veering again. We're going to end with a west wind, but too late to matter." He met the quartermaster's glance with anxious eyes. "I don't like the drift of this. Seems like we're getting a fall tempest, three whole months out of season." Neither man belabored the obvious, that with the archipelago of Islamere lying east, a westerly gale might force *Moonless* north to gain leeway.

"Bad luck," murmured the quartermaster.

Fast as a whipcrack, Corley answered. "Do you think so?"

The officer paled above the spoked curve of the wheel. "What else? Demons cannot shift weather, and Anskiere's bound in ice."

A gust struck. Stressed canvas boomed in protest, and *Moonless* flung into a heel. Water pressed against her rudder, and the wheel creaked, slipping in the quartermaster's grasp. Corley reached and caught the spokes, adding his own weight to maintain the brigantine's heading. For a moment the two men strained, feet pressed to the wet planks of the deck. Then the wind eased, and the pressure abated.

"Boatswain, send a man to assist with the helm!" The instant the deckhand arrived to relieve him, Corley took a log reading and retired below.

Returned from Taen's cabin, the steward found his captain in the chart room. Light from a gimbaled oil lamp flickered over Corley's shoulders, flashing and sparking through salt crystals in his hair as he bent with dividers and pen, working out the running fix. Patient, the steward waited until his master looked up.

"Captain, you had best come. The Dreamweaver is ill. I cannot rouse her."

Corley's eyes steadied, dark with decision. After a moment he spoke softly. "By the Great Fall, that's bad news." If the Vaere had chosen this to penalize her for breaking her oath to return, the timing couldn't be worse.

He straightened and blew out the oil lamp. Crossing to the companionway ladder which led onto the quarterdeck, he cracked the hatch cover. The chilly smells of rain and seawater swirled into the cabin as he shouted against the storm. "Bring *Moonless* about. We're going to have to run northeast."

With the gale closing from the west, no other choice remained. Islamere's jagged shoals lay too close for safety, and no time remained to beat clear of the southernmost reefs; frustrated, concerned, Corley saw his hopes for a fast passage balked. The Isle of the Vaere lay due south.

The captain banged the hatch and hastily secured the fastening. "Fetch the healer," he snapped at the steward, and without pausing to shed his damp cloak, he headed for Taen's berth.

~ VII ~

Dream-storm

Gale winds whined through masts and rigging, and *Moonless* tossed, spray flying from her bow like foam from the jaws of a beast. Sprawled loose-limbed against the lee board of her berth, Taen Dreamweaver heard the thud and rush of seas whipped to fury by the storm. She struggled to determine whether the sensations were reality or another sequence of the nightmares which had beset her since the morning Jaric disembarked at Landfast. Yet as if her senses were locked in shackles, her mind remained in darkness.

A hinge creaked, stiff as the door to the cottage Taen had known as a child. Orange light suffused her awareness, centered by a pinpoint of flame. A male voice called her name. Powerless to respond, she did not answer. The light moved closer, fell blinding across her face, and she smelled the hot reek of oil.

"Taen Dreamweaver," repeated the man. Cloth rustled, very close by. "You're right, she's not sleeping. What in Keithland could be ailing her?"

Taen had heard that voice before. She wrestled to identify where; for an instant an image like an acid etching formed in her mind, of the Kielmark flinging chart after chart across the table in his study at Cliffhaven castle. Then the veils of delirium closed over her once more, and words bounced like echoes across the dark.

" . . . something decidedly amiss."

Someone's fingers closed over Taen's wrist. Shapes slashed her awareness, inspired by a presence edged and dangerous as sword steel. The Dreamweaver cried out from the depths of trance. Gasping, she at last perceived that the person who touched her was no nightmare born of a troubled mind but solid flesh and blood. His concern pierced the depths of her until her dream-sense rang with echoes. The grip shifted on her arm, transferring her limp weight into the care of another whose self was a warm muddle of worry. A cup brushed Taen's lips. Stinging liquid ran down her throat. She stirred and choked, but after a moment the elixir cleared her mind. Taen quivered and opened her eyes.

Awash in a flood of lanternlight, she saw faces crowded against the low beams of the cabin: the wrinkled visage of the healer, the cabin steward's bald head, and the Kielmark's bearded captain, salt-streaked and mettlesome, the violence of character which had prompted her vision of swords held flawlessly in check.

Corley spoke before the others could react. "Kor's grace, she's come to." His hands pressed deep into the blankets by the Dreamweaver's side as he leaned close, openly ignoring the healer's request to give her space and air. "Girl, what ails you?"

"No ordinary sickness, that's certain," snapped the healer from behind. "Let me through."

Corley waved him silent. "Taen?"

"I don't know." Dizzy and confused, the Dreamweaver wished she sounded less like a lost child. "My dream-sense seems overturned. I have visions . . ." Her voice trailed off, and she was terrified by her own words. *What had happened to her mastery?* Yet the fear cleared her mind a little. Her voice became stronger. "Corley, whatever happens, take me to the enchanted isle. Tamlin of the Vaere will know how to help."

"You'll get there." Corley straightened with an expression unexpectedly grim. He left the bedside abruptly and ducked through the companionway, but not before Taen sensed his thought: *how could he tell her that an out-of-season storm had diverted the brigantine's course due north?*

Relieved of the captain's bothersome presence, the healer jutted his bearded chin and took charge. "Out!" he snapped at the cabin steward. "The child needs no gawkers hanging about."

Taen stirred as he chivvied the steward past the bulkhead. "I don't mind," she said.

"Oh, sure." The healer thumped his satchel of remedies on the sea chest in the corner and testily shook his head. "You'll be that much better without yon gossip poking his nose into corners."

The elder arranged his brazier on a slate. The shuddering toss of the brigantine appeared to cause him no difficulty, for he spilled none of his phials as he concocted a bitter-smelling potion of herbs. Taen drank the mixture with heroic distaste, at which point the steward reappeared with a tray of hot soup. The healer admitted him grumbling, and lingered to make certain she ate. At last he packed up his satchel and left. Taen slept. For several days no dreams returned to trouble her.

But the storm grew worse. The wind reached gale force, screaming like a demon out of the west, and battering the wave crests into streaming tails of spindrift. Stripped to bare spars, *Moonless* reeled and tossed, seawater rolling green through her waist. The off-watch crew huddled wet as seals in the forecastle. Lashed beside the helmsmen, Corley oversaw his command night and day from the quarterdeck.

Taen learned to disregard the monotonous clang of the bilge pumps. She ate cold fare with the crew; seas were too rough to permit any fire in the galley, and, lacking that central place of warmth, the brigantine became dank and cheerless below decks. Still, Taen was a fisherman's daughter. Inured to the discomforts and the perils of the sea, she badgered the sailhands until they laughed, and put red pepper in the cook's jerky so he would stop carping about the fact that his food was never hot. Watching her bright spirits light the brigantine from stem to stern, not even the healer guessed her dizzy spells had returned. Taen fought to stay active. Burning resources and wit like festival candles, she knew if she returned to her berth to sleep, the dreams would overwhelm her once again.

But a morning arrived two days later when the dawn watch entered the galley dripping rainwater. They shouted coarse jokes about wet weather causing ringlets, and one by one fell silent as they noticed Taen sprawled against the woodbox, her skin dry and burning to the touch. Neither noise nor shaking could rouse her.

"Inform the captain," snapped the boatswain.

Dragged unceremoniously from his hammock, the healer rammed a path through the gawking crewmen to Taen's side and found Corley newly arrived from the quarterdeck.

Unkempt from ceaseless exposure to wind and water, the captain paced until he heard the healer's prognosis: this time the girl had drifted too far for mortal efforts to avail. Her cure, if any existed, lay with the Vaere.

"See her to a berth." Corley shut red-rimmed eyes, for a moment overcome by fatigue. Then he shivered like a dog and added, "Storm's lifting. By daylight we should be able to put about and resume a southern course."

But weather balked his plans again by midday. The heavy clouds broke, replaced by a sky the clean cobalt of enamel. Capricious winds shifted and winnowed and stilled. *Moonless* wallowed becalmed over a round-topped procession of storm swells. Her gear crashed and banged aloft, and the smoke from her galley fire rose straight as a spire overhead. Silent, Corley took sun sights and consulted his charts. Tempest and current had set *Moonless* far to the east and north, leagues from her desired course. The Isle of the Vaere presently lay twenty days' sail under perfect conditions; but without wind for her canvas, the brigantine rolled dead as a gaffed fish in the water. Suddenly sensitive to every ache in his tired body, the captain laid his dividers aside and bellowed for the officer of the watch.

The man arrived tardily. Curt to the point of rudeness, Corley demanded the reason, and received a second round of ill news. Inspection of the hold revealed casks worked loose by the storm; most of the water stores had been fouled with seawater.

As the officer delivered his report, Corley resisted a consuming urge to cover his face with his hands. *Moonless* would need to make landfall within eight days to take on water, else the crew would suffer shortage. Kor defend the innocent, thought Corley; the girl who had kept his sailhands grinning through a bout of the most evil weather he had seen on the Corine Sea would now have to wait on more than the wind for help.

Taen never felt the hands which lifted her from the galley deck and carried her, wrapped in blankets, to the narrow berth in the aft cabin. Lost in a maze of dreams, she knew nothing of the healer's attempts to rouse her, nor did she react to the thumps and shouted commands from the hold where the sailhands labored to secure the ruined casks. Her mind assumed a course all its own. Personalities deflected her, temporarily flooding swirls of color and dimension across her inward eye; then they passed, and the images ran together into a world of twilight and shadows. Taen drifted, time and self forgotten.

Later the light faded entirely. Muffled in night like felt, Taen sailed through an eddyless void. Neither moon nor stars pricked the depths, and no lantern shone to mark any haven or dooryard where she might find peace and rest. How long she drifted could not be measured, but imperceptibly, the quality of the blackness changed. She perceived a spark of illumination. Distant, but warm as candle flame the light drew her like a moth.

Blindness lifted from Taen's dream-sense. She found her awareness centered in a dusty attic chamber stacked with books. There afternoon shadow streaked a copy table where Jaric bent over parchment and a scroll with handles of gold-stamped wood. A brief shiver gripped him. Though the room was neither cold nor dark, he paused, laid his pen aside, and reached with ink-stained fingers for the striker to ignite the oil lamp.

"Never mind, boy." A scribe with rumpled silver hair shuffled out from behind a row of shelves. "No sense burning lights, now. If your eyes are tired, you can finish translating that treatise in the morning."

Jaric rubbed a crick in his neck. "You don't mind, Brother Handred?"

The elder unhooked his cane from a chairback and limped across the chamber. Through dust-streaked cuffs and an assortment of ancient food stains, Taen saw that he wore the deep blue robe of Kor's Brotherhood. "The master in residence told me you stayed all night."

"I was reading," Jaric admitted. "I didn't start copying until dawn."

"Well, then you're plenty tired." Head cocked like a bird, the priest thumbed through the pages piled at Jaric's elbow. The script was clean and straight, and probably without errors; whatever the scarred state of his hands, this boy had been trained well. "You've done enough for one day."

Taen felt the ache of Jaric's weariness cut through the dream-link as he rose to his feet. "I can go?"

The priest nodded. "Eat. Get some sleep. You'll work the better for it come morning."

But rest never entered Jaric's mind as he pushed back his stool and picked a path through the stacks to the door. The boy *Moonless* had delivered to Landfast was changing, Taen perceived. The teaching of Corley and another swordsman called Brith had bent Jaric's mind toward a mold which accepted no excuse for weakness. More and more, necessity forced him to set aside the fears which had poisoned his childhood at Morbrith. He remembered to buckle on sword and dagger before he entered the streets. Now better acquainted with Landfast,

Jaric chose back streets and alleys least traveled. Within minutes he reached the dockside.

"Alms, young master," called a one-handed beggar who leaned on a bollard. A mangy tomcat crouched by his feet, and clothes already patched shapeless needed another round of mending at elbows, knees, and cuffs.

Jaric tossed the fellow a silver with the unthinking reflex of habit.

"Thank'e." The beggar jammed the coin in his boot and straightened with a crooked grin. "Boat's bailed for ye, master. Best check the starboard bowline. She's chafed a bit, from the storm."

Jaric paused while a wagon rumbled past. "I came as soon as I could." He reached into his pocket, groped for another coin.

"Leave be, boy." The beggar shrugged. "I do well enough by you."

Jaric tossed a copper, spinning, into the air. "Take it for the cat, then. I've no family to feed."

"Right, aye, then." The beggar caught the coin with the speed of a striking snake. Taen saw him stare after as Jaric ran down the dock to the slip where *Callinde* lay tied.

Linked through the dream to the boy's concern, the girl stepped aboard the ancient boat. After a hasty glance to ascertain whether the floorboards were dry, Jaric ducked around the headstay and ran anxious hands over the dockline the beggar had mentioned. Frayed plies scraped under his fingers; the rope must certainly be replaced. Squinting against the low sun of afternoon, Jaric bent and unfastened the aft locker. He reached beneath the folded canvas of the headsail in search of his store of spare cordage, and froze suddenly in mid-motion. Taen felt a chill jolt through him. Startled, she shared the apprehension which tightened his chest as he dug under the sail and dragged forth an object that *could not* have been there, yet was. Jaric sank against the thwart, the cold, pale length of an ash flute clenched hard between his hands. Inlay flashed silver as he turned it. The breath came fast and dry in his throat.

Moved to concern, Taen probed him and encountered stark edges of fear. She never learned why. As if roused by her dream-touch, Jaric stiffened. He flexed his wrists in sharp denial, and the delicate shaft of the flute snapped. Splinters glanced in the sunlight, fell whispering to the deck; and Taen cried out, for as the ash wood broke asunder, a wail of purest sorrow echoed within her mind.

She protested without thought. '*Jaric, no!*' The makers of the flute offered their gift without malice. They wished only to aid him, defend him from harm.

But the words of the Dreamweaver in his mind only caused the boy to start up in alarm. With a guilty gesture, he tossed the broken instrument into the harbor. As it sank from sight, Taen saw that memory of its origin was linked to another event Jaric had determined to hide. Reflexively she pursued the reason; and the dockside where Jaric tended *Callinde* vanished, swept away by the whine of wind across desolate acres.

Taen looked down from the carved archway of a tower and saw a place of treeless rock. Bare except for scabrous splotches of lichen, hills fell away to a gray horizon. Trapped by dreams, the girl knew she gazed from a window far distant from Landfast, beyond the borders of Keithland itself. Even as she wondered how a thought from Jaric's mind would lead her here, she sensed movement in the chamber behind her.

'*He will be all you hoped for, and more,*' said a voice whose overtones grated like rusty metal.

The words formed no language spoken by man, but, gifted with a Dreamweaver's talents, Taen understood the meaning. Touched by nameless dread, she turned from the window to view the chamber behind her. Within a vaulted hall of stone, crimson carpets covered a raised, central dais. A mirror pool of black-veined marble reflected a table and carved chair whose yellow-eyed occupant possessed no human features.

'*Bring him hither,*' bade the demon on the dais. His tone whistled like flutes. He leaned forward, rippling skin all mottled and scaled like a lizard's. Orange spines tipped fingers, ears, and the armored plates visible beneath the hem of the garment which swathed his spindly torso. Gold chains winked above spurred ankles.

'*I enter, Lord Scait.*' The original speaker strode from the shadowed depths of an antechamber. It moved with the raddled gait of a hunchback, followed by others who supported another apparently ailing or injured. By the fleshy curves of their gill flaps, Taen recognized the toadlike Thienz, empaths whose kind had allied in the attack against Cliffhaven. All but blind in daylight, the demons advanced on rubbery, webbed feet. Crested headdresses clinked, beads and jewels keeping time to their ungainly stride. The party stopped by the poolside, reflected upside down in the water as they offered obeisance to the figure seated on the dais. Taen took a careful look at the other, who bowed woodenly in the grip of wiry Thienz fingers. And her heart twisted terribly inside, for there stood no demon but a human male in ragged, salt-stained clothing.

Black hair lay tangled against the filthy cloth of his collar. His sea boots were torn with wear, and his face a dead mask of exhaustion. Granted a clear view of his features in the pool, Taen felt the vision tighten like a noose around her mind; for the man held between the hideous bodies of the Thienz was Marlson Emien, her natural brother, last seen when he had fled Jaric's sword beneath the Tower of Elrinfaer. But Emien's expression of lifeless uninterest was one his sister had never known before.

'This is the dissident who succeeds the witch, Tathagres?' said Scait from the dais. *'He came of his own will, you say. Is that so?'*

Emien gave no sign of recognition. His eyes remained fixed, a cold and passionless blue, while the demons discussed him in images which translated in no tongue spoken on Keithland's soil.

'Lord, that is so.' The spokesman for the Thienz stepped to the lip of the pool. Beads clinked on either side of its jowls as it bobbed its blunt head. *'This Emien-that-was desired the power of his mistress-now-dead. He did murder to claim it. See, Lord, mighty-and-greatest, there are burn scars on the man-flesh of his hands. By this be certain the crystals once-stolen-from-Llondelei ensure our permanent domination of his body. His fate is yours to command.'*

Scait's lips curled, revealing razor rows of sharklike teeth. *'Has he talents? Information? Bring him hither, that I might test his mettle.'* The lizard demon flicked spiny fingers and beckoned.

The Thienz-demons clustered tightly together. Though small and awkward of movement, they proved surprisingly strong. Webbed, toadlike fingers propelled Marlson Emien past the mirror pool, pressing him prone on the carpet before the dais.

The Demon Lord arose, and with the detailed horror of nightmare, Taen realized his throne was comprised of preserved human remains. Wishing to turn from the image, but unable to abandon knowledge of her brother's fate, she whimpered in the depths of trance, even as the demon ruler of

Shadowfane set spurred hands against the sides of Emien's head.

The probe must have been cruel, for despite the restraint of the Thienz, the boy's body arched against the floor. His scream echoed piteously off the vaulted ceiling of the hall; but no mercy was shown him. Scait Demon Lord arose from his examination with the satisfaction of a scavanger sated upon carrion. Yellow eyes glittered with excitement as he transmitted his findings to the Thienz.

'He has abilities, this manling stolen from Keithland! A sorcerer's latent potential, did-you-not-see: had he not forsaken loyalty to his kind, he might-have-gone to the Vaere and caused-us-sorrow, even as Ivain and Anskiere before him.' Here the demon croaked in sour irony. *'Now he is ours. Let him be called Maelgrim, for when his talents are mature, he will both be deceived, and act the part of deceiver, our tool and the bane-of-his-kind.'*

The group spokesman cleared its throat with a croak. *'Lord-mightiest, there is more. Marlson-Emien-Maelgrim has a sister of equal talent. She has trained already with the Vaere, and walks Keithland as Dreamweaver.'*

The demon on the dais swore in slit-eyed fury. 'Corinne Dane, *Accursed! How can this be?'* Spurs clashed against ankle ornaments as he sprang precipitously to his feet. *'Explain!'*

The spokesman for the Thienz bobbed in deference. *'High-mightiest, when the shape-shifter, Tathagres'-ally, perished during the assault on Cliffhaven, it sent a message most-strange through its death-link. The Karas claimed it was Dreamweaver-betrayed. This boy has memories of a sister who proves-this-was-truth.'*

Listening, Taen felt as if a sliver of ice pierced her heart. She struggled to influence her dream-sense, bend it away from the horrors of this place; but her effort dissipated, smothered by dark. Powerless to control her Sathid-enhanced talents, she had no choice but observe as Scait bent for the second time over the prone form of her brother. Emien flinched from the touch. He whimpered and writhed as the Demon Lord ransacked his mind for information. The Thienz before the mirror pool clustered together, trembling and hissing softly among themselves. Their discomfort translated across the link and oppressed Taen's dream-sense with foreboding.

Yet even this did not prepare her for the violence of Scait's reaction. His spurred grip tightened on Emien's flesh, almost drawing blood. Then, as the import of his findings registered, he recoiled as if burned. His whistle of alarm struck echoes off vaulted stone ceilings; beneath the dais the Thienz stilled utterly as their overlord's yellow eyes lifted and fixed upon them.

'*Cowardly toads! Fools! The sister-Taen-Dreamweaver is no threat to Shadowfane, dying as she is of her Sathid. But the other, Ivainson-Firelord's-heir-Jaric! That one could inflict death and sorrow upon-us-all.*' Scait bared his teeth and, agitated as never before, raised his long hackles before inferiors.

The Thienz wailed in alarm, almost tumbling over each other as they shrank from the wrath of their lord. Scait harried them with imprecations and curses, but Taen ignored their meaning. Terrified for Ivainson Jaric, and consumed with the need to warn him, she struck out with all her strength against her prison of dreams. Yet her struggle accomplished no more than the frenzied wingbeats of a moth. Taen felt her dream-sense ripple, darken, and refocus on the same stone chamber at Shadowfane.

On the dais, Scait flexed his spurs and crouched once again over Emien. '*The sister can show us where. Weakened as she is by changes in her Sathid, she might be vulnerable if we seek to manipulate through the affinity that remains between her and this, her brother.*'

The Thienz spokesman whuffed its gills. '*Your will, mightiest.*'

Stillness fell, broken by a rasping scrape as Scait honed the edges of his teeth by grinding his jaws together. As the Thienz pressed closely around him, he reached a last time for Emien.

Taen never felt the Demon Lord and his minions combine their powers. She knew only a moment of red-hazed perception, as the minds of Kor's Accursed encompassed her brother. Then their probe struck, a blazing arc of force that stabbed like sword metal into her awareness. She recoiled, unable even to cry out. The defenses that should have answered her Sathid mastery failed utterly, sundered as she was from control. Demons snapped her frail web of denial. With a thrust like pain, they seized upon the subject of their desire and plundered. Two words they tore from her, *Cliffhaven,* and *Landfast;* both would be searched for the purpose of destroying Ivainson Jaric.

Taen barely noted Scait's fierce crow of triumph. Dazed by

the demon's whirlwind withdrawal, her battered human awareness grasped only fragments of the instructions he gave to his underlings; vaguely she understood that the demon compact at Shadowfane would meet to hear tidings. Emien would be trained as a weapon against Keithland, and assassins would sail to hunt Jaric. This was the will of Lord Scait.

The Thienz wailed mournfully in consternation, for saltwater immersion was a hazard to them. But their spokesman groveled before the dais without protest. *'Your will, Grandmightiest.'* Its crested headdress rattled as it shuffled back among its colleagues. Then, croaking among themselves, the Thienz gathered Emien between them and marched him unprotesting from the hall.

The impact of implication became too much for Taen to endure. Grief for her lost brother and fear for Ivainson Jaric momentarily upset reason. She cried aloud, every fiber of her being reviled by the betrayal she had been entrapped to commit. Sundered by the violence of her rejection, the thread of the vision snapped. The demon's vaulted council hall vanished, swept away in the torrent of her Sathid change. Sound beat against Taen's ears, shrill as wind through winter branches. Orientation crumbled with it; the girl's awareness tumbled over and over, banished into darkness and primordial cold. Ice cracked like old bones around her, shackled her feet to bedrock stillness. Stars sprang into being, needle pricks against an endless field of night. Solitary, aching, Taen sought but found no landmark from any place she knew. No effort availed her. Again and again she spun thought, only to strike against impenetrable bounds of nightmare. The strange words spoken by demons whispered and sighed through her thoughts, uncipherable as the tracks of ghosts.

'. . . *Dreamweaver . . . no threat . . . dying as she is of her Sathid. . . . Ivainson-Firelord's-heir-Jaric . . . could inflict death and sorrow upon-us-all. . . .'* And always, with a tearing edge of pain, her concern circled round to Emien. '. . . *came of his own will . . . did murder. Let him be called Maelgrim . . . our tool and the bane-of-his-kind.'* Horror and memory blended, until one became inseparable from the other.

Taen struggled afresh to escape her prison of dreams. But the images she wrestled muddled like ink only to blossom anew in her mind. Her endeavors earned no respite. Dreamsense returned nothing but the desolation of absolute emptiness, and in the end, frayed to a febrile sleep of exhaustion, she drifted forgetful of her purpose.

The presence stole upon her unawares. A soft chink of bells and the click of beaded feathers at first passed unnoticed, an insect rustle of sound teasing the limits of awareness. Nailed to immobility by the vacuum brilliance of the stars, Taen ignored the interruption. But the disturbance waxed insistent, and was joined after a time by a ruddy glimmer of light. The girl felt her consciousness caught and bridled by a touch so light she never thought to protest. Dream-sense aligned like mirrors in her mind. Light cut like a blade across blackness. Taen recovered self-awareness like a sleeper wakened, and found herself in the presence of Tamlin of the Vaere, the same who had trained her in the ways of power.

Fey, impertinent, the creature had changed not at all since her departure for Cliffhaven. Scarcely half the height of a man, he stood with his clay pipe tucked amid an unkempt nest of whiskers. Skin crinkled around eyes unfathomable and dark as jet. From folded arms to stitched calf boots, Tamlin radiated an impression of quickness and reprimand.

"Girl-child, you broke faith. That's trouble." The tiny man shrugged in irritation, and bells and beads danced on the thongs laced through his sleeves. "I warned you, made you swear. You should have left Cliffhaven long since."

Tired to the marrow of her bones, Taen had to gather energy simply to answer. "I had to stay."

"Did you so?" Tamlin snorted through his pipe, and smoke rings lifted, silvered by the light of his presence. "Now your life is endangered."

A spark of resentment rose in Taen. "Would you rather the demons won Landfast? Had I left, the Kielmark's defenses would have fallen. Who would have guarded Mainstrait against invasion then?"

"You're ignorant. Foolish as well." Tamlin twirled the end of his beard between his fingers, and a thoughtful crease appeared between his brows. "Listen now, or perish. Your dream-sense has become unbiddable because you left my guidance before your cycle of mastery was complete. The Sathid crystal you bonded to extend your talents now reaches maturity within your body. The process should have been overseen by the Vaere. Yet you left Cliffhaven too late for our helping."

Taen felt cold touch her heart. *"I can't awaken out of this?"*

"Be silent." Tamlin bit down on his pipe, hands stilled against the fawn cloth of his jacket. "Remember this, whatever befalls. If you cannot reach the enchanted isle, seek the makers of Jaric's flute. They alone can save you."

"Riddles?" said Taen, frightened now, for Tamlin's presence had suddenly begun to fade. The glow of his pipe reddened like a coal, and slowly diminished. Sharp in the ebbing twilight, the Dreamweaver recalled an image; again she saw the scarred fingers of Ivainson Jaric tense, twist, and the delicate shaft of a holed instrument snap into splinters and bent wire.

"Tamlin, the flute you mention is broken!" Taen's protest echoed across emptiness; the Vaere was gone. The darkness of his passing closed over Taen's head, even as the green waters of Landfast harbor had once swallowed the fragments of the flute which offered her sole hope of survival.

～VIII～

Search

The days lengthened toward summer, and in Landfast, oldest settled city in Keithland, the fruit sellers' stalls smelled fragrant with ripe strawberries. Unmarried girls wove ribbons in their hair for the dances to celebrate the planting, and though the season made them eager for courting, Jaric could only stare wistfully at their smiles. Days he spent copying manuscript in the towers where the archives were stored, and in the long hours before twilight, he met Brith in the training yard for arms practice. His sailor's tan faded, but his calluses did not. He cleaned and oiled his steel each night as the lampsmen made rounds to light the wicks along the Lionsgate stair. Then, as Brith and his cadre of off-duty guardsmen gathered, laughing, to visit their alehouses and taverns, Jaric slung his weapons across sweating shoulders. Bound by Anskiere's geas, he stepped into the gathering dark to begin his search for means to safeguard the Keys to Elrinfaer.

He went first to Kordane's shrine. An acolyte met him within the tiled arches of the forecourt. The man wore a robe of blue, the single gold star which adorned his collar showing he had sworn life service barely one year past. He could not have been much beyond Jaric's age, yet he carried himself with an arrogance that seemed common to all junior officials in Landfast. The acolyte regarded the baldric, sword, and dagger slung across the visitor's shoulders, and his lips pursed with disdain, even as he executed the bow of ritual welcome.

"Have you come to worship?" The alcoyte straightened, chin lifted for the negative he expected would come.

Jaric stared at him, the disappointment inspired by such brusqueness politely kept hidden. "I wish to speak with the head priest."

"*Head priest?*" The alcoyte sighed, loftily amused. "You're backlands-born, aren't you, soldier? We have no head priest here. Only his holiness the Master Grand High Star."

Jaric accepted this without the least sign of discomfort. His hands gently shifted the sword belt. "Does he have a shorter title?"

"'His Eminence' will do." Nettled by the chime of steel cross guards, the acolyte added, "You don't need those in here."

"But I didn't come to worship," Jaric reminded. "If his Eminence is too busy with devotions, please mention that the matter concerns Keithland's defenses."

The acolyte raised his brows at this, as if he doubted any connection a boy with a north-shore accent might have with the preservation of civilization. Still, the single star on his collar was no match for sharpened steel if argument arose; he spun with a flap of dark robes and jerked his head for Jaric to follow.

The anteroom of Kor's shrine was lamplit and chill, the walls being faced with black marble, and the floor polished stone with no carpets. Dark hangings with the gold-sewn sigil of the priesthood seemed to swallow what little light was available, and the raised dais with the reliquary and public altar were shadowed and dim with mystery. Footsteps and voices echoed under lofty vaulted ceilings; the few worshippers clustered by the offering chests spoke in whispers, and acted apologetic if their children made noise or their sandals scraped inadvertently. Jaric waited where his guide indicated. Still holding his weapons, he dropped no coins in the offering chest; nor did he ask the attendant on duty to light any lamps for loved ones. Taen deserved such a courtesy, he knew. But the thought of crossing the chamber was daunting; and a particularly demanding practice with Brith had left his muscles in knots. Weary, hungry, and anxious to be quit of the Keys, Jaric debated the propriety of sitting down on the floor where he stood. Then the acolyte returned and beckoned him through a door into the inner sanctuary.

Beyond lay a drafty expanse of stairwell. The stonework was pierced at intervals with lancet arches open to the outside, and by the lack of glass Jaric guessed the acolyte had led him through the oldest portion of Kor's sanctuary. Here at one time the openings would have been covered by siege shutters, for the walls were dressed and buttressed like a fortress, and the risers worn by the generations of tramping feet.

"Tell me your name," wheezed the acolyte. Since he was a

man unaccustomed to exertion, his second ascent of a very steep climb exacted a punishing toll.

"Kerainson," Jaric replied, and winced inwardly as his tired legs protested the length of the stair. Yet he managed with better grace than the acolyte, and finally took pity as the man began to gasp. "If you tell me where, I can go on my own."

The acolyte rolled his eyes. "His Eminence would send me to fast. Don't tell him?"

Jaric shook his head, then memorized what seemed an unduly complex set of directions. Three flights and two corridors later, he knocked on the one door he found that had the Brotherhood's star and fireburst inlaid in gold into ebony.

"What!" barked an impatient-sounding voice from within. "If it's the accounts from the grain tax, leave them for tomorrow, will you?"

"I'm not the accountant," called Jaric. Gently he lifted the latch.

A gray-haired man in a rumpled smock jumped up and peered over the papers piled on his desk. The lamp which burned by his elbow lit apple cheeks, a harried frown, and hands better suited to a farmer. "Ah, the visitor, yes, do come in."

Jaric took a startled step into the room. "You're his Eminence the Grand High Star?"

"Eh? No." The man noticed the sword and dagger slung across his visitor's shoulder and blinked. "You don't need those in here." Then, belatedly remembering the question only partially answered, he said, "I'm his Eminence's secretary. Tell me why you came, and if the matter warrants, I'll refer you."

The boy made no move to lay aside his blades. Neither did he speak, but instead reached one-handed to his collar and lifted a sweat-stained thong over his head. A small leather pouch dangled from the ends. He loosened the drawstrings with his teeth, then dumped the contents onto the only square of desk not littered with paperwork.

A heavy object tumbled out. Black, cube-shaped, it clattered like a die and stopped with a device inlaid in one side uppermost. Lamplight flickered over the triple circle and falcon, sigil of Anskiere, once Stormwarden and sworn defender of Tierl Enneth. The secretary sucked in a surprised breath, then bit off an exclamation as a second item settled with a whisper of sound beside the first. Scratched wood framed the black-and-gold-barred length of a stormfalcon's feather; even here, fenced by papers and pens and the clutter of sheltered living, the spell-wrought thing radiated the chill of gales driven by sorcery.

"Kor have mercy," murmured the secretary. He directed a nervous glance at Jaric, as if seeing him for the first time. "Where did you come by those? Are you the Stormwarden's emissary? You knew his powers leveled Tierl Enneth? Four thousand people drowned, they say. Should Anskiere ever again set foot on any isle of the Alliance, he stands condemned to death by fire."

Jaric said nothing. For an extended interval, the flash and gleam of lantern flame over Anskiere's gold seal was the only movement in the room. Then the secretary jerked open a drawer, raked out a pair of spectacles, and jammed them over his ears. "Wait here, boy. Wait." And near to shaking with agitation, he burst through the door behind his chair.

A taller man stepped through a moment later, the secretary tagging anxiously behind. The newcomer wore no robes but trousers and shirt close-fitted to his body. The fabric was knit rather than woven, the emblem of office in sewn silver and indigo on his chest. More agile than the secretary, with a face barely wrinkled and hair dusted gray at the temples, he turned sharp, dark eyes upon Jaric, then glanced at the desk, to the items isolated between tiered stacks of accounts.

His voice proved as authoritative as his attitude. "Kerainson? Pick those up and bring them in."

Brisk but not unkindly, he held the door open while the boy filed past. The chamber beyond was sumptuously carpeted. White-painted walls contrasted with polished stone sills; but Jaric had no eyes for the view of Landfast which sparkled four stories down, alight with lanterns and life. He stared instead at row upon row of bookshelves laden with gold-stamped bindings and rare texts. The lettering was scribed in religious runes, which he lacked the schooling to decipher. Yet the promise of new knowledge offered fascination enough; surely Kordane's Brotherhood possessed means of holding the Keys to Elrinfaer secure from demons.

"You're standing on the sacred symbol," admonished a voice at his back.

Jaric started, and belatedly noticed he had strayed beyond

the carpet. The floor beneath his boots was configured like a seal. A polished mosaic of lapis lazuli and agate depicted Kordane's Fires as they first arced across Keithland's sky, condemning mankind to exile until such time as the last demon was vanquished or killed.

"I'm sorry." The boy stepped back with an embarrassing chime of sword steel. Painfully diffident, he stilled his swinging blades and found the Grand High Star smiling at him.

"You don't need those in here," said his Eminence softly. "But keep them by you if you feel the better for it. Only sit, please. I've a stiff neck from looking over accounts, and watching you walk circles is a distraction I'd rather avoid." Strong, pale hands lifted a chair from the corner and thumped it on the carpet before the books. The Grand High Star seated himself on a nearby divan, his attention apparently fixed on the wrought-brass candlestand which supported the only light in the chamber.

Jaric slipped his baldric from his shoulder. He looped the leather over the chairback and settled stiffly on the seat, the Keys to Elrinfaer and the stormfalcon's feather clenched in white knuckles in his lap. Then, granted audience with the man in the highest echelon of Kor's priesthood not sworn to seclusion, the boy struggled for words to begin.

The Grand High Star rescued him from discomfort. "You are the heir of Ivain?"

Jaric flinched, wishing he had the courage to lie; but the eyes of the priest on the divan were unforgiving, behind their kindliness. "Eminence, how did you know?"

"You look like him," the Grand High Star said bluntly. "And Cliffhaven's news ofttimes travels in the gossip of sailors. The priesthood has heard that the curse pronounced by Anskiere at Northsea had been loosed within Keithland."

"I never knew either sorcerer," the Firelord's son admitted miserably. Wariness showed in his bearing as he opened his fists and bared the Keys to Elrinfaer and the feather.

"No, boy," said the Grand High Star. "The Brotherhood cannot shelter those things in your care."

Jaric returned a stricken look. "But—"

The Grand High Star waved him silent. Then he rose and crossed to the doorway. After a few quiet words to the secretary standing without, he nodded, shut the panel, and promptly returned to the divan.

"Ivainson, the works of Kordane's Brotherhood and the

doings of sorcerers have never intermixed. By oath an initiate must maintain, nurture, and defend. But sorcerers, particularly ones trained by the Vaere, seem compelled to meddle, so far to the detriment of mankind. The destruction of Elrinfaer should have taught your Stormwarden the futility of challenging demons. It did not, and four thousand more innocents died at Tierl Enneth."

"But I have no wish for a sorcerer's powers!" Jaric burst in. "Instead I seek means to avoid them."

The Grand High Star tapped his signet with its carven seal of office. The boy seated hopefully before him never moved, even as he sighed and spoke. "Firelord's heir, the priesthood cannot help."

That moment a knock sounded at the door. Jaric started, hands tightened convulsively on the Keys to Elrinfaer. But the panel only opened to admit his eminence's secretary. The man carried a tray laden with sweet pastry, cheese, and ale. He set this on a side table and, with a bow to his superior, departed.

The Grand High Star smiled as the latch clicked shut. "You seemed hungry," he said to Jaric. "If my order can do nothing else, at least I could be certain you got supper."

The solicitude was impossible to refuse. Jaric returned Keys and stormfalcon's feather to the pouch on the string at his neck. He reached tentatively for the cheese knife; and the Grand High Star of Landfast waited without speaking while the boy shed his self-consciousness and ate. Only then did his strength become apparent, innate, but too often obscured by uncertainty. His hair needed a trim, and his clothing was simple, but the manner in which he broke his bread would not have been out of place in a king's hall.

Anxious not to tax his host's attentiveness, Jaric soon set his ale mug aside. "The sanctuary towers of Landfast are the most secure stronghold upon Keithland. Why not safeguard the Keys to Anskiere's wards there?"

"Because demons covet the breaking of those wards, Jaric." The Grand High Star settled back. Carefully, patiently, for he understood the disappointment his words would bring, he explained that the knowledge stored in the sanctuary towers was too vital to be risked. "The priests who enter there stay for a term of life, and not even I know what secrets they guard. Were they to add the wards of a Vaere-trained sorcerer, demons might attack to gain possession of them. Better the

Keys fell to Shadowfane than that the legacy of mankind became jeopardized."

Jaric forgot the half-eaten pastry in his hand. "But I thought the outer defenses—"

The Grand High Star seemed suddenly burdened with sadness. "Jaric, what I'm about to tell you is unknown to men on the streets, and in peril of your soul you'll never repeat it. But the ward you encountered upon entering Landfast waters was no defense at all, only a screen maintained by the more talented initiates of the Brotherhood to detect the presence of demons. Should Kor's Accursed send spies, or even an attacking army, no disguise will shelter them. Our citizens will gain warning of invasion. After that, defense of this city must rely upon ordinary force of arms."

Crumbs jumped as the pastry dropped from Jaric's hand onto the tray. He stared, shocked, at the haunted countenance of the Grand High Star, and suddenly understood: this man's fatalistic serenity and Ivain Firelord's contempt of the priesthood both stemmed from the fact that mankind's survival hung balanced on the most fragile of threads. The impact of implications stunned the mind. For if this priest spoke honestly, the bulwark of Landfast's defenses was based on bluff. In all of Keithland only the Vaere-trained owned effective powers against demons. The enormities of Elrinfaer and Tierl Enneth gained a new significance, and, almost, the Cycle of Fire seemed less a mad recourse, and more a remedy of desperate necessity.

Jaric forgot courtesy. Miserable with fresh doubts in the one place he hoped to find solace, he rose and grasped his sword belt. But his move to depart was caught short by the steely voice of the Grand High Star.

"Ivainson Jaric, listen well. You came to Landfast to gather knowledge. Wise or not, your quest shall not go unsupported. There are treatises in the secular archives pertaining to Keithland's defenses. These will be made available to you for study."

Jaric spun just short of the doorway and bowed. "I am grateful, Eminence."

"Don't be." The priest seemed suddenly remote behind the badges and signet of his office. "I must also restrict your stay here, since your presence shall inevitably draw unwanted attention to this city. Felwaithe's royal seer already warns that the compact at Shadowfane seeks your whereabouts. You have

leave to remain until the fall solstice. After that, I recommend
you apply to the enclave of wizards at Mhored Kara, and beg
them to offer you shelter.''

Jaric accepted this banishment with startling poise. His
dark eyes remained steady, and the hand on his sword no
longer trembled. "Like you, the kingdom conjurers can warn.
They have little ability to guard. If demons overtake me, and
the Mharg fly free, how long do you think your sanctuary
towers will stay standing?''

The question was impertinent; the highest-ranking priest in
Landfast answered through white lips. "Until eternity or man's
salvation, by the grace of Kordane's Fires.''

"I hope so," whispered Jaric. And he spun with the reflexive grace of a swordsman and departed.

All the way home, through streets bustling with Landfast's
frenetic nightlife, Jaric thrashed through the facts revealed by
the Grand High Star. Jostled by sailors on shore leave, and
whistled at by more than one aging prostitute, he shut his
eyes, sweating and cold and angry by turns. Who enacted the
greater injustice against mankind, he wondered: the priests
with their fabrication of illusions, or the Vaere-trained, whose
perilous powers sometimes killed the innocent? The question
nettled like a thorn, his own fear a litany beneath. The only
surety in Keithland was the tireless hatred of the demons.

"Anskiere forgive me," murmured the boy, surrounded by
strangers; for like the righteous, ignorant populace of Keithland, he had condemned what he had not understood. Tierl
Enneth's deaths might perhaps be justifiable; but in terror Jaric
knew he could not accept such responsibility for his own. The
Cycle of Fire was a curse he would escape if he could. And he
would, he must, though the demons crushed him to powder as
he tried.

Ivainson Jaric never spoke with the Grand High Star of
Kor's Brotherhood again, but the next day after sword practice, he called back at the shrine. Now the acolyte at the entry
greeted him with solicitous respect, and conducted him to the
librarian in the chamber of secular archives. There, by the
command of the Grand High Star, an impressive collection of
documents and books had been compiled. All were bound in
black leather, and not a few had locks.

Though the chamber that housed them was vaulted with
high, airy domes, large enough to diminish the tallest of men,

Jaric felt confined. Here, for the first time he could remember, he found no security in a place of knowledge and learning. The evil and the doom threatened by Shadowfane's compact seemed to poison his heart against hope. Inexplicably he thought of Taen, even as he perused the first titles. Haunted by growing doubts that his search would prove futile, he barely noticed the librarian behind him raise crossed wrists in the traditional sign against evil. Need to escape the Cycle of Fire overshadowed any social stigma of Ivain's inheritance. Jaric lifted the first book from the shelf and retired to an alcove overlooking the merchants' wharf. There he wedged his sword in a notch between cushions and, with feet braced against a worn corner of wainscoting, began to read.

Sundown came quickly. Beyond the window the city towers streaked shadows across the hump of Little Dagley Islet. Carts rumbled away from the dockside, and as the harbor beacons glimmered orange through twilight, the whistles and shouted jokes of the longshoremen faded as they sought their wives, or refreshment in the taverns. Jaric squinted in the failing light, and barely glanced up as the librarian brought a stand and two spare candles. He managed a nod when the man retired for the evening, leaving instructions concerning the visitor for the night watch.

Jaric read as if the treatises and the essays were not long-winded, or repetitive, and tediously interrupted with religious overtones or outright misconceptions. He dared do no less. A paragraph carelessly skimmed might contain the one fact he needed. Some of the works on the hilltribes' rites were available nowhere else on Keithland; the wild clansmen who practiced them were easily provoked to killing, and their ways were little known to outsiders. Evangelists of Kor's Brotherhood were among the few to venture among their camps. Jaric studied until his eyes stung and the light wavered. He finished the first book in time to light a fresh candle from the failing wick of the last. He reached next for a collection of essays, absently kneading a cramp in his thigh. The words were archaic and stiff, difficult to follow. Jaric persisted, while the second candle burned down to a dribbled stub. In time, the third and last of his lights flickered out. The glow of a rising quarter moon lit his way as he returned the books to the librarian's desk.

Jaric pushed open the wide double door, and caught the watchman napping at his post.

"It's after midnight, boy," groused the man as he shuffled yawning to his feet. He fumbled at his belt ring and the rattle of his keys echoed down deserted corridors as he unlocked to let Jaric out.

The streets outside were equally empty, except for scavenging dogs and disreputable sorts who rummaged in trash-bins for their livelihood. Ivainson walked between shuttered houses, past lamps with their wicks trimmed low. He kept one hand on his sword to deter footpads, but his thoughts were detached as he contemplated the rites of the clansmen, whose chosen high priestesses were ritually blinded as maidens. The barbarities described in the texts were disparaged by the priests; yet the visions experienced by the women after their cruel initiation were indisputably true seeing. They possessed power to unmask demons, even shelter their folk from the malign influence of dream-image that Kor's Accursed some-times employed to lure isolated humans to their deaths. Whether the Presence behind the springs that were the center of the clan priestess's devotions truly held power to guide, advise, and protect was a claim no devout missionary dared endorse without risking trial for heresy. The point was moot, from Ivainson's standpoint. Valid as a religion or not, the clan tribes' beliefs were not adequate to safeguard the Keys to Elrinfaer, or stay frostwargs and win Anskiere's release.

Jaric's curse of frustration rang in the emptiness of weavers' alley. His quest was a vain one, surely. If the clans-men, or any conjurer, priest, kingdom, or alliance within Keithland held force or knowledge enough to suppress the demon compact, *they would have done so*. Unbidden, the thought followed, that Anskiere and the Vaere-trained who preceded him had courageously endeavored the same, despite the mistakes at Elrinfaer and Tierl Enneth.

"No," said Jaric aloud. An alternate to the Cycle of Fire *must exist*. Yet the suspicion his conviction was false drove him into a run.

His baldric and weapons chinked faintly in the dark, and his footsteps echoed like whispers against the locked doors of the buildings. Rats dashed from their scavenging, and the glassless lanterns of the poor quarter flickered to the disturbed air of his passage. The boy pushed harder. Sweat stung his eyes, and the breath rasped his throat. The pouch on its knot-ted thong swung to his stride, the Keys to Elrinfaer banging painfully into his breastbone. Jaric closed his hand over sharp corners of basalt with a half sob of panic. Why should he be chosen to shoulder such a burden? As a child, he had been weak, ridiculed by his peers, and inept at anything resembling conflict. What talent had his mad but gifted father owned, that the pain of a sorcerer's legacy should fall to a son he had never known?

The empty streets held no answer, only the reminder of humanity's fragile and inadequate defenses. Still running, Jaric could not escape facts. Centuries had passed since Kor's Fire had fallen from heaven. Demons whose numbers had once been small had multiplied, even as men had; Shadowfane's strength increased with each passing year, while mankind's defenses had evolved very little. One day the balance would swing. The compact would strike, and under attack by powers of mind and sorcery, men would strive and perish. Was he, Ivainson Jaric, by himself responsible for light and darkness, good and evil, survival or death? The question ripped him with anguish and doubt, and he ran faster, his feet a blur over the cobbles. The poor quarter fell behind; smells of sea-rotted timbers and waste faded, replaced by hearth smoke and new paint. The houses of rich merchants arose on both sides of the street, each with stoutly shuttered windows and inset dooryards planted with shrubs. Sometimes a light shone through, where a man or his wife tallied accounts in the lateness of the night. Oblivious as insects before the killing advent of frost, they went about their industries unaware of the doom which threatened. Jaric gasped. His chest burned with exertion, yet he raced onward, past a crossroad with a shrine to the Sacred Fires. Beyond, scrolled columns rose amid pools of lamplight; a wrought-iron gate spanned the roadway between, blocking the path of his flight.

"Halt!" cried a voice from the shadows.

Jaric stumbled, caught short of a fall by unyielding bars of iron. He hooked his fingers to stay upright. Dizzy from exhaustion, he recognized the perimeter defenses of the sanctuary towers guarded by the highest of Kordane's priests.

"What passes? Are you in trouble?" demanded the sentry on duty. Pressed against cold metal, and numb to most else, Jaric lifted his head. Thinking the boy fled from footpads, the soldier had stepped from his post to survey the street for thieves, or maybe a murderer.

"I'm alone," said the boy between gasps.

The soldier returned a puzzled look.

Jaric chose not to explain. He leaned his cheek against the gate to recover his breath, his eyes fixed on the tiled court beyond. Torches blazed over the entry to the towers where priests guarded knowledge too precious to risk to demons. The brightness seemed to sear his eyes. He closed them, even as the grief of a sorcerer's inheritance ached in his heart. Willing or not, Ivain's heir must answer to his father's legacy; accounting would be exacted for Keithland's need.

"You can't linger here, boy," snapped the sentry. He lifted his halberd to prod, and Jaric nodded.

Certain of nothing but his own weaknesses, and the inescapable probability that his search of the libraries was wasted endeavor, he loosed his grip on the grillwork. Anskiere's curse would never leave him. By burden of blood relation, he must act; but only when hope was exhausted. Responding at last to the impatient shove of the sentry, Ivainson Firelord's heir straightened. He began the long walk to the boardinghouse, where a bed waited, and the transient oblivion of sleep.

Yet now even that peace was denied him. The leathery smell of aged books followed Ivainson into rest, and that night, for the first time, he dreamed of demons. They sailed in black boats, toadlike forms with webbed fingers hunched in silhouette against the lacy foam of the swells. Pale eyes glinted in the dark of the open sea, and the hissing croaks uttered in place of language threaded menace through Jaric's sleep. He tossed in his blankets, threatened by a purpose remote and pitiless as the constellations which shone unchanging overhead. Elusive, evil, dangerous in the extreme, Thienz demons lifted blunt snouts to the south. The thrust of their intent stabbed outward, searching, circling, frustrated to bitter and repeated fury by the wards which protected the isle of Landfast. 'He is there,' Shadowfane's chosen whispered among themselves, mind-to-mind, as one being. 'Ivainson Firelord's heir hides there.'

And from the boats on the open sea, cold reached out and touched Jaric, sending chills over his sweating skin.

The vividness of the nightmare wrenched him awake. Soaked and shaking, he threw off his sheets and paced the floor. But the worn pine boards beneath his feet did not reassure. The solidity of the boardinghouse walls seemed somehow less substantial than the lift and hiss of waves beneath the keels of Shadowfane's black ships.

Jaric perched in the window seat. He wrapped his arms

around his knees and regarded the towers of Landfast, while sunrise burned the gray east to red, and finally to gold as bright as Ivain's command of flame. On this day, as any other, farm wagons and drays laden with fishmongers' barrels rumbled through the streets, bringing produce to market. The whistles of the milk sellers called buyers to their doors to haggle, and the bell towers sounded carillons at daybreak. Yet the familiar wakening of Landfast reflected precarious tranquillity. Warned by the Llondel on the ice cliffs, and the visions of Felwaithe's seer, Ivain's heir no longer dared presume the black ships and their searchers were anything other than real. More weary than ever he could remember, Jaric reached for boots and tunic. He needed all the courage he possessed simply to face another day in the libraries. As he tied his laces, his hands clenched in terror. Where, for love of all he knew in life, would a backlands scribe like him find strength to combat such as the Thienz, with their ability to steal thought and override the living will of a man?

Five days after the storm the Kielmark's brigantine, *Moonless*, drifted still in the northwest reaches of the Corine Sea. Far from any land, she lay like a speck upon water flat as sheet metal. The sky glared cloudless indigo overhead. Shirtless, his shoulders bronzed by pitiless sunlight, Corley paced the quarterdeck, the tap of his booted feet measured against the nerve-wearing creak of cord and timber. He strode from wheel to compass to railing, and back, repeatedly, until his officers adopted tact and fell in step with their captain as they reported. The slow-witted who did not received sharp words and a glare biting as frost.

The ship's healer paused at the head of the companionway ladder; absorbed in his own troubles, he called out without first gauging the prevailing mood. "Captain? I think you should accompany me below."

Corley spun on his toes, hands poised as if he expected attack. "Best tell me why." When the healer hesitated, he snapped, "Quick, man! Is the Dreamweaver dead?"

The healer shook his head, fed up with eddyless air and the captain's dicey temperament. "Not yet. But without help she soon will be."

"Kor's *Fires!*" Corley's tone blistered. "Do you think I can raise the wind? We're no slave-bearing galleass, to row our way out of a calm."

The healer gripped the rail and stood in steadfast silence. Presently Corley raised his brows, and his hands dropped loose to his sides. "I'll come. But nothing under Keithland's sky that I do will be any use."

Shadow pooled under his feet as he stepped to the companionway and followed the healer into the airless confines below decks. Taen lay on a pallet in the healer's quarters, her hair spilled like ebony silk across the sheets. Her eyes were open, but misty and unfocused above the curve of her cheeks; worse, her perfectly motionless limbs made her seem a sculpture in wax. Never had Corley seen a girl look so vulnerable. With her indomitable spirit absent, the fact that Taen was a child inhabiting a woman's body became arrestingly plain.

"Kor's grace, is she breathing at all?" Corley knelt by the pallet in alarm.

The healer coughed uncomfortably by the companionway, his head bent beneath the beams. "Her life signs are very weak."

Corley lifted the girl's wrist from the sheets. Her bones felt frail as a bird's, and the pulse raced shallow and quick under his finger. But where the consuming restlessness of his character had once driven her awake through a touch, now not an eyelash flickered. Close up, Taen's skin was feverish and dry, the hollows of her face a shadowed, translucent blue.

Corley raised helpless eyes. The healer, who could not face him, sighed and shook his head. "I don't *know* what's ailing her. Only the Vaere could say."

At that the Kielmark's sternest captain settled Taen's wrist back upon the coverlet with unabashed regret. *"Damn* the wind! After all Taen did for Cliffhaven, she deserves better." He paused, his lips thinned with conflict. Then he met the healer's glance, and all trace of profanity vanished from his speech. "You know it's too late, now, for the Isle of the Vaere. If the wind came up this minute, I have no choice. *Moonless* must run straight to the nearest shore for water."

The healer remained mute. The captain's decision was not made callously; with empty casks, not a man of *Moonless*'s company would survive to reach the Isle of the Vaere.

Corley's boots scraped against wood as he rose. "This will haunt me the rest of my days." He smacked his fist to his palm in frustration. "The Vaere warned her, yet she chose to stay and defend. The Kielmark will be bitter when he hears."

Aware that his voice was painfully altered, he stopped, pushed past the pallet and departed. The healer stared mutely at Taen's face, death-pale, but still possessed of an innocent and unearthly beauty. The girl was doomed, surely; for the closest landfall was the deserted shore of Tierl Enneth.

ᑲᑐ IX ᑕᑐ

Ash Flute

In a fourth-floor garret of Landfast's main library, a single candle guttered, and wax dribbled and froze like old ice against the base of the stand. The flame flickered out as Jaric closed the book he had finished reading. He made no move to strike a fresh light, but lifted another volume from the table and hitched his stool closer to the window. Far beneath the sill, blots of shadow underhung the people and wagons which jammed the square; diminished by distance, the noise of the traffic through Lionsgate sounded thin as the clatter of toy figurines. Jaric paid no heed. Propped on one elbow with his fingers jammed into tangled hair, he leafed through the pages of yet another history of the Great Fall. This book was far older than the others. The covers were cracked and worn, and the text archaic. Jaric touched the lettering, felt a texture that differed from inked parchment of reed paper. He knew a moment of excitement. Perhaps this account contained information the others lacked. Driven by the conviction that time was growing scarce, the boy perused the older writing eagerly. Hope died as he read. The most ancient record in Landfast's stacks only repeated the same events, beginning with Kordane's Blessed Fires which had seared down from the divine province of Starhope and set men and demons upon Keithland to contend for survival. There followed the usual lists of First Elders and their offspring, who had dispersed and settled, establishing the civilized bounds of Keithland.

Defeated, Jaric bit his lip. His eyes ached, and his stomach cramped with hunger; in the weeks since his audience with the Grand High Star, he had neglected meals and sleep while he poured every spare minute into studying the records of Landfast. As he had guessed, his efforts brought him no nearer to safety than the moment he had encountered the Llondel demon upon the rocks of Cliffhaven. Tired and disheartened, the boy flopped the book closed and buried his face in his hands. The spiel of a fish seller drifted through the opened casement, underscored by the clatter of hooves and wagon wheels. In daylight, amid the bustle of Keithland's most populous city, his beginnings at Morbrith felt very far away; Emien and the perils of Shadowfane seemed unreal as the tales told by firesides to frighten children. But at night, dreams of black boats and demons continued to break his sleep. Then the leather bag which held the Keys to Elrinfaer weighed all too heavily. Ivainson stirred and dropped his hands. As he reached dispiritedly to replace the book on the stack, his fingers snagged an edge where the glue had loosened on the binding.

The damage made him pause out of instinct. His earliest training had been by an archivist concerned with the preservation of ancient records, and repairs had been part and parcel of the daily chores. Jaric examined the worn place, and discovered a protruding corner of parchment that logically should not have been there.

The leaf was yellowed and flecked with age. Jaric bent closer and perceived traces of lettering, faded nearly illegible. Certain the fragment was not an integral part of the book, he tugged it gently free. The parchment fell into pieces as he uncreased its tight folds. He lined up the edges in the sunlight, and saw lettering. Written in an informal hand rather than the script of a trained scribe, the message itself proved cryptic.

"What I write here is forbidden, since the charter established by the Landfast Council. But how else can a man protest what he knows to be futile? With the Veriset-Nav unit lost in the crash, no ship can find the way back to Starhope; the heritage so carefully sealed in the sanctuary towers will inevitably prove useless. If the Council's policy endures, will our children's children ever know their forefathers ruled the stars?"

Jaric frowned, fingers tapping anxiously on the tabletop. Nowhere within the records had he encountered anything to match the context of this strange note. No archives mentioned an artifact called Veriset-Nav unit; Anskiere might command wave and weather, but how could a man hold influence over stars? Even the sorcerers knew them as lights in the sky, changing with the seasons, and useful only for navigation. Perplexed, Jaric considered the city beyond the window. The Landfast Council still ruled the Free Isles' Alliance, but the sanctuary towers were the perpetual domain of the priests. Now, as never before, he distrusted the platitudes of the Grand High Star of Kor's Brotherhood. Their secrets were perhaps deeper than anyone guessed. The knowledge he sought might indeed lie locked within the great, cream-colored spires which notched the sky above Lionsgate.

The door latch clicked sharply. Jaric started from contemplation and glanced around as a blue-robed priest entered the chamber. He strode toward the table by the window with an air of querulous admonition, his mouth pursed and his brows drawn into a frown.

"Young man, why are you idle? Does our guild pay you copyist's wages to sit staring at sky?"

Jaric leaned on his forearm, covering the scrap of writing he had found; the note's contents were certainly heretical, and if he wished continued access to temple records, the Brotherhood must never find reason to question his faith. Jaric met the priest's suspicion with a show of boyish innocence. "I thought Brother Handred was making the rounds today."

The priest sniffed. "You're impertinent. Brother Handred is busy. Now answer me. Where are your pens?"

Jaric sighed. "This is my day off." Slowly, surreptitiously, he closed his fingers over the parchment.

The priest coughed. "Well then. Who gave you permission to disarrange the stacks and leave books piled all over the library?"

"Brother Handred," Jaric said sweetly. With the paper safely crumpled in his palm, he rose. "I'm finished anyway." In a move designed to provoke, he reached across the table and lifted a book by its pasteboard cover.

The priest flinched. "Stupid boy!" He snatched the volume from Jaric's hand and smoothed the pages closed. "Brother Handred will hear about this! How ever did you get hired without knowing the proper way to handle a book?"

Jaric shrugged, then flexed his wrists, that he might appear more like a sailhand caught out of his element than a trained copyist.

"Well," huffed the priest. "Get along, boy. I'll tidy your mess." He clutched the piled books protectively against his chest, and glared until Jaric passed the doorsill.

In the cool shadow of the stairwell, Ivainson paused and slipped the parchment with its strange writing into the bag along with the stormfalcon's feather and the Keys to Elrinfaer.

He tugged the drawstrings taut and replaced the thong beneath his collar with a curse of sharp frustration. Lacking an initiate's training and vows, he had no way to gain entry to the sanctuary towers of Landfast. The guards and fortifications that surrounded them were enough to daunt a small army, far less a determined thief.

Light slanted steeply through the doubled arches at the base of the stairwell, showing noon was now past. Jaric hastened across the tiled foyer, wary of being late for sword practice. Brith's lessons were always tougher when his students forgot to be punctual. Midday glare whitewashed the marble paving beyond the main floors. Jaric stepped out into heat and the busy press of traffic. Sweat slicked his back beneath the thick linen of his tunic. Startled to remember that solstice lay barely a fortnight off, he realized a full year had passed since Anskiere's geas had driven him from Morbrith Keep.

"Boy! Watch yerself!" A carter's whip cracked, and his team of draft horses curvetted sideways with a deafening rattle of hooves. Jaric dodged the spinning rims of the cartwheels. No longer intimidated by the press in Landfast's streets, he passed the snapping row of pennants which marked the council hall of Landfast, then turned into the street of the potters' guild. The guest house where he had lodgings lay in the alley beyond. Hoping to avoid the landlady's chatter, the boy ducked through the pantry entrance; usually the kitchen was deserted at this hour of the day.

Jaric grabbed a fresh roll from the bin. He chewed with wolfish appetite as he climbed the back stairway to his garret room. From the chamber opposite, he heard the carping voice of the downstairs tenant complaining of moths in the blankets. The landlady returned an epithet and tartly suggested he admit his paid woman through the door instead of the casements; then perhaps the insects wouldn't fly at the candles and end up nesting in the bedclothes.

"But I put the flame out *before* I let her in!" whined the tenant; a silence developed as he realized what he had been tricked into admitting.

Jaric grinned and gently closed his door. He threw off sword belt and tunic and piled them on his bed. Then, with one hand busy loosening laces at his throat, he opened the lid of his clothes chest and rummaged inside in search of summer-weight garments. The shirt he wanted lay folded beneath his trapper's woolens. Jaric tugged impatiently. The cloth pulled free of the chest, and a light, slim object tumbled out, clattering hollowly across the floorboards.

Breath stopped in the boy's throat. Chills pricked his neck as the Llondian flute he had smashed and sunk in the harbor rolled to a stop beside his knee. Shell inlay gleamed in the light from the dormer. The delicate wooden shaft lay unmarked, as if no breakage had occurred. Jaric shuddered. With the shirt balled up in his fist, he settled back on his heels. The forester, Telemark, had once told of a Llondian demon which had waylaid him after a storm of sorcery had destroyed the contents of his cabin. When the forester recovered from the encounter, he had found his shattered flasks miraculously mended and restored to the shelves, and every displaced item in his cabin set to rights. Now, confronted by the flawless surface of the ash flute, Jaric wondered whether Telemark had trembled with fear as he did now. The powers of the Llondelei were beyond human comprehension.

The shirt slipped from the boy's hand as he reached to retrieve the instrument from the floor. The instant his trembling fingers touched the wood, Llondian images snared his mind. His perception of walls, floor, and room buckled, replaced by a lonely, wave-washed shoreline. The hills beyond stood crowned with jaggedly gapped walls, and houses that were roofless and forsaken to the elements. Gulls dove and swooped against empty sky. Pilings thrust blackened stumps through the seethe of the swell, the wharves and shops they once had supported torn cleanly away. Jaric understood he viewed the ruins of Tierl Enneth, the city blasted to wreckage by the powers the witch Tathagres had stolen from Anskiere's staff.

Yet, through Llondian perception, the boy observed that the landing of what had been the richest city in the Alliance was not deserted. A ship's boat drove through the booming froth of the breakers, her oarsmen trained and steady, and their stroke expertly timed. The man in the stern was *Moonless*'s boatswain; and as if Jaric's recognition were a cue, the Llondian image tightened and focused solely upon the boat.

The craft held other familiar faces. Hatless, his shoulders glistening with spray, Corley sat in the bow with a cloak-wrapped form in his arms. By the strands of black hair which looped his wrists, Jaric realized whom the Kielmark's captain sheltered. In anguish he cried out Taen's name; the empty beach and dismembered dwellings beyond echoed his despair over and over to infinity.

'Not dead,' soothed the Llondel presence in his mind. 'Yet your Weaver of Dreams is very ill. The landing you view will not occur for another fortnight, but unless you sail to the shores of Tierl Enneth, and there summon help with the ash flute, Taen will perish. Heed well, little brother of your race. Should the Dreamweaver die, the hopes and the efforts of your forebears will have been in vain.'

The image of the longboat wrenched out of existence, replaced by the screams of frostwargs etched against the silence of ice-bound caverns. For an instant, Jaric shared the icy vigil of the Stormwarden of Elrinfaer. Then his perception turned, vanished, and coalesced into the peat-smoke dimness of a fisherman's shack where the niece of Mathieson Keldric grieved for an uncle buried in the tide. Cut by a keen edge of sorrow, the boy cried out and abruptly wakened to the touch of a hand on his shoulder.

"Are you ailing, boy?" Solicitous with concern, the landlady smoothed the hair from his brow.

Jaric drew back from her touch. "I'm all right. Just tired." Worried lest she notice a demon artifact beneath her roof, he glanced at the floor. But the ash flute no longer lay on the boards beside his knee.

Skirts swished softly as the landlady straightened. "You work far too much, you know. Boys your age should be carefree. Haven't you the time for a girl?" She clasped her hands at her waist and ran an appreciative glance over Jaric's muscled shoulders and the finely drawn line of his brows. "That's a pity, don't you see?"

"No." Embarrassed by the elderly woman's regard, the boy spoke curtly. "I've troubles enough without adding girls to the tally." He reached to recover his fallen shirt and froze as he discovered the flute beneath the cotton.

The landlady retreated to the door. "Well, boy, I'll allow you the wisdom in that. Some men spend their whole lives, and never learn." With a snort of annoyance which had more to do with the downstairs tenant than any vagary of Jaric's, the woman ducked into the hallway and departed.

Her step faded on the stair. Jaric rose swiftly. He unwrapped the flute and tugged the thin shirt over his head. Leaving the lacings at cuff and collar untied, he pulled cloak and sea boots from the closet. Concern for Taen left no room to question the Llondel's intentions. Jaric emptied the clothes chest and tossed his few belongings into the folds of his cloak. As he knotted the wool into a bundle, his thoughts leaped ahead to the difficulties of passage between islands. Tierl Enneth lay eighty leagues to the north across a shoal-ridden strait. Safer waters lay eastward, around the tip of the archipelago, but that route might take too long, particularly if the wind blew from the north. *Callinde*'s shallow draft was better suited to avoiding reefs than making time on a windward heading. Grimly Jaric buckled on his sword and dagger. He left a neat pile of coins on the clothes chest to pay for his bed and board, then slipped out by way of the pantry stair.

Determined to avoid the bustle in the streets, Jaric hurried into the tortuous maze of byways and alleys which riddled the districts between thoroughfares. Because his route lay shadowed by gables and the clustered spires of the town, he never noticed the man who emerged from the arched gate of a nobleman's entry and followed his steps. Preoccupied with concern for Taen and intent upon reaching the harbor before the turn of the tide, the boy raced over puddled brick and ducked under the dank stone of cross-bridges. As he crossed a slash of sunlight between houses, the man who pursued caught sight of the cloak bundled under Jaric's arm; he swore and redoubled his chase.

Jaric rounded a corner. Confronted by a five-way intersection where several alleys converged around mossy foundations of stone, he hesitated and, unsure of his bearings, chose blindly. The man who dogged his tracks saw his quarry run down a known dead end. He chuckled and slowed to a jog, confident he could reach the harbor ahead of the boy.

Minutes later, Jaric leapt over the rotting boards of a tavern's rear stair and found himself blocked by the mortared bricks of a courtyard wall. Too winded to curse, he whirled and retraced his steps. One turn-off led to the locked gates of a root cellar; another sent him sliding and panting over a refuse heap. Broken glass skittered under his boots, startling a starved dog which foraged among the garbage. Jaric gave the snarling animal wide berth, nostrils revolted by the smell of rotten meat. Ahead, sunlight stabbed down through the grate of a culvert; beyond rose the lampposts which flanked the entry of the Lanterns Inn. Restored to familiar territory, Jaric continued at a run. He sprinted down the street of the spice grinders and, still sneezing from a cloying miasma of cinnamon and pepper, arrived breathless at the quayside.

Sea air slapped his face, damp and fitful, and straight out of the south. The boy squinted to windward and frowned to find a low band of clouds beyond the crosshatch of ships' rigging. The breeze might favor a crossing to Tierl Enneth, since *Callinde* sailed best on a downwind heading; but weather from that quarter invariably brought rain. Passage might be miserably wet. Jaric waited while a beer cart rattled past, then bolted for the wharf where his boat lay tied.

The tide had just turned. In the harbor, a cargo bark raised sail; sailors' gruff voices blended in a chantey, accompanied by the rattle of anchor chain through the hawse. Anxious to catch the current to his advantage, Jaric threaded his way through the jam of commerce on the docks. Half running, he rounded a mass of piled fish nets and all but impaled himself on the point of an unsheathed sword.

"Kor!" Jaric bounded back. Cloth spilled from his arms as he dropped his bundled belongings and drew his own blades from their scabbards.

"Why the haste?" said Brith, in precisely the tone he had used the first time they met. Unlike the sessions in the practice yard, his mouth showed no smile beneath the brown tips of his mustache. The eyes he fixed on his pupil remained cold and steady.

But Jaric was no longer the timid boy who had cowered from a fight on the steps before the scribes' towers. Desperate with worry for Taen, he lifted his sword and attacked.

Brith's block met him, effortlessly executed and seemingly solid as stone. "Where were you off to, boy? Didn't we have a practice scheduled this afternoon?"

Harried backward by a fast attack, Jaric managed a breathless reply. "I haven't time. Why concern yourself? Fires! Sometimes I think you have nothing better to do than follow me around!"

Steel clanged vengefully against Jaric's guarding blade. Stung by the force of the blow, the boy guessed at once that this encounter was no spar for sport. Brith's eyes were narrowed slits of annoyance, and his attitude that of a man who fought in earnest. Pricked by intuition, Jaric feinted and kicked clear of the nets at his heels. "You've been following me. Why?"

Brith drove into a lunge and recovered with his habitual neat footwork. "Where were you *going*, boy?"

"Sailing!" Jaric twisted to avoid a rolling cask. A long-shoreman cursed and ordered him out of the way, then sprang back as Brith's sword whined through the air and clashed against the boy's cross guard.

"No, boy." Brith beat at Jaric's guard, driving him toward a stacked pile of lumber. Steel clanged and shivered under the force of his offensive. "I'm paid the Kielmark's gold to keep you safe at Landfast. Won't see my hide roasted by his first captain because I broke my trust. Put up now." Jaric wrenched clear of a bind; Brith cut at his fingers and scored a glancing touch. "Drop your sword, do you hear?"

Stung, bleeding, and angered beyond reason, Jaric exe-cuted a whistling riposte. After Anskiere's demands, the Kiel-mark's high-handed attempt to meddle became an intrusion not to be borne. Only the innocent would suffer; distressed by the threat to Taen's life, and incensed by Brith's superiority, Jaric felt something snap within his mind. He focused every ounce of his being on the fight. As his sword battered against Brith's guard, his lips curled with a grim understanding. Un-like the weaponsmaster, he was under no constraint of the Kielmark's; if he must, he would strike to kill.

The shift in the intensity of Jaric's style caught Brith by surprise. The swordmaster deflected a fast cut to his chest and escaped with a tear in his tunic. In the exchange which fol-lowed, he lost two steps. When the boy beat and lunged and nearly maimed his face, he was forced to recognition; some-how, Jaric had lost his inhibition against fighting. "Kor, boy! Had you applied yourself like this earlier, I might have taught you something worthwhile."

Icily silent, Jaric continued to attack. Brith abandoned speech. Although the boy was still too inexperienced to best him, for the first time the guardsman required total concentra-tion to defend himself.

Swordsman and pupil circled like dancers across the dock, the flash of parry and riposte licking between obstacles. The belling clang of swordplay carried stridently over the bustle. Longshoremen loading a nearby lighter rolled their casks upright and perched on the rims to observe the fight. Brith and Jaric wove back and forth. Unaware of their audience, they skirted pyramids of stacked barrels, baled cloth, and the heaped mounds of fish nets. Other workers joined the long-shoremen, and presently a crowd formed. Coins clinked in callused palms as the sporting ones among them exchanged wagers, then energetically joined the spirit of the dispute by shouting encouragement to whichever duelist they favored to win, the seal-dark man with the fast sword, or the blond boy who met superior skill with determined defiance.

Idlers gathered and the crowd swelled larger. At any moment their commotion would draw the attention of the town guard. Brith redoubled his efforts, aware he must subdue the boy at once or risk getting fined for brawling in public. Steel rang dissonantly. Brith hammered at Jaric's guard, then, in a twist, caught the boy's sword in a bind. Through the sliding ring of blade on blade, he sensed the tremor of flagging muscles. The boy could not last much longer. Though competently executed, his technique was now wholly defensive. As the weapons wrenched apart, a fast feint and a lunge might corner him against the lumber pile. Confident of victory, Brith drove in with the agility of a fox.

Jaric parried the attack, twisting to avoid a step back. His elbow snagged on a plank. The wood fell with a boom onto the dock. A moth-eaten cat shot from a cranny just as Brith lunged. His boot struck the animal a glancing blow in the ribs. The cat yowled and fled. Distracted, Jaric glanced sideways for a fraction of an instant. Brith's blade hooked his cross guard and, with a single stroke, disarmed him. The sword pinwheeled from the boy's hand and fell ringing onto wood. Deafened by a chorus of cheers and groans from the onlookers, and pressed hard against the lumber by the points of his opponent's steel, Jaric panted and shifted his dagger to his right hand.

"Desist," snapped Brith. He also breathed heavily from exertion. "You're beaten now. If you don't quit, I'll have to hurt you." His sword flicked like a snake.

Flattened against stacked planks, Jaric missed his parry and, trapped in another bind, caught a warning scratch on the wrist from his opponent's dagger.

"Drop your knife," commanded Brith. His sword arm flexed, bearing painful pressure against the boy's stressed wrist.

Still Jaric refused to relinquish his weapon. "How many times did you warn that chance can ruin a victory?" And his brown eyes showed a hint of laughter as a board thrown from the sidelines struck the weaponsmaster squarely in the back of the neck.

Brith buckled at the knees and crashed at Jaric's feet. The

swordmaster's head had barely struck planking when a familiar, one-handed figure darted from the crowd and piled squarely onto his shoulders. Breathless, the beggar lifted his face to the boy. "Kicked my cat, this lout sure did."

"I saw." Jaric grinned. He bent wearily and recovered his sword, then gathered up Brith's weapons as well. "Can you hold him long enough for me to cast the lines off my boat?"

The beggar raised both eyebrows and answered with a gap-toothed smile. "Surely, boy, surely."

"Thanks." Jaric flexed bleeding fingers, and hurled the swordmaster's weapons over the lumber pile. They plunged with a splash into the shallows by the breakwater. Brith could find them easily enough, but only at ebb tide. By then *Callinde* should be well beyond the harbor. Jaric could buy provisions in one of the fishing villages north of Landfast; after that the rain would hide him from further pursuit. Ivainson tossed a silver to the beggar, collected his bundle of belongings from the dock, and shoved through the bystanders who now argued loudly over the validity of winning bets, since the beggar had clearly foiled Brith's victory. By the time the boy boarded *Callinde,* the shouts had transformed to a brawl. As a uniformed guard on a war-horse thundered over the docks to intervene, none but the beggar noticed the fishing boat slip her docklines and hoist sail for the open sea.

In keeping with the advent of summer, weather from the south brought low clouds, and then mist which lowered clinging and gray and turned finally to drizzle. Light winds held *Callinde* to an easy, northerly course, but she was not the only craft to ply the Corine Sea. North and east, on a close-hauled course for the heart of the Free Isles' Alliance, a scarred old fishing boat with no flag of registry sailed under orders from Shadowfane. Her sails were gray with mildew and her hull dark; the face of her helmsman was the toadlike countenance of a Thienz. Alone of seven companions, it hunched over the compass, rain dribbling runnels over the ornamental crest of its headdress. Yet the others huddled in the lee of the mainmast were not sleeping. Joined mind to mind, they bent their thoughts toward Landfast, whose barrier ward shone to their perception as an icy halo of light. This no demon could cross without rousing the wrath of men. Though their quarry lay on the other side, this difficulty did not distress the Thienz, who tuned their every resource to the hunt. Humans by nature had short memories for trouble; sooner or later they grew complacent and misjudged, and for the day such folly overtook Ivainson Jaric, the Thienz waited with a patience no human could match.

Night fell. Rain blew cold in the face of the helmsman, and he rose with a whuff of his gill flaps and shook droplets from his headdress. At his movement the tranced Thienz stirred from their huddle. They shambled to ungainly feet and sought a meal of fish, snatched live from a barrel by the masthead. Then, with backs hunched against the gunwales, they gnawed through scales and fins and cartilage. The youngest of them whistled soulfully, deploring the salt in the flesh. Its elders rolled tiny, half-blind eyes in shared sympathy. Though water was the natural abode of their kind, the deep pools of fresh streams and lakes were their proper element. Boats were a curse to limbs designed for swimming, and the surrounding sea an evil best not mentioned. Its rich solution of minerals could leach the gills of an immersed Thienz, bring death by poisoning and suffocation. For seagoing brothers, awareness of mortality permeated every lift of the swell. Yet Lord Scait commanded. The company sent to hunt Jaric licked fish from webbed hands, oppressed and silent with a distress they dared not express.

At length the Thienz who had served as helmsman groped its way to a nook by the mast. One of the others took its place in the stern, knuckles gripped to the tiller and its snout lifted to the wind, since it maintained course by senses unknown to humans. The rest of the Thienz finished their meal and, picking scales from pointy teeth, drew together to resume communion with their purpose. Collective consciousness pooled, focused as always upon the ring of defenses surrounding Landfast. The hard lines of the wards lay unchanged, and, surrounding the fringes, the clustered flickers of illumination that were men and the crews of wooden ships scattered like beads on dark velvet. Thienz-memory recalled a time when ships had been metal, albaze with the brightness of energy fields. The mighty star fleets of ancestors once had tracked such sparks of light through the vast deeps of space, and all but obliterated humanity. But the remembered glory ended in captivity and cruelest exile, and survival became a thing steeped in hatred. For that, Thienz braved oceans and sour fish and at last found reward for their patience.

A light-mote brighter than the others emerged from the glow defined by Landfast's wards. As it cleared the energy barrier, its pattern grew more distinct, and, with a hiss of triumph and malice, the Thienz narrowed the focus of their search. They knew, without mistake. The aura of this man brightened and blazed, a hard-edged beacon that seared sensitive perception almost to pain. So did humans with a sorcerer's potential appear to the minds of demons. The Thienz-eldest croaked, shivering with ecstatic anticipation. The perilous vigil had ended. For whatever reason, Ivainson Jaric sailed beyond the protection of Landfast.

The Thienz collective flicked thought to the helmsman, who flung the tiller hard over. Two youngest left the link to adjust sail, and the dark boat scudded into a heel, gunwales pressed into a reach. Her course was set now to race, for from Jaric's untrained, unshielded thoughts the demons had pried the required facts. He sailed in haste for Tierl Enneth, his hope to spare Taen the agonies of the Sathid death.

The night fell close as ink over the Corine Sea. Droplets rolled like sweat over the face of the Thienz helmsman, and its wiry limbs trembled. Tierl Enneth lay seventy leagues off, against a contrary wind. Yet the shores of that isle housed a ruin, empty of all but the bones of slaughtered men. With diligence, and determination born of hate, Thienz might win two prizes, Ivainson Jaric, Firelord's heir, and Marlsdaughter Taen, who might yet make a weapon to pair with the brother already in thrall to Shadowfane.

Though fitful and unsteady, the winds blew from the south throughout Jaric's passage from Landfast. Drenched by intermittent rain, and exhausted by the pull of the steering oar, he muscled *Callinde* through the narrow strait which separated the mass of Tierl Enneth from the splinter islet of Hal's Nog. Shaking drenched hair from his eyes, the boy clung grimly to the helm. He had been twelve days at sea. Now, in the final hours of crossing, the channel was treacherous with rocks. Current ran counter to his course, and a single miscalculation could sliver *Callinde*'s stout timbers, leave him awash in the hammerblows of breaking swells.

Gulls looped and screamed above the yard as daylight failed. Overcast skies blackened into night like starless ink. Jaric blotted dripping fingers and groped in a locker for the flint to strike the compass lantern. He longed for the safety of anchorage. Every sinew ached with exhaustion. Waves crested and boomed to starboard, carving crescent swirls of foam which warned of submerged reefs. Yet Corley was due to make landfall with *Moonless* the following afternoon; Jaric had no choice but run the strait's perilous waters in darkness.

Sheltered by the damp folds of his cloak, the lantern wick flared and caught. The boy latched the glass closed, knuckles stained red by the glimmer of flame within. The air smelled heavy with rain. Dreading reduced visibility, Jaric bent strained eyes upon the waters off *Callinde*'s bow. While the waves remained dark, he sailed safely in the deeps of the channel. But should a faint slash of spray suggest the presence of whitecaps, he hauled on his steering oar and dragged in the sheets, setting his frail craft to weather to claw clear of the shoals. He lost count of the number of tacks he made long before midnight. Left only guesses and the glimmer of the compass lamp to guide him, Jaric fought to stay alert. More than once he caught the cloying scents of earth and wet grass, as his course strayed close to the shore of Hal's Nog.

The rain held off until dawn, then resumed with wretched persistence, turning waves and whitecaps a pocked, leaden gray. Jaric huddled in his cloak and blinked droplets from his lashes. With visibility reduced to scant yards, he dared not relax vigilance, even for a second. Beaten with exhaustion, he never knew the precise moment when he cleared the straits and entered the wide, safe harbor of Tierl Enneth.

Yet, in time, he noticed that tidal currents no longer kicked and curled around *Callinde*'s steering oar. The swells under her keel silvered and flattened into wavelets, the first sure sign he had reached protected waters. Weeping with relief, Jaric abandoned the helm. He set his anchor, dropped canvas, and settled to rest under the partial shelter of the mainsail. Wind through the rigging lulled him. He slept finally, unaware that two additional vessels bore down upon the harbor where *Callinde* took shelter. One was Corley's command, *Moonless*, bearing a battle-trained crew of eighty. In the other, a black vessel seen only in dreams, eight Thienz licked their teeth, driven onward by Scait Demon Lord's directive to kill.

~·~ X ~·~

Tierl Enneth

Mist rolled across the harbor of Tierl Enneth and cloaked the ruined city in gray. The drizzle which began at dawn still fell in the early afternoon when, like a phantom haunting waters where moored ships once swung with the tide, *Moonless* ghosted in under the whispered flap of her staysails. Her deckhands sang no chanteys. In somber silence, they dropped anchor, furled canvas, and swayed two longboats out. The first craft they loaded with empty casks which bore recent marks of repair. Corley commandeered the second. Scowling, his maroon tunic darkened with damp, he accepted the blanket-wrapped weight of the Dreamweaver from the healer's anxious arms. Leaving command of *Moonless* to the first mate, the captain descended the side battens one-handed and settled in the stern seat of the boat. He arranged Taen in his lap, and paused a moment to look at her. Rain beaded her lashes like tears; pale as a porcelain doll, the girl barely seemed to breathe.

The healer glared reproachfully down from the waist and tried one last time to object. "She ought not to be moved."

Corley ignored him. With a curt jerk of his head, he ordered his sailhands to proceed. The boat jostled under the added weight as four brawny men stepped within. They positioned themselves on the benches and threaded oars through rowlocks in subdued silence.

"Take her ashore, then," murmured Corley. His eyes never lifted from the girl in his lap. Looms lapped into water. As the Dreamweaver's head rolled with the pull of the first stroke, the Kielmark's most hardened captain bit his lip and wondered whether he was right to trust the dream which urged him to convey the failing girl to land. He had no fey skills; only a sure eye for weapons and a knack for managing men. But when his sleep had been torn into visions four nights in a row by an image of Taen dying in screaming agony unless he carried her with him into Tierl Enneth, Corley chose to act. He had nothing to lose. Barring a miracle, the Dreamweaver was already lost.

The oars dipped and lifted like clockwork; expertly handled, the longboat hissed through the waters of the harbor. Surrounded by the smell of sweating men and damp wool, Corley regarded the landing of Tierl Enneth, once Keithland's most opulent trading port. Flotsam-snarled sands and wrecked dwellings now sheltered no life but seabirds. Crabs picked at the pilings of the emissary's dock, where past generations of royalty had debarked to fanfares of trumpets. If Landfast was the seat of government and antiquity, Tierl Enneth had nourished the arts, until Anskiere's sorcery smashed city and inhabitants without warning.

The oarsmen threaded a careful course between the shorn bollards of the traders' wharf, and the boat grounded on the strand. Men leapt from the bow to steady the craft against the curl of the breakers as Corley rose from the stern. Bearing Taen, he stepped over the gunwale and, careless of the water which swirled over his boot tops, waded shoreward while the crew beached the longboat.

The ruins loomed ahead, gray stone tumbled like bones against the lighter gray of the mist. Corley stood dripping on the seaweed at the tide mark. Uncertain what to expect, he scanned the slivered ramparts which remained of the harbor gate. The sculptures of eagles had been torn from their niches, and the great arches rose gapped and broken against the sky, spoiled past memory of design. Weeds presently grew where gilded four-in-hand coaches had thundered over marble paving.

Despite the company of the men at his back, Corley shivered. He tightened his fingers in the blankets which sheltered Taen, and suddenly realized Tierl Enneth was not entirely deserted. A figure in a dark cloak walked amid the looming mist of the ruins.

Corley tensed. Taen's helpless weight prevented a fast reach for his sword. On the point of tossing her into the arms of the nearest oarsman, he saw the approaching stranger throw his hood back. Sun-bleached hair tumbled in the wind, and with a shock of surprise, the captain recognized the face.

"Jaric! Kor's Fires, boy, what are you doing here?" Corley strode briskly forward, his uneasiness transformed to annoyance. "Brith was under orders to keep you safe at Landfast!"

Jaric paused by the crumbled breakwater, brows knotted with an anger all his own. "I owe no loyalty to the Kielmark, nor any of his hired henchmen. I came here for Taen."

As the boy leaped down to the strand, Corley sensed changes; Jaric carried himself with an unthinking self-command. If he had sailed to Tierl Enneth for the sake of the Dreamweaver, how could he possibly have known *Moonless* would make landfall there of all other ports in Keithland?

Jaric drew nearer; Corley noticed the scabs of a recent fight on his knuckles. "Did you best Brith?" he demanded in surprise.

"No." The boy looked worn, exhausted utterly from his passage. His clothing and hair sparkled with salt crystals, and his hands were chapped from the sea. "He tried to stop me." Reluctant to elaborate, Jaric bent over the blankets and studied Taen. "How long has she been like this?"

"Too long." Corley hefted the girl and settled her more comfortably against his shoulder; her cheek rolled limply against his neck. "Do you know how to help her?"

Jaric looked up, eyes darkened with sudden and painful uncertainty. "I've been instructed. But by Kor's divine grace don't ask anything more." He lifted his arms to take Taen.

Concerned by the boy's fatigue and by his studied lack of comment on his encounter with Brith, Corley shook his head. "Wherever you're going, I'll carry her."

Jaric stiffened, distrustful of the captain's motives. He might face another fight should Corley try to balk him; and delay would cost dearly. Taen's still limbs and cold flesh warned how near she lay to death.

Corley sensed the boy's suspicion and softened his tone. "I won't stop you, Jaric. Just show me where to go." With crisp decision, he addressed the crewmen who lingered nearby. "Return to *Moonless*. Tell the mate to post an anchor watch until I return. I'll signal for a longboat by lighting a fire between the pillars of the harbor gate."

Jaric watched with trepidation as the sailhands moved to depart. "Do you act for the Kielmark?"

"No." Corley qualified without pause. "I act for the Dreamweaver who once spared every soul on Cliffhaven from Gierj-demons."

"Then leave your sword and knives behind," said Jaric.

Deison Corley clenched his teeth with a visible jerk. His lips tightened to an expressionless line, and for a long, dangerous moment he regarded the boy on the strand before him. Yet Jaric stood his ground with staid resolution; and something about his stillness disarmed the captain's affront.

Without speech, Corley hefted Taen, and transferred her limp weight into the arms of the boy. Gravel crunched at his back as his men busied themselves launching the longboat; unwilling to leave his blades unattended on the strand, Corley reached swiftly to unbuckle his sword belt.

But Jaric impulsively changed his mind. "Never mind, I'll trust you."

Corley looked up. He searched the boy's troubled expression through windblown strands of Taen's hair, and suddenly understood. Probably Jaric's guidance came from a source as fathomless as the dreams which had entreated the captain to bear the Dreamweaver ashore in Tierl Enneth. Sympathy filled Corley for the upheaval caused by a destiny too weighty for even a sorcerer's heir to encompass. "You won't be sorry," he said gruffly.

With an emotion very near to gratitude, Jaric restored Taen to the captain's capable arms.

Thick fog muffled Tierl Enneth. Its whiteness erased the outline of the beach head, and the hiss of unseen breakers turned ghostly, a mirage of disembodied sound. The forms of captain, Firelord's heir, and Taen Dreamweaver became lost to the eyes of the crewmen aboard *Moonless*, yet the limits of visual perception were not shared by demonkind. Aboard the fishing vessel dispatched to destroy Ivainson Jaric, the Thienz assigned as watcher observed the exchange on the shore. Even as Corley accepted the limp weight of Taen Dreamweaver and turned with Jaric to bear her toward the ruins, the demon signaled its companions.

'Man-fools, we have them, with-certainty.' The Thienz ruffled its crest, amazed and elated by the hapless ways of humans. For the Dreamweaver lay unguarded, unconscious to danger; and though the presence of latent power wrapped a haze of confusing energies about the Firelord's heir, the Kielmark's captain had a mind decisive as a sword's edge. His intentions were plain: directed by Ivainson Jaric, Corley planned to bear Taen Dreamweaver to an unspecified place, and upon his given word, the Kielmark's men at arms were to stay behind.

The companion Thienz whuffed their gill flaps, pleased-for-Scait, while the watcher showed them Corley turning toward the ruins. The captain and the two-who-were-prey turned unsuspecting toward deserted dwellings where no-human-ally-now-lived.

'*Ours,*' hissed the Thienz at the helm, its reference to the Firelord's heir. It clicked sharp teeth and pulled the tiller with anticipation, even as the response of its companions swirled and buffeted its awareness. The harbor must not be risked, with the vigilant presence of eighty men at arms. But the landward side of Tierl Enneth's ruins was unguarded since the devastation unleashed by Anskiere's powers. Thought-forms flickered with rising excitement as the demons plotted. The sloop could be landed under cover of the mist, then concealed in a cove beyond view of the brigantine's sentries. Thienz would creep ashore. On dry land, well removed from the accursed dangers of salt water, the Kielmark's captain and his blades could most-easily be overwhelmed.

'*Then shall Ivainson-Firelord's-heir perish, to the sorrow of mankind and the Vaere.*'

Whetted for the kill, a Thienz crew member sprang to harden sheets. Fingers ill suited for handling rope slipped and gripped in eagerness to tease the sails into perfect trim. The sloop responded, rounding to the slight breeze and swinging shoreward. Yet as the sails snapped gently taut, the watcher hissed warning from the bows. Wide lips curled back from small, back-canted teeth, and its thought-lash of startled annoyance slapped through the minds of its companions.

'*Men move beyond the walls of the city-now-fallen, many-men, stop-see; they might bring danger.*'

Two Thienz abandoned the lines. They crowded around the spokesman and at once melded awareness to scout this new development. Chafing, almost reckless in their haste, they pressed to sample the human minds who presently converged upon the meadows beyond Tierl Enneth.

The demons' probe met the taste of dust, and beast-smell and the sweaty reek of oiled flesh. Wagon wheels creaked, and somewhere a singer intoned a chant in queer, quarter-tone intervals that jarred the eavesdropping Thienz with unpleasantness. Shadowfane's minions delved deeper to escape the irritation. Beneath the surface patterns of sensory perception, the enemy minds they touched were strangely unstructured by logic. Their thought-colors blazed like beacons, twisted to resonance by fierce countercurrents of emotion. The watcher-

Thienz saw and sorted implications, even as a presence among the humans noticed the eddies generated by demon meddling. Warned off, the Thienz withdrew. Their probe dissolved without trace well before that guardian awareness coalesced and stabbed out in challenge.

The dark boat rocked gently in the mist, its occupants stilled to listen. *'Clan tribes,'* hissed the watcher. *'They gather to celebrate the solstice, and with them rides she-who-sees-truly, a sightless-one trained to read memory.'*

A wail arose from the helmsman, echoed in octaves by its companions. Thienz could not pass that way, for clan priestesses never failed to detect the presence of Kor's Accursed. Other Thienz paused in their tasks, turning wide, near-blind eyes toward the shadow the watcher's body imprinted upon the air. *'Trouble for us, but also hindrance for Corley-Jaric-Taen,'* they intoned in return.

The shared song of the hill tribes' enthusiasm swelled yet again. Wild clans on the move might complicate the will of Lord Scait, but all was not lost. The humans hunted by Shadowfane would be forced to travel far afield, since clan tribes celebrating solstice would be dangerously inclined to violence. Strangers who trespassed upon the rites quite often got themselves murdered.

The dark boat rocked as the Thienz turned hands to their sailing. They bailed, and eased lines, and cheerfully bickered over who-next-should-share-helm-watch; while, as a descant to physical action, they braided words and mental musings into plans for night landing followed by ambush in the misty fells past Tierl Enneth.

Poised at Corley's side with one foot on the breakwater wall, Jaric felt as if he stood at the edge of the unknown. The Kielmark's captain would keep his word, though his life became the cost; yet the boy fretted, wondering how Corley would react when he discovered they acted under influence of the Llondelei demons. Distressed that Taen's life should depend on the whim of Kor's Accursed, Jaric slipped one hand beneath his cloak and touched the shaft of the ash flute. Contact roused a cold tingle of energy; a presence touched his mind, urging him quickly into the mist-choked ruins of Tierl Enneth. Aware no choice remained but to trust in such a guide, the boy drew breath and started forward.

Corley leaped the shattered stone of the breakwater.

Trained to move in silence, he followed the boy's lead across cobbles slimy with moss. Except for the fact the captain carried Taen, Jaric might have forgotten the presence of his companion. Once within the city, cracked walls rose up on either side, the hiss of breakers echoing between like the mournful whisper of ghosts. Wind sighed over tenantless thresholds, and gull droppings streaked the fretwork of sills and chimneys. To Jaric, Tierl Enneth was a city haunted by the resonance of misused powers. Only bones remained, scattered by scavengers; once he tripped over a skull, and eye sockets clogged with fungi stared accusingly at his back as he passed.

Distressed by the emptiness and the mist, Jaric whispered unthinkingly aloud, "Why weren't they buried?"

"Too many dead," said Corley, and the boy flinched at the sound of a human voice. "Very few had relations left living to care."

Shocked speechless, at last Jaric understood the undertones of sorrow which had haunted the Stormwarden's manner; Tathagres' transgression had permanently cost Anskiere his peace of mind. Amid the smashed houses of Tierl Enneth, the boy's doubts resurfaced with vicious intensity. Evidence of tragedy wider than his worst imagining confronted him on all sides. The silence, and the empty, gaping doorways, infused fresh desperation in his need to escape the Cycle of Fire. What were Vaere-trained sorcerers if not evil, that demons could deflect their formidable powers against mankind? Shaken numb by the catastrophic scale of Anskiere's failure, Jaric stumbled through dooryards and gardens overgrown with briar as he followed the ash flute's directive.

Late in the day, the sun broke through the fog. Purple shadows slanted across the western lanes of Tierl Enneth. Wreckage was less evident on the landward side of the city; yet even those dwellings left whole sheltered no inhabitants. Windows gaped fireless and black, and alleys lay deserted. Guided by the Llondian artifact, the Firelord's heir and the Kielmark's captain reached the far wall of the city in the wan light of the afterglow. Darkness obscured the arch of the trade gate which pierced the inland fortifications. Above, the battlements rose intact, notched like the spine of a dragon with scales of green ivy. Jaric stopped briefly to admire the pair of eagles which capped the portal, their outstretched wings tipped in gilt.

Corley paused and shifted Taen's weight to his opposite shoulder. "Are we going through?"

Jaric nodded. Though twilight was nearly spent, the tingling pull of the ash flute showed no sign of diminishing. Dogged by rising uneasiness, the boy pressed on toward the arch.

Shadow closed around him, dense as spilled ink. Corley followed on his heels. The air smelled of damp and moss, and the stone deflected the sound of their footsteps into echoes. Directed through darkness by no more than the mental pull of the ash flute, Jaric hastened his pace. Suddenly his shoulder crashed into rock. He gasped in near panic.

Corley spoke calmly over the boy's shoulder. "Turn left. Before the city was destroyed, an iron gate was kept barred during the night. The tunnel on either side was built with a crook to foil siege engines."

Jaric pushed away from the stone, his fear changed to regret. The finest of engineered defenses had not spared Tierl Enneth; the survivors of the cataclysm had chosen to relocate rather than rebuild their homes. A few paces ahead, Jaric brushed past the rusted remains of the grill. Then the corridor bent once more. The far arch loomed ahead, scattered across with clusters of orange light.

"Kor," swore Corley in disbelief. "Could those be campfires? I can't believe it!" He lengthened stride, reached the far entrance of the tunnel, and, with Jaric at his side, looked out over the countryside beyond.

Blurred by streamers of mist, the valley that nestled between ruins and hills lay riddled with hundreds of torches. Music wafted faintly over summer's chorus of crickets, cut across by raucous shouts. Painted wagons, lighted stalls, and the packed earth where dancers circled all formed a familiar pattern. Jaric needed no words to qualify; identical seasonal gatherings had occurred beneath Morbrith's walls each solstice throughout his childhood. Tierl Enneth itself might lie deserted, but wild clansmen from the hills still gathered there for summerfair.

Corley shifted his weight, settling Taen in the crook of his elbow. Her face appeared as a pale oval against the mouth of the tunnel. When Jaric did not speak, the captain scuffed his boot irritably against the cobbles. "We have a problem." Clansmen were distrustful of strangers and quick to anger at any time; when they were drunken and euphoric from the rites of the solstice, their belligerence became unmanageable. "We could wait for full dark and perhaps slip past without being seen."

"No." Jaric released a quivering breath. The Llondian flute directed him straight toward the heart of the festivities. Aware as his companion of the dangers, and agonized by Taen's helplessness, the boy resisted an urge to fling the artifact to the ground.

"Carry the Dreamweaver, then," said Corley grimly. "Before long we'll both be glad my blades weren't sent back to *Moonless.*"

The mention of weapons earned no response but an unreadable glance from Jaric; the boy made no effort to accept the burden of the unconscious girl. And frayed to a nervous edge by the prospect of crossing a summerfair on the very eve of the solstice, Corley's great hands knotted. Taen's blankets pulled taut, and a lock of her hair tumbled free and streamed in the wind.

"Wait." Jaric stepped back and, with abrupt decision, reached beneath his cloak. "Steel may not be necessary."

Had Corley been amenable to religion, the boy might have begged a blessing from Kordane for understanding. But from a captain trained on Cliffhaven, Jaric knew he could expect no better than a split second of reason before a sword stroke. Wary of the consequences, he pulled the ash flute from his belt.

Inlay glimmered with the iridescent gleam of shell; not even fading light could conceal the stops, which numbered twelve, too widely spaced to suit even the longest human fingers. Corley studied the artifact, then glanced at Jaric's face.

He spoke with controlled gentleness. "That's Llondian, am I right?"

Jaric nodded, openly distressed; mere possession of demon handiwork was heresy punishable by death should he ever stand trial under the priests.

But Corley made no outcry. "Well," he said quietly, "if you think that thing will protect us from quick-tempered clansmen, by all means use it." At Jaric's startled silence, he shrugged. "Boy, the ways of a sorcerer trained by the Vaere are not those of a man. Anskiere consorted with Llondelei. Even the Kielmark knows."

Jaric lifted a hand and carefully tucked Taen's fallen hair back under the blankets. "You're not afraid?"

The captain drew a quick breath. "All right, yes, I'm afraid. Did you think me a brainless fool? I've a half sister who's a hillman's get, and still I can't fathom their ways. But this much I'd bet. Alone, without help, we'll surely end up spitted on clansmen's daggers."

Relieved, Jaric summoned courage and struck out from the archway. Corley followed, tense and beginning to sweat. Thornbrakes and meadow grass had overgrown the trade road beyond, muffling their passage to a sibilant swish of undergrowth; dew spangled their boots at each stride. Corley lifted Taen to his shoulders to keep her blankets dry. Silent but for an occasional grunt of exertion, the captain stayed close to Jaric's side until the light of the clansmen's bonfires streaked their faces like ceremonial paint. Close up, the smells of roasting meat and incense mingled with the odors of sweat and the manure of horses. A bowed instrument rasped arpeggios to the stamp of dancing feet. Ragged, painted, and scantily clad in the furred skins of animals, the clansmen and their women spun like shadows between a circle of torches lashed onto poles. Both sexes carried steel. Daggers, short swords, and quoit rings gleamed from belts and shoulder scabbards, and bone-hilted knives protruded from the tasseled fringes of boot tops.

A stone's throw from the perimeter, Jaric tripped on a branch. Sticks snapped beneath his feet as he scrambled to maintain balance. Corley grabbed his elbow and steadied him, too late. By the fireside, a man whirled and broke away from the dance. He spotted the intruders, pointed, and raised a yammering shout of alarm. The music died as the revelers laid aside their instruments.

Corley froze between steps. "Use your whistle, boy." He pitched his words with urgency, for the interlaced patterns of dancers unraveled like torn knotwork. A fist-shaking mob coalesced around the first man. Shoulder to shoulder with their husbands, women tossed braided hair over their lithely muscled backs. Steel flashed in the torchlight as one clansmember after another drew knives.

Jaric raised the flute to his lips. He made no attempt to seek the stops, for the Llondel demon by the ice cliffs had instructed him to sound the highest note on the scale. The crowd charged from the fireside with an eerie, quavering scream, just as the boy drew breath and blew into the mouth-piece.

The flute sang out with a tone so pure it pierced the clamor like a needle through cloth. The very air seemed to shatter. The note swelled, deepened, raising resonant harmonics beyond the range of hearing. Vibrations spread outward like wind, touching the living essence of plants and livestock, and fraying the thoughts of men into patterns never meant for mortal minds. The attacking hillfolk jumbled to a halt and fell silent, knives forgotten in their hands; and like ripples settling from a stone tossed into water, the seething hordes of the summerfair quivered and stilled and quieted.

Jaric lowered the flute, leaving the crisp snap of torch flames isolated in a pool of silence. His head rang and his limbs trembled. Somehow he retained the presence of mind to stumble forward. Trusting Corley to follow on his heels, he entered the summerfair; and the torches burnished his hair like gold struck by sunlight.

That moment an eldritch cry split the stillness. An ancient woman burst from the mass of clansmen. Clothed in garments of knotted leather, she raised fleshless arms and swayed toward Jaric. Corley hung back as, in the singsong syntax of trance, the crone raised her voice and spoke in the tongue of the clans. Her guttural syllables chilled Jaric like the touch of winter ice. His step faltered, and he stopped, alone within the ring of flame-light. He knew whom he faced. A year past he had met this woman's counterpart in a backlands settlement called Gaire's Main; the prophetic words spoken then still broke his sleep with nightmares. As priestess of the spring on the isle of Tierl Enneth, the woman was crazed through a lifetime dedicated to ritual dreams and oracular vision. Her word superseded all law among the clans, and should she speak against them, very likely he and Taen and Corley would perish at the hands of her maiden initiates.

The woman uttered one last word and snapped her jaw shut. Beaded locks of hair rattled around her shoulders as she stamped her foot, spun around, and ran to the tailboard of a wagon piled high with wreathes of ceremonial flowers. Nailed to the wagon's crosstree was the traditional offering to the blessed Flame, a circlet braided from the fire-lilies which bloomed only at solstice. Jaric held his breath as the priestess leaped, snatched, and landed bearing the sacred circlet. Before he could move a muscle, the woman whirled. For a single suspended instant, his frightened gaze locked with the blind pearl-white of her eyes.

Then the priestess stamped again. She whispered in the common tongue of Keithland, yet her words reached the boy as if she spoke in his ear. "Aye, so, ye are the one." And she threw the wreath.

Orange, gold, and butter-yellow, the flowers fluttered through the air and landed squarely on the crown of Jaric's head. The clansmen gasped. Though not a man among them spoke, they knelt as one on the packed earth. Only Jaric and Corley and the blind priestess remained on their feet in the torchlight.

Corley stepped swiftly to Jaric's side. "Best move on. The Lady has granted us safe-conduct."

The boy roused with a start. Fire-colored petals tangled with strands of his hair as he twisted to face the captain. "Do you know what she said?"

Corley answered with reluctance. "Yes." But to his surprise Jaric did not demand a translation.

In a voice half-choked with misery, the boy said, "Please, if you can, will you tell them to *get up?*"

Corley swore. Clutching Taen closely to his chest, he shouted in the coarse tongue of the clans. With a ragged rustle of movement, the people rose to their feet. Someone shouted at the far edge of the crowd, and a drum boomed through the night.

"Go now," said Corley in Jaric's ear.

The drumbeat quickened, then broke into wild rhythms of exultation. Though Jaric longed with all his heart to flee, he forced himself to step forward with dignity. Painted, braided, and reeking of sweet oil and the exertion of their revels, the clansfolk parted and deferentially permitted him to pass.

With Corley at his shoulder, the boy strode through a living corridor of flesh which extended the breadth of the summerfair. Hands plucked at his clothes; children peeped with unblinking eyes from the fringes of their parents' leggings, and grandmothers murmured over the blanket-wrapped Dreamweaver cradled in Corley's arms. Dazzled by the glare of the torches, Jaric kept on, though his knees trembled and his knuckles blanched against the shaft of the ash flute long before he crossed the final perimeter of wagons.

Darkness closed over him on the far side. The priestess shrieked again at his back, and flutes and fiddles joined the drums' rejoicing. The hillfolk resumed their solstice dances beneath torches which smoked and streamed in the wind. Jaric plunged gratefully through the dew-drenched grass of the meadowland. He did not speak, even as the summerfair shrank behind, and the campfires dwindled to orange glimmers down the valley. The land became rough, cut by ravines and small, rock-strewn streams. At length the moon rose, round and full in the east. The pine forest which bordered the fells loomed ahead, outlined in silvery light. Still Jaric showed no sign of slowing. Corley shifted aching shoulders and wondered whether he dared to pause for a rest. Suddenly, with a queer and desperate violence, Jaric stopped.

He yanked the wreath from his brow. The soft bells of the fire-lilies crushed between his fists as he drew breath and demanded to know the meaning of the priestess's prophecy.

Aware how close the boy was to breaking, Corley answered with patience. "She called you Firelord and Demonbane. She said danger would track you as winter follows spring." Slowly, with painstaking care, he eased the Dreamweaver to the grass and continued. "She told her people not to obstruct us, for the sake of the girl who would defend all men from the Dark-dreamer yet to come."

Something in the captain's manner cued Jaric to the fact that there was more. "Go on."

Stooped over Taen's still form, Corley sighed. "The Lady said one day you will go forth and steal power from the very heart of Shadowfane. If you survive that quest, mankind will endure to see Kor's Fires rekindled in the heavens."

Jaric hurled the wreath to the ground with a wrenching cry of anguish. "Shadowfane?" His voice held a raw edge of fear. "Do you know how misguided her faith is? Great Fall, I'm *no man's savior!*"

"You're Ivain Firelord's heir," Corley said matter-of-factly.

The scent of mangled flowers hung heavily on the air between them. Jaric twisted his face away, eyes shut hard against tears. "Ivain was a murderer. I've no intention of following in his footsteps."

Corley, who knew men, had wisdom enough to keep silent as Jaric whirled and ran. Aware the boy must come to terms with his fate by himself, the captain sighed and gathered the Dreamweaver from the ground. He followed at a walk toward the forest.

The Llondelei waited at the edge of the pines, their gray

cloaks mottled like smoke in the moonlight which spilled through the boughs. Confronted by a hiss, and movement, and a glowing circle of eyes, Jaric started back and slammed into Corley.

Both humans froze as thought-image knifed into their minds. *'Danger stalks from behind.'* The Llondelei dealt a shadowy glimpse of creatures rustling through what looked like scrub grass. Before their meaning entirely resolved, they added a fleeting likeness of Taen's face, the glossy black of her hair crowned with myrtle. Silent, impatient, the tallest of the three demons lifted six-fingered hands toward the girl.

Pressed tight to the captain's side, Jaric felt Corley shrink in the dark. "Let them take her," the boy said quickly. The demons would use force if they resisted.

Yet already the Llondelei had sensed the captain's hesitation. They acted without warning. Jaric felt a jab in his head like hot wire. He tumbled, his eyes full of moonlight, and never felt his body strike the ground. Two Llondelei stepped across his prone form; they caught Taen as Corley's knees buckled. Thought-images passed briefly between Llondian minds. Then, with a mournful whistle, the female among them bent and stripped Jaric of his sword and dagger. She grasped the wrists of the Firelord's heir and hoisted him onto her back. More silent than the rustle of a leaf, she bore her burden after her fellows and vanished into the forest.

Corinne Dane

Corley awoke to birdsong and the cold trickle of dew down his collar. Daybreak brightened the tops of the pines, and a six-legged tree pecker rattled the branches overhead, stabbing for grubs beneath the bark. Alarmed to discover Taen and Jaric missing, the captain rolled to his feet and gasped at the pain of stiffened shoulders. Fully alert, and frantic with concern for his companions, he searched the ground for sign of the Llondelei. Yet the surrounding mat of pine needles showed no trace of a track. Only a sword and dagger of Corlin steel remained; surely, after his experience with Brith, the boy would not have abandoned his weapons, except under duress.

Corley swore and brushed twigs from his hair. Whatever beneficient connection Anskiere might have with the Londelei, Taen and Jaric lay in demon hands with no human weapon to safeguard them. The captain would not give them up without a search. Though his stomach was pinched with hunger, and his body ached from his night in the open, Corley never hesitated. He gathered Jaric's weapons from the ground and set out to seek his companions.

Mountains thrust like the armored spine of a lizard down the length of the island. The forests cloaking their slopes proved dense and seamed with gullies, too rough for a single man to cover effectively. Faster, more efficient than most, Corley quartered acres of remote dells, occasionally crossing the rutted tracks cut by the clan tribes' wagons. He startled satin deer from their grazing, and brush pheasant from their nests, but encountered no sign of the Llondelei.

Only as the day wore on, he felt increasingly unsettled, as if he sensed something following. Time and again he checked his back trail, yet nothing arose to justify his suspicion. Slowed at last by hunger, he paused by a stream to whittle snares in the late afternoon. The facts of his predicament were not reassuring. If the demons intended Taen and Jaric harm, by now no man could help them. Yet the Kielmark's orders had been explicit; Corley saw no alternative but to return to the harbor and wait. If his two charges survived, surely they would return to Tierl Enneth and *Callinde*.

In a place of purplish twilight, shadows danced in patterns on tree trunks. Wind rustled through alien foliage; no, Jaric decided, the sound he heard was *not wind*, but spring water singing over pebbles in an underground channel. Enveloped in the overlapping images generated by collective Llondian consciousness, the boy strove to separate dream from waking reality. He lay on a mat woven of rushes, surrounded by the earthy confines of a cavern that was surely the Llondian demons' burrow. Yet even as his mind framed the concept, an influx of images contradicted; *this here-now dwelling was a place of misery and exile*. Home raised memories of moist air and shadows, of endlessly whispering breezes and lacy tendrils of vegetation. That wood was *other*, a place inconceivably distant from Keithland's forests. The sun there shone red, little more than a dim star overhead.

Jaric puzzled to fathom how any sun might resemble a star. Disoriented by the waking dreams of the demons who sheltered him, and troubled with concern for Taen, he propped himself on one elbow. An oil lamp shaded by panes of violet glass dangled from a chain overhead. A weak flicker of flame illuminated a chamber bare of furnishings, except for the grass mat and a clay ewer of water cradled in a three-legged stand nearby. The earthen floors were beaten smooth. Walls shored with timber bore incomprehensible patterns of carving, and scarlet hangings curtained the archway to an alcove beyond. Uncertain whether he was prisoner or guest, Jaric wondered whether the structure concealed a door. According to Kordane's Law, prolonged exposure to Llondian imaging could drive the human mind to madness. Yet the boy would not consider leaving without searching for Taen.

Leave, Kordane's Law; Llondian consciousness plucked fragments of thought from his mind, and the unfathomable caprice of their kind melded the concepts. The illusions the demons employed in place of spoken language overwhelmed Jaric's senses, and the cave's board walls shattered into a starburst of light. Disoriented, the boy fell back on the mat. He threw his hands over his face, but the light endured. Indelibly impressed on his mind's eye, he saw the conflagration streak earthward acrosss blackness spangled with stars. A roar like thunder filled Jaric's ears. Deafened, his vision blistered by forces too awesome for comprehension, he endured as Llondian memory unveiled the glory of Kordane's Fires at the time of the Great Fall.

'Corinne Dane, *probe-ship*.' Borrowed human words strained to encompass inconceivably strange concepts. '*Stole Llondelei from Homeworld*,' that place of soft shadows and rich soil and magnificent, towering trees. Jaric experienced a withering flash of hate. '*Your kind, stole us away, Homeworld*.' Star-sun, lost sun, red as a stab wound in the sky. Wrung by hostile emotions, Jaric cringed and cried out.

The image shifted like a jarred kaleidoscope. '*Peace; this human is Ivainson Firelord's heir, let him be*.' Restored to the unthreatening interior of the cave, the boy felt the demons' enmity subside.

Shaking, Jaric unclenched his hands. He pushed sweat-soaked hair from his eyes and sat up. Two coals of orange glowered from the alcove where the curtain hung; a Llondian demon watched him from the dark.

Jaric forgot his fear. "What have you done with Taen?"

'*She who spins dreams?*' The Llondel stepped into the chamber, a gray, six-fingered hand extended to steady the boy as he rose. '*Come*.'

Jaric shrank from the demon's touch. He reached his feet unaided and discovered with distress that his weapons were missing. "Where's Corley?"

The Llondel hissed. Its spurred fingers flinched into a fist, and, like a slap, Jaric received an impression of a sunny forest glade. There crouched the Kielmark's chestnut-haired captain, toasting fish on a stick over a campfire. Yet the image did not reassure. Disquiet troubled Jaric, as if something evil lurked in the shadows beyond Corley's campsite. But the Llondel allowed him no chance to explore the premonition.

The image dissolved abruptly into dark, lit by baleful eyes. '*Follow*.' The demon pushed the curtain aside and beckoned.

A narrow corridor extended beyond, minimally illuminated by lamps paned with the same violet glass. Left no choice but to obey, Jaric stepped forward. His heels clicked against tiles of glazed ceramic. Unable to see as well as the demon who guided him, and curious what might lie behind the doorways which opened at intervals off the hallway, the boy lagged slightly behind. His footsteps reverberated within the burrow, bewildering his ears with overlapping layers of sound; imperceptibly, his self-awareness frayed into dreams. Jaric stumbled. He pressed a hand against the wall for balance as, adrift in the flux of Llondelei consciousness, his mind crossed the far borders of Keithland. Inside stone towers at Shadowfane, he perceived a young man crouched with his arms locked over his ears. A strange, reddish aura shimmered over his form; unsure if the phenomenon was induced by imagination or Llondian prescience, Jaric looked closer. Through the shifting curtains of light he saw scarred fingers and a familiar tangle of black hair.

"Emien?" he called, though he had not intended to speak aloud.

Hard, spurred fingers clamped Jaric's wrist. The connection broke before the man in the tower could answer, and Ivainson felt himself jerked backward, into the violet-tinged shadows of a corridor beneath the earth. '*Stay close*,' admonished his Llondian guide. '*Heed, or risk your mind. If you stray, I cannot shield you from the dream-melding of the burrow.*'

Jaric shared the jumbled reactions of many in the instant before the demon released him. '*Ivainson, Firelord's heir; strong-willed, yes? Look, he seeks the Dark-dreamer before time.*'

"Dark-dreamer?" the boy said aloud. "Do they mean Emien?"

The Llondel hurried forward without answer. Presently it paused, pointed through a side door, and jabbed Jaric's mind with a fleeting impression of Taen Dreamweaver's face. The boy needed no further incentive. He entered the chamber hard on the demon's heels and stopped, blinking in the glare of unshielded candles.

Forced to squint as his vision adjusted, Jaric made out the hooded forms of three Llondelei clustered around what appeared to be a wooden tub filled with hot water. Through the steam which drifted and coiled above the rim, he saw a dark, wet head, and the flushed features of the girl whose memory had haunted him since the moment they parted at Landfast.

"Jaric?" Taen's voice was weak, but tinged with unmistakable reproach. "Corley said if you followed *Moonless* from the Free Isles, he'd skin you with the dullest of his knives."

"Well, he didn't. After four weeks of worry over you, every blade on *Moonless* had an edge that would split a cat's whisker." Astonished by the tightness in his throat, Jaric rushed to embrace her. Quickly as he moved, the demons reacted first. One behind caught him by the shoulder and yanked him back, while two in front sprang to their feet and caught his hands. Spread-eagled and helpless, Jaric struggled to reach Taen; but Llondelei thought-forms hammered his protest to silence.

'Never you touch, not now.' The command was qualified with an impression of his inner self perpetually locked into sympathy with Taen's powers as Dreamweaver. Jaric saw his potential as Firelord's heir rendered impotent at a stroke, *all because he had ignorantly embraced the Dreamweaver before her illness left her.* Llondian images detailed a ruinous sequence of catastrophes which mankind could suffer as a result: cities burned, refugees starved, and civilized Keithland crushed before an onslaught of demon foes.

Released with a suddenness that jarred thought, Jaric stumbled to his knees. Shaken, afraid to rise, he searched the demons' inscrutable eyes. Then, rubbing a cut where a spur had accidentally scored his wrist, he appealed at last to Taen. "I don't understand."

"How could you?" A trace of an impish grin touched her lips. "I don't guess the mysteries of the Vaere are part of the Landfast archives."

"No." Jaric responded to a prod from the demon at his back, and seated himself on a mat at Taen's side. Though the glistening skin of her shoulder was close enough to touch, he clenched his hands tightly in his lap.

"The Vaere were desperate when Cliffhaven was endangered by demons. I was sent to intervene," Taen said. "At the time, my Dreamweaver's mastery was incomplete."

But Jaric knew she left out details to spare him. Taen had been dispatched to Cliffhaven to preserve his own life from the combined effects of Anskiere's geas and the Kielmark's unpredictable temperament. Against the will of the Vaere, she had stayed on and engaged her talents in Cliffhaven's defense so that he could recover the Keys to Elrinfaer in safety. Anguished that Taen's suffering had begun with disobedience in his behalf, Jaric covered his face with callused palms.

"Ivainson, no, you can't blame yourself!" Taen rested her cheek against the rim of the basin. Wearied by the inadequacy of speech, she engaged her craft as Dreamweaver.

Her thoughts touched Jaric's mind as softly as a falling

leaf. Gently she made him share an understanding she had only recently acquired through the Llondel who cured her illness. The powers of the Vaere-trained were created through a bond with a living matrix called Sathid. Upon maturity, the crystals caused an incompatibility with the body, which developed into a coma. At that time, the crystals would procreate by transforming the living tissues of the body into seed-matrix. Death was the usual result. Yet since Llondelei also derived their imaging abilities from Sathid bonding, they knew ways to separate the mature crystal from the body without harm. The process was easily disturbed; physical contact at the wrong moment could cause the matrix to cross-link, augment the imprint of a second mind alongside that of the first master.

Demon thought-forms defined the matter further. Swept into an explanation of dreams, Jaric observed that the Stormwarden of Elrinfaer's formidable control of wind and wave derived from two Sathid matrixes. The crystals formed the foundation of his powers, and to protect them from enemy meddling, he sank them in a capsule beneath the polar ocean. Driven beyond the icy deeps, the boy traversed a series of interlinking associations called forth by Llondian consciousness. In a whirl of past events, he saw enemies march from Shadowfane. They murdered Llondelei guardians and stole the last of their native stock of Sathid matrix. The crystals were pure, never having bonded previously; no others could replace them, except on Homeworld under the scarlet star. Once returned to Shadowfane, hostile hands experimented with the matrix and discovered what Llondelei always knew. At the time of separation, Sathid crystals could bond again; any who attempted to share the influence of an impressed matrix risked total subjugation to the will of the original partner. And since the matrix itself inherited the experience of each successive master, the crystal itself grew stronger, wiser; it, too, might contend for mastery. Thus had Jaric nearly destroyed a balance when he tried to touch Taen, and thus did the compact at Shadowfane create pawns to commit atrocities against mankind.

Freed from the imaging, Jaric recalled the caustic burns which had disfigured Emien's hands since the hour he had murdered his mistress, Tathagres. Abruptly he remembered Taen's presence. He stopped his speculation, but not before the Dreamweaver caught the direction of his thoughts.

"My brother stands in grave danger. The Llondelei know Tathagres served Shadowfane. She carried Sathid already impressed by demons in a collar of wrought gold. Though the witch herself was not matrix-linked, the enemy controlled her by the crystal's influence. Through her they channeled their designs against Anskiere and Cliffhaven. But when Emien broke the band from her neck, the matrix contacted his skin. Very likely he will succumb to direct possession. Any talent he has could be developed to the detriment of our kind."

Jaric felt the breath constrict in his throat. For a suspended interval he studied Taen's face through the steam which clouded the tub. The girl's eyes showed fatigue, their color shadowed under lashes like ink; but her expression reflected concern rather than grief. As yet she seemed unaware that Emien was held captive at Shadowfane. Dry fingers brushed Jaric's arm. He started and found a Llondel crouched at his shoulder.

'Once, she saw,' sent the demon. Its touch intensified in his mind. *'The girl received the image in delirium, and for the sake of health, we let her believe she experienced a nightmare. But she cannot be kept ignorant much longer.'* Slitted nostrils flared; and drawing the boy into sympathy, the creature inclined its head toward the Dreamweaver.

Jaric beheld the chamber and its inhabitants through the altered perception of Llondian eyes. Candlelight threw off a hurtful, greenish cast; and Taen's person shimmered with the blue-violet aura which accompanied the maturing presence of a Sathid bond. Its pattern radiated changeless and clean as light refracted through dewdrops at dawn, then vanished, blotted into darkness by a second view of the black-haired captive huddled within Shadowfane's walls. In contrast, the patterns emanating from Emien's form gleamed an angry scarlet, contorted as a hillwoman's knotwork.

The image faded away. Subjected to the expectant regard of the Llondelei, Jaric realized the demons expected him to intervene. Logic demanded that he develop his sorcerer's potential to combat the anguish Emien would unleash against Keithland. But the revelation that all Vaerish powers, even the Cycle of Fire itself, were derived from mastery of a Sathid matrix changed nothing. Tierl Enneth's plight had affirmed his aversion to sorcery more deeply than ever before.

Frustrated to despair, Jaric challenged. "Why should you care what becomes of Keithland? Kordane's Law holds all demons alike. What separates your kind from the builders of Shadowfane?"

The Llondelei hissed with affront. Taen cried aloud, but her warning went unregarded. The demon at Jaric's side caught his wrist in a crushing grip. Its spurred palm drove deep into his flesh, and he tumbled headlong into an inferno of heat and violence.

The night-dark forests of Homeworld exploded into fire, slashed by energy weapons carried by invaders. Jaric watched a stand of torched trees buckle and fall. Droves of batlike fliers took wing, shrilling piteously as the flesh seared from their bones. A small band of Llondelei fled the conflagration. Driven from their burrow in confusion, blinded by smoke, and disoriented by the cruel brilliance of the flames, they ran only to be captured. Darts tipped with drugs whined through cascades of airborne sparks and struck the running forms. One after another, Llondelei tumbled to earth and lay still.

White-suited creatures advanced across the swath of smoldering vegetation. Their bodies resembled a man's, but instead of faces, their heads were glassy, featureless windows with blackness inside. Jaric screamed in terror. Yet the dream did not relent. Bound to memory of Llondian disaster, he watched helplessly as the enemy piled their stunned captives in a fearsome metal wagon. The vehicle jolted into motion with a roar, and the dream-image went dark. Jaric endured a period of jostling movement and noise. Then, like a beacon in a sea of confusion, he heard a human voice.

The woman's accent was foreign, her tone openly distressed. "Commander Keith, I must protest! The inhabitants of Llond's world aren't dangerous. My God, they don't even have space travel yet!"

A gruff voice replied. "They register psi strong enough to ruin us. That's enough to list them among the enemy. Complaints don't count a damn since Starhope was besieged. And God? If *Corinne Dane*'s mission fails, if mankind doesn't find a defense against powers such as your Llondelei possess, the only human survivors will be those colonies enslaved by the Gierj. Since the Book of Revelation didn't mention that ending, you can assume the rest of old Earth dogma was fiction also. Now get back to your post!"

Jaric strove to make sense of the words. Denied sight, and confused by religious references whose meanings seemed

strangely skewed, he puzzled over the term *Corinne Dane*.
Llondelei consciousness caught the name in his mind, and the
dream upended, flung him with sickening vertigo into a vista
of blackness and stars. Adrift in the vastness of space, Jaric
beheld a vast, metal engine. Its surface was cluttered with
incomprehensible symbols, and a shiny, bewildering array of
struts and vanes and lights. 'Corinne Dane, *star-probe-ship*,'
sent the Llondelei who imaged the dream. An explosion of
blue-white light followed; the engine shot forward like a me-
teor, scribing a line of fire across the dark.

Tumbled through sequence after sequence of images, Jaric
at last understood; the Blessed Fires praised by Kordane's
priests were nothing more than a corrupted reference to this
same ship, *Corinne Dane*, which once had sailed the vast
deeps of the heavens. The Llondelei granted no time to examine the impact of this discovery. Images patched Jaric's
thoughts like mosaic work. He saw scores of Llondelei caged
in metal while *Corinne Dane*'s mighty fires transported them
across inconceivable distance. Twelve races gathered from
other worlds shared the confinement of the Llondelei. Gierj,
Karas, Mharg, Thienz, and frostwarg, and other demons
whose shapes Jaric did not recognize: all huddled imprisoned
in the ship's dungeon. With restless thoughts and endless
hatred they plotted against the humans who had captured
them; humans whose lonely, isolated minds made them such
easy prey that now their last outpost among the stars battled
desperately to stave off extinction.

Joined with Llondian consciousness, Jaric shared the suffering of captives who pined for the forests of Homeworld. He
cringed from the tortured scream of machinery as other
demons' vengeance wrenched *Corinne Dane*'s guidance sys-
tems out of sequence. Rudderless as a ship in a storm, the
great craft hurtled through the atmosphere of a far, uncharted
planet. Smoldering wreckage smashed and scarred a barren
landscape with the marks of the Great Fall.

Jaric screamed as his sight again went dark. Beset by the
pain of Llondelei survivors, he breathed air that was dry and
thin, hurtful after the moist damp of Homeworld. One with
demon memory, he crawled from the wrecked framework of
Corinne Dane, a castaway on an unknown world. Forced to
forage for fish and lichens, Jaric endured cruel cold and blizzards. He knew the discomfort of seasons set out of harmony
with his anatomy. Sorrow and despair beset him as compan-

ions weakened and died. Weeping for release, he suffered the hardship of the Llondelei who survived and reproduced. Even after the humans at Landfast seeded the first forests upon the barren hills of Keithland, the exiles never ceased to mourn for the lost land of their ancestors.

Jaric screamed. Battered by generation upon generation of Llondian grief, he recalled the thoughtless words he had uttered before the images trapped him. *"Why should you care what becomes of Keithland?"* As if his guilt keyed release, the dreams fled from him like shadows before light.

He recovered awareness, shivering on his knees in yet another underground cavern, but this chamber was smaller than the one which had sheltered Taen. Jaric raised himself shakily from the floor. Wetness slicked his thumb, blood from the stinging puncture left by a Llondian spur. The demon who had inflicted the wound waited at his shoulder, motionless in the violet light of the lamps. It offered no image as the human boy recovered his composure; and shamed to the core, Jaric was too embarrassed to speak. He stared at the far wall, and there saw a board laid generously with bread and fruit.

The Llondel bade him sit down. The boy complied, startled to awareness of his own hunger. But the influx of alien thought-images had left him feeling vaguely queasy. His awareness seemed oddly separate from his physical body. Perception of solid reality frayed at the edges, unintegrated as oil on water. Aware that time spent among the Llondelei could only intensify such disorientation, and that madness lay at the end, Jaric buried his face in his hands.

He did not hear the demon rise at his back. Its feet made no sound as it stole from the chamber, leaving the curtain open for another who entered in its stead. Unsteady on her feet, one hand braced to the wall for support, Taen Dreamweaver tugged at the wool robe the demons had loaned her. She regarded the bent head of the Firelord's heir and managed a wan smile. "Why don't you eat? Illusions don't smell like peaches, and if I tried, I could count the knobs on your backbone from here."

Jaric spun around. "Taen?" He scrambled awkwardly to his feet and hesitated, arrested by uncertainty. "Are you . . ."

"On the mend," Taen finished for him. "Except this darned wool itches like the thistle cloth we used to rub down goats." She stepped to his side, bringing freshness and a calm that dispelled the nausea brought on by demon thought-image.

Abruptly suspicious, Jaric helped her to sit on the mat. "You aren't using your powers to steady me, are you?" Through the contact he felt her trembling. The weakness of her appalled him.

"No." Taen picked up a peach and bit into it. "A Dreamweaver's aura can heal. Had you forgotten?"

"Yes." Recalled to manners, Jaric reached for a loaf and broke a piece off for the girl. "We have to get out of here."

Taen looked at him with her mouth full. A tinge of color had returned to her cheeks, and her blue eyes were laughing. "You make a terrible sailor," she observed. "Always wanting to change the wind. Will you eat that chunk of bread, or are you just going to sit there bleeding on it?"

Jaric dropped the crust with self-conscious embarrassment. He looked for a napkin to blot his thumb, but found none and had to settle for a strip from his cuff, which was torn anyway.

Taen continued as he bound his cut. "The Llondelei will free us in their own time, I think, but not before the Sathid matrix expelled from my body fully crystallizes."

Jaric regarded the board as if the bread were an enemy that had betrayed him. "We might have been here days already."

Taen punched him, ineffectively, but with the fire of her usual spirit. "It's only nightfall outside. That makes one full day, and the last without supper. Eat, or I will use my powers. You'll need your strength. If my legs don't stop wobbling by tomorrow, who else do I have to carry me back to *Moonless*?"

The Llondelei returned when the last of the peaches were consumed. Two of them escorted Taen to a place where she could rest; illness that preceded the maturation of her Sathid matrix had left her exhausted, and even through his preoccupation, Jaric noticed she had difficulty keeping her eyes open. Though he would rather have sat with her while she slept, the Llondel who remained forbade him.

'*Follow.*' The image that touched the boy's mind was tinged with urgency and an indefinable weight of regret.

Taen's presence had eased the immediacy of his despair. Jaric dusted bread crumbs from his shirt and went where the demon directed.

It led him deep into earth, yet the timber-shored walls of the burrow held none of the dank chill he might have expected. The tiled corridor they traversed was dry and warm, if eerily lit by the violet-paned lamps. With no image offered in explanation, the Llondel guide stopped and flung open a door. Jaric entered the chamber beyond at its command, his feet rustling through a mat of sweet rushes. The room was large, even more sparsely furnished than the others he had seen. Here the air had a close smell, as if animals were kenneled nearby. Suddenly, in the gloom of the far corner, Ivainson saw movement, Llondelei; but these differed from any he had observed so far. Four gray-skinned youngsters tussled like puppies on the rushes, and something about the savagery of their play set his hair aprickle.

The human boy held still, awaiting a cue from the demon at his side. None came. Except the Llondel young noticed Jaric and broke apart with whistles of surprise. Lankier than human children, their silvery skin ridged with sinew, they approached with trusting curiosity. The grown Llondel made no effort to exchange images with them, but stood motionless. At last, confused by the adult's poised stance, and driven to uneasiness by the wild, animal innocence reflected in the eyes of the young, Jaric spoke. He hoped he would not offend. "Why have you brought me here?"

Gray cloth rustled. The Llondel's furrowed face turned toward him. Beneath the embroidered cloak hood, Jaric saw the creature's slitted nostrils widen; the light in its eyes shone subdued and sad. *'No Sathid.'*

The image rang with tragic overtones; cut to the heart by forced empathy, Jaric felt helpless tears blur his eyes. At his feet the cublings squealed and scattered playfully. With breathless, gleeful whistles, two smaller ones pounced upon the largest, and presently the entire group tumbled into a knot of fists and knees. Puzzled by the incongruity of the youngsters' behavior in the presence of opposing emotions in the adult, Jaric found his answer; since Llondelei communicated entirely through shared mental images, spoken language did not exist among them. Any Llondian young born since Shadowfane's theft of the Sathid were deaf and blind to their own culture. Even if words could be made to compensate for the loss, the ancestral memories of Homeworld would be forgotten within a generation. Priceless heritage, and the cherished identities of forebears who lived before the Great Fall, would become irretrievably lost.

Jaric pressed his bandaged thumb to his side. Reduced to silence by the weight of tragic consequences, and saddened by the Llondelei cublings who cheerfully hammered each other with six-fingered fists, the Firelord's heir strove to lighten the plight of the Llondelei. "What of the Vaere? If the sorcerrs they train are Sathid-linked, another source of the crystals must exist."

The Llondel lifted spurred hands and pushed back its hood. It turned a rounded, earless head and regarded Jaric with anguished eyes, then answered. Like Kordane's Law, the Vaere held all demons alike. The Llondelei far-seekers had searched in vain for their isle. Though Taen could reach Tamlin with a thought, the far-seekers received only silence.

Jaric tried again. "But Anskiere was Vaere-trained. Would he break his loyalty to consort with Llondelei?"

'*Yes.*' The demon's images turned forcefully emphatic. '*Anskiere was born a prince among men. Where he perceived injustice, he had strength to follow the dictates of his heart.*' In a condensed rush of pictures, the creature showed Jaric the far-seeker who had befriended the sorcerer, and the pact sworn between Stormwarden and Llondel in the twilight seclusion of a forest glade. He heard words spoken as Anskiere of Elrinfaer promised to intercede with the Vaere in behalf of a wronged species. But hope was brief. Wrung by disappointment and a sweeping change of scene, Jaric perceived the tragedy of Tierl Enneth, then the towering prison of ice which prevented the keeping of that oath.

'*Keeper of the Keys, Firelord's heir, are you blind to destiny? The survival of your people, and also Llondelei, lies with your mastery of the Cycle of Fire.*'

"No," whispered Jaric. But his denial proved futile. Out of patience, the demon overturned his senses with brutal abruptness.

He saw himself ringed with the Sathid aura of a sorcerer's craft, but blindingly brilliant, stronger than even that of Anskiere of Elrinfaer. *Centered within a nexus of power, his flesh charged to near incandescence, he would make war upon Shadowfane's demons.*

"No. Ivain my father went mad!" Jaric's shout echoed through the cavern, scattering the Llondelei cublings. But the images battered into him without surcease.

By the Firelord's grace, Corinne Dane'*s fires will rise once more, bearing Llondel and human to the stars in peace.*

Jaric exploded into white-hot anger. He broke the demon's hold upon his mind and flung back a step. "No! There must be an alternative!"

The Llondel answered in words, underscored by finality irrevocable as death. *"Ivainson Firelord, for that you are already too late."* Eyes flared like coals beneath the cloak hood. The adult demon trilled a mournful seventh, and Jaric felt his will milled under like sand in the teeth of a storm tide.

ᖰᖱ XII ᖲᖳ

Destiny

Caught in a moment of wrenching disorientation, Jaric blinked to clear eyes that were stung by change. He looked upon night and the orange glow of a fire. The Llondel allowed him an instant to recognize the campsite where earlier the Kielmark's senior captain had toasted a fish for supper. Then demon thought-image swept away self-awareness, and Ivainson Jaric *was* Deison Corley, waking from sleep with the hair on his neck prickling with the sense of impending danger.

Even as Corley closed hands over his daggers, shadows moved, studded with the glint of eyes touched by firelight. Theinz-demons come hunting from Shadowfane closed in to take their prey, not the Firelord's heir they sought, but another: the chestnut-haired captain who had set up the Kielmark's counterattack during Kisburn's assault on Cliffhaven. Because of Corley, a Thienz, six Gierj, and a Karas shape-changed to human form had been slain. The demons reached for the captain's mind to initiate their attack. As they melded awareness with his thoughts, their eagerness seeped through the contact; and chilled by an influx of malice not his own, the captain jerked his first dagger from the scabbard. He had no chance to throw. His human will suddenly reeled under a demon-inspired compulsion to turn his blade against himself.

In the nursery chamber of the Llondelei burrow, Jaric cried out, the sound of his own voice unheard in his ears. He never saw the cubs who scattered away, eyes flaring in alarm, from the dimness of the far corner. Trapped wholly in Corley's awareness, the boy knew only desperation as the Thienz drove the captain toward suicide.

But the trained instincts of the fighter were not easily overpowered. In the moment Corley raised his knife, Thienz-bound against himself, the unconquered portion of his mind rebelled. He seized the only available recourse, and shoved his left hand to the wrist in live coals.

Pain came white-hot and immediate. Entwined in rapport with their victim, eight Thienz suffered equally. They screamed as one. Their hold upon Corley sundered, and even as reflex jerked the man's scorched flesh from the flame, he whipped back his knife hand and threw. The blade caught the nearest Theinz in the throat. Its death-dream diverted its fellows a split second, enough for Corley to close his fingers over the cold hilt of his broadsword. He yelled, shattering forest silence, and drew. His first stroke sliced two of his antagonists in half.

The survivors scuttled frantically into the night-black thickets. Corley could not see them. But Thienz-demons would sense each other; their counterattack would be sudden and coordinated, and against five he would be lost. The captain struck blind. Twigs and small saplings sheared under his blade. Slashed greenery whipped straight to jab him as he pressed forward, each step taking him farther from the fire that had been his salvation. Yet he did not hesitate in false hope. He had read the histories. Repeat tactics never worked on a Thienz. His only chance was to cut them down before they managed to regroup.

Yet his enemies had melted like ink into the night. Corley shook back sweat-soaked hair. His seared hand throbbed, and his breath rushed raggedly through his throat. Necessity forced him onward. His sword stroke stayed even, a scything lethal arc he had practiced to mechanical perfection. With wry fury, he wondered whether his corpse would continue the motion after the Thienz had crushed his spirit to whimpering defeat.

Then, without warning, the captain's inner musing became wrenched away and replaced by another reality.

Jaric smelled sweetrushes. Yanked back to separate awareness, he dimly recalled falling to the floor in the nursery of a Llondelei burrow; but as dream-image bound him deeper into night, he could neither tear free nor influence the demons who manipulated his mind.

'Firelord's heir, you were cautioned long ago on the ice cliffs: now Shadowfane's minions come hunting, and Keithland holds no haven.' Revelation followed, cruel as death: Jaric and his companions had nearly been overtaken on Tierl Enneth. Only because Llondelei influence had directed them across the midst of the clansmen's summerfair had they been spared from attack. Since the tracking Thienz had presumed

civilized humans would never attempt such a course, the ambush they prepared had been foiled. Cursing, yowling among themselves, Shadowfane's hunters lost precious time and their prey by going around, beyond range of the blind priestess's sensitivity to demon presence. Now, with Firelord's heir and Dreamweaver out of reach, the Thienz vented their frustration upon the luckless person of Deison Corley...

Their next strike battered the captain to the edge of unconsciousness. The sword flew spinning from his hand. He crashed after it, landed heavily on his shoulder. Briars tore his face. His teeth gouged up a mouthful of dirt, and his vision went utterly black. Still he fought. But now his enemies were guarded; pain could no longer free him. All he had left were the knives concealed on his person, though he might only get the chance to use one. Trapped like a rabbit in a warren, Deison Corley reached for the blade snugged in the sheath against his thigh. Around him, the Thienz closed in.

Jaric twisted, savaged doubly by Llondelei accusers. "You'd let Corley die!" he charged in return. "Your kind saw his peril, and yet did nothing to save him."

The Llondel returned no mercy. Unlike the heir of Ivain and the Dreamweaver, the life of Deison Corley held no consequence to the far-seers of their burrow. The man's continued well-being concerned the Llondelei not at all; *Jaric had disregarded all warnings; that the Kielmark's captain should die was just consequence*. The guilt cut like a whip.

"No!" Jaric's anguished denial rung without echo within the burrow's earthen walls.

'Then who else among mankind shall end contention?' The Llondel showed him Corley, struggling in the night with his dagger in the guts of a Thienz who had strayed within reach. Human and demon thrashed over and over in leaf mold, entangled and sticky with blood. Jaric tasted salt. Dream-image and self muddled together, his own tears indistinguishable from Corley's sweat as the captain fell limp, mind-bound victim of the four Thienz left living after the ambush.

Jaric felt his face ground on the rushes. He whimpered, flayed raw by remorse as the demons closed, vindictive in their desire to maim. Still he could not snap the fear which rejected Ivain's inheritance. Though he shared the suffering and the death of a friend, the bones of four thousand unburied corpses bound him to horrors far worse. The multitudes slain by sorcerers' mistakes shackled the heir of Ivain against action, and for this the Llondelei named him coward.

"More than one captain died at Elrinfaer and Tierl Enneth!" Jaric flung back. "Must human endeavor be limited to Vaerish mysteries and the Cycle of Fire?"

As if in vindication, an arrow slashed the dark. The shaft struck and buried to the feathers in the neck of the Thienz who crowded to kill. It tumbled thrashing to the ground. The demon beside it spun with a snarl toward the brush. This one was mature enough to carry venom, and Jaric saw the glint of poison sacs distended to bite.

Then, beyond the thicket, a shadow moved. The creature staggered and fell, the beaded leather haft of a hillman's dagger stuck in its chest. As one, the Thienz survivors abandoned Corley. Flight availed them nothing. As Corley threw off the effects of their hold, ten leather-clad tribesmen dashed silently from the thickets. A hail of javelins transfixed the last two Thienz from behind.

Relief lent Jaric the boldness to repudiate the judgment against him. "There, humans *can* kill demons without sorcery!"

Llondelei consciousness denied nothing as Corley rose from the ground. Half-dazed, cut in a dozen places where branches and Thienz claws had mauled him, the captain still retained presence of mind to thank his rescuers in clan dialect.

The leader of the foray hid surprise at the fact that an outland captain spoke his language. He jerked his dagger from the nearest corpse, feathered ornaments trembling at his wrists as he raised the bloody blade. "No thanks are due, seafarer, and none accepted. Our Lady sent us hunting for Thienz, not to win tribe-debt for sparing the carving of city-man skin."

Corley bent with a grunt, retrieved his longsword from the leaves, then leaned heavily on the cross guard. Tired, battered, and stinging, he regarded the clan chief entirely without rancor. "Health to your horses, then," he said.

The hillman raised painted eyebrows; here stood a townborn wise enough to tribe ways that he returned insult with blessing; this from a warrior great enough to slay four of the enemy before he succumbed to their mind-tricks. Guardedly acknowledging respect, the clan chief turned his fist outward in salute. Then he and his fellows spun soundlessly and the image of their leaving vanished utterly into dark . . .

* * *

Jaric's reprieve ended, his awareness of Corley ripped away by a tide of contempt. *'Foolish boy, did you think peril ends here?'* Without waiting for answer, Llondelei consciousness tore away his defense, stripped him vulnerable before self-evident truth: young Thienz were the compact's lowliest and most expendable resource. Their auras were least detectable to humans, which made them suitable as errand runners to Keithland; but before the mighty of Shadowfane, the powers of these were insignificant. Angered now, the Llondelei tightened their net. Cruel as the death of hope, they toppled Ivainson Firelord's heir headlong into nightmare. . . .

Images hammered into him with the force of physical blows. The Dark-dreamer emerged from Shadowfane. Commanding the same powers Taen employed for good, the brother spun ringing webs of nightmare. Misfortune harrowed the people. Farmsteaders on the northern borders of Hallowild died screaming in their cottages; others woke crazed from sleep and butchered their families. Cattle and crops died of neglect in the fields, and weeds wove shrouds through the bones which lay whitening in the dooryards.

"Spare them," whispered Jaric, but his words became the sated croak of scavenger birds. He heard laughter as demons praised their chosen, one called Maelgrim who had once been born a fisherman's son on the isle of Imrill Kand.

A demon hissed, and stone walls crumbled. Jaric saw dead men at arms in Morbrith livery stare open-eyed at the sky. Within the bailey, amid a litter of shredded parchment, the master scribe who had taught a lonely boy to write pleaded on his knees for mercy. Yet the Dark-dreamer saw into the victim's mind and there encountered memories of Ivainson Jaric. Maelgrim spat in the dust, and the ascending whistle of Gierj-demons rang across the valley where corpses rotted in the sun. Parchments ignited into flame, and Jaric's scream blended with that of the archivist at Morbrith, who burned alive on a pyre fed by his own life's works.

"No!" But the images spun faster, slivering the soul of the Firelord's son to agony: Taen dead, spitted on the knife of her brother, *all because a recalcitrant boy refused the fate of his father!* Black hair clotted in a pool of scarlet where she fell. Her death brought an end to the powers of the Vaere-trained, and the demons advanced unhindered.

The eastern kingdoms of Felwaithe and Kisburn did battle and failed, proud cities razed one by one to rubble while the countryside smoked with the burned-out shells of farmsteads. The wizards of Mhored Kara came singing to the field and perished, slaughtered beside their familiars without any bard to commemorate their passing. The images continued, relentless. Gierj-demons sang in another place, and fire swept across the thornbrakes of Cliffhaven. Bleeding, riddled with burns, the Kielmark howled curses as he and his men roasted like slaughtered animals. On the north-shore cliffs, dirtied tons of ice softened and slithered seaward with a roar like a spring avalanche. Bloodthirsty whistles echoed over the roar of flames. When the heat subsided, the frostwargs scuttled to freedom, and their segmented legs scattered the bones of the Stormwarden of Elrinfaer who had once confined them. Roused, murderous, crazed to insatiable frenzy, the creatures rampaged across the straits. No Firelord stood forth to curb them.

Broken at last by grief, Jaric wept. Yet the images knifed through his tears with terrible clarity. Landfast became desecrated by demons. Priests died, disemboweled, and the knowledge preserved by Keithland's first, star-faring generations was torn from broken towers. Forever ignorant of their heritage, the townsmen trapped in the streets suffered diabolical torment as the Dark-dreamer culled the weak from the strong. Demons bred the survivors for slavery.

Jaric's tears became the salt-wet tumble of storm waves. Crouched in despair over *Callinde*'s rail, he cast the Keys to Elrinfaer into the sea, that Kor's Accursed might never recover them. Yet atrocity did not end. Maelgrim Dark-dreamer and his pack of Thienz chased down their final quarry, the heir of Ivain Firelord whose latent masteries held Keithland's last chance of recovery. Winded and beaten after a long, hopeless flight through the wilds, Jaric stumbled to his knees against the granite cliffs of Northsea. His captors closed in, Emien among them, his eyes bereft of all trace of humanity. Jaric gasped air into burning lungs. At bay and cornered, he stared at the sword blade which quivered in triumph at his throat.

"You showed mercy and granted me life, once," said the brother whose hand had murdered Taen. "I survived to know my true masters. Shall I offer you the same courtesy? The Keys to Elrinfaer are lost, but your talents might yet unbind the Mharg."

Jaric tensed, his final, desperate act an attempt to throw himself on his enemy's blade. But the Dark-dreamer engaged his mastery and slapped him aside unharmed. Captured alive, and bound by the Thienz, *Ivainson saw himself delivered to Shadowfane.*

"No!" His protest echoed off walls of windowless stone. Demons came. They slashed Jaric's flesh with a knife, and poured the dissolved crystals of the living Sathid into his wound. Shackled by demon malice, Jaric experienced the first unbearable torment of the Cycle of Fire; *if he survived, Kor's Accursed intended to command his powers. Their will would become his own, and he himself would betray Anskiere's trust, break the wards over Elrinfaer Tower, and release the horrors within.*

"*No!*" Jaric howled in the throes of insufferable anguish. Flame consumed his limbs. The blackened flesh of his hands peeled from splayed bones. "*No!*" Tendons popped and sizzled, and sparks shot through the eye sockets of his skull. "*No!*" Riven by madness, the son of Ivain would raise fire and sear the last human life from Keithland. "*No, no, no!*"

"Jaric!" Taen's voice echoed through a roar of flame. *Taen Dreamweaver, who died bleeding on the dagger of her brother.*

"No, Jaric, will you listen?" A girl's cold fingers reached through curtains of fire and grasped his shoulder. Charred muscles burst under her touch. Jaric screamed in mortal agony.

"Ivainson Jaric, *wake up!*" The fingers tightened, shook his body with desperate violence.

Jaric moaned and opened his eyes to the gray folds of a Llondian cloak. He flinched and started back, but small hands caught him close. Taen's face loomed over him, backed by sky and the sun-dappled leaves of a forest.

"Jaric?" With a tenderness that tore him to the heart, the Dreamweaver smoothed the damp hair from his brow.

Tatters of nightmare fled, but waking thought could not disperse their memory. Jaric drew breath into a throat stung raw from screaming. Shattered, shivering, he clung to her, afraid to close his eyes; afraid if he lost sight of her for an instant, he might drown in the morass of despair inflicted by Llondelei far-seers.

"Kor's grace," said Taen unsteadily. "That was bad." She endured the grip of his hands, though his fingers gouged into her back. Patient, and near to crying herself, she numbed the worst of his anguish until equilibrium could return.

Jaric steadied under her touch. His quivering gradually subsided, and he loosened his locked muscles with an effort that was visible. Pressed against Taen's side, he twisted at last and examined his fingers. The skin was tanned and healthy, unmarked by any trace of burns. With a final shiver, he said, "You know what they tried to tell me."

Taen met his eyes. Now she could not prevent the tears which coursed down her cheeks. She said nothing. But Jaric knew that through his dream, the Llondelei had permitted her to discover the fate which awaited her brother.

Tortured by her steadiness, Jaric lowered his gaze. "Kor! I *can't* try the Cycle of Fire, do you understand?" He rammed his fist into the chilly dampness of last season's leaves, and watched a spider scurry in panic across his knuckles.

"I understand what will happen if you won't," said Taen in a voice kept painfully calm.

Jaric rolled away from her and wrapped his arms around his knees. He would not ask if she knew of the attack upon Corley; not immediately. "Where are the Llondelei?"

"Gone." The cloak borrowed from the demons rustled as Taen shifted position. She did not touch him. "Once the Sathid finished crystallizing, I was free to leave. They released you in the forest a short time later. I used my dreamsense to find where."

But her words became background to echoes of the nightmares wrought by Llondelei. Their meddling in Jaric's mind had offered warning. Dared he proceed without heeding? Eight hunters from Shadowfane lay dead, but their kindred at Shadowfane would already have sensed their fate. More attacks would follow; if demons overtook *Moonless* in force, Corley's crewmen would be no match for them. Aware through deep disquiet that the Dreamweaver had stopped speaking, Jaric hid his face in his hands. His words emerged muffled. "You're well, then?"

Taen reached out and tugged his wrist until he surrendered. With a smile so genuine it caught the breath in his throat, she placed a small amber stone in his palm and closed his fingers over it. "There. You hold the foundation of my power as Dreamweaver. Tamlin has urged that I hide it, lest demons use it against me. Why must you believe the legacy of the Vaere-trained is an intolerable burden?"

Jaric sighed. His emotions felt threshed over and over until only the husk of feeling remained. Yet his expression softened slightly as he gathered the girl close. "If anyone on Keithland could convince me, little witch, you would be the one." He paused then, too lacerated to hide the fear which tangled his inner self. The Llondelei had shown him horrors. Terrorized by another possibility, that Keithland might also fall to ruin because he embraced the Cycle of Fire only to repeat the madness that had made Ivain devastate Elrinfaer, Jaric fixed on the last place his quest had left unsearched. "I have one more plan left to try."

He returned the crystal to Taen's hand. Then, looking down into her trusting blue eyes, he found himself caught by an irrational rush of desire. Flushed to the roots of his hair, Jaric resisted an urge to kiss her. "Will you help?"

The words came queerly strangled from his throat. Aware of his discomfort, but not the turmoil which prompted it, Taen replied with a brave attempt at humor. "Help do what, you fish-brained scribe?"

"I need to subvert the priests and break into the sanctuary towers of Landfast," said Jaric. Driven in his need to escape destiny, the idea firmed, a shelter against a future too terrible to contemplate. If a defense against demons existed, it surely must lie within the heritage of the first men of Keithland; records might still survive from the ship, *Corinne Dane*. But to break the security of the priests was treason of the first order, a direct violation of the Landfast Charter. Smudged with dirt, with his shirt torn and small sticks hooked in his hair, Jaric braced his shoulders in anticipation of rebuke.

Taen grinned. Then the incongruity between his request and his appearance broke her control; she burst into peals of laughter. Jaric's brown eyes widened with hurt. Before he could retreat, she sobered and caught his callused hand. "I can do better than that. If you want, I can pick secrets from the mind of the Supreme High Star himself. But first I think we should get back to *Moonless*. If we delay much longer, a certain captain I know will be whetting his knives down to needles."

Sensitive to the signs that weakness lingered yet from the Dreamweaver's harrowing illness, Jaric controlled his impatience to be far from the burrows of the Llondelei; he matched his pace to Taen's as they hiked through the breezeless summer morning. Noon came and went. By afternoon, the pair reached the forest's edge, where they rested. Withdrawn and broodingly silent, Jaric stared across open meadows. The broken towers of Tierl Enneth lay etched against the skyline beyond, blue with haze, but eloquent with still-remembered tragedy.

Braced against a tree trunk, Taen Dreamweaver plucked a tassel of pine needles from her collar. The intensity of Jaric's stillness disturbed her. "You're very quiet."

The boy shrugged. Distressed by his reluctance to answer, Taen sounded his mood with her talents. Jaric felt her touch. He jerked back, tensed as if to move on; and balked by his restlessness, the Dreamweaver could discern nothing of the reason for his worry.

She spoke of ordinary things to disarm him. "The Llondelei didn't keep your weapons." Attuned even to particulars, she shrugged her cloak from her shoulders and qualified. "Corley carried your sword and dagger safely back to *Moonless*. I contacted him to be sure."

Yet mention of the captain seemed only to intensify Jaric's silence. "He knows you're safe? Then he'll want you back on board as soon as possible."

Taen frowned, now certain that the stresses implanted by Llondelei dreams absorbed Ivain's heir still. A glint of pure mischief lit her eyes. "You can't fret all the time. I won't let you." Without warning she launched herself at him, piling shoulder first into the hardened muscles of his middle.

Caught unprepared, Jaric gasped. He overbalanced, fell rolling into soft grass with Taen clutched in his arms. Her hair tangled in his shirt laces, then scattered across his face, fragrant with the herbs used to sweeten her bath. Wakened to the fact that the touch of her was pleasing, Jaric ceased struggling and lay back with her warm weight sprawled across his chest.

Taen spoke, her words muffled by the cloth of his sleeve. "Do you mind if we take a nap first?"

At a loss to answer, Jaric swallowed. Her nearness disoriented him. He could feel the pound of his heart against her cheek, and the pressure of her hip against his groin stirred his blood with desire. Abruptly he tried to pull away.

"Don't, Jaric." Taen shifted and caught his ears between her fingers. "You're not a scrawny apprentice anymore. And if I were a serving wench from Morbrith, I'd treat you differently than you remember." With an impish grin, she released him and began to tickle his ribs.

Jaric broke into laughter. Yet his mirth caught in his throat,

transformed to a wrenching sob of despair. Llondelei warnings
had cornered him, unveiled a painful sequence of destiny no
sane man could tolerate. Aware how sorely he needed release,
but not that he feared for her safety, Taen applied her mastery
and deftly overturned his control. Immediate tears flooded his
face. With the last of his pride, Jaric twisted his face into the
grass and wept.

Taen curled next to him, her arm across his shaking
shoulders. She said nothing, offering only the comfort of her
presence. But when he finally steadied, his expression no
longer seemed a mask of agonized endurance. Though the
grief instilled by the Llondelei visions had not left him, now
he observed the summer meadow with calm; the strength and
the life in his limbs could be appreciated without shrinking in
horror of tomorrow.

"You cheat like the daughter of a Landfast merchant," Jaric
accused the Dreamweaver at last. Yet he spoke without rancor.

"Daughters of Landfast merchants don't roll in the hay
with vagabonds." Taen climbed to her feet and shook grass
seeds from her fallen cloak. "Are you going to spend the rest
of the day on the ground with the ants?"

"I should." Jaric grinned and rose also. "The worst they
ever do is pinch."

He caught Taen and pulled her into his embrace. Then, too
embarrassed to express himself, he opened his hands and
whirled abruptly eastward toward Tierl Enneth. Taen fell into
step at his heels. Reassured that the quality of Jaric's mood
had changed, she did not badger him from silence.

Except for occasional gullies, the terrain offered easy
walking. Still, sundown spilled shadow across the hills by the
time Dreamweaver and Firelord's heir reached the site where
the clans had celebrated summerfair. The painted wagons had
departed, leaving torn earth and the dried mounds of horse
droppings. Jaric and Taen trod a flattened expanse of grass
where dancers had celebrated solstice. But the desolation of
the place now was total, with the tenantless dwellings of Tierl
Enneth brooding black against amber in the afterglow.

The pair hastened their pace. They entered the wall through
the damp mouth of the arch, Taen wrapped in the Llondian
cloak, and Jaric shivering in his torn tunic. Dusk deepened
over streets and towers; in time their legacy of bones became
veiled kindly in darkness. Taens grew weary. Jaric caught her
stumbling; he supported her lagging steps, then carried her

outright. This once her physical nearness did not move him. Now more than ever before he had no wish to linger amid ruins whose sole testimony was a sorcerer's failure to protect.

At last Jaric heard the rhythmic wash of breakers ahead. The lane he traversed widened and joined the avenue which led to the sea gate. The harbor glistened silver in starlight beyond the gapped span of the arch. Blackly outlined against sandy shore, a boat waited with four oarsmen lounging by the thwarts.

A man's voice called from the breakwater. "Jaric? The Dreamweaver warned me of your arrival." Corley leaped the wall and extended brawny arms toward Taen. His left hand was poulticed, and on his wrists the scars of old battles were scribed across with fresh scabs. Overset by remembrance of what might have resulted had the clansmen not interceded, Jaric lost all inclination to speak.

As he surrendered the Dreamweaver to the captain's care, Corley added, "I saved your sword and dagger, boy, but, Kor! I'll flay you with the dullest knife on *Moonless* if you ever again give up weapons without a fight."

The tapers burned low in Shadowfane's great hall in the early hours before dawn. Shadows crawled grotesquely over the skulls used as end caps on the posts of Scait's tall throne, but the Demon Lord did not sit. He paced, the click of his spurs upon stone an uninterrupted rhythm since the news which had drawn him from council. Back and forth he passed across the dais; no underling dared to approach. Finally he flicked a thought-query at the Thienz who knelt with snout pressed to forelimbs at the foot of the stair by the mirror pool.

'What passes in Keithland, one-who cowers-beneath-my-feet? The report from your underlings at Tierl Enneth is carelessly overdue.'

The Thienz raised features gone yellow and creased with age. Too experienced to be cowed by its overlord's irritable insult, it whuffed air through its gill flaps and chose words. "Lord-mightiest, I offer news of a mishap."

Scait stopped poised between steps. The long hackles at his neck ruffled aggressively, a warning noticed at once by those favored advisors gathered across the hall. They stopped murmuring and lifted their eyes from the wax model of Landfast which had preoccupied them through the night.

"Speak," commanded the Sovereign Lord of Shadowfane.

A neat movement spun him round, and he sat very stiffly on his cushions.

The Thienz repeated its bow, then rose on ridiculous feet. It offered image to explain. Scait received with narrowed eyes; sharing the view of a woodland dell in the highlands of Tierl Enneth. Between innocuous thickets of greenery lay the dismembered remains of eight Thienz sent to apprehend Jaric. Insects had hollowed the bodies; bones showed white through shriveled flesh, but decay did not affect the feathered tokens staked through the victims' torsos.

"Clansmen," hissed Lord Scait. His hackles bristled in displeasure, and his spurs scraped reflexively over the skulls. "How did this happen?"

The Thienz sang a mournful note. "Treacherous are the tribes of Tierl Enneth, Great-Lord. Their seeress sees much we wish would stay hidden. They dissipated the death-dreams of the fallen; most-unforgivably, little memory survives."

Scait's body stilled. At his silence, the boldest of the favorites abandoned her fellows and joined the Thienz by the dais. "Lord," she intoned. "If Taen and Jaric sought the burrow of the Llondelei on Tierl Enneth, what-chance the Dreamweaver survived?"

Scait's eyes flicked up. He bared teeth to silence the nattering of his underling, for her noise added nothing. Why the Llondelei should support humans was not fathomable; but that they might have chosen to spare Taen Dreamweaver from Sathid death must not be lightly dismissed. In the deep, chill hour before dawn, Scait weighed options. His next move must be planned with boldness, or mankind might gain another Vaere-trained sorcerer as ally. The boy Ivainson Jaric must be apprehended without thought for losses.

"Here is my command," said Scait. The favorites straightened to hear, and the Thienz swiveled small, half-sightless eyes toward the throne. "Send forth underlings to steal boats from human fishermen. The victims must be carefully chosen, isolated from their families and far from any harbor, for the rulers of Keithland must not be made to suspect." Here Scait paused and narrowed his focus upon the Thienz. "These boats you will load with a venomed elder, and those of your kind who have least seniority. They shall sail south into Keithland at the earliest opportunity."

The Thienz rocked in keenest anticipation. Though the

young who were appointed would receive such orders with trepidation, that Taen-Dreamweaver-who-killed-brothers-at-Cliffhaven might be found and ripped apart was cause for joyful sacrifice.

Yet even as the Thienz rocked in anticipation, Scait sensed the cause of its jubilation. He sprang from his throne, crossed the dais in two steps, and descended the stair beyond at a bound. "You will *not* set the hunt after Taen Dreamweaver."

"Lord!" objected the Thienz, then abruptly smothered its protest as the spurred thumb of its overlord flicked out and pricked its neck.

"The boats will seek the Isle of the Vaere." Gently, cruelly, the Lord of Shadowfane bore down. Blood beaded around his spur, and the Thienz twitched, even as it received its instructions. "At all costs your siblings must find and kill Ivainson Jaric before he finds his way there."

Pinned and helpless, the Thienz repressed an ingrained reflex cower. "Mightiest-high-one, your will shall speedily be done. But if the Dreamweaver has recovered her powers, she will cloak the prey from our sight. What means shall locate the one-you-desire-killed?"

Scait withdrew his spur and delicately licked the point.

Since the slightest taste of blood could stimulate the insatiable appetite of his kind, the Thienz scuttled in terror from underfoot. But the Great Lord's feeding instinct remained quiescent as he turned lambent eyes to his favorites. One or two waited with short hackles raised, as if they questioned his judgment concerning Taen; perhaps their hidden thoughts contemplated something more grave than disapproval. In the annals of the compact, combat had been called against rulers with less provocation than this.

But Scait dismissed such threat and turned his back, challenging belligerence with contempt. "The girl is nothing at this time but distraction. Dally for her now, and we risk facing a trained Firelord."

One among the favorites dared a small sound of dissent.

Scait whirled, deadly and graceful and utterly sure of his dominance. "Against Taen Dreamweaver, we have her brother. Had you forgotten? His powers will begin to stabilize within the next few days. Then shall a ruse be framed to snare the sister." The Sovereign Lord of the demons slashed the air with his spurs, and the long hackles at his neck bristled fully erect. "This is my plan. Who among you dares disapprove?"

Dawn spilled gray through the high windows of Shadow-fane's great hall. In its light, the tapers smoked and guttered, while with manes smoothed in agreement, the sycophantic circle of demons all bowed to the will of their overlord.

ᕦᕤ XIII ᕦᕤ

Maelgrim

After rest and food and an accounting of events in the Llonde-lei burrow, Corley put away his whetstone and sheathed the impeccable steel of his knives. To the relief of his crew, he ceased to pace the quarterdeck through the night and the day while Taen recovered from the exhaustion of her ordeal. Still, watches were kept with strict regularity, and a scout network continued to quarter the shoreline for Thienz-sign. Since they discovered nothing more threatening than a fishing boat abandoned in a thorn thicket, *Moonless* remained at anchor off Tierl Enneth.

But Jaric's restlessness would not abate. More silent than usual, he avoided company, and even Taen had difficulty drawing him out.

"Sulk in peace, then," she retorted in exasperation when for the second time in an hour the boy retreated into the chart room. After that the Dreamweaver resorted to card games to fill her time. The sailhands resurrected their stakes from knotted stockings and sea chests. More than a few groused that dampness had transformed their former winnings to sprouts. For a time, the cook found it necessary to forestall looters by barricading the bean stores in the galley. Loud-voiced, boastful, and vociferously protective of the Dreamweaver who teased them to laughter, the off-watch crew aboard *Moonless* settled comfortably back to routine. Corley reviewed reports from his scouts between stints of cursing the healer. When the persistent, meddling fool finally stopped worrying at his scabs, the captain channeled his own excess energy into resuming Jaric's education at arms.

Corley then drove his charge relentlessly to assess the effects of Brith's teaching. He found Jaric's attitude changed in more than technique. Where once the boy had handled his blades with a tentative, even fussy finesse, he now struck out boldly. Gratified by the belling clang of solid blocks and parries, Corley grinned, then pushed the boy harder. But now the captain added occasional words of praise between epithets. That teacher and pupil both used the practice to vent their internal frustrations did not matter; in a short time, the Firelord's heir would be capable of defending himself with a fair degree of skill.

By the seventh day, Taen had recovered equilibrium enough to resume command of her Sathid-born powers. Jaric endured his morning sword drill with evident impatience; the instant Corley excused him, he hastened below decks and tossed his sword on his berth without pausing to oil the blade. At last, Taen could turn her talents to dream-search the secret knowledge of the priests who lived in seclusion at Landfast. Pitched to feverish anxiety, Jaric hurried to the Dreamweaver's cabin, only to find her absent.

The captain's steward reassured him. "Taen said you'd ask for her. You'll find her waiting in the chart room."

Jaric voiced a breathless thanks. His steps slowed as he made his way aft and stepped through the chart room door. The lantern swung gently over a table cleared of maps. Taen sat with closed eyes, her breathing gentled in the peaceful rhythm of sleep. Jaric saw with trepidation that she had already focused her dream-sense and begun the tedious search; for amid Landfast's populace, few minds held knowledge of the mysteries guarded by Kor's Brotherhood.

Jaric eased the door closed. Too restless to sit, he paced, his head bent to accommodate the low ceiling. Nerves and the stifling heat thrown off by the lamp made him sweat. The sanctuary towers had been sealed by the founders of the Landfast Council; to break their edict consitituted treason. Yet should demons conquer the Alliance, that same knowledge would be threatened. The heritage and purpose of Keithland's forebears might surely be lost. Burdened by the horrors of Llondian prophecy, Jaric crossed and recrossed the space between table and chart locker. Only one fact mattered: if the sanctuary towers failed to yield answers, all that lay between Keithland's continuance and mankind's survival was himself, and the Cycle of Fire.

Hours passed. The lamp burned low and finally flickered out. Smoke spindled up from its spent wick. Jaric struck a spark to a candle he found in a locker, then sat and busied himself with oil flask and wicking string. With the meticulous care learned under a forester's guidance, he cleaned the lantern and set the flame burning once more. A golden circle of light illuminated the cabin. Across the breadth of the chart table, Taen lay motionless in trance. Her hair spilled over her wrists, ink-black against pale skin. The curve of her cheek lay tilted toward Jaric; if her lashes and brows seemed delicate as a master artist's brushstroke, any image of perfection was marred by the broken thumbnail which peeped beneath her chin. Devoid of jewel or artifice, clad in a shift of plainest linen, the girl owned all the spare beauty of a wild creature of the wood. Jaric felt his breath catch.

He set aside the knife he had used to pare wicks. As if the smallest disruption might break the spell and rouse her, he clamped his oil-streaked fingers in his cuffs. Earlier he had been unable to keep still; now, if an enemy burst in and challenged him with a naked blade, he would have found it impossible to move. Blood rushed through his veins. His skin went hot, then cold, and he swallowed painfully. This girl had been all things to him: betrayer, confidante, a friend who had badgered him until he laughed, and a kindred spirit who had eased him through times of anguish; but suddenly, in the undefined space between one breath and the next, this same girl became the one treasure in all Keithland that he could not bear to lose.

Jaric regarded Taen with a hunger he never knew he possessed. The lamp burned lower by his elbow. Memories of the matronly ridicule he had suffered at Morbrith faded until, almost, Jaric imagined he could touch this woman and receive her welcome. *Moonless* swung against her anchor line, disturbed by a breath of wind. Draft from the hatchway tumbled a strand of hair across the pink curve of Taen's lips. She stirred, her brows pinched into a frown. The same breeze eddied across Jaric's sweating skin. He shivered and abruptly recalled his fate. Between himself and the girl across the table lay futures too terrible to contemplate: the bloodied knife of the brother who would kill her, or the madness of the Cycle of Fire. And if he hesitated in his choice, if he delayed one day or one hour too long, Thienz might destroy them both.

Jaric shoved violently to his feet. He stifled a raw cry and braced his fists against the bulkhead. No alternative offered relief. Of the countless cruelties Ivain had inflicted upon Keithland in his madness, his mistreatment of women was least forgivable. Jaric understood that to complete his father's heritage, he must first sacrifice his feelings for Taen. On this,

his self-control wavered dangerously. If the search of the sanctuary towers failed him, he wondered whether he would have strength enough to leave her, as he must, since the presence of the Firelord's heir would inevitably draw enemies. Jaric stared down at his hands. He dared not look toward the chart table. If he did, even once, the sight of the girl would break him.

No hand moved to trim the lantern wick. At length the flame trembled, thinned to red, and sparked out. Taen sighed in the darkness. Warned by a rustle of cloth, Jaric knew she awakened. He waited with taut muscles, yet failed to hear her step. The first he knew of her presence was a feather-light touch on his shoulder.

"Jaric?"

He whirled, backed against the unyielding frame of the bulkhead.

She could not read his face in the darkness. "Jaric? What's wrong?"

Ivain's heir fought his voice level. "You surprised me."

Blind himself in the shadow, he heard her sandal scrape the deck. Then the striker snapped. Haloed in the light of new flame, Taen closed the glass shutter and stretched on tiptoe and hung the lamp from the hook above the chart table.

She faced him then, and he saw her eyes were full of tears. "I didn't find what you need."

Pained by her anguish, Jaric took a moment to understand the import of her statement.

"The minds of the priests in seclusion are beyond my reach," Taen resumed. "I cannot tell why. Perhaps the stone of sanctuary itself forms a defensive barrier." She hesitated, and the disappointment she felt on his behalf cut Jaric to the quick. "I turned from the towers, and tried the mind of the Supreme High Star, whose sacred title is Guardian of the Gates. He alone knows what secrets the tower protects. Jaric, you'll find no help against demons at Landfast."

Safe beyond range of her touch, the boy lifted brown eyes to her face. "Tell me why."

Taen answered reluctantly. "The sanctuary towers contain keys to Kor's Sacred Fires, also answers to the riddles of eternal space and time. But by divine decree, that knowledge must be withheld from man until all demons are vanquished from Keithland."

Jaric closed his eyes. Sweat on his skin caught the lamplight like gilt, and his chest heaved as if he had been running.

Taen had phrased her findings in religious terms, but through Llondian memory, Jaric perceived more. Almost certainly Landfast preserved plans to the engine *Corinne Dane,* heritage of mankind's origin among the stars. How many would be slaughtered if demons knew such knowledge still existed? Even now the anguished words of the starprobe's long-dead captain echoed in Ivainson's thoughts. *"If* Corinne Dane's *mission fails, if mankind doesn't discover a defense against powers such as your Llondelei possess, the only human survivors left in creation will be those colonies enslaved by the Gierj."*

Corinne Dane had flown, and crashed like a stricken bird on hostile soil. Jaric swallowed, dangerously near to weeping. His last hope had failed, left him lightless in the shadows of his weakness. In a moment of gritty honesty he admitted he had built dreams only to delay, for since his interview with the Grand High Star at Landfast the truth had been apparent. Had a weapon against demons existed, *Corinne Dane's* band of castaways would never have formed the Landfast Council, nor drawn up their charter of secrecy; they would have rebuilt their broken ship and brought rescue to their beleaguered civilization among the stars. Instead, for a span of centuries, Keithland's people had struggled for survival, precariously defended by the talents of Vaere-trained sorcerers. Jaric drew a shuddering breath. Safe haven no longer existed. If he asked passage to the Isle of the Vaere, or fled from *Moonless* to spare Taen from the Thienz who tracked him, already he might be too late. Racked by indecision, Ivainson Jaric opened his eyes.

The lantern flame wavered, recently brushed by a draft. The chart room stood empty. Attuned to the depth of his distress, Taen had possessed the wisdom and the tact to leave him in solitude.

Corley ordered *Moonless* under way at the turn of the tide. The clank of the capstan and the rattle of chain through the hawse reverberated the length and beam of the brigantine, yet Taen barely noticed the din. Weary from her dream-search of Landfast, she sat on her berth in the darkness, her heels tapping restlessly against the wooden locker beneath. She needed no Dreamweaver's talents to sense Jaric's apprehension of the Cycle of Fire. Distressed that she could not console him, and afraid if she sought counsel from the Vaere that Tamlin would command her to intervene and force Jaric to accept his father's heritage, she longed for the wise comfort of Anskiere of Elrinfaer.

Moonless shuddered as her anchor ripped free of the seabed. The rhythm of the capstan's pawls quickened, and feet thumped on the decking overhead as sailhands rushed to man sheets and braces. "Steady as she goes!" yelled Corley from the quarterdeck. The brigantine lifted into a heel as yards of unbrailed canvas caught the wind. Taen settled with her back against the bulkhead. She did not weep. Though emotions knotted the core of her being, she was the daughter of an Imrill Kand fisherman, born to hardship and loss. She had learned early to temper misery with practicality. If Jaric refused the Cycle of Fire, not even the Vaere could change his mind. To wish for the guidance of an absent sorcerer would not cure the problem; and the effort of the morning left her drained. Aching, and unsettled by problems too great for her powers to encompass, she rested her head against the bulkhead.

Light sleep claimed her unawares. The security set about the sanctuary towers at Landfast had been complex, taxing in the extreme to unravel; concern for Jaric had driven her to an imprudent outlay of energy. Now, drifting directionless in dreams, Taen failed to safeguard all her channels. A compulsion crept in, not her own, but threaded through her thoughts with a tact that could only come from one who had known and loved her. Slowly, subtly, the intrusive presence blended with the essence of her will; and presently subtle prompts became conviction.

Since the demons' strike against Keithland involved the brother they held captive, Taen saw clearly where duty lay. In the past, she had failed to save her brother from the guilt-ridden misery which had pressured him to forsake his own kind. Now the only option left was to prevent him from becoming a weapon against humanity. She must engage her mastery, contact Emien in the heart of Shadowfane, and attempt to break him free of the demons' influence.

Spray sheeted across *Moonless*'s stern as she rounded the headlands of Tierl Enneth and jibed for the open sea. Jounced against the bulkhead as the spanker boom slammed onto starboard tack, Taen centered her awareness. She did not feel the draft which spilled through the grate, nor did she smell the sea breeze, spiked with the scent of impending rain. Never did she imagine that her intent had been molded by enemies who shaped a snare. Unwary, and drawn by love, her dream-sense carried her awareness across the wild barrens beyond the borders of Keithland.

Gusts whined across the stone spires of Shadowfane; echoes like the keening of grief-stricken women penetrated even the depths of the dungeon where Taen found Emien. The man she recongized as her brother crouched in darkness within the barred confines of a cell. His face was hidden behind scarred fingers while a Sathid matrix cross-linked to demon masters deepened its grip upon his mind. Careful not to disrupt his equilibrium, Taen extended her dream-sense and tentatively encompassed his thoughts.

At once, she knew nightmares. Prompted by the crystal's guidance, Emien relived events from his past as vividly as the day they occurred. Taen merged with his consciousness as fluidly as water flowing into a pool. Through her brother's dreams she observed a storm-lashed vista of ocean. Wind screamed, blasting the wave crests into spray, while the sibling she remembered clung with wet hands to the gunwale of a pinnace. Numbly he watched the galleass he had abandoned founder among the swells. Though the vessel was half-veiled in sprindrift, Taen recognized King Kisburn's flagship, *Crow,* which had borne the Stormwarden in chains from Imrill Kand. She, a girl of ten, had stowed away to free him. Emien had boarded later, with a vow to bring his sister safely home; instead he had lost her.

Now the demon-controlled Sathid he had inherited from his mistress compelled remembrance. Battered by storm winds of Anskiere's making, Emien watched the galleass settle beneath the waves. The Dreamweaver who shared his memory felt the grief and sick anger which thwarted him from tears; for the boy believed his younger sister was still trapped in the galleass' hold. The blame for her death was entirely his. Wretched with loss, he knew guilt; *the familiar, terrible guilt he had suffered when his father drowned in the net his own carelessness had entangled.* Mourning could not absolve him; crushed beneath an overwhelming weight of responsibility, Emien sought release in vicious anger against the Stormwarden who had lured his sister into danger.

Taen saw her chance, but lost any opening to act.

The demon-controlled Sathid which supplanted her brother's will arose like a cyclone of force. It splintered

Emien's spirit like a hammerblow. The self-inflicted anguish of a sister's death became multiplied tenfold, twentyfold, twenty hundredfold, until agony became the sum of his existence. Taen lost her grip. The torment which harrowed her brother sucked her deep into the recesses of his mind, and through his mouth she screamed and screamed again. Emien's cell rang with echoes while slowly, painstakingly, Taen recovered a semblance of control.

But for the brother entrapped at Shadowfane, the agony continued. Tortured beyond reason by despair, he sought oblivion. Power blocked his desire. Demon voices addressed him through the Sathid link which bound his conscious will.

'As Emien, you suffer needless loyalty for a sister who later betrayed you. As Maelgrim-demon-honored, you can spare yourself. Would you choose to renounce this memory?'

Thrashing in unbearable anguish, Emien whispered hoarsely. "Yes. Set me free."

'So be it. Become Maelgrim.' A sigh like wind passed across the link. Bound to the consciousness of her brother, Taen perceived a series of sparkling flashes. Storm-tossed ocean frothed beneath the pinnace's keel; exactly as before, Emien regarded the foundering pinnace. Only the remorse he once had felt for his lost sister was gone. Now the anger and hatred for Anskiere remained, resonating through Maelgrim's awareness like the tireless toll of fog bells.

Prompted by the Sathid, the boy dreamed on, of the whitehaired witch whose incomparable beauty had captured his loyalty. He noticed no eddy as the sister who shared his vision drew back from his mind. Horrified by the demon's meddling, and utterly careless of risk, Taen delved into her brother's memories with every shred of her skill. There she found that the sibling she had known and loved during childhood had changed beyond recognition. Where Emien should have recalled his mother and his home on Imrill Kand, his sister found gaps braced by bitterness, resentment, and malice; his inborn humanity was shattered nearly past hope of mending. In time, Taen saw that all compassion would perish, leaving a demon abomination named Maelgrim.

That transformation must not happen undisputed. Roused to outrage and fury, the Dreamweaver focused her will. As her brother cried out under a fresh onslaught of torment, she raised a veil of resistance across his mind to block the demon's designs.

For an instant Emien's screams ceased. Sharing his moment of reprieve, Taen knew the drafty damp of a cell where a lost, beloved voice cried out. "Sister?"

Then with the subtlety of a chess gambit, Shadowfane's minions narrowed their trap. Power arose, a storm song of force terrible as the wail of the damned. Slammed by a barrier of limitless dark, Taen mustered resistance; the vigor of her own Sathid link answered the demons' challenge. Her offense struck their barricade with a tortured flash of sparks. Forces thundered and spun like a cataclysm unleashed. The restraints set upon her by demons shivered, thinned, and finally tore asunder. Taen blazed through the gap, prepared to defend Emien's mind.

But the ravaged entity which remained of the brother she had loved did not stand in her support on the other side. *The entire sequence had been a ruse, designed and intended to imprison her.* Whirled haplessly into the destructive malice of Maelgrim, Taen felt herself seized and mangled by rage which understood no limit. Frantically she tried to withdraw. Her defense came too late. Demons controlled Maelgrim; and since their servant had been born her brother, his talent potentially matched her own. Even as Taen sensed the roused awareness of his matrix, demons assumed control. They urged the cross-linked Sathid to attack. Energies surged across the link and attempted to manipulate her own powers against her.

Taen bolted in terror. Should the enemy succeed in awakening her own Sathid's awareness, she would be crushed, her will extinguished as swiftly as a candle in a gale. The consequences of defeat stopped thought. Blind with panic, and still depleted from her session that morning with Jaric, Taen mustered her remaining resources into a flare of raw power. She strove, yet failed to snap the dream-link. Harried across distance by the malevolent entities of Shadowfane, Taen tried to quench her powers within the circle of her own awareness; surely no evil could challenge her within the security of her cabin on *Moonless*.

But the assumption proved false. The demons retained their hold. As Taen dissolved ties with her brother, enemies reversed the polarity of the link with a stinging lash of force; and for the space of a heartbeat, the Dreamweaver became Shadowfane's puppet. Through her consciousness, the enemy assimilated all, brigantine, crew, and captain. Taen experienced a savage flash of annoyance as the demons recognized

Corley; his machinations had cost them a victory at Cliffhaven, as well as the lives of eight Thienz on Tierl Enneth. Yet Shadowfane's minions did not pause to strike. Instead, voraciously hating, they discovered one they despised more, one they hunted because in time his talents might mature to threaten their designs: Ivain Firelord's heir sailed on board a brigantine whose destination was the Isle of the Vaere.

Taen screamed aloud. Unable to endure any threat to Jaric, she convulsed and ripped into the depths of her being. Lifeforce itself became tinder for her rage, and the conflagration raised a white flash of power. The result tore through the demons' hold, and she woke disoriented in darkness.

Panting in the dampness of her own sweat, blinded and choking on tears, Taen took several seconds to recognize her surroundings. *Moonless* reeled in the throes of a squall. Waves thudded against the brigantine's sides, shivering timbers and keel, and wind shrilled through tackle and rigging with the savagery of a witch shrieking curses. Ragged with exhaustion, amd tormented with self-reproach for the dangers brought on by her lapse of discipline, Taen pushed herself upright. That moment the companionway door banged open.

Deison Corley burst across the threshold. A lantern swung from his fist and his bronzed hair dripped rain. "Kor's grace, what's happened?"

"Demons." Taen fought to steady herself. "The compact at Shadowfane has taken over my brother. His powers are theirs, and through him I was lured into contact. Kor's Accursed attacked me across the link."

Corley swore; shadows spun crazily across the cabin as he raised the lantern to a hook set in the deck beams overhead. "List the damage. Quickly."

Taen drew a shaking breath. "The enemy knows *Moonless* is bound for the Isle of the Vaere."

"Destinations can be changed," snapped the captain. "What else?"

"Jaric," Taen began. As Corley surged forward in alarm, she backed her voice with a Dreamweaver's compulsion. "No! Things aren't that desperate! The demons have no knowledge of Jaric, except what they could sort from my brother's memories." Taen qualified with an image drawn from the past, and Corley shared the immediate impression of a frightened, diffident boy, flattened at swordpoint against a thorny tangle of brush; so had Jaric appeared to Emien upon the shores of

Elrinfaer at the moment the Keys were won. Taen's meaning was poignantly clear; without the support of a Dreamweaver's mastery on that day, Ivain Firelord's heir could never have completed the Stormwarden's bidding.

"Jaric's changed a great deal since then," Corley conceded. "But you know that's stinking little protection. Won't count a dog's damn against the might of Shadowfane. The boy must be warned."

He snatched down his lantern and moved to go; and Taen's perception caught the concern which filled the captain's mind. When Corley had entered the chart room to plot his course, Jaric had learned *Moonless* would sail for the Isle of the Vaere. A brief but stormy confrontation had resulted; reflexively, Taen reached out for Jaric's thoughts, her intent to measure the impact of the captain's insensitive rejoinders. The quality of the silence which met her all but stopped her heart.

"Wait!" Frantic with worry, Taen Dreamweaver leapt from her bunk. "Corley, wait, I'm coming with you."

She bolted through the companionway. Rain slashed her face, backed by a howling wind. Hard on Corley's heels, the girl struggled to climb the wet and heaving ladder. Even as she gained the quarterdeck, a shout from the officer on watch hailed the captain.

"Boy's gone overboard."

"Quartermaster, hard alee!" Corley bellowed. He thrust the lantern into the startled grasp of a sailor, then bolted for the rail. His brawny hands snatched up the line which secured *Callinde*. "Boatswain! Stand by to man the tackles!"

With a stupendous heave of muscles, Corley dragged the towrope in hand over hand. Coils flaked across the deck, and presently *Callinde*'s dark shape loomed through the squall. Gold against the white of the waves, a head broke the surface of the sea. Jaric shook the hair from his face and clung like a limpet to *Callinde*'s prow. Even as the Kielmark's captain sought to drag him back, Taen arrived, slight and soaked like an otter beside Corley's great bulk. She saw steel flash in Jaric's hand. The line sang, short and sharp, and splashed slack into the sea.

Corley dropped the severed rope and swore. With barely a break in motion, he threw off his sword belt and began to strip his person of weapons. He intended to swim for the boy, Taen saw.

She caught his elbow as the first of his knives clattered to the deck. "No! You must not follow him!"

Corley jerked free, a dagger in each hand and a murderous frown on his face. "Why not?"

The Dreamweaver raised her voice over the flapping din of canvas as the brigantine rounded to weather. "Jaric's pushed to the edge already, can't you see? And aboard *Callinde* he'll be safe if demons strike at *Moonless*."

Corley cursed, on the brink of diving overboard.

Taen shouted. "Not even the Stormwarden dared force Jaric to the Cycle of Fire! Would you break his mind trying?" And she braced herself to protect with her Vaere-trained powers as enchantress.

Rain slashed across wood and oilskin and the flogging yards of canvas overhead. Finally Corley jammed one knife, then the other, into the sheaths at his wrists. "Kor's eternal Fires, girl. If I could lay hands on that boy's hide, I'd flay him quick. Will he *ever* learn not to jump ship without his weapons?"

Shivering, her hair fallen wet around the delicate lines of her collarbone, Taen stared after the vanishing shape of *Callinde*. And shocked back to reason by the stricken expression on her face, Corley caught her close.

"Jaric's tough, you know that, girl. However hard he's pushed, I never yet saw him run." A gust caught the spanker even as he spoke, recalling Corley to his neglected command. Belatedly he remembered he must chart a new course for *Moonless*, away from the southerly heading Shadowfane's compact would expect him to hold for the Isle of the Vaere.

Taen sensed his thought. Suddenly she longed for the village of her birth, a harbor so remote that Anskiere himself had chosen the site as a refuge after the disaster which destroyed Tierl Enneth. Imrill Kand as a haven made sound sense. Warned and alert to her peril, she would never again let her defenses slip; and if demons did trace *Moonless*, a northwesterly course might provide a foil for Jaric and *Callinde*.

"Put me down," she demanded of Corley. "Then sail me home. Please. Put about and go east to Imrill Kand."

The captain regarded her with the level attention he usually granted to equals. "You're sure? Luck won't forgive if your judgment's sour, and to sail that course will be in defiance of the Kielmark's orders."

Taen tilted her head with a shaky ghost of a smile. "The

same tired argument? I thought we wore that one out on the night of your master's victory party." .

Corley sucked air through his teeth; irritation and laughter warred on his rain-drenched face as he released the Dreamweaver abruptly. "Don't ever count on that one, girl." After an interval trading glares, his humor finally won out. "The day I give over my command to a cheeky, wet snip of a girl, those dogs in the forecastle will be sewing my carcass into sailcloth. Now that fact's understood, will you go get dry? You've given *Moonless*'s healer and my steward enough gray hair without adding pneumonia to their troubles."

ᴄ~ᴏ XIV ᴄ~ᴏ

Hunted

Dawn broke between squalls. Sunrise peeped through the last, low-flying clouds and scattered an arching magnificence of rainbows, but Jaric regarded their loveliness with little joy. *Moonless* and Tierl Enneth had long since vanished over the horizon. Alone upon the sea, the boy huddled in *Callinde*'s stern with both hands clenched to the steering oar. West winds drove his boat on a broad reach. Once he cleared the archipelago beyond the point of Tierl Enneth, he would turn south to Landfast and every indulgence a port city could provide. Until then, during a fortnight-and-a-half passage through mild summer weather, Jaric had solitude and too much time to reflect. He sailed *Callinde* and tried desperately to keep thoughts of Taen from his mind.

The night fell calm and star-studded. Jaric hove his boat to and ate a meager meal from his stores. Rocked upon the face of the sea, he slept only to waken screaming in horror of the Cycle of Fire. Later he tried tending the steering oar from sunset to dawn; but fatigue inevitably betrayed him. Against his will his eyes closed, and nightmares caught him at the helm. *Callinde* bore off her course; time and again the rattling crash of jibed sails battered Jaric back to wakefulness. In despair he buried his face in his hands and wished for stormy weather. The present, changeless blue of water and sky reminded him endlessly of Taen's eyes.

Conditions remained fair, though the wind rounded to a southwest heading. Forced to tack, Jaric revised his course and beached on a wild spit of land west of Islamere. There he trapped game, foraged tubers for the food locker, and refilled his water casks. Since *Callinde* sailed poorly to weather, he camped four days until the winds blew easterly, then crossed the final leagues to Landfast under gathering sheets of cloud.

Lightning laced the sky and thunder crashed when at length he rounded the islet of Little Dagley. Torrents of rain dimmed the light beacons on the jetties to weak haloes. Worn to exhaustion, and harassed by the pound of the squall against the sails, Jaric threaded a cautious course between the anchored ships and mooring buoys which cluttered the inner bay. He rounded *Callinde* to windward and at last dropped sail by the harbormaster's shed.

A dock lackey in fresh-looking oilskins caught *Callinde*'s lines. Jaric jumped ashore. He failed to note that the servant eyed him with wariness. Drenched, bearded, and ungroomed after a three-and-a-half-week passage, the boy warped his boat to the bollards. Muscles bunched under his wet skin, and the scars left from recent sword cuts shone livid and red across the knuckles of his dagger hand. Preoccupied and weary, Jaric ducked past the lackey and barged through the doorway of the harbormaster's shed to negotiate dockage for *Callinde*.

The master on duty leaped to his feet so quickly the beribboned beret which displayed his badge of office slipped down across his eyes. "You again! Fires, and what could you want *this* time?" He straightened the hat, revealing a droopy mustache and an anxious frown.

Jaric stopped in his tracks. Water dripped from his tunic, spattering the swept boards of the floor. "I want dock space for a fishing boat ten spans in length."

He raised a hand to his belt. The official flinched, but the boy drew no weapon. Instead Jaric pulled forth a leather bag and spilled a flood of coins on the counting table. Silvers bounced, rolled, and clanged into stillness, while the man behind the table slowly turned pale.

"Well?" Jaric gestured impatiently. "Are you deaf and blind? I said I want—"

The official lifted a trembling hand. 'I *heard*. And I remember. You're master of *Callinde*?"

Jaric nodded.

"Kor!" The man dropped into his chair as if his legs had failed him. "Would you ruin me? That boat's marked in the Kielmark's registry. *No fee*. Do you hear?"

Jaric made no move to retrieve his coins. "I swore no fealty to Cliffhaven." But the anger in his tone made the ribbons in the man's hat quiver all the more.

The official swept the silvers into a heap and shoved them across the table with a rasping jangle. "Corley himself named you for the Kielmark's exemption. I won't be jeopardizing the trade of every guild in Landfast, knowing that. D'you think I

want to hang because I brought Cliffhaven's retribution, and
only a wharf fee to show for it? No. Get out. *Callinde* docks
free until I'm personally informed otherwise."

Jaric shifted his weight to depart. But the harbormaster
bolted from his chair and plucked at the young captain's sleeve
in sharp distress. "Boy, please. Don't be leaving any coin."

Jaric swore. "If honest silver bothers you, then give it to
the one-handed beggar with the tabby cat."

The official released him in dismay. "Which, the one who
got arrested for striking the guards' master of arms?"

Jaric jerked and stopped, hands knotted into fists; and the
harbormaster recoiled into the table, inciting a tinkle of coins.

"Arrested?" The boy sounded strangely heartbroken. *Must
everyone who befriended him come to harm?* The beggar who
had downed Brith had probably saved Taen's life. Grief
caught Jaric off guard, twisted, and became anger. "Send the
silver to pay the beggar's fine, then!" he shouted at the dockmaster. "Tell him to spend what's left, along with my apology
for the prison charge."

The official drew breath to protest. But the boy stormed
through the door, leaving water puddled on the floorboards, and a
troublesome pile of silver on the table. The harbormaster swore.
He called the man on dock watch in from the rain and, with
utmost distaste, dispatched the fellow to the town prison with
Jaric's coin and orders to free a one-handed beggar and a cat.

Rain glazed the slate roofs of Landfast, and cold, whipping
wind chased the run-off into currents across the cobbles. Jaric
slogged through the storm with his head down. He had no
particular destination, only a driving need to forget the leather
bag full of sorcerer's wards which swung at his neck, token of
the destiny set on him by a father and a weathermage he had
never known. That he could not compromise his fate without
losing the black-haired enchantress who had captured his heart
caused him pain beyond bearing. Jaric splashed through puddles until he found himself by the Docksider's Alehouse.
Drenched and morose, he pushed the door open and entered.

The taproom was crowded with patrons from every walk of
the waterfront. Tracking footprints across brick that was already wet, Jaric pressed between a knot of dice-throwing sailhands and two merchants who argued with a captain over bills
of lading. A pot boy stoked the fire on the hearth beyond, his
face flushed red as nearby longshoremen shouted unflattering

comments about his skinny frame. Once Jaric had been the butt of such jokes. Unaware how greatly he had changed since his initial passage from Cliffhaven, he hurried to the bar, where he tallied what remained of his coin. He spent all but two coppers on a wineskin. Then he retired to an uncrowded corner and sought the oblivion of drink.

When he was a scrawny apprentice at Morbrith Keep, unwatered wine invariably caused Jaric to fall asleep. Now, in the smoky air of a Landfast alehouse, the remedy chosen to drown his sorrows did not take immediate effect. Ivainson hunched in his dripping clothes, while the talk of a dozen groups of men swirled around him. He listened to debates over prices of silk and wool, a discussion of shipping hazards, and several rounds of sailhands' tales relating mishaps at sea. All the while, rain drummed on the roof shingles, relentless as Keithland's doom. The afternoon wore on. Gradually the wineskin grew flatter. Jaric regarded the ebb and flow of patrons with owlish eyes. He sat unresponsive when the one-handed beggar his money had freed burst in, jubilantly flipping coins while the tabby on his shoulder batted playful paws at the flash of the silver. The vagabond ordered beer for himself and his pet, and half the men in the taproom burst into laughter.

Jaric settled his chin on his fists. Too moody to respond when the redheaded barmaid paused by his elbow to flirt, he closed his eyes. The girl's smooth skin reminded him unbearably of Taen. Presently the barmaid plied her charms elsewhere. The wineskin lay empty beneath the boy's hand, and at last the drink overwhelmed him. Jaric settled into sleep that felt like death.

The boy woke to coarse words and a hand shaking his shoulder. He blinked, stirred, and found a burly man in a leather jerkin standing over him, shouting.

"Get up, tar-knuckles. Time to lock the doors. This isn't an inn, and nobody stays the night."

"I'm no sailor," Jaric muttered. He tried to straighten, groaned, and pressed both hands to his aching head.

"Don't matter what," said the man. He caught the boy's tunic and yanked. "Out with you."

Thrust to his feet, Jaric stumbled. His clothing reeked of wine, and movement made his stomach heave. He started on unsteady legs toward the privy behind the bar.

The man in the leather jerkin wasted no breath on warnings. He seized Jaric by the collar, propelled him forcibly across the tap to the door, and pushed him into the night. The boy tripped over the steps and sprawled face first into a mud puddle. He raised himself, shuddering, while the door boomed closed, them promptly fell, sick to his stomach. When the nausea subsided, Jaric settled his back against the tavern stoop and took stock of his position.

The rain had ceased. Stars glittered like frost overhead, gapped by the black silhouettes of the Landfast towers. Wretchedly alone, and chilled with the aftermath of sickness, Jaric wiped mud from his face. He rose clumsily to his feet and turned down the alley toward the dockside and *Callinde*.

The lane between the tavern and the shoreside warehouses loomed black as a pit. Dizzy from the wine, Jaric walked slowly, one hand braced against the alehouse wall. Refuse and run-off from the storm squelched beneath his boots. Between a cranny in the foundations, he heard the furtive crunch of a rat gnawing a bone; the sound ceased as he passed, then resumed. Jaric stopped. Overtaken by nausea, he crouched in the street once again. Yet instead of wet paving, his hands brushed the icy flesh of a man stretched prone in the alleyway.

Jaric recoiled with a cry of surprise, all sickness shocked from him. He explored further, felt a length of torn cloth and a sinewed arm. Suddenly a furred creature threaded between his knees. Jaric started back. He lost his balance and sat sharply on the cobbles, just as the beast leaped into his lap. It rubbed against his chest and meowed.

Recognizing the beggar's cat, Jaric shivered in relief that swiftly changed to worry. He pushed the animal away and bent over the man who lay prone in the street. Lanternlight flickered at the mouth of the alley. Dimly Jaric made out the form of the beggar, his one empty cuff pressed wet to the cobbles. Bruises mottled his face.

"No," whispered Jaric. He required no imagination to deduce what had happened: the beggar had carried silver into the alehouse, then boasted of the wealth and the freedom bestowed upon him by a young swordsman who had returned to pay his fine. Probably footpads had attacked him as he left, beat him senseless for his money, and dragged him into the alley to die.

Jaric touched the old man's face, felt cold skin and a flaccid mouth. No roguish, world-weary smile animated those lips now. Wrenched to the heart, Jaric bowed his head.

"No," he repeated. Grief overwhelmed him. Another friend lay dead. Unbidden, the boy remembered Taen and the fate mapped out for her by Llondian dream. Jaric felt a smothering sense of panic. Dreams had shown him death. But never until now had he experienced the reality. These cold hands, *her cold hands, Maelgrim would knife her;* the cat huddled forlorn in the alleyway; *himself, bereft.*

"No!" Jaric's shout rang, echoing, through night-dark streets. The fears twisted inside him changed, transformed to cruel regret; the chance he might cause a catastrophe like Tierl Enneth paled to insignificance by comparison. Ivainson did not hear the jingle of mail, or the footsteps which approached. Slammed hard against the end of dreams and hope, he wept to realize that nothing in life could wound him so deeply as the eventuality of Taen's murder.

That moment the cat streaked away. A dazzle of lantern-light fell full across his face, and an authoritative voice demanded, "What's happened here?"

Jaric opened his eyes, squinted, and felt the steel of a guardsman's sword prick his throat.

The blade jerked. "Quick, thief. Answer sharp. Did you murder for money?"

"No." Jaric lifted empty hands, spoke around the pressure against his larynx. "Search me. You'll find no coin."

The guardsman spat. He did not lower his weapon, but seized the boy with a gauntleted fist and hauled him to his feet. "Perhaps I caught you too soon to find coin, yes?"

Sickened to the core, Jaric stiffened. "Search us both, then! This man was my friend."

The guardsman bashed him back against the building and raised the lantern. Flame-light flickered over the sprawled form of the beggar, opened eyes and bloodied jaw glistening like macabre paint. Jaric turned away.

The guardsman grunted. "Some friend. That's old Nedge. Thief himself, did you know? The executioner chopped his hand as lawful punishment." He released his hold on Jaric and sheathed his sword in disgust. "Kor curse his flea-ridden corpse. I'll have to clear him out before he starts to stink."

Distastefully, the man at arms prodded the beggar with his toe. "How long's he been dead, d'you know?"

"No." Jaric rubbed his wrists, outraged by the guard's callousness. No matter what his crimes, no man deserved to die without the pity of his fellows. As that thought turned in

Jaric's mind, logic drove him one step further; unless he mastered the Cycle of Fire, Anskiere would perish similarly, deep under the ice cliffs with no friend to care.

That moment the beggar stirred. A snore escaped his lips. Steel flashed as the guardsman started back with a curse. "Kor, the stupid sot! Got himself drunk, didn't he? And probably bashed his silly head passing out in the street."

Jaric almost shouted with relief. *He had not caused the beggar's death.* The sudden, lifting rush of departing blame snapped a barrier within him. Self-doubt imprisoned him no longer. Offered the reprieve of a second chance, he seized the freedom to choose. He would go to the Vaere. No failure, no loss, and no fate carried worse penalty than the guilt of a loved one's death. If he could act to spare Taen, the risk of his father's madness must be accepted.

"Get on your way," said the guardsman curtly.

Jaric lifted his chin, his hair glinting gold in the lantern-light. "One moment," he said. With deliberate defiance, he loosened the laces at his throat, drew off his linen shirt, and spread it over the beggar who lay in the street. "This man is my friend, thief or not. Let him sleep in peace." And with a level glance at the guardsman, the heir of Ivain Firelord rose and strode off, to seek *Callinde* and the open sea.

Summer haze hung a moon like a yellowed game piece over Cliffhaven when *Moonless* returned to her home port. Despite the late hour, her crewmen furled sail with matchless efficiency. Yet the anchor had barely bitten into the seabed when signals flashed from the light tower caused Corley to yell for a longboat. No man dared delay direct summons from the Kielmark, far less a message coded urgent.

Blocks squealed in a night of oppressive stillness. The instant the boat splashed into the harbor, Corley departed for shore with all the speed his oarsmen could summon. Too impatient to wait until the craft drifted to the dockside, he leaped a span of open water to the wharf.

An officer with a lantern met him. His skin sparkled with sweat above his unlaced collar, and his chest heaved, as if he had been running. "Best hurry, man. Kielmark's in his study, pacing."

"Kor," said Corley sourly. "He wouldn't by chance be in a dicey temper, now would he?" Without pause for answer, he stripped off his own tunic and shirt and sprinted through close, late-season heat.

Except for an occasional sentry, the streets by the wharf lay empty. Corley raced past closed shops and darkened houses with only the echo of his footfalls for company. The stair which led to the fortress left him winded after long weeks confined to a ship's deck. Yet when the guards waved him through the gatehouse, he did not slow down to walk. If the Kielmark sent for audience demanding all speed, he would be counting every second with resentment until his captain arrived.

Corley passed the repaired portals of the great hall, then hastened down the corridor which led to the study. The door burst open as he rounded the last corner, and the Kielmark thrust his head out.

"Kor's Fires, another minute, and I'd have ordered you spitted, captain." The Lord of Cliffhaven spun and paced savagely from the threshold.

Corley followed into the candlelit clutter of the study. Breathless after his run, he bent a keen gaze upon his master. The Kielmark was stripped to leggings and boots in the heat. He paused before the opened square of the casement, the muscles of his back and shoulders quivering with suppressed tension. Throwing knives gleamed in a row upon his belt, and both hands were knuckled into fists. Suddenly he whirled from the window. The eyes he trained upon Corley shone ice-pale with anger. "Demons take judgment, man, *what were you doing in the north?*"

Corley ignored the question. With an expression of mild inquiry, he lifted his wrist and blotted sweat from his brow. "What happened here?"

The Kielmark surged forward with a frenetic burst of energy. He drew one of his knives. A flick of his wrist spun the blade the breadth of the room, to strike quivering in the stacked logs by the hearth. As if the violence steadied him, the King of Pirates leaned back against the sill. "Thienz-demons came hunting. Now tell me where Taen Dreamweaver is, and quickly."

"She's safe." Corely qualified promptly. "Though not on the Isle of the Vaere, as you ordered."

The Kielmark straightened with warning speed. "I said, where?"

"Imrill Kand." Corley smoothed the crumpled cloth of his shirt and tunic, and draped the garments across the back of a nearby chair. Then he sat. "Between a run of contrary weather, an illness related to the maturity of her mastery, and a vagary of Jaric's, the original plan had to be abandoned. Taen asked to go home. I saw no reason to prevent her."

"Kordane's Blessed Fires!" exclaimed the Kielmark, his consonants bitten and sharp; then without warning he burst into laughter. "Made the damned demons chase themselves, snouts to tailbone, you did."

Corley slipped a dagger from his boot and the inevitable whetstone from his pocket. "You say? How?"

The Kielmark pushed off from the window. He bent, wrenched his throwing knife from the log, and thoughtfully tested the edge of the blade with his thumb. "Shore patrol here captured a fishing boat off North Point. They found it crammed to the gunwales with Thienz-demons who thought they could drift off Cliffhaven's shores with impunity, even spy and pick the thoughts of *my* following. The stinking toads!"

Corley's steel sheared acrosss stone. "Thienz lurking inside the bounds of Keithland? That's bold. I trust you taught them a lesson."

The Kielmark raised murderous eyes, the knife haft poised in his fist. "I lost a man bringing those Accursed in. Two demons I killed outright, for that. The third died very slowly. It talked before the end."

Cautioned by his master's tautness, Corley stilled his hands. "Was that wise?" With a single thought, a Thienz could relay its suffering clear back to Shadowfane.

"Then their masters will think twice before they send another such envoy, won't they?" said the Kielmark. When Corley offered no comment, the King of Pirates turned on restless feet to the window. Moonlight silvered the curled hair on his crown as he continued. "At first I thought that demons came seeking the Dreamweaver. But the Thienz I tortured said differently. Shadowfane seeks to locate the Isle of the Vaere. They tried tracing *Moonless*. Only my most reliable captain sailed them all over the Free Isles' Alliance, every place but the southwest reaches where she belonged. Man, I sweated and I counted hours until you made port. Thank Kor the weather went contrary. If my original orders hadn't been balked, who knows what might have resulted?"

The Kielmark considered his captain, and frowned as he noted that whetstone and knife lay motionless. "So?" he said softly. "The Dreamweaver is on Imrill Kand, alone, but she can cloak herself with her craft. I trust Jaric remains under a guardsman's protection, securely inside the Alliance's defenses at Landfast?"

Corley placed his weapon on the bare wood of the table, then faced his master with steady eyes. "Five weeks past, Jaric went to sea with *Callinde*. Not even Taen would say where he went."

The Kielmark exploded from the window. The candles in the sconces guttered furiously as he crossed the carpet. "Great Fall, were you daft?"

"No." Corley smiled. Another man might hang for such a transgression; but he had stopped enemy knives at the Kielmark's back so many times, they might have been the same flesh, so tightly did their loyalties interweave. "That boy is marked by fate. I saw a hill priestess name him Demonbane at the summerfair rites on Tierl Enneth. Her clans paid him homage like a holy one. He went, Lord. I doubt a man could have stopped him without causing him injury."

The Kielmark hefted his knife, impaled it in the trestle next to his captain's, then shrugged his massive shoulders in resignation. "Either Jaric will return one day with a Firelord's powers, or else he'll wind up dead. I cannot shepherd every sorcerer's brat who rebels against fate. But Taen is another matter. Cliffhaven's debt to her is too great. You will dispatch five ships to safeguard Imrill Kand."

"The fishermen there won't like interference," Corley pointed out.

The Kielmark slammed the table with his fast. "Bedamned to the fishermen! Choose the finest crews in the harbor. Then return here and deliver your report."

Corley rose to depart with troubled thoughts. Unless the demons' true quarry was the Firelord's heir, why should Thienz risk themselves within the borders of Keithland seeking the Isle of the Vaere? No chart listed its position; even to find the place required the talents of a trained sorcerer. Now, too late, the captain regretted the fact that he had yielded to Taen's request. Jaric should never have been permitted to sail without escort.

Night fell swiftly in Keithland's lower latitudes. Braced against *Callinde*'s sternpost, Jaric chewed a strip of dried meat and watched the afterglow of sunset dapple the western waters gold. Around him the sea stretched to the horizon, empty. A fortnight had passed since the peaked profile of Skane's Edge

had disappeared astern. Still the boy found no trace of the
fabled Isle of the Vaere. Jaric swallowed the last of his savor-
less meal and rubbed his hands on his breeches. The water
flasks were nearly empty. If he encountered no land in the
next three days, he would be obliged to head about and return
to Westisle to restock his supplies.

A glance at the compass showed the wind steady from the
south. Jaric ran a calculating glance over the mild swell and
the clear arch of the sky, then sheeted headsails and spanker
on opposite sides. With the mainsail furled on the yard, *Callinde* would ride out the night hove to. After a quick check to
be sure all gear was stowed, the boy settled in his accustomed
nook in the stern.

Twilight deepened over the face of the ocean. Rocked upon
the waves, Jaric lay still and listened to the slap of *Callinde*'s
halyards. Stars pricked the cobalt of the zenith overhead. The boy
watched them brighten, and wondered whether Taen watched the
same sky many leagues to the north. Presently weariness overcame him. His eyes fell closed. Of necessity, Jaric slept lightly at
sea; even a slight change in weather could endanger him if he
failed to rouse in time to adjust *Callinde*'s sails.

Alone in a world of wind and waves, Jaric rested dreamlessly. When the late-rising summer moon lifted above the
horizon, a presence brushed his mind. Gently, furtively, it
probed his sleeping thoughts for information. Jaric stirred
against the stern seat, vaguely aware the disturbance origina-
ted elsewhere.

"Taen?" he murmured, wondering whether she might have
tried contact. But the presence subsided at the mention of her
name. Jaric sighed. He nestled his head in the sun-browned
crook of his elbow and settled back into slumber. The moon
rose high over *Callinde*'s starboard quarter, tracing silver
highlights over the wave crests. But Jaric no longer drifted
alone. A whisper of foam sheared the water. A tiller creaked,
and a dense black triangle of sail eclipsed the sky. As *Callinde*
plunged into shadow, a wiry figure leaned from the newcomer's rigging and snagged the smaller craft's stay. Frog-
like hands caught her thwarts. In silence, two other figures leaped
across the water between the rails.

Callinde rocked under the stealthy weight of boarders.
Jaric roused in the stern, eyes opened and alert. Dark as ink
against the stars, he saw two crested, lizardlike heads. Blunt,
smooth-skinned faces trained toward him, revealing a glint of

gimlet eyes and no nostrils at all. With a jolt of fear, Jaric recognized the Thienz. The creatures had been hunting since Taen's encounter with Shadowfane; but Jaric's stop at Landfast had muddled their search. Thienz had overtaken *Callinde* much farther south than they planned. Though the demons' eyesight was all but useless, they would stalk prey by sensing the thoughts in their victims' minds.

Desperate and frightened, Jaric fixed his attention upon the innocuous memory of a book he had copied as an apprentice scribe. The text had expounded at boring length upon the particulars of planting; in hopes that farming might mask his intent from the Thienz, the boy eased back his sleeve, where he kept a knife to slash rigging in emergencies. The haft slipped coldly into his palm. One Thienz stiffened in the bow. Jaric jerked his blade from the scabbard and threw.

Steel flashed and struck. Air whuffed through the demon's gill flaps. It staggered backward, the knife buried to the hilt in the folds of its broad neck.

Expecting the swift, crippling attack upon the mind which had brought down Deison Corley, Jaric kicked off from the stern seat. He could not know that, even untrained, the intensity of his inborn potential made his awareness difficult to grapple. His hands shook as he tripped the latch on the locker beneath the steering oar and snatched the spare rigging knife from its bracket. Bitterly he regretted the sword left on *Moonless* as he confronted the demon who remained.

It carried a short, curved saber, unsuitable for throwing, but deadly enough against a man armed with nothing but a knife. Jaric moved forward with caution. Frantically he reviewed the strategies taught by Corley and Brith. The Thienz did not wait. Disadvantaged by poor eyesight, and sensing murder in the boy's mind, it raised its blade to cut the head stay and bring down mast and rigging in a tangle to trap its adversary.

Jaric launched himself with a shout. Unable to clear the mast before the demon's blade fell, he sawed frantically at the headsail halyard just above at the cleat. Plies popped and parted, and the line snapped. Loosened canvas slithered in a heap over the bow. Knocked off balance, the Thienz tumbled across the thwart with a croak of surprise. Its sword flailed clumsily through the air as *Callinde* swung into the wind. Jaric lunged and stabbed it in the back. Flesh shuddered under his hand as he jerked his steel free for a second strike, then a third. The slick heat of the creature's blood on his hands caused the breath to gag in his throat. Half-sick with shock, Jaric stumbled back from his dying enemy. He shrank against the thwart and only that moment noticed the boat which trailed *Callinde*, a second party of demons poised by her rail to board. Moonlight glanced off blowguns and darts pinched in demon fists. Jaric freed his feet from the miring folds of the headsail. Even with his enemy half-blind, numbers threw the odds against him. Very likely the darts carried poison.

Wind ruffled the spanker. Slack canvas slammed taut, and, lacking the balancing force of the jib to hold her hove to, *Callinde* sheared ahead. Only one refuge remained where Thienz could not follow; undersized forelimbs hampered them from swimming without their heads immersed, and their gills did not function in salt water. With a short gasp of fear, Jaric caught the jib sheet on *Callinde*'s lee side. He flipped it overboard. Then, in full view of the demons, he leaped the other rail and dove.

As he struck the water he heard a wail from the Thienz. Their dismay touched his mind like dream-sense; they had expected the weak, indecisive boy Emien recalled from Elrinfaer, not a strapping young man who threw knives. Their mistake would not be repeated. Even as sea water closed over the boy's head, the demons relayed their discovery to colleagues at Shadowfane.

Callinde gathered way. Jaric swam under the keel and surfaced to leeward. His hands scrabbled frantically over planks. If he missed the sheet line he had thrown, his boat would sail past, and demons would have him at their mercy. Jaric thrashed, felt rope snake past his shoulder. He grabbed and clung. The jerk as the plies whipped taut stripped the callus from his palm, but he dared not cry out. Aware that *Callinde* would swing and jibe against the drag of his weight on the line, Jaric thrust his dagger between his teeth.

He hauled himself in hand over hand. Foam swirled to his chin, slapped his face, and set him choking. Jaric struggled for breath, and felt a mental stab as Thienz sought his mind. He ducked fast, sucked salt water around his blade on the chance that demons might think him drowning. All the while his hands stayed busy on the line. Fighting the drag of the water, Jaric hauled himself alongside *Callinde*, then kicked and hoisted himself up to the jib sheet block.

Over the rail he glimpsed Thienz beginning to board. *Callinde* swung, delaying them; her spanker flapped sullenly as her sternpost crossed the wind. Jaric dangled with his feet in the sea. Hanging from his hands, he worked aft along the thwart while the yard carved an arc across the stars. *Callinde* balanced between port tack and starboard, then jerked as the enemy entered her cockpit. Jaric caught the knife from his teeth. Waiting with his mind locked on images of darkness and sea water, he felt the boat turn further. Wind blew cold on his cheek. Then air filled the spanker with a thunderous flap of canvas. The boy yanked himself up, reached over the thwart with a desperate heave, and slashed the spanker sheet at the block.

The boom swung across the cockpit with killing speed, smashing the Thienz where they stood. Darts showered in the moonlight, to fall rattling amid floorboards and a flailing mass of demon-flesh. Jaric jammed his knife between the thwarts. He hauled himself bodily on board and, with the breath burning in stressed lungs, plunged across the cockpit. Barring his heart against mercy, he stabbed and cut throats until the last, toad-fingered hand fell limp.

At the end, he leaned gasping against the stern seat. Blood streaked his arms to the shoulder, and his tunic dripped sea-water dyed red. Pilotless, *Callinde* jibed again; the shadow of her sail scythed across the deck, then passed, exposing carnage drenched in moonlight. Overtaken by horror at the killing his hand had engineered, Jaric cried out. He doubled up over the rail and retched until his stomach emptied. His nausea took a long time to subside. When at last he raised his head, he saw that the demon ship drifted aimlessly. No helmsman took her tiller to resume chase.

Yet Jaric dared not assume all the Thienz lay dead. *Callinde* wallowed over the swells, littered with corpses and the silvery needles of spilled darts; she could not sail until cut lines were spliced and set right. Jaric pushed himself to his feet. With shaking hands he set about the task of lashing the spanker boom and clearing his decks of the dead.

~ XV ~

Stalkers

Morning came in a wash of copper and gold, with *Callinde* sailing briskly on a southwest heading. Jaric crouched over the helm, both eyes gritty from sleeplessness, and his fingertips raw from splicing lines. The attack and its aftermath had left him spent, and though at dawn he had grappled to make certain none of his enemies remained, empty decks failed to reassure him. The demons would be back. Jaric dared not rest until *Callinde* was well away from her present position.

The breeze slackened as the day warmed. Jaric set about the repeated task of lashing the helm, then shook the last reef from the main and changed to the larger headsail. Then he fetched a biscuit from his dwindling stock of supplies and munched while he made a restless survey of the horizon.

The sea stretched empty, except for the saffron-dyed sails of a fishing boat out of Innishari. Yesterday the presence of other craft would have been a welcome reassurance that *Callinde* did not fare alone upon the ocean, but now any boat might carry enemies. Jaric lost his appetite. To sail the empty south reaches with no more weapon than a rigging knife suddenly seemed a fool's errand. If he were killed or taken, the Keys to Elrinfaer and Anskiere's wards over the Mharg would become a fearful liability to Keithland. The boy tossed his crust overboard for the fish to finish, then freed the steering oar and brought his boat about. His search for the Isle of the Vaere must wait. The level in *Callinde*'s water casks was getting low anyway. Since Westisle lay four days' sail due north, Jaric decided to visit the markets there. Perhaps by trading every belonging he could spare, he might arm himself well enough to repel boarders.

But his plan lasted no longer than the span of a still afternoon. The wind died to a breath, and the waves rolled, varnished by calm. Stopped dead in the water by the caprice of the weather, Jaric cursed, and longed for Taen, and finally exhausted himself with worry. He shipped the steering oar in frustration. Curled in the slanting shadow of the headsail, he slept with his head on crossed wrists.

He woke in the silver chill of twilight. Early stars pricked the zenith, the sea an expanse of darkened indigo beneath. Jaric rose and stretched the stiffness from his limbs. He splashed seawater on his neck and face to relieve the sting of sunburn, then stepped to the bow and leaned on the headstay to reconnoiter. South, the boundary of water and sky met in a line unbroken by any sign of life; but to the north, between *Callinde* and the direction of Westisle, spread the pen-stroke silhouettes of nine masts.

Jaric's skin prickled warning. No fishermen he ever saw would drop canvas in a calm and risk missing the first change in the wind. Occasionally the Kielmark's vessels used such a ploy to conceal themselves in the dazzle of sunlight reflected on water. But only the most inept of pirates would sail in fishing smacks and sloops, far from the wealth of the trade routes. What bore down from the north could only be Thienz drawn by the death-dreams of last night's slain.

Jaric shut his eyes to forestall panic. He resisted the first, overwhelming impulse to spring headlong for the steering oar. The compulsions of Thienz traveled poorly over water and at present *Callinde* lay distant enough to keep him beyond reach of demon manipulation. Jaric forced himself to think rationally. He must wait until dark to put about. Then the stalkers from Shadowfane might not see his boat change heading, and if luck blessed him with wind, *Callinde* might flee beyond the horizon before morning.

But the waiting proved painfully difficult. Jaric paced and sweated as the sun lowered, the last rays staining *Callinde*'s sails bloody red. The afterglow faded slowly from the sky, and with it went sight of the masts which loomed to the north. Jaric assumed the stern seat in cover of darkness. Sweating in icy fear, he took up the steering oar and sculled *Callinde* around. No breath of air steadied her keel on the new course, an easterly heading he hoped would enable him to tack and make port in Harborside on Skane's Edge. The presence of the Thienz made landfall there all the more necessary; his mug now scuffed bottom when he had dipped into his cask for a drink. If the enemy kept him at sea after his stores ran out,

thirst and starvation might kill him without the inconvenience
of a fight.

Left no task in the calm but to battle his own apprehension,
Jaric stared north until his eyes stung. His vigil was lonely, a
solitude more relentless than any but a sailor could know.
Nothing met his search but night-dark waves, broken by the
occasional sparkle of phosphorescence where schools of fish
disturbed the surface. The dark had swallowed his enemies.
No means remained to determine whether the drift carried
their boats near or farther off. Every noise made Jaric start,
even the slat of *Callinde*'s gear as she wallowed windless in
the swell. By the time the constellations turned to show the
harvester overhead at midnight, the boy's nerves were sawed
raw. Light would have helped. But the glow of the masthead
lantern would mark his position like a beacon, and very likely
draw the demons to try a mind-probe to bind him. Recalling
Corley's evasive action with flame when Thienz had meddled
with his thoughts, Jaric fetched the lamp from a locker. He
cleaned and trimmed the wick by touch, then made certain the
reservoir was filled with oil. As a final precaution, he dug
deep in the aft locker and removed a cask of oakum, a mix of
pitch and fiber used by shipwrights to caulk the seams between planking. At need, the stuff would burn mightily; to set
such a fire on shipboard would be an act of extreme desperation, but better *Callinde* were destroyed than to let demons kill
him for the Keys. Jaric wedged the cask beneath the stern seat
with a muttered apology to the shade of Mathieson Keldric.
Then he sat with striker and rigging knife near to hand, and
thought of Taen between fervent prayers for breeze.

Wind answered in the dark before dawn, but weather came
with it, blotting the summer sky with sheets of low-flying
cloud. For once not cursing the threat of moisture in the air,
Jaric hardened his lines. *Callinde*'s sails banged taut. She
gathered way, driving forward into the swell. Spray shot from
her bow, and sternward her wake trailed a comet tail of phosphorescence. Her young helmsman leaned into his oar and
smiled with fierce exhilaration. Rain would hide him; if he
rigged the spare sail with a catch basin, run-off could replen-
ish his cask. Stormy weather might lend him resource to
thwart both thirst and the Thienz.

Yet fortune granted only small favors. The clouds lowered
and spilled thick, misty drizzle, and the wind slacked to the
barest hint of breeze. Jaric hunched over the steering oar.

More wet seemed to trickle down his neck than ran off the spare canvas to fill his catch basin. By dawn barely enough air moved to fill *Callinde*'s sails, and beyond ten yards, the waves lay swallowed in drifts of featureless gray. The possibility that Thienz might lurk unseen at any quarter of the compass preyed upon Jaric's thoughts, wore at his spirit until he was angered enough to want to shout and cry by turns. Instead, he lashed *Callinde* on course, fetched out whetstone and rigging knife, and returned to his post at the helm. With the oar clamped in one elbow, he resorted to Corley's habit of sharpening steel to pass the hours.

Day brightened over *Callinde*'s yard. Still the mist did not lift. It mantled waters the gray on gray of dull metal, and damped the shear of steel across stone as Jaric whetted his blade. He continued long after the edge was keen, just to keep his fingers busy; but as the morning progressed, that remedy was not enough. The fog swirled ghost-shapes around his boat and strung jeweled droplets on his lashes. He blinked them away, yet in time this seemed too much effort. His eyes grew heavy. His hands stopped the motion of whetstone and blade, while his mind strayed unnoticed across the borders of waking, into dream. . . .

Waves and the dull red of *Callinde*'s sails lost color, became the whiteness of snowfall in Seitforest. Jaric failed to arouse at the transition, wrought as it was by the touch of the enemy upon his mind. Cold and stillness lulled him. His senses knew nothing but the slow spin of flakes whispering through bare branches, the soundless settling of snow into hollows. In time the leaf-patterned forest floor became featureless as spread linen. Even the creeks froze and drifted over, the trickle of water over rock silenced until the season's distant changing. Winter bound the land, and Jaric, into tranced peace. His body assumed the numbness of extreme cold, and his mind became lost in ice-white landscape. Enspelled by dreams, he did not feel his fingers loosen, or hear the clatter as his knife fell to *Callinde*'s floorboards. Nor did he notice when his arm slipped from the steering oar. *Callinde* lost way, her sails slatting fretfully aloft. Beaded with droplets from the mist, the compass needle wandered in circles as his boat drifted rudderless over the waves.

And the dream-cold deepened. Knife-keen, it pierced the very mantle of the soil and touched the trees to the roots, freezing the dormant life within. Boughs bent, burdened under cruel shackles of snow. Wood gone brittle with chill snapped, eerily soundless in the wintry air; frost chewed through the bark like acid, and ice crystals pried and pressured, and burst the fastness of stone. Soon the whiteness ruled supreme. Sprawled like a corpse against *Callinde*'s thwart, Jaric felt no pain. He knew no alarm, no sorrow, no feeling at all, even as the cold penetrated his body and reached to stop his heart.

Near the end another sound intruded. Faint with distance, and sweetly brittle in the still air, the chime of goat bells penetrated the Thienz-wrought tomb of cold. Sluggish with trance, Jaric fumbled after the source. The white which blanketed his vision thinned slightly, and insubstantial as ghost-image overtop he saw a hillside patched with wildflowers and heather. The land was rough, torn in places by weathered spurs of granite. There a black-haired girl sat amid a milling herd of brown goats. The vision of her was indistinct, as if viewed through the shallows of a running stream. But her warning rang clear as the bells through the winter chill which gripped him.

'*Jaric, the Thienz have set a dream-spell on you! Jaric!*'

But the whiteness rendered the words as sound without meaning, a disturbance that floundered and died into silence. The girl's image dissipated, and the hillside with its cloak of heather and fern dimmed to wispy shadows. Before long the void devoured them entirely. Thienz-bound, Jaric drifted reasonless as a stone.

Yet the presence of the Dreamweaver did not entirely fade. With all her skills, Taen gathered herself and struck out against the cocoon that demons had woven around the awareness of Ivainson Jaric. Her urgency pried like a knife, and this time broke through.

Jaric roused. The workings of his mind and body felt swathed in a tide of whiteness and he could not orient. Uncertain whether the presence he remembered was a temptation of demons designed to weaken him, or illusion born of longing and his own imagination, he murmured Taen's name.

Her answer brought raw-edged fear. '*Jaric, you must break free!*' At last allowed foothold in his conscious mind, she spun dream-sense and attacked. The demon's prison shivered before the impact of her powers. Taen struck again, utterly exhausting her strength. Unable to maintain contact, her touch faded, even as the barrier of numbness which threatened the life of Ivain's heir weakened and suddenly collapsed.

Cold needled wakened senses with an onslaught of terrible pain. Jaric recoiled. Ripped by agony into full remembrance of *Callinde,* the ocean, and the fishing boats laden with enemies determined to take his life, he doubled over in the stern seat. His brow cracked unwittingly into the steering oar. His howl of shock and surprise was torn away by wind, and he roused fully at last, brought around by the maddened thrash of canvas. The weather had changed, totally. Mist had given way to clouds and driving rain. Water streamed in streaks off sails and spars, while *Callinde* pitched over white-capped waves, her lines lashing untended through her blocks. Panting like a distance runner to regain the air his slowed lungs had neglected, Jaric made no move to remedy his lapse of seamanship. He reached instinctively to rub his bruised forehead, then stopped to stare at his hands. The flesh was barely cool to the touch. Yet to the eye the skin was mottled purple-white, as if exposed to extreme cold. The inner ache and the agony of returning circulation were quite real, and the effects wrung Jaric to dizziness. The illusion of winter that Thienz had used to ensnare his mind had apparently afflicted his body with all the effects of frostbite.

The implications terrified, that Thienz he could not see might bind the human mind with visions potent enough to kill. Jaric stuffed his aching fingers under the tail of his tunic, but more than cold touched his heart. His search for the Isle of the Vaere had nearly ended here, adrift on the lonely ocean. Ivain's inheritance and Taen's hope of life might have been wasted before his potential could be challenged by the Cycle of Fire. Frightened to action, Jaric rose upon shaky legs. Since the machinations of the Thienz did not carry efficiently across water, the demons who had tried murder would not be far off.

Shivering and alone, the heir of Ivain Firelord sprang forward and hardened *Callinde*'s slackened lines. As his boat rounded, her sails punched taut by the wind, he bounded back to the steering oar and strained every muscle in his arms resetting his interrupted course. He shied from thinking of Taen, whose need had inspired him to seek the Vaere, and whose intervention had certainly spared his life. He dared not consider the headache which tormented him, nor the lingering ache of frost that gnawed at his fingers and toes. He bound all his resources to sailing, and the north-northwesterly heading that would see him safe to Skane's Edge.

The squall came on suddenly. Between one gust and the next a downpour lashed the waters, flattening the wave crests and kicking up spray in opaque white sheets. Jaric sailed by his compass, his hands clenched fast to the steering oar, for the storm left him blind. No visibility remained to show whether he sailed toward freedom or the heart of the demon fleet; and as the wind shifted round to the north, he fought the buck of the swell. Clinging to the helm, he drove *Callinde*'s bow windward to the limit of her sturdy design. Then the squall passed. The skies hung moiled and black, and the sea foamed angry spray beneath. Jaric squinted through the spray which sheeted off the bowsprit, but no trace of mast, sail, or spar marred the waters ahead. Storm still curtained the sternward horizon, hiding any presence of Thienz pursuit. Since Jaric saw no sign of the demon fleet, he concluded he must have drifted past their location in the calm, and only Taen's intervention and the cover of the fog had spared him. Afraid to leave the helm even for a drink of water, he sailed, while nightfall darkened around him.

Clouds smothered the stars, and the ocean heaved black as a pit. Jaric huddled in damp clothing, the play of wind over *Callinde*'s sails his sole means to hold course. On a clear night with the polestar visible, such crude measures might have worked, but not now. Squalls and mists meant changeable weather, and under such conditions the wind would not blow consistently from one direction. Sooner or later, Jaric knew he must take a compass bearing to check his course. The lamp he had trimmed and tended earlier waited, hooked still to *Callinde*'s thwart. The tin shutters were latched closed, and the wick dry and ready; still his hand shrank from the striker. Loath to make a light lest he give his position away to the Thienz, he made no move from the helm.

Callinde sailed on through the dark. Slave to the demands of his boat, Jaric rested his head on crossed wrists while the thrum of water over the steering oar translated through bone and flesh. Despair ate at his heart, though no Thienz appeared to attack. Staring, morose, at the tail of phosphorescence kicked up by the keel, Jaric saw a brief flicker of lightning astern. A squall moved in from the east, sure sign the wind had shifted radically. The compass check could no longer be delayed, unless he wished to risk doubling back and sailing head on into the demon fleet. Bending with the taste of fear in his mouth, Jaric reached for striker and lamp.

He slid aside the shutter on the lantern, the grate of metal on metal a scream against the natural sounds of water and wood and canvas. Jaric's fingers shook as he snapped a spark. He gave the flame barely an instant to catch and steady before he snapped the shutter down to a slit. Light yellow as a pen stroke parted the blackness of the night. Jaric wrestled the steering oar into the crook of one elbow, then raised the lantern over the binnacle. The compass revealed a disappointment. *Callinde* currently sailed due west, and had done so for an unknown span of time. Until the stars or sun could be seen for navigation, Jaric could not fix his position. Worse, to reach Skane's Edge, the old boat's poor performance to weather would force him to tack.

Jaric hardly bothered to curse the cruelties of the sea. With the breath gone ragged in his throat, he hauled the steering oar round, then burned his forearm as a chance wave jostled the heated frame of the lantern into his flesh. Reflex made him flinch, and another jerk as *Callinde* wallowed broadside over a swell caused the north-facing shutter to slide open. Light slashed across the water; it caught like sparks on a shear of foam, and the wet-black glisten of timber. Jaric stifled his scream of terror. Not a stone's throw off his thwart sailed one—no, two—*no, three* Thienz vessels. How long they had stalked him in darkness he could not guess, but that they were within range to attack was beyond all remedy. As if the weather mocked him in his weakness, the wind lay in favor of the demons.

Jaric slammed the shutter back over the lantern. He looped the carry ring over a hook, even as Thienz yammered their cry of attack. Their collective psychic assault ripped his mind as he slammed his full strength against the steering oar. The effort came too late. Jaric's defenses sheared away like slivers under a joiner's chisel. The demons knew his inadequacies; through the frenzy of their bloodlust leaked the satisfied memory of the night they had stalked and studied him. No cranny of his mind was unknown to them, no weakness, no strength, and no resource. The force of their compulsion was beyond any power in Keithland to deny, for the Thienz had shielded against outside intervention. This time no Vaere-trained Dreamweaver could break through to wrest their quarry away.

Ivainson-Firelord's-heir-Jaric-Thienz-quarry would perish now, for the compact and the glory of Scait.

The boy wept tears of fury and frustration, even as his hands disobeyed his inner will and did the bidding of enemies. The steering oar turned on its pins, and *Callinde*'s bow swung obediently through the eye of the wind. Jaric thrashed, in vain. He owned no Firelord's defenses to counter the grip that shackled his will. *Callinde*'s prow turned inexorably south. Her sails whipped taut and she shouldered ahead, directly toward Thienz who lusted to rend the son of Ivain Firelord limb from limb. Their excitement charged the contact, bruising their victim with images of blood and torn flesh; once he was aboard their black boats, his dying would be horrible and slow. Spurred to inspiration by extremity, Jaric attempted the unthinkable. He stopped struggling against his captors, without warning pitched his efforts into concordance with theirs. His own added strength drove *Callinde*'s helm hard over in the direction their compulsion demanded. The abruptness of her swing caught the demons by surprise. With a yammering yell of dismay, they slackened their designs upon Jaric, but already the heavy, curved prow of Mathieson's fishing boat sheared wide of the course they intended.

The great, patched main caught wind with a bang. *Callinde* lurched and Jaric slammed forward. His shins barked into the sail locker, yet he clung to the oar, dragging his boat another two points to port. The grand old vessel responded, gathered way, and lumbered into a heel that parted the swell, straight for the Thienz vessel that centered the enemy fleet.

Wails arose from Thienz crewmen. Demons unraveled like crochetwork from their perches on the rails, while the helmsman of the centermost boat jerked the tiller hard starboard to avert collision. The sloop jibed, but not handily enough. The iron-banded edge of *Callinde*'s keel post hammered crunching into her side, while Jaric slammed head-first into the steering oar. The force of the collision stunned the Thienz hold upon his mind.

Bleeding from a cut lip, and confused by the hellish toss of shadows thrown by the lamp, Jaric retained barely enough presence of mind to keep his grip on the helm. He reacted on nerves and instinct. With his boat locked still to the enemy's, he kicked the heavier *Callinde* into a jibe.

Timber grated and shrieked. The bolted iron fittings which reinforced *Callinde*'s bow savaged the lighter sloop. Splinters gouged up; pale and pointed as knives in the lamplight, they showered into the foam. Jaric glimpsed the riven boat. Its attendant pack of Thienz were very close, the eyes of each gone wide and liquid with fear. The malice of their curses slapped stingingly into his mind. Then a swell shouldered the locked craft. The high curve of *Callinde*'s prow grated another point to port and hooked a stay on the enemy boat. The Thienz who manned the sheets shrieked alarm.

Strain snapped water like smoke from the cable. Jaric had only an instant to brace his body before the floorboards shuddered and the following wave heaved up and under *Callinde*'s bow. The stay on the demon boat snapped with a whipcrack report. Thienz crew scrambled over themselves in attempt to slacken lines, but none could act swifter than wind. A gust thundered into the sloop's mainsail; canvas bellied and her unsupported mast screamed and cracked. Thienz wails rent the air. The backstay knocked the helmsman flying as the shorn timber scythed sideways. Canvas braked its descent, lent a stately, deceptive grace to impending disaster; then spars and tangled rigging bore downward, plowing a furrow of death among the Thienz. They scattered across the deck, tripped by ropes and battered down by trailing blocks. Jaric watched the carnage with numb horror, while the sloop's tackle and sails settled toward the waves.

The impact kicked water sixteen spans into the air. Billowing yards of canvas followed and scooped sea with a jerk that ripped the sloop's chain plates from her bow. The Thienz vessel heeled, glistening like a fish. The following swell drove her hard against the butt end of her fallen mast, impaled her timbers with a boom like a battering ram. Dark toad-shapes spilled screaming into the waves. Salt water burned the tender flesh of their gills, smothered their cries to silence. The ranks of demon survivors abandoned the energy patterns of coercive attack. They moaned in communal anguish as the boy who had been their quarry clung to *Callinde*'s backstay. He shouted in savage elation, while drowning Thienz spun death-dreams before the waves extinguished their memories forever.

Callinde drifted free, her timbers gouged with scars. Old Mathieson's craft mark had been sturdiness, not style, not speed, and not grace. Jaric could have wept for love of the quirks of north-shore fishermen, but two other boats filled with Thienz gave no surcease. Even as one vessel hove to in an effort to rescue the demons still clinging to the wreck, the

second jibed and bore down on *Callinde;* now the heaviness of
her hull worked against Jaric. The sloop the enemy had stolen
from the more affluent fisherfolk of Felwaithe was lighter,
leaner, and faster. To race her with *Callinde* would be the
errand of a fool.

Jaric did not try. As the Thienz drove their craft to take
him, he bent and wrestled his cask of oakum from beneath the
stern seat. The lid proved stuck fast. He pried and split his
fingers on the seal, to no avail. The gabble of Thienz voices
drew inexorably closer. Spray carved up by the sloop's bow
dampened the boy's cheeks, even as he swore and reached for
his rigging knife. He hammered the cask top with the blade.
Splinters gouged his skin as he ripped through and seized a
tarry mass of caulking compound. By now the Thienz vessel
shadowed *Callinde*'s quarter. Only seconds remained before
the death-dreams of the less fortunate ceased to preoccupy
those enemies who pursued.

Jaric straightened just as the demons grappled his mind.
His hand jerked toward the sheet line, urged by Thienz compulsion to let the sails run free and allow them to overtake and
board. The boy resisted. Crying out for the pain, instead he
closed his fingers over the lantern ring. Nerve, bone, and
sinew, his will was resisted by the Thienz. Determined,
whipped onward by fear and love for Taen, Jaric heaped
oakum through the shutter and onto the flaming wick.

Pitch-soaked fibers flared like lint. Seared by a wash of
flame, Jaric felt the Thienz within his mind shift beyond reach
of his pain. He seized the small instant of reprieve, spun, and
flung the lantern.

It arced hissing over water. The moment of flight seemed
to span eternity, or the dark end of time. Then the brand
crashed tumbling against the headsail of the oncoming Thienz
vessel. Flaming clots of oakum spattered forth, to cling and
burn and ignite.

The Thienz squalled in fury. Backlash through their mind-
probe stung Jaric like a whip, and energies savaged the channels of his nerves. The torment unraveled his control. He
crashed backward against the stern seat, gasping. The shaft of
Callinde's steering oar jerked abandoned circles above his
head. But the wood stood in stark silhouette against leaping
veils of flame. Powerless to move, Jaric wept in triumph. His
enemies were defeated. The Thienz sloop burned, sails and
rigging, and presently the hatred that gouged the boy's inner

awareness receded as the attacking demons were forced to abandon their prey and contend instead for survival.

Battered, bruised, and sticky with pitch from the oakum, Jaric crawled to his feet. No Thienz engaged to prevent him. He set blistered hands to the steering oar, and tenderly swung *Callinde*'s bow downwind. Her main filled with a bang that stung his ears, and the lines whumped taut. Spray shot from the bow, jeweled carnelian and ruby in the light of the conflagration astern. Then old Mathieson's boat did what she was best suited for: she gathered herself and raced before the wind.

The oar steered to a feather touch downwind. Jaric sank wearily against the sternpost, his feet stuck to the decks by spilled gobs of oakum. His only knife lay buried somewhere beneath the tarry mess, which would have angered Corley. Jaric closed his eyes. His imagination showed him Taen, teasing like a harridan over the black pitch that would rim his finger and toenails throughout the coming fortnight. But the humor and the exultation suddenly soured. Thought of the Dreamweaver's reaction to the fate he had narrowly avoided caused Jaric to shudder, then explode into racking sobs. Almost he had lost everything, the Keys to Elrinfaer and Keithland's future. Aftershock overturned equilibrium, left him feeling reamed and empty and lost. But throughout the tempest of reaction, the boy clung to his purpose. *Callinde* held to her course like a bird migrating before the killing storms of winter.

The glare of fire receded astern. Jaric shook tangled hair from his face, surprised to find that hunger pinched his middle. He had forgotten meals for what seemed like days. Determined to concentrate on the ordinary, he pried sticky fingers from the helm and sought out the biscuit cask. But once the food was in hand, he found himself too frayed with exhaustion to eat.

Spray waterlogged the hardtack in his fist. He licked at salty crumbs and adjusted lines, and stubbornly refused to look back in the direction of the carnage his hand had wrought among the Thienz. The boat which remained would come for him. Of that he had no doubt. Somehow, against hope, he must be ready when demon attack carved his inner will into a weapon. Jaric forced himself to take sustenance. He sailed, wary with nerves and determination, and never guessed so inconclusive a victory might alter the stakes against him.

* * *

Callinde had vanished over the horizon by the time the Thienz had rescued their last survivor from its perch on a floating spar. They hauled it on deck, where it crouched dripping and mewled of its misery, for waves had splashed it, and its gills burned unmercifully. Fluid clotted its lungs from even so brief an exposure, and perhaps-near-to-certainly its companions would be sharing its death-dream by dawn. At last, irritated, the seniormost Thienz cuffed it to silence. The chastened one scrabbled sideways into a corner and licked its webbed fingers, while companions undamaged by salt water laid out the crushed bodies of their dead, communed with their wounded to ease the pain, and crooned laments for the lost. The night was all but spent before the survivors who were Jaric-defeated gathered beneath the mainmast to pool resources and send word of their plight to Shadowfane.

The content of their news roused much consternation. Scait's favorites and the senior members of the compact convened hastily in the main hall. Though the Lord of Shadowfane was feeding, none dared assume the risk of leaving him uninformed. A wailing junior Thienz was dispatched through the door of the dining pit to summon him. It lost an arm, before the meaning of its message penetrated the instincts that drove Scait's frenzy. Reason returned to the Lord's savage eyes. He bridled his appetite before he succumbed to the urge to slash the errand-Thienz' throat; but the anger roused by its message spiked the Lord's hackles with malice. He granted the underling's heroics no reward, but left it moaning and bleeding amid the hacked remains of his meal.

The Sovereign Lord of Shadowfane stalked from his dining pit and joined at the meeting in the great hall with his lips and his foreclaws unwashed. His jaws still crunched the finger-bones of the underling who had informed him of Jaric's escape, and only the most ambitious of his favorites were not cowed. Those bold ones watched with predatory patience as he strode across the floor.

'So, Ivainson-Firelord's-heir-Jaric is a human with courage to be reckoned with.' Scait paused, licked his teeth, and glared at the rows of cringing favorites. 'A curse on the seed of his father, he must be dealt with.'

No demon stirred around the mirror pool as their overlord ascended the dais and sat. Claws scraped softly on cured human flesh as he settled on his throne and glared down at the wizened Thienz who hastened forward to crouch at his feet.

'Show me Jaric's aura, Thienz,' commanded Scait. 'As he lives now, *not the inadequately translated memory of Taen-brother-Maelgrim.*'

Beads clashed as the Thienz elder rose. It blinked wrinkled lids at the Lord on the throne and insolently flapped its gills. Then, having established the fact that it had not been intimidated into compliance, it squatted and offered an image.

Scait shared with his eyes narrowed to slits. Thienz-memory gave him Jaric, poised by lanternlight on *Callinde*'s decks; to the eye he was still a human boy, muscled from his hours at the helm, and tanned and tangle-haired from exposure. But demon senses perceived more than flesh. Surrounding Jaric's form spread intricate patterns of energy startling for their complexity.

The Lord of Shadowfane bared his teeth. Seven decades he had studied the enemy. In that time, he had arrogantly presumed to claim knowledge of humanity's native endowment for psychic development. In depth he had dissected the inborn talents of Merya Tathagres and, most recently, Marlson Emien. He had once even gazed upon a Thienz-wrought image of Taen Dreamweaver. But never before had the aura of a man birth-gifted with a Vaerish sorcerer's potential been unveiled to demon sight prior to training and mastery. For the first time, Scait realized how rare, and how precious, and how *fearfully strong* was the ability latent in the individuals chosen for dual Sathid bonding. Yet, paired with the staggering capacity for power, this boy who sailed to claim his right to the Cycle of Fire owned a naïveté, a defenselessness born of the fact that he had yet to access the well of resource within him.

This observation bent Scait's thinking into change. His eyes stayed hooded, but his favorites did not mistake the expression for sleepiness. Their Lord's very stillness bespoke warning, and the experienced among the council waited in poised anticipation for their master to stir and straighten.

Scait chose speech to communicate, which confirmed that he plotted deep, yet would not confide indiscriminately in his underlings. The risk he intended to take was perhaps a greedy one, but Jaric's talents offered possibilities whose dangers were two-edged. More than the Keys to Elrinfaer might be won for humanity's downfall. If Ivain's heir were captured alive, the compact might develop and enslave his vast potential through bonding to a previously mastered Sathid. Then all his Firelord's powers might be used to rip Keithland into chaos. The vengeance planned for centuries against humans might be completed at a stroke.

Scait's lips widened into a leer as he spoke his will to the ancient Thienz. "You will assemble a third fleet to sail in support of the dozen vessels still quartering the south reaches." A murmur arose in the chamber, stilled by a gesture of Scait's forelimb. "No more inexperienced young will be entrusted. By my command, only the strongest and eldest Thienz will embark upon this voyage, for I wish the pawn Maelgrim to go along. He will use his training to secure my desire. Let him not fail. Ivainson-Firelord's-heir-Jaric is to be captured and delivered living to me."

Storm of Crossing

Gusts off the sea jangled the wind charms the Imrill Kand fishermen hung from their eaves for protection against ocean storms. By that sound, and by the shouts of the children who chased the goats through the streets to pasture on the tors each dawn, Taen woke aware that she was home. Although she opened her eyes to the loft that she had known as a girl, with the same faded counterpane tucked beneath her chin, the present allowed little chance for reminiscence. Too much had changed during the year of her absence. The brother who had slept in the cot across the loft was now forever lost to demons.

Taen rose. She dressed hastily in trousers and tunic that had once been Emien's, with a cast-off shirt of Corley's thrown overtop for warmth. This she gathered close with a belt of knotted string, tied as a gift by *Moonless*'s sailhands. Her Dreamweaver's robes of silver-gray stayed folded away in the cedar closet, as they had since her arrival. To the Imrill Kand villagers, the garments were uneasy reminders that she had returned to them an enchantress, transformed by the mysteries of the Vaere from a crippled child of ten to a grown woman in little more than one year's time. Accustomed as Taen was to isolation, this new alienation was a misery she tried not to dwell upon. Briskly she combed and braided her hair, then descended the ladder to the kitchen.

Her mother heard her despite the fact that Taen no longer had a stiff ankle to drag and clatter over the rungs. Marl's widow never looked up from kneading dough, but called out to her daughter with her back turned. "Here's you going barefoot again. Step on something sharp, or catch chill, and don't come crying to me for pity."

"Now who's acting the witch?" Taen jumped to the floor, grinning. "My boots are by the stove, drying, since last night. You didn't see them when you made fire for the bread?"

The old woman made a sound through her nose. "'Twas

before daybreak, then, girl. And you shouldn't stay out on the tors after nightfall. Could come to grief on the rocks."

By the smell, the first loaves were baked through. Taen twisted the tail of Corley's shirt around her fingers and retrieved the pans from the oven. "I know," she forestalled, even as her mother drew breath to warn that her sloppiness was bound to cause burns. No matter that a moment later she banged the bread pans down with a clatter and ended licking a blistered thumb.

"Stubborn." Marl's widow set her dough in a bowl to rise, then turned around, wiping her hands on her apron. Careworn, and aged by sorrow from the loss of husband and son, she regarded the daughter the Vaere had changed into a stranger she barely knew. "You'll be going to the tors again?"

Taen nodded. She preferred to work alone, where she did not have to watch folk she had known since girlhood making the sign against evil behind her back.

"Might be rain later," said Marl's widow. She brandished a damp fist at Taen, who had twisted a corner off the fresh loaf and crammed it into her mouth. "You're old enough not to do that."

"That's what the cook on *Moonless* said." And Taen sighed as the cooling bread was removed beyond reach; the barley and smoked fish her mother offered instead made a dull substitute. The Dreamweaver picked at her plate without enthusiasm. Jaric's danger, and the threat of the demons who tracked him, fretted at her thoughts always; but this burden must not be shared here, for the sake of the brother whose betrayal shadowed this house like cobwebs. Of necessity, Taen kept to the ordinary. "What was Uncle Evertt bellowing about?"

Marl's widow raised offended eyes to the window which overlooked Rat's Alley. "Wants the Kielmark's brigantines gone from these waters. No matter that they're here to defend. I told him to save his grousing for the tavern."

"And he didn't," said Taen, but without bitterness. Times had been hard for her uncle, even before Emien had lost the sloop. Even plain barley was a commodity on Imrill Kand. Taen scraped her bowl carefully, and wrapped the fish in linen for her lunch. "I can bring back herbs for the pot," she offered as she rose.

"Won't be back in time for supper, and ye know it." Marl's widow vanished into the pantry and reappeared with her sewing basket, just as Taen stamped her feet into damp boots.

"Take this, child. The cold's coming, and you'll need something against the wind."

Taen looked up, saw the cloak in her mother's outstretched hand. The fabric was woven of fine-spun goat's hair, russet, with borders of blue to match her eyes. The gift left her speechless, for she knew better than any that coppers were scarce under her uncle's roof. Taen searched her mother's face, and her delight withered before the certainty that the fabric could not be spared.

Her mother noticed the hesitation and frowned. "Not fine enough for ye, then?"

Taen recognized the look, and forced a lighthearted grin. "Only if you stole it." Then, lest she cry on the spot, she threw her arms around her mother's floury middle and squeezed.

"Settled with the weaver with the money I earned darning sweaters," Marl's widow confessed. "Evertt can't throw his weight around over that, and I'll sleep maybe, knowing my girl is warm without taking handouts from pirate captains' mates."

Taen exploded backward. "Corley?" she said incredulously, and ended sneezing the flour she had inhaled in her outrage. "He's Cliffhaven's top-ranking officer, and nobody's lowly mate."

"Go," said her mother. "Now, before I slap your backside for tearing the end off the new bread." And she bundled Taen and the cloak through the door, into the puddled brick of Rat's Alley.

Bemused, the Dreamweaver ran her fingers over the cloth. Then she smiled with the sweetness that had won the hearts of the roughest of the Kielmark's captains. "Thank you, Mother," she called, and started to pin the collar with a brooch of plain copper.

That moment the door flung open again, and a linen-wrapped packet of herring sailed out and struck her in the chest.

"Forgot your lunch," said Marl's widow. She banged the latch closed, but not before her daughter glimpsed her tears.

That, more than any other thing, impressed upon Taen the change her life had taken since Anskiere had sent her to the Vaere. She had come home, yet Imrill Kand retained little claim upon her loyalty; the villagers and their bitter struggle for sustenance seemed sadly diminished in significance. As a girl, she had longed for healing so she could work on the decks of a fishing sloop; how little she had bargained upon the fact that such simple dreams would lead her to join the Vaere-trained as guardian of Keithland.

The wind blew cold, ruffling the puddles in Rat's Alley; overhead, the luck chimes jingled in warning of autumn. Taen clutched the edges of her whipping cloak and left her uncle's door stoop. She passed the weathered-board stalls of the fishmarket, and the docks, and the Fisherman's Barrel Inn, and, remarked by a weaving, squalling flock of gulls, wended a tortuous path through a fish-stinking expanse of drying nets. Beyond lay the goat track which led to the upper meadows, and the rock-crowned heights of the tors. The gulls sped away on the breeze. Taen climbed quickly, where once she had limped. The shingled roofs of the houses diminished beneath, and clouds raced tattered and damp across the crags. Wind and the bells of the goats were the only sounds she could hear when at last she chose a sheltered cranny and settled herself within.

The sea spread like hammered silver from the shore, unbroken but for flyspecks of fishing craft, and the distant masts of a patrol ship from Cliffhaven. Secure in the knowledge she was guarded by vigilant men and weapons, Taen closed her eyes. Her dream-sense answered her readily now that she had gained experience. Within seconds her vision of harbor and village melted away, replaced by wider vistas engendered through her Sathid-born talents. The boats were specks no longer, but craft with crews who labored with sails and nets. Each man reflected his own pattern of fears and dreams; of emotions and desires and hopes that blended to fashion the spirit of an individual. Although Taen could sift the contents of men's minds with the same fascination that an archivist might show while studying books, she passed by. Her attention extended outward, across the wide waters between Hallowild and Felwaithe. She encountered no demon-sign; only one ship flying the Kielmark's blazon, and a ragged patch of mist. Except for that the seas appeared empty.

A prickle of intuition caused Taen to linger. She had been raised by the sea; all through childhood she had known weather to descend unexpectedly from the northwest, bringing peril to the fishing fleets, and silence in the houses where wives and mothers awaited their menfolk's return. The moods of storm and sea were studied and known and feared; yet something about this isolated fogbank roused the Dream-weaver to uneasiness. She sought the reason, and felt her hair prickle in alarm. This mist was not natural, but drifted purposefully south across wave crests buffeted by winds blowing due east.

Alerted to danger, Taen probed further. Fog hampered her dream-sense, clinging white and impenetrable. The swells crested and foamed, strangely muted, and the air felt oddly dense. Suspecting the handiwork of demons, the Dreamweaver quartered the area with care, yet nothing came of her search. No shadow of a boat moved within the murky mass. She drew back, cold, and prepared to try another pass; then she reconsidered. If demons sailed in strength, with resources forceful enough to blind her dream-sense with illusion, she would be foolish to expose herself further. The most she could accomplish from Imrill Kand was to warn the enemy of the fact that their presence had been discovered. Far better such trespassers were caught unsuspecting, and dealt with before they could cloak themselves and escape. Grimly Taen gathered her dream-sense. She sought across the waters for the irascible presence of the Kielmark's acting officer in command, master of the brigantine *Shearfish*.

She found the man on his quarterdeck, arguing with the cook over an infestation of weevils in the porridge. Taen repressed a smile, for the beleaguered cook cursed his captain under his breath in wildly original oaths before he raised his voice in defense.

"Man, you ask too much, when it was yourself came blundering into the bread room looking for crewman's contraband and sliced the sacks what held the oats." The captain of *Shearfish* glowered, but by now those deckhands within earshot were watching. As if his manhood were at stake, the cook pressed hotly on. "O' course the dighty weevils moved right in, could you ask them to forgo a bite with such plenty sprinkled about for the taking? Lucky I found the bag, I say, or we'd be eating bugs and their leavings the rest o' the way back to port."

"Enough!" snapped the captain, so abruptly the nearer deckhands jumped. The cook went suddenly pale. Taen chose that moment to intervene. She sent a warning and a plea to *Shearfish*'s master, to investigate the unnatural fog to the north; and out of respect for the services she had already rendered to Cliffhaven, her request carried weight. The subject of weevils died with alacrity. Even as Taen relayed details, the captain transferred his shout to the quartermaster; the great wheel spun at his command and *Shearfish* put about with a thunderous flap of sails.

Taen and the cook sighed with relief. While crewmen ran to polish weapons, the Dreamweaver withdrew. She sped her awareness southward as she had each day previously, to resume her watch for *Callinde* and Ivainson Jaric. Now the sick worry hidden within her burst free of constraint. Her last sight of the Firelord's heir had been the night she had discovered him under attack by demons. She had exhausted her powers to break the Thienz' hold upon his mind. By the time she had rested enough to resume her watch, she had encountered no trace of Ivainson or Mathieson Keldric's old fishing boat, though she had tried ever since, repeatedly.

First Taen swept the seas southeast of the Free Isles' Alliance. She had found a strayed trade vessel blown off course from Skane's Edge, and two small fishing fleets. No sign did she encounter of Firelord's heir or *Callinde*. That in itself should not have been discouraging. The Isle of the Vaere was a fey place, elusive to mortal perception and not always visible to the eye; no charts would show its position. Though any trained sorcerer could sense its location, Jaric would be sailing blind; and by now Taen was forced to assume he plied waters far off his intended course. The past day she had expanded the limits of her search. Still she found nothing. Her dream-sense encountered lifeless vistas the breadth of the southeast reaches, and now she fought against loss of hope. Logic insisted that continued effort was futile; stubbornly she held out. If Jaric had abjured his inheritance, or if storm or demon possession had interrupted his quest, the consequences and Keithland's peril were too final for thought.

Now Taen quartered the seas lying west and north of the fabled isle. She dream-read sailors in the ports on Westisle and Skane's Edge, but their minds held no memory of a fair-haired young man with an antique fishing boat. South she found nothing, not even traces of wreckage. Now only the wide waters to the east remained, the least likely place for a man sailing alone with a small craft and limited provisions.

Northerly gusts blew cold across the tors of Imrill Kand, moaning around crannies in the rocks where Taen sheltered. Her new cloak protected her body, but she barely cared that her fingers and toes were numb. With her awareness centered across the breadth of the Corine, she knew only seas that were patched gray and cobalt beneath the breaking cover of rain clouds. There the wind blew warm and damp from the west, its smell scoured clean with salt.

Presently another scent intruded. The taint was so faint she might have imagined it, the barest suggestion of something acrid. Taen paused, tightening her focus. A moment later, her heart quickened in alarm. The smell traveled clearly on the east breeze, now identifiable as smoke from charred cordage and timber. The source, when she traced, proved swathed in heavy mist, identical to the patch she had diverted *Shearfish* to investigate in the waters to the north off Felwaithe. Taen's dream-sense shrank in reflexive warning. The evidence overwhelmingly indicated demon-sign and battle; and what reason for both in this desolate stretch of ocean, if not Ivainson Jaric?

Pressured now by fear, Taen added caution to her search. Worse than discovery, she dared not let demons detect her probe, tap into it, and gain further knowledge of Jaric. Her mistake with Emien aboard *Moonless* must never be repeated.

The Dreamweaver entered the mist with the subtlety of snow drifting through air, and the net she wove to trace was fine-meshed enough to draw minnows. The fact that she might be helpless to intervene should she find Jaric in demon captivity made her palms sweat and her breathing shallow. But the tenacity of her Imrill Kand upbringing shored her spirit against heartbreak. To find him alive would bring hope, however dire his circumstances.

She pressed deeper, found a drift of burnt timbers but nothing else, only an icy, unnatural emptiness which made her flesh crawl. The mist pressed close about her dream-sense. It cloaked the wave crests and coiled like smoke through the troughs. Taen detected no life but schools of scavenger fish come to investigate the flotsam, yet her foreboding only intensified. Something lurked just past the borders of her perception, like movements glimpsed in a mirror. Her skin prickled as if she were watched by hostile eyes; despite the fact that she sat in the distant north, surrounded by rock and soil and thin grass grazed by goats. The entity which lurked in the mist seemed somehow *knowing*, as though her presence had been expected.

Taen paused. Even as she sought to refine her probe, a force brushed light as feathers down her spine. Suddenly she felt an overpowering urge to pull back, leave this stretch of

ocean, and forget the traces of wreckage she had found here.
Yet Imrill Kand offered no haven if the Keys to Elrinfaer fell
to enemy hands. Certain her compulsion was demon-inspired,
Taen braced to fight; if the Thienz who came hunting from
Shadowfane saw fit to hide their machinations, she refused to
be cowed. Power smoldered within her, cleaving the mist for a
target to strike. Yet her dream-probe encountered no Thienz;
only the sudden, unexpected awareness of Ivainson Jaric.

The shock wrenched a cry from Taen's throat. Ablaze with
unshed power, and poised for battle, she yanked back. Cold
rock bruised her spine, yet discomfort to her body became
insignificant before the whetted edge of wariness within her
mind. Quite certainly the Firelord's heir had been unveiled
because it suited the purpose of demons for him to be found.
Yet Jaric was not taken captive. He sat alone at *Callinde*'s
helm. His hair was sodden and wind-tangled, and his eyes
stinging from lack of sleep.

The energies Taen had woven in search of him were still
intact. Power flared in answer to his presence; she dampened
the force instantly, but not before a spark of contact leaped
through.

Jaric raised his head. "Taen?" he said, and the hope and the
confusion in his tone almost broke the Dreamweaver who
huddled in the cold in Imrill Kand. That narrowest instant of
pity proved fatal. The enchantress hesitated, and the trap she
feared, the threat that instinctively cautioned her against
maintaining any thread of rapport, overtook her. Thienz grappled a foothold through the contact.

Taen screamed in fear and pain. She slammed up defensive
barriers, too late. Her compassion for Jaric ran deep, and the
grip of the demons had penetrated through to its source. They
had breached that innermost psyche where she was unguarded
and their attack was engineered with devastating precision.
Jaric had been used as bait, left free and in solitude expressly
that demons might snare her. Once Taen Dreamweaver was
rendered impotent to defend, her powers would not foil the
demon's final possession of their quarry. The last living heir of
Ivain Firelord would be taken as surely as a wheat stalk razed
by a scythe. The pain of that ripped Taen open to more cruel
revelation still: the guiding mind behind this most deadly plot
had been not that of a demon *but that of the brother she had
lost to Shadowfane*.

"No!" Taen's cry echoed over the tors of Imrill Kand. She

struggled to repel the hold upon her mind, even as power flared and burned her resistance away to nothing. The being who now was Maelgrim had no mercy; all that remained of his humanity had been carved into a weapon for killing. He traded upon ties his sister would harbor, the same loyalty and stubborn love that had made her hesitate to strike him down once before on the heights of Elrinfaer. Maelgrim thrust through the Thienz net to cripple her.

Yet Taen did not crumple. Weeping bitterest tears, she mustered and deflected the killing blow. Her dream-sense flashed white under the paralyzing agonies of conflict. Her mind reeled under the backlash, and the suffocating hold of the Thienz released. Taen reached immediately to retaliate, to strike at the source of Keithland's peril before Jaric could be captured or slain. But no force answered. She had dangerously overextended herself, and her powers were utterly spent. Sapped of energy, Taen opened her eyes to gray mist, and a wind that scoured across the rocks of Imrill Kand. Pain and cold wracked her body, and her eyes ached from tears.

She tried to stir, and could not. Her limbs felt locked in lead. Afraid now, for the chill might certainly kill her, she struggled to lift her head. Her vision became patched with darkness. Dizziness wrung her senses like grass stalks swept up in a whirlpool, and a fierce attack of nausea left her gasping. Jaric, she thought weakly, but could not rouse enough to focus her warning into dream-call. As the void swirled and engulfed her, Taen heard laughter from the man she had once called a brother. Then the sound shattered to echoes. Her awareness slipped sickeningly into night, even as the last terrible fact crackled across the link: the Demon Lord of Shadowfane wanted more than the Keys to Elrinfaer. He had commanded that Jaric be taken alive. Ivain Firelord might have been hated, even cursed for his cruelties and his malice. But the son bequeathed to Keithland might do worse; enslaved by demons, the boy and his prodigious potential for a sorcerer's mastery might be turned like a cataclysm against his own kind. A Firelord dedicated to destruction would surely end hope and extinguish humanity's chance of survival.

Had Taen retained even a glimmer of consciousness, she would have wept for sorrow, that the greatest fear of Jaric's heart should now so terribly become real. But her awareness extinguished like candle flame slapped by a downpour.

* * *

Night fell over the tors of Imrill Kand. The broken clouds of afternoon fused into darkness and whipping rain that slashed the rocks, and beat in icy sheets over mats of flattened grass. Bracken bent to the storm, and run-off drummed over a mud-spattered goat-fleece cloak that only that morning had been new. The Dreamweaver of Imrill Kand lay beneath, unmoving. Her hands glistened with rainwater when the lanternlight fell across them; the hair plastered sodden to her cheek swallowed reflections, seemed a shroud cut from the very cloth of death.

"Fires, she's here, then," said a soul-weary voice edged with bitterness.

A shout followed, and a rustle of oilskins, as the small band of searchers clustered together around the site.

More light flooded the cranny in the rocks where Taen lay. Evertt stamped mud from his boot soles to be sure of his footing on the rocks. Grim as the granite he trod, he set his storm lantern in a cranny. Then he bent and gathered his niece in his arms exactly as he would have hefted a net of fresh-caught cod, except that his movements were awkward with a grief only his dead brother might have recognized.

Her skin was very cold.

"We're too late," someone murmured. Already the dour men with their flickering lanterns dispersed to descend the tor.

"Perhaps." Evertt lowered his head against the driving rain, the girl cradled limply against his chest. "She breathes, but her spirit rides the winds." He said no more until he reached the doorstoop in Rat's Alley where Marl's widow waited in an agony of silence, even as she had for the husband and the son fate had torn from her before this.

Now, the same as then, Evertt could not meet her eyes. He stepped full into the light which spilled from the kitchen, Taen bundled loosely in his arms. The mud and the wet spoiling the cloak which had not protected made the mother gasp, but she did not ask. Still, beaten and worn with years, she did not ask.

Her aching, terrible courage made Evertt feel inadequate. Rage at his helplessness made him gruff, for he knew no other way to treat the humiliation, and the endless, grinding tragedy of life as he understood it. "Found her on the tors," he snapped. Then, sorry for his harshness, he tried to ease what he could not change. "Taen is too small for her task. But like her father, she won't believe it."

Which was Evertt's timeworn bitterness finding expression, as it always did, that his brother had been born knowing how to find joy in the face of adversity.

Marl's widow stiffened. "The sorcery could not kill her, any more than the storm did Marl." Bravery had, though, and now might do so again. Abruptly Marl's widow discovered she was not too hardened for tears. "Bring her in, then."

Evertt stepped into the dim warmth of the kitchen, and for once he was not nagged about the mud he tracked in with his boots.

Taen wakened to dry blankets and the dull red glow of the hearth fire. She lay on a cot by the settle. Her cloak hung on a chair, filling the air with the reek of damp wool, while wind and rain slashed the windowpanes, jangling the luck charms intended to ward storm violence from those within. Taen stirred under the coverlet. Her eyes stung. Her body ached, as if savaged by fever, and her heart bore a burden of pain greater than any she might have imagined when she accepted her training from the Vaere.

"Don't speak," said Marl's widow.

Taen turned eyes that were too old for the years she actually carried. Restless on her pillows, she framed a tortured question. "How long?"

Marl's widow found herself crying again, not in relief, but for the mysteries which burdened her daughter she would never again understand. "Your spirit has ridden the winds through a day and another night."

Taen grew very still. Her blue eyes acquired depths that wounded, before she closed them. *Too late, too late for Jaric.* Thienz had taken him as she slept, and the Keys to Elrinfaer with him. Even as the Dreamweaver's mind encompassed the knowledge, she sensed the demon boats which dragged *Callinde* in tow. Defeat had sharpened her dream-sense to knife-like clarity, and an image formed, of Jaric battered helpless by the vindictive triumph of the Thienz. His body lay wrapped in sailcloth, trussed in spare cordage purloined from *Callinde*'s lockers. But far worse, his mind was left aware. The fate he would embrace at Shadowfane was known to him, and the horror of his knowing was reflected inward over and over by the mirrorlike spell of his prison. The demons could not kill him, by Scait's express command; but in bloodless malice they tortured the mind of their victim past bearing.

Taen could not penetrate Thienz' defenses with her dream-

sense; that she saw at all was a cruelty arranged by the one
Shadowfane named Maelgrim. Powerless to intervene, ravaged by the failure of her talents as never, ever before, the
enchantress knew Ivainson Jaric well enough to guess the
depths of suffering he could not express. Behind the glassy
blankness of his eyes, his heart was screaming.

"When the net grows too heavy, the wise fisherman seeks
help," said Marl's widow from the shadows by the cot in
Evertt's cottage.

Taen swallowed, willing the images to leave her. She
opened eyes flooded now with tears and forced her hands to
unclench. "Who is left to help?" She stared at the roofbeams,
hating the whipped sound of her words even as she spoke
them.

Marl's widow leaned forward and rested work-weary arms
upon the shelf of her knees. "The sea itself, if the powers
beneath so choose." Then she abandoned the solace of proverbs with a sigh of exasperation. "Daughter, must you always
seek to bend the wind?"

The words were very near the ones a Dreamweaver had
offered Jaric in the burrow of the Llondelei. Now that time
felt far distant, a child's dream of happiness. Taen kicked the
memory to quiescence, before sorrow could choke her heart.
The Keys might be taken, but the Mharg had yet to fly;
leagues of ocean remained to be crossed before Jaric reached
the dungeons of Shadowfane.

"So like your father you are," Marl's widow began, and
stopped, for a glance toward the pillows made her breath
catch. Taen's tears had stopped. Her face was no longer that
of a girl, or even a woman, but that of an enchantress trained
by the Vaere. Power rang from her, even as sound reverberating from steel under the hammer falls of a smith's shaping.
Yet even now the familiar was not entirely lost; the Sathid-born force of the enchantress held that fierce, indomitable
hope with which Marl had tempered the hardship of his days
upon Imrill Kand.

"The sea will help, if the powers beneath so choose," Taen
repeated. She turned a shining look to her mother. *"Callinde's*
provisions were low, her casks nearly empty. *If the demons
bear the Firelord's hair to Shadowfane, they must make land-fall, somewhere, for water."*

Her mother made the sign against evil, for the mention of
perils beyond her understanding. She turned diffident eyes to

her daughter, who was no longer of Imrill Kand, but inextricably bound to the turning of the world beyond. Only Taen did not see her mother's uncertainty. Her Dreamweaver's mind was already far removed by the powers that marked her craft.

Taen's awareness sped outward from Imrill Kand, straight as an arrow's flight. She wasted no time with openings, but roused the captain of the Kielmark's brigantine *Shearfish* with an urgency that shot him bolt upright in his berth. He narrowly missed slamming his head into the deck beams overtop, but purpose overrode his annoyance.

'Weaver of Dreams, I have patrolled the northeast reaches in the area you named,' he thought in answer to her query. *'My men saw no mists. If there were demons, they are gone.'*

But the negative report was a thing Taen had expected, since learning that Maelgrim's talents directed the powers of the Thienz. He would surely be sailing where her dream-sense had seen the fogs of cloaking illusion, and through mind-trance with the second fleet of Thienz to the south, his powers had augmented the trap that had sprung on Jaric. The eyes of men would see no trace to mark the boats which sailed from Shadowfane; but a Dreamweaver might. Taen bent her focus to Cliffhaven. If *Shearfish* bore her south, and the Kielmark mustered his men at arms, the chance existed that she might track the demon fleets. Though the sea was too wide, too open, to launch an attack upon enemies men could not see, on land, with the aid of her dream-sight, an army might manage an ambush when dwindling provisions drove the Thienz ashore.

The Kielmark sat at dinner. Before his table, an uncomfortable merchant captain stood with the bare steel of two captains pricking the back of his fine brocade doublet. He had thought to run the straits with impunity after sending ingots lined with lead in his tribute chests, and now was regretting his scam. Though the meats and the wines were very fine, the Sovereign Lord of Cliffhaven was not eating. For the merchant, that sign boded ill, but the judgment awaiting him was summarily put off. The King of Pirates sprang to his feet even before Taen had completed her message. Wine sloshed in the goblets as he shoved away from the table, yelling for his captains to leave the merchant in irons, and follow him afterward to the bailey. The Dreamweaver's rapport faded as he called for the saddled horse. Shouting commands to his captains even as he gained the saddle, the Kielmark wheeled his mount with a crack of hooves and galloped for the harborside gates.

Taen relayed another of his orders; and far north, the brigantine *Shearfish* came about with a crack of canvas and steadied on a new course for Imrill Kand.

But in the end all the flurry of preparation proved useless. When the Dreamweaver turned her perception south, the demon fleet which guarded Jaric did not ply a northerly course for Shadowfane, as anticipated. Natural wariness perhaps made them shun the lands of men; their stores might be too depleted to reach the mainlands which lay between the south reaches and Felwaithe's distant shores. But far and away more likely, with the Keys to Elrinfaer taken at last, the demons intended to ply north to free the Mharg. Taen saw with bitterness that the black ships with *Callinde* in tow sailed due east, for the southwest shores of Elrinfaer. No army could be gathered there to do battle for the rescue of the Firelord's heir; those lands had been stripped of habitation since Ivain's betrayal, and Anskiere's contention with the Mharg.

Skilled as the Kielmark's captains were, they could not outsail the winds. No fleet and no fighting men, no matter how well trained, could possibly cross the Corine Sea in time to matter. Even the wizards at Mhored Kara could not help, with trackless leagues of wilderness lying between their stronghold of towers and the western sea. Beaten, cut by cruelest despair, Taen rebalanced her powers. Nothing remained but to recall the Kielmark's brave ships. Afterward, defeat like ashes in her mouth, she gathered weary resources to frame one final message. This one sapped her in more than content, twisted as it must be across barriers of space and time. Tamlin on the Isle of the Vaere was last to learn of her failure. Once the demon fleet sailed from Elrinfaer, no force in Keithland could prevent Maelgrim and his Thienz from delivering Ivainson Jaric to the Lord of Demons at Shadowfane.

↶XVII↷

Lady of the Spring

Taen's sending reached the Isle of the Vaere in the still hours before dawn, yet no shadow of night darkened the grove on the fabled isle. As always, the oak trees stood without a rustle in silvery, changeless twilight, where nary a grass blade stirred. No little man with clothing fringed with feathers and bells manifested in response to the Dreamweaver's tidings; yet the being known as Tamlin of the Vaere received word of Jaric's peril and the Keys' loss nonetheless. The extent of the damage was no sooner understood when the entity which inhabited the grove sent a second call forth into Keithland. Directed to a certain spring in the forests southeast of Elrinfaer, this was a summons of desperation; for even the Vaere could not be certain the initiate of the mysteries there would accede to the demands of necessity.

The storms in the south reaches of the Corine eventually broke, but the swell took far longer to subside. The black fleet from Shadowfane tossed on a beam reach, and the jerk as *Callinde* rolled and snapped short on her towline became torment without surcease for Jaric. Each surge of the sea fetched his limp weight against the comfortless angles of wooden ribs and floorboards. His cheek and shoulder quickly chafed raw from the pounding. He could not move to ease his misery, even to turn his head. Demons had trussed him in sailcloth and cord. They had lashed his wrists to the mast, then imprisoned his mind with ties more ruthless still. Fully aware of his battered and aching body, Ivainson Jaric was deprived of any control of his limbs. His thoughts were left free to agonize over his helplessness.

Defeat and humiliation became suffering from which no surcease existed. The Thienz sailed for Shadowfane, to deliver him alive to Lord Scait, along with the cloth sack which contained the stolen Keys to Elrinfaer. The seals over the

wards which imprisoned the Mharg now hung at the neck of a
demon; more terrible still, the critical potential for his Firelord's mastery would be enslaved, even as the Llondelei far-
seers had forewarned. Jaric cursed the wind that bellied the
black boats' sails. As *Callinde* was dragged inexorably northward, he ached for Taen, whose death at the hand of her
brother would proceed undisputed. He thought often of the
Stormwarden, whose geas of desperation had failed to bring
rescue, and whose doom in the ice now was sealed. All the
while Jaric's Thienz captors gabbled among themselves. They
praised each other for the defeat of Ivainson Firelord's heir
and they jabbed energies at his mind to taunt him. A day and a
night passed before they gave him anything to drink, and then
he suffered the indignity of rough handling as they poured
water down his throat. The demons did the same with the
food, an ill-smelling paste of raw fish that they chewed first to
soften, their poison sacs sphinctered shut to prevent contami-
nation that might inadvertently kill him. Had Jaric been left
any physical response, he would have gagged rather than
swallow; but even that reflex was denied him.

The winds held fair from the west. Spray fell full in Jaric's
face, and his hair trailed in the bilge, which unavoidably came
to reek of urine. The Thienz seemed unfazed by the stink.
They gloated, and they trimmed sails, and they checked often
to see that the towrope dragging *Callinde* and the lines binding
their prisoner did not chafe.

Day followed day in a misery of animal suffering. Nights
became a terror-ridden procession of nightmares as, over and
over, Jaric relived the destruction of Keithland as foretold by
the Llondelei dreamers. He saw Taen bleed under the knife of
her brother; Anskiere's bones became trampled by frostwargs;
and the jewel-bright scales of the Mharg flashed in sunlight
over withered acres. Other times, his captors crafted images to
torment him, of Scait Demon Lord on his throne of human
remains, and of the dank dungeons carved beneath the foundations of Shadowfane. There, most horribly, the heir of Ivain
would come into his inheritance; in mind-rending agony he
would suffer the Cycle of Fire for the vengeance of demons
against humanity. Powerless to move, unable to weep, and
denied any means of dying, Jaric endured. He burned in the
sun's harsh glare and shivered, drenched, through the squalls.
There seemed no relief, except at rare intervals when exhaustion overcame discomfort, and he slept. Then his wretched-

ness receded before a dark like the void beyond eternity.

During such a time the Thienz reached the westernmost coast of Elrinfaer, their purpose to refill depleted water casks. Jaric did not rouse when the lookout croaked from its perch in the rigging. He did not feel the short, sharp tugs as *Callinde*'s towline was snubbed short, nor the bang of sails as the black ships jibed to run before the wind. The first he knew of the landfall was the jar and the grinding scrape as *Callinde* grounded on the shoaling sands of the barrier bar. The Thienz at her steering oar responded clumsily; the heavy craft slewed sideways, and all but broached as breaking surf boomed and exploded into spray against her portside thwart. Jaric was thrown hard on his back. Impact knocked the wind from him, and his bonds jerked his arms at excruciating angles beneath his body. He could not curl to protect himself. *Callinde* rolled queasily through the trough, while the Thienz at the helm whuffed alarm and tugged to straighten the helm. Before it succeeded, a second wave hammered down. Bruised against the mast, Jaric choked helplessly on the flood of water through the bilge. Soaked and limp as flotsam, he felt Mathieson's forgiving old fishing boat swing and plow like a dolphin for the shore.

She grounded with a jolt in the shallows. Jaric lay gasping as his captors seized the towline and dragged the ungainly craft ashore. Dazzled by the glare of noon sunlight, he heard the thumps and bumps as others boarded. Soon busy, toad-fingered hands untied the lashing which secured *Callinde*'s casks. More Thienz scrabbled over the gunwales, these to stand guard while the others searched for a clean spring ashore. Jaric endured their cuffs and their kicks, his opened eyes filled with sky, and the sour, reedy smell of marshland strong in his nostrils. Flies crawled on his scabs, and mosquitoes stung his face. Swarms clouded the air around the Thienz also, but the insects seldom fed, for the demons snapped their jaws and ate them. Queasy from thirst and days of unsuitable food, Jaric wished desperately for the freedom to close his eyes voluntarily.

That moment, a shriek rent the air. The nearest of the Thienz toppled over, its limbs thrashing in agony. It crashed heavily against Jaric's leg, even as the demon standing watch in the stern snapped straight, a feathered arrow pinned through its gills. It fell without outcry, while its companions shrilled the alarm.

Jaric noticed clan markings on the arrow before cries and screams rent the air and a spear stabbed, quivering, into *Callinde*'s sternpost. Another ripped through a Thienz trying to board. More demons swarmed to replace it, jostling and shoving to launch the craft bearing their prisoner back into the sea. Arrows fell in a hail to prevent them. Thienz crashed thrashing into the salt sting of the foam, while others dove to raise the sails. More shafts sleeted among them. *Callinde* lurched. A javelin struck the deck not inches from Jaric's ear, and a stricken demon clawed him in its death throes. *Still he could not move.* That he had need to was certainty, for hill tribes on a raid against Kor's Accursed were known to slaughter with berserk fury.

Callinde slewed in the lift of an incoming wave. Jaric fetched up against the pinrail. Then the mast tipped; the boat dragged seaward, spinning, the Thienz at her helm toppled with an axe in its back. The one at the bow who fought to shear the towline died next, of a dagger thrust to the groin. Then an eldritch scream rent the air, bone-chilling for its anger. The sound cut through the minds of the demons like a knife, and those closest wailed aloud in consternation. Jaric felt the bindings upon his mind give slightly. His heart flared with hope as a feather-and-fur-clad clansman leaped *Callinde*'s thwart. Then the boy's view was eclipsed by the head of the Thienz elder who commanded the fleet of black boats. An arrow transfixed its forearm; blood twined channels through its creased flesh, and its eyes were dark with pain, but its hands were vengefully strong as it tugged Ivainson upright by the hair.

'*Die in torment, Firelord's heir.*' Gills gaped red as wounds beneath its jowls as it opened its mouth. The venom sacs behind its foretongue discharged as it bit, sinking needle fangs into its victim's shoulder.

Jaric did not see the axe blow that severed the attacking Thienz' neck. His mind exploded in a haze of anguish. The poison racked him, each tear in his flesh a heated rivet of agony; and whether the fetters of demons still bound him became immaterial. He lacked recourse to recoil or even to scream. Riven through with suffering, he received the impression of a hillman bending over him with a scarlet axe. He tried to warn, to beg that the Keys to Elrinfaer be sought out and recovered from the hands of the demons who had stolen, all for the ruinous release of the Mharg. But words would not come. The sky and *Callinde* overturned, pitched him headlong into pain.

Sounds receded, overlaid by a roar like surf. Jaric knew vertigo, then the bitter tang of salt on his tongue. Somewhere an ancient, wrinkled crone lay dying. The vision of her body lying crumpled in white sand was imprinted sharp as sorrow through his torment. Almost he could count the knots in the interlaced leather of her garment; but why he saw the death of a hilltribe's seeress remained a mystery. His skin went from fire to ice to fire again, and his breathing seemed to rock the earth. Then came a jolt, and he saw clearly, a flat gray vista of swamp reeds and scum-caked pools. The feathered heads of the bullrushes seemed to advance upon him, twisted and tossed by wind that made no sound. Seed tips brushed his bitten shoulder and agony flamed from the contact. Darkness flooded his vision. His mouth went bitter and dry as ash, and his feet seemed to float. Taen, he thought, but her image ran like wax in his mind. For a very long time he knew nothing but the jumbled dreams of delirium, boats that sailed over blood-dark seas, and the grinding crash of masonry as the towers of Landfast were falling, falling, blasted to rubble in flames raised by sorcery.

In time the dream changed texture. Dry heat gave way to darkness and moisture, and a grinding, tumbling roar filled Jaric's ears. Behind that endless, rolling crescendo of sound he heard the treble clang of hand cymbals and chanting. The words were not intelligible, but by the inflection, Ivain's heir knew. The speakers mourned the devastation of Keithland. Where the cities had stood, curtains of red light were falling, falling into absolute dark where Mharg-wings knifed like razors . . . and though his guilt could never be absolved, in time he realized that the sound, and the ritual, and the plummeting curtain of illumination at least were real.

He lay on his side in a place that smelled of moss and cured fur. His limbs were unresponsive as dead meat, and his shoulder throbbed beneath the weight of an herb compress. Though his head swam with dizziness, Jaric determined that he lay in a cavern recessed behind a waterfall. The cascade roared and shattered into fine rainbows of spray not three yards from him, and on his other side a coal brazier spattered highlights like jeweled fire over walls of natural stone. The chanting swelled and receded, changeless as breaking surf; somewhere in the background a woman keened in grief. Jaric fought to control his muddled thoughts. Powerless to stop the flight of the Mharg and reverse Keithland's doom, powerless even to prevent the tears which traced his cheeks, he watched the falls and wondered why, if life elsewhere were ending, his own wretched existence continued.

A sonorous voice interrupted from the shadows at his back. "The sorrows of the grievers are not yours, Keeper of the Keys."

Had paralysis not shackled his reflexes, Jaric would have flinched at the name given him by Llondelei. Yet not even his eyelashes flicked. Helplessness forced him to think, and analyze, and finally determine that the speech was heavily accented, not stilted with images as a demon's would have been.

The Firelord's heir labored through pain to understand more, when the speaker gently qualified. "The lament is for the ones who fell to Thienz-*cien* on the shores of the great sea, and under blessing of the Presence you lie in the Sanctuary at Cael's Falls."

Jaric knew a spinning moment of vertigo. Disoriented and hurting from the after effects of Thienz venom, he tried vainly to move, to turn and face the unseen speaker. His experience at Tierl Enneth and the treatises in the archives of the Landfast priesthood offered scant understanding of hilltribes' culture, but this much he knew: the Lady who kept the Sanctuary at Cael's Falls was word and law among the clans. Her will was supreme over all other seeresses and chieftains throughout Keithland. On a whim she could order him killed.

But struggle did nothing to alleviate the Firelord's heir's distress. At his back, the speaker uttered a phrase in clan dialect, and a person left the cavern with a soft rustle of leather. Jaric felt shadow chill his body as someone else passed between his pallet and the brazier. Then light and warmth returned and only the crash of the falls remained.

A hand touched his shoulder. He could not recoil or protest, even as the fingers gripped and pulled him inexorably onto his back. Then he did break into a cold sweat, for he had expected the wrinkled crone from the Llondelei dreaming of Anskiere's past. Instead, the Lady of the Spring at Cael's Falls was a girl with russet hair braided and coiled back from a waiflike face. Her age might have been twelve. The ceremony of her initiation had to have been recent, for her eyes were swathed in cloths that smelled strongly of healer's unguents.

Her touch upon his flesh was unsteady. No doubt she still felt the ache of the knife which had taken her sight.

"The Lady of the Spring died on the strands with the others," she murmured, as if her mind tracked his thoughts. Once again he recalled the crone he had dreamed, her bone-thin face outlined in a wreath of dry seaweed.

The child bending over him qualified with a reproach that stung. "I am her appointed successor."

Her words seemed to shimmer with reflections: of knowledge withheld, and sorrows laid bare. Called to account for his delays at Landfast, Jaric thought of Taen, and then, sharply, of peril and his own helplessness. Again he tried to move, only to lose himself impotently in vertigo left by the Thienz venom. The falls hurtled around him, the churning maelstrom of their waters a sound like the grind of the wheels of fate. Turning, they would crush him, and Keithland would burn. . . .

The seeress stiffened. She snatched her hand from his shoulder and uttered a phrase in dialect, her tone all ice and hostility. Young she might be, but the power at her command was shatteringly evident. Jaric's delirium cleared before a surge of raw fear.

Energies he did not understand tingled across his skin. The seeress arose. She whirled, and the knot-worked leather of her garments fanned a chill over him even as the embers in the brazier flared white-orange. Hallucinations touched off by the poisons made her shadow seem to caper as she strode to the back of the cavern. Drapes hung there, fashioned of woven cloth, and sewn with pearl chipped from the shells of river mussels. The clan seeress whipped these back and cried out in a pure, singing tone that shivered the air like a bell. An ache suffused Jaric's bones; uncertain whether this was an effect of his sickness, or the resonance of unknown powers, he fought for breath. Black patches danced before his eyes. Through them he saw a slab as black as a pool under starless night. Intricate patterns were worked in gold upon its surface, concentric circles with interconnecting whorls that dazzled and confused the eye. Silhouetted like a spider on a web, the seeress sank to her knees. Like one tranced she raised her hands and touched the disc at the very center. No visible phenomenon resulted, yet Jaric felt a force vibrate upon the air. Unseen energies whined along his nerves, and the hair prickled at the base of his neck.

The sensation ceased when the seeress lowered her arms. As she broke contact with the slab she staggered slightly. Small and suddenly very frail, she dragged the curtains closed and then sank down until her cheek rested against the stone of the cavern floor. "You shall have help," she murmured to Jaric. "By the life of my people, I swear you shall be cured."

The bandages over her eyes seemed to run red, accusing him of crimes and suffering beyond hope of redemption. Whether this, too, was an illusion born of delirium, the heir of Ivain could not say. The thunder of the falls swelled around him until he screamed and toppled backward into night.

He roused choking, the bitter taste of herbs on his tongue. Someone supported his head; horny calluses dug into his cheek, and guttural voices spoke above a white, never-ending hiss of sound. Jaric felt the cold rim of a cup pressed to his lips. Stinging liquid filled his mouth, and he coughed and turned feebly aside.

"Ciengarde!" The exclamation had an acid inflection; and though the language was strange, Jaric understood. They called him by his name, the same name spoken by another seeress at midsummer, under the shadow of the ruins at Tierl Enneth.

"Demonbane!" called the voice again, compelling. "Drink of the elixir and live."

Again his mouth was poured full of liquid. The taste was acrid. Jaric swallowed and drew a gasping breath. His chest ached. He wanted, terribly, to run, but his legs were beyond feeling. The hands shook him, pinching him cruelly.

"Ciengarde, answer! Resume the burden of your fate."

Weakness washed through him. Aware Taen's life depended upon his reply, Jaric struggled, snatched air into lungs that were racked like a drowning man's. But his tongue would shape no sound.

His eyes filled, and he wept. As if his tears were a catalyst, he saw the ancient predecessor of the seeress. Robed in knotted black, her crabbed hand raised and pointing, she spoke no word. Yet her accusation struck Jaric like a blow. Each hour he had dallied at Landfast had engendered tragedy; the life of the boy recovered from demons on the southwest shores of Elfrinfaer had been measured and bought in blood.

No. But even in recoil, Jaric could not escape the will which summoned him.

The fingers that gripped his body tightened their hold without pity, and the living seeress's command rang out like a whiplash. *"Ciengarde!"* his hard-won core of conviction transformed to a stinging agony of guilt. "Answer!"

Jaric flinched. The seeress's hand moved as if to slap him, even as a mother might reprimand a stubborn son. Such presumption of authority moved the Firelord's heir to rage. Air dragged like sand across his lacerated throat. "I am here."

His words seemed to fall into a pool of blackness. The restraint loosened from his limbs. He sank, utterly spent, into drowsy warmth.

"He will live," someone pronounced in a girlish treble, while the roar of the falls hammered into echoes that swallowed light.

He woke next to daylight and the faintly rancid scent of the white bear pelt that covered him. Even the softness of the fur seemed harsh against his flesh, and the hand and wrist lying crossed over his chest flared an angry, congested red. There were scabs left from the ropes. Jaric closed his eyes, listening to the tumble of Cael's Falls. He smelled the moisture upon the air, a sweetness not unlike rain-washed moss, and he thought of Taen's laughter. Then memory returned, of a tavern, and too much wine, and a shame that cut to contemplate. He tried to close the fingers of the hand that lay upon the coverlet, his left, which he had lain upon through the long days of his captivity. A blaze of pain answered. But the fingers quivered, and slowly, ever so torturously, closed into a fist.

Jaric felt sweat drip down his temples. He gasped in shallow breaths and tried to move the other hand, the one he could not see, the one attached to the shoulder the demon had bitten.

"Ach! No!" And without warning, the female who had chastised him reached out and pulled his hair.

Jaric opened his eyes. The seeress of Cael's Falls bent over him, the bandages over her face replaced by a veil of woven straw. Through the chinks he glimpsed blind, scarred tissue, and a girlishly vexed frown; then the seeress turned and called to someone else beyond his view. An attendant wearing deer-hides arrived and fussed with the dressings on his shoulder. By the ungentle twists and tugs of the older woman's hands, the heir of Ivain Firelord understood that his efforts to move had knocked his poultices awry, and that his healers were mightily displeased.

Jaric struggled to turn his head. "How long?" he whispered, unable to manage more.

But as always, the seeress anticipated him. "The days number ten and six that the Presence has guarded your spirit."

The news struck hard, now that hope had been reborn. Jaric forced air into his lungs and attempted to inquire of the Keys to Elrinfaer. Words grated painfully in his throat. "Tell me—"

Yet before he managed more the seeress turned away. She knew what he would ask, and more plainly than words the line of her back indicated an unwillingness to answer. Jaric persisted. With a wrenching effort of will he raised his left hand and hooked her garment. "Please."

The touch was a breach of etiquette. The attendant sucked air through her teeth with a hiss; in shocked reaction she grasped his wrist and snatched back his offending hand. Incensed, the seeress spun like a cat and faced him. Only the trembling lip that showed beneath her veil reminded that she was but a girl, alone and frightened as he. "When you are stronger, she that the Presence names Dreamweaver to Keithland will reveal those things you must know."

Jaric subsided against the firs, white-faced. Taen apparently was safe; but for how long? And what in Keithland had become of his trust to Anskiere, that he must wait to hear? But no further questions were possible, for the seeress turned stiffly and left his presence.

The attendant remained, fussing over his dressings. She accompanied her ministrations with scolding clicks of her tongue, until, provoked to rebellion, Jaric sought clumsily to muffle his ears with the furs.

The attendant prevented him, allowing his dignity less regard than the bother of a swarming gnat. "Lie still." And she finished with an epithet in clan dialect.

Jaric ripped out a protest. "I never asked for help."

His obliqueness required no definition. The hillwoman stopped, lightless black eyes fixed on his face. Her back was stiff, and her muscled shoulders scarred from what looked like an injury inflicted by antlers. She answered finally, in a stilted, broken accent. "The Lady is never asked. She acts only by the will of the Presence."

"And never questions," Jaric whispered, for even so small an outburst had left him limp.

The clanswoman bent brusquely to her bandaging. "To question is to die, *Ciengarde*."

Angry, debilitated, and faint with pain and worry, Ivainson Jaric turned his face to the falls. When at last the seeress's attendant finished dressing his shoulder, he hardened his will with determination, then struggled to flex his legs.

The attempt served only to tire him. Hot with fever, he tumbled into dreams that rang with the powers of the Presence. He saw torches, a circle of leather-clad clansfolk who chanted laments for the dead. The deceased presented in state at their feet lay covered with dark cloth, sewn and knotted with abalone into the sigil of the seeress. Except this Lady's hair was not aged and white, but auburn; neither were her bared features those of a girl. The tribes of Cael's Falls mourned a grown woman. In flickering flame-light, Jaric observed that the leather ceremonial mask which covered her blindness was stained dark with new blood, the ritual of initiation itself the cause of untimely death.

Beside the bier stood a girl-child who might once have been sister, or daughter, or niece, but who now bore the mark of successor. She was robed without ornament in white fleece. Her feet were bare, and hair of matching auburn blew unbound in the wind. She lowered a torch with trembling hands. As she touched the ceremonial shroud of her predecessor into flame, her eyes remained vivid and steady. Through the closing rites of the ceremony, while the flesh of her kinswoman burned, she neither shrank nor wept.

Fire obliterated the scene, then smoke smothered flame into shadows.

"To question is to die, Ciengarde," cried the voice of recent memory.

Jaric sweated on his bed of furs. The dark closed over his mind like a pool, and somewhere a very young girl screamed once in terrible agony.

Soon after, the vision lost coherence. Jaric tossed, adrift in a half trance between waking and sleep. Dimly he was aware of hands that raised him up, forced broth between his locked teeth. Once, when the falls danced white-etched in the lightning of a late-season storm, he sensed the seeress at his side, the Sight she had gained in place of vision trained intently on his face.

His lips shaped speech with great difficulty. "Was that your sister, or mother, who failed the old one's legacy?"

The Lady gave no answer.

Jaric drew a ragged breath. Though uncertain whether the storm-lit figure was a dream, an apparition, or a delusion born of strong drugs and poison, he persisted. "Someone close to you died. If you suffered the old one's inheritance in her stead, and my actions are to blame, I am sorry."

The hill priestess stirred, the sigh of her knot-worked robes all but lost in the rush of the falls. "Power cannot bend to sorrow, *Ciengarde*."

Jaric wrestled for strength to sit, but fingers reached out and bore him down. His helplessness that moment became a torment worse than pain. "Is threat to Landfast, to Keithland, to every living tribe under your protection not cause enough? Lady, I must know. What became of the Keys to Elrinfaer?"

His plea met implacable silence. Whether out of pique, or the inborn distrust of her kind, the seeress departed without reply. Dreams closed once more over the mind of Ivainson Jaric.

When next he awakened, he remembered, and did not ask again. Hillfolk came and went, tending his daily needs and changing his fouled dressings. The wounds in his shoulder gradually ceased to fester, and his intervals of delirium receded before increasing hours of lucidity. Yet the crippling weakness lingered. Jaric lay all but motionless, his senses filled with the crash and tumble of falling water. Two thoughts turned in his mind: had he claimed his inheritance sooner, his present suffering might have been avoided; since he had not, in his frailty only one argument remained that could force the seeress to break silence.

For all his determination, a week passed before he was able to try. Even then, he had to wait for the brief interval when the eldest of several healers assigned to watch over him fell asleep. At the first of her wispy snores, Jaric rolled on his good side. He tossed off the suffocating furs. The Thienz venom had left him devastatingly weak; the slightest movement left him breathless, his forehead slick with sweat. Still he drove himself, quivering, to his knees. There he paused, while dizziness sucked at his balance. He waited, eyes closed, for the vertigo to subside, which took a fearfully long time.

Perspiration cooled on his body and made him shake. Jaric

bit his lip, forced his unwilling limbs to bear weight. The grotto wall lay barely two paces away, yet he reached it gasping as if he had run an endurance race. The curtains of the falls tumbled not an arm span distant. Backlit by moonlight, the water shimmered like faery silver, elusive and cold and forbidden. Jaric dragged himself upright against the stone and inched his way to the ledge.

Spray showered over him like needles of ice. Jaric licked his lips for the clean, wild taste of it. His knees were trembling. Beyond his feet the water poured in thunderous, down-sweeping torrents into darkness. Defying vertigo, Jaric watched droplets bounce off his toes and whirl unseen over the brink. A mapping text read long ago in the Kielmark's library claimed Cael's Falls dropped three hundred feet into a cauldron carved into rock. A second, newer work claimed the drop to be triple that. With a scholar's curiosity, Jaric wondered which was true.

A sharp intake of breath cut short his reverie. Rough hands caught him back from the ledge, and he toppled in a heap at the feet of the Lady of the Spring. She wore no veil. Half-healed blind eyes seemed to sear him with reproach.

"*Ciengarde*": the word pure anger at his recklessness; had he fallen, the future of humanity would have found oblivion with him.

"Tell me what I need to know," demanded Jaric, though he had spent all his strength, and that moment could barely manage speech.

The seeress stamped her foot. Attendants rushed into the grotto, and at her command, they half carried, half dragged Jaric back to his furs.

When he woke the next morning, a pair of clan warriors armed with axes stood guard at his feet. Humiliated, and wretchedly infuriated by his failure, Jaric shouted out loud to the seeress, who was not present, but who most assuredly was listening. "Am I a prisoner, then?"

Yet when she answered his challenge, he started, for the roar of the falls had masked her approach. "No prisoner, *Ciengarde*, except to the fate which binds you." She stepped into view from the shadows behind his head, black-clad, and looking nothing like the child she actually was. Rooted in total acceptance of the powers which had torn her from youth, her poise was an embarrassment. Solemnly she extended his sword; knotted around the cross guard were the thongs of a familiar leather bag, darkened now with bloodstains. With a gesture of newfound respect, the seeress added, "No prisoner, son of Ivain Firelord. Never that."

Driven by a wild surge of relief, Jaric reached for the weapon. He had been sixteen when he learned of his inheritance; seventeen when he assumed Anskiere's geas. Now, at eighteen, he had seen the greatest of his responsibilities ceded to the judgment of a twelve-year-old child whose courage left him disgraced. Jaric forced himself not to buckle. The weight of the steel bore down upon him and emphasized how thoroughly the Thienz venom had devastated his vitality. He let the cold length of the blade settle across his chest, then, with fingers that trembled, fumbled and felt the hard edges of Anskiere's basalt block. The Keys to Elrinfaer had been recovered. Drained with release, Jaric gripped the sword and its burden of wards until his hands went white. "Thank you, Lady," he managed at last in a whisper.

The seeress watched with impassive, stony silence, as if a weight of sorrow measured her gift. Unmanned and desperate under the intensity of her gaze, and humbled by a debt he could not express, Jaric turned his face into the furs. She left finally without speaking, but the guards at his feet remained.

Another week passed. The days all dawned gray behind the tumbling cataract of Cael's Falls. Jaric labored at lifting his sword. Then as his hand began to steady, he tentatively attempted forms, while his guards commented in grunts upon his progress. Betweentimes they played at knucklebones, and for Jaric the rattle of the game pieces seemed to keep time to his pain. In time his persistence must have earned the clansmen's approval, for when the healers came to change the dressings on his shoulder, or feed him, or perform other less agreeable tasks, his guards offered him privacy by turning their backs. Night and day Jaric fought to recover the health the Thienz venom had sapped. Gradually his tissues began to heal; his pallor left him first, and then the debilitating tremble. Dexterity returned, and slowly, grudgingly, balance and the beginnings of strength. In time, steadied between the shoulders of the warriors, he was permitted to stand, and then with difficulty to walk.

The moment he could cross the chamber unassisted, he demanded access to *Callinde*. The seeress denied him, until, by words and vehement gestures sketched upon the air, he made her understand that two fortnights' neglect should not be stretched out into three. His boat had fared poorly as a Thienz prize; ripped sails and rotted cordage might delay his sailing as surely as a relapse, and the demon hunters from Shadowfane would not wait to allow repairs.

Yet five more days passed before the priestess granted grudging consent. Jaric arose on the following morning and neatly rolled up his furs. He donned his cleaned and mended clothes, and buckled on his sword. The two warriors assigned to attend him were barely old enough for beards. They flanked his steps as he left the seeress's grotto and made his way down a passage whose left-hand partition was a perpetual curtain of water. The stone underfoot was glazed with damp, polished smooth by centuries of erosion. The wall on the right bore paintings of Kor's fall, and scenes of beast hunts and rituals whose meanings Jaric could only wonder upon. At last the corridor gave onto a ledge, and he stepped out into sunshine for the first time in thirty-seven days.

The dazzle of reflection off the falls seared his vision. Blinking until his eyes could adjust, his shoulder pressed to the cliff face for support, Jaric made out a series of wooden rungs slotted into notches in the stone. The breeze smelled of balsam and leaf mold, woodsy scents familiar from Seitforest. Below, the falls roared and spattered off jutting shoulders of granite, to dash into lace-fine drifts of spume in a cauldron far, far beneath. To a sailor's eye, the second of the texts had listed the distance more accurately. Jaric swallowed, sweating to recall the time he had stood swaying on that brink, and the seeress's just anger in the moment she pulled him back.

Behind him a warrior spoke in dialect, asking whether he was afraid of heights. Jaric shook his head. Below, like a model made of matchsticks, lay a scattering of huts and gardens, and the inevitable beaten circle of earth where wagons and teams of horses were picketed. Cael's Falls was a shrine rather than a settlement. Tribes came to consult their seer, or to leave offerings of food and fur for the staff who remained in her service. Beyond lay forests broken by pale marshlands and the russet basins of reed pools baked dry by late summer heat.

"How far is the sea?" Jaric inquired, in what stilted bits of dialect he had managed to master during convalescence.

The warrior in front of him grinned, his teeth very white against his weather-tanned face. "Follow."

Never certain whether the oblique answers of hillmen were the result of his poor pronunciation, or the perverse reticence

of their kind, Jaric made his way down the ledge toward the
rungs. The drop beneath was sheer. Not at all sure his strength
would last the descent, he swung his weight out, over air, and
laboriously started down.

There were alcoves with railings where climbers could
pause and rest. Curled panting and sweating into the topmost
of these, Jaric cursed his Thienz-weakened body while the
warriors who accompanied him lounged upon the rungs above
and below, laughing at a joke between themselves. Long before the ache in his muscles subsided, the Firelord's heir
forced himself to his feet. He finished the climb this time
without stopping, though the effort half killed him. He collapsed in a heap by the pool at the bottom, whooping air into
taxed lungs. The fingers of both hands spasmed uncontrolla-
bly, and his vision spun.

"A fool for courage, you are," said one of the warriors, but
whether he spoke out in mockery or disgust, Jaric never knew.
The next instant he was scooped up in sinewed arms. Struggling not to inhale the ornamental feathers which trailed from
his bearer's wristbands, he felt himself deposited on the
withies of a skin boat. The floor tilted crazily as the second
clansman stepped aboard and shoved off. Then the current
snatched the frail craft from the bank.

Whirled dizzy, and further disoriented by a spinning view
of sky and wind-tossed treetops, Jaric fought an unseamanlike
urge to be sick. In time he recovered enough to notice the
warriors paddling furiously, spray and sweat lending a patina
to their bronze skins. The roar of the falls receded, replaced in
time by another thunder as the coracle jounced and skated
over the cross-currents of a rapid. Jaric managed, between
dousings, to sit up. "How far is the sea?"

"Not far, *Ciengarde*," assured the warrior in the stern. He
nodded forward.

Jaric turned to look as the coracle ducked and shot like a
pinched melon seed into shallows. He raised himself to the
gunwale in time to see a wall of dry reeds coming straight for
his face. He yelped, ducked, and managed not to fall out as
the coracle rammed and braked to a stop in an explosion of
cattail down.

The warriors slapped their knees and laughed. Then, amid
a confusion of gestures, they thrust broken reed stems into
Jaric's hands and drew lots to determine who should drag the
mired craft free.

The loser claimed his reed was a liar. Half in frustration, and half carried away by the exhilaration of the first freedom he had known in weeks, Jaric leaped the thwart to do the job himself. He no sooner touched bottom when he sank to his waist in brown muck.

The warriors stared at him, suddenly silent. Then the nearer one spoke. *"Ciengarde,* we usually use the pole wedged under the seat for this labor."

"Oh, Kor's Fires," exclaimed Jaric. "Did your seeress tell you I'd perish at the touch of a little water?" And he shoved the coracle so hard that both of his escorts overbalanced and fell with a smack into the brackish water of the reed bed.

They came up spitting mud, reeds pinched in the soaked draggle of their skin garments.

"How far is the sea?" Jaric demanded.

"Oh, very close," said the nearest, and with a wicked gleam in his eyes, flipped the coracle back and keeled him over full length in the swamp.

ᏀᎧ XVIII ᏀᎧ

Fabled Isle

The three occupants of the coracle reached the coast at noon, slapping at insects and scratching chafed patches where damp leathers had irritated their skin. By now Jaric wore one of the warrior's wristbands. The young man who had offered the gift had received in exchange the cuff torn off Ivainson's second-best shirt. Yet whatever ebullience had developed between clansmen and Firelord's heir during the coracle ride down the creek dissolved upon arrival at the estuary. The two warriors became broodingly silent from the instant they stepped ashore. While the gulls screamed and dove overhead, they sauntered onto the beach head, stripped, and without a word or a glance at Jaric, began to scour their muddy leathers clean with sand.

Left at a loss, and worn more than he cared to admit by the journey, Jaric finally searched out *Callinde*. She rested a short distance up the shoreline, beached dry above the tide mark. At first glance, little aboard her appeared amiss, but a stone's throw off her bow, between water and the ribbed detritus of weed left by the sea, lay a blackened patch in the sand. A great fire had burned there not long in the past. Abruptly Jaric felt a chill roughen his flesh.

Sand rustled beside him. He looked up to find one of the warriors at his side. "Tell me what happened," Ivainson said softly.

The clansman regarded him with expressionless eyes. "This is not a thing for telling under the daylight, *Ciengarde*."

Wind blew, stirring Jaric's hair; the plumage stitched to his tribal waistband twisted right and left against his palm. The sun overhead suddenly seemed too hot, and the air, inexpressibly icy. "Tell me," he repeated. "In the dark or the light, as *Ciengarde* I have the right to know."

The clansman bowed his head. As if signaled by the gesture, his companion down the beach shook sand from his leathers and arose. He walked still naked to his tribe fellow's side, and incongruously, Jaric realized they were brothers.

"We wait, then, for the twilight," said the elder.

Jaric nodded, and without speaking strode off to tend *Callinde*. He spent the afternoon sanding away splinters where arrows and spears had scarred her planking, and scouring the odorous stains left by half-devoured fish heads. Then he set lines and sails to rights, and mended the worn shank of a stay. In time the sky reddened. As the sun sank beneath the western rim of the sea, a high, keening wail called him from his labors. The hillmen stood upon the beach, their shadows trailing across the blackened area where fires had burned not forty days before. They sank to their knees and squatted as the last sunlight died, and Jaric joined them. The cries of the gulls faded in the air. Twilight silvered the shoreline as, in words and stilted pictures scrawled in chilly sand, the heir of Ivain Firelord learned what the tribes of Cael's Falls had sacrificed to save him.

The clansmen ended their account with a ritual song of lament. Then, unwilling to bed down in a place where blood had been shed, they arose and silently disappeared into the woods. Full dark had fallen. Jaric knelt motionless in the starlight beside the dead circle of ash. For a long time he listened to the rush and boom of incoming tide. Throughout he agonized for each and every life his reluctance had destroyed; the months he had tarried at Landfast searching for an alternative to his inheritance had been paid for by the deaths of thirty-eight men and women, and twelve children, without counting the old seeress's first successor, who had perished during her ritual of initiation.

Jaric regarded the ashes, black as a pit in the darkness. Once he would not have understood the loyalty of the clans of southwest Elrinfaer, who had answered a summons that forced days and nights of travel with little food and no sleep, all for the sake of a stranger. That children had fallen ill under the hardships, and a wife had been left by the wayside in the throes of childbirth, could not be permitted to matter. The seeress had called the clans for a cause that brooked no delay. Jaric closed his hands into fists; the time was too late for regret. So said the young clansman who had recounted the struggle on the strand, where every tribe answerable to the shrine of Cael's Falls had stood forth to challenge the Thienz. The demons had guarded the Firelord's heir in force, and the powers they exerted upon the mind were by far too dangerous for a small band of raiders. Even children were needed to preoccupy the enemy. Unless Jaric was recovered alive, Shadowfane's triumph over humanity would inevitably follow, and even a single Thienz survivor might escape with the Keys to free the Mharg.

Victory had come to the clans, but at cost. The old seeress had died breaking the hold upon Jaric's mind. Her second, surviving successor was gifted with great talent, but woefully undertrained. Much knowledge had been lost. Admitting this, the young clansman had shrugged. "The sea will wear away the strongest shoreline, but *Ciengarde* must sail if the land is to remain fertile. Can a man abjure the will of the Presence, and live?"

Jaric traced a finger through the ash that remained of the thirty-eight who had died, among them the father and the sister of the brothers who had escorted him to *Callinde*. He drew a shuddering breath, but did not weep for the young boy who later had run himself to exhaustion and death, to bring the herbs and minerals the Presence had named to the priestess, that an antidote for Thienz venom could be mixed to keep hope alive. Once the burden of such relentless sacrifice would have broken Ivainson Jaric. But not now; he had changed profoundly in the months between Landfast and his striving for the Isle of the Vaere. Now Jaric laid his palms upon gritty earth and quietly swore his oath to the dead. *Callinde* would sail at dawn.

That night, wrapped in the damp shelter of the mainsail, he dreamed of black ships, a fleet so vast that the ocean was sheared into foam by the streaming lines of wake. Wind moaned through a cabled forest of rigging, and through its dissonance, Taen's voice cried warning: Maelgrim Darkdreamer sailed with these Thienz. If Jaric was overtaken by the brother enslaved to Shadowfane, Keithland's future would be irrevocably lost. Then the voice of Taen was joined by the wails of the hilltribes' dead. And always, relentlessly, the demon ships converged upon the southwest reaches.

In the dream, Jaric hardened lines until his hands bled. He guided *Callinde*'s steering oar with hairsbreadth precision, and coaxed maximum advantage from each gust. Yet old Mathieson's boat was too clumsy. The demon fleet gained effortlessly. Enemy sails swelled and eclipsed the sky, blanketing Jaric in shadow. Somewhere he heard Taen shouting frantic instructions; but the dark smothered her words beyond all understanding.

That moment, someone kicked his ankle. Jaric started, roused, and shot upright amid a clatter of sail hanks. He blinked sweat from his eyes, breathing hard, and by the canvas that slid loose around his shoulders recalled that *Callinde* lay beached on the shore of south Elrinfaer. The seeress of Cael's Falls stood over him. Her scarred eyes were tied with a veil that streamed in the breeze like smoke; stars shimmered faintly through gauzy folds, jewels for the unseen face beneath.

"*Ciengarde, you are leaving at sunrise.*"

Startled afresh by her prescience, and wrung with the horrors left by dreams, Jaric nodded. He dragged himself warily upright and braced his weight against the back-canted shaft of the steering oar. "I must, Lady."

But the seeress had not come to deter him. "You seek the Vaere, *Ciengarde.*" Away from the echoing grotto, her voice seemed unfamiliarly thin. Yet with none of the uncertainty of the young, she raised her blowing veils and regarded him with eyes that saw no living boy but a spirit-world of mysteries.

Jaric shivered.

The seeress ignored his discomfort. As if speaking to air, she repeated a directive given her by the Presence within the shrine of Cael's Falls. Then her dispassionate recitation ceased. With the faintest rustle of gauze she lowered her veils and departed.

Jaric watched her go, a shadow against the scrolled curl of waves breaking upon the sands. In time her form merged with the black circle of ash, and she seemed to vanish from the face of the earth.

Her presence might have been a vision; Jaric regarded the lift and surge of the breakers, and the sliding, silvery rush as the backwash slid seaward to mesh with the foam of incoming waves. He wept then, not for the dead, but for the aching rebirth of hope. Without doubt the black ships and Taen's warning had been true dreaming; the Lord of the Demons had sent Maelgrim Dark-dreamer forth from Shadowfane to hunt him. But the most powerful priestess to serve the Presence had spoken from her shrine for the second time in the long memory of the clans, to grant a city-born the most significant guidance so far received from any source. It might, perhaps, be enough to thwart the Dark-dreamer and the designs of his demon masters. In terms a sailor could understand, the Lady of Cael's Falls had given Ivainson Jaric the location of the Isle of the Vaere. She had not done so for the sake of dead clansmen, nor even for the continued security of humankind. She had gifted the Firelord's heir because he had learned to embrace his destiny, fully and finally, for his own sake.

Jaric surged to his feet. He banged open the chart locker and rummaged within for a map of the seas south and to the west of the Free Isles. There and then in the starlight he made a calculation, and estimated a crossing of three weeks, provided the winds held fair. Too restless to sleep, he arose and checked *Callinde*'s stores; then, grateful for the water and provisions already laid in by the generous hands of the clansmen, he stamped on his boots. West winds tumbled the feathers on his warrior's wristband as he rigged blocks to drag *Callinde* toward the sea. Jaric set his teeth against the lingering weakness of the Thienz venom. Determined, pressured by hope and the bitterest of goals, he labored through the effort of launching.

At last, sweat-drenched and panting and ready to board, he stood in the shallows and looked back. The beach spread pale by starlight, blighted by the fire scar that had honored the bravery of thirty-eight dead. Jaric repeated their names one by one, then hauled his tired frame over *Callinde*'s high thwart. His hands trembled as he shook out canvas, and his head swam with dizziness. Slowly, painstakingly, *Callinde*'s bow swung. Her sails slapped taut to the wind. With apparent reluctance, Mathieson's ungainly craft responded to the shove of the breeze and gathered way, her wake a faint lisp over the deeper boom of surf.

Jaric turned his face to the sea. No longer did he sail for Taen alone, nor for the civilization so precariously preserved within the painted towers at Landfast. The wild tribes of Keithland had sacrificed loved ones for a future. To them he owed a blood debt that only the Cycle of Fire could absolve; lastly, for himself, nothing less could bring peace.

In the morning, when the two brothers assigned watch over Jaric returned to their post, they found the beach deserted. The dark, seared circle left by the fire for the slain was slashed across by the white drag mark left by *Callinde*'s keel.

The early part of the crossing passed smoothly. Mild weather lingered, and the winds blew steadily from the east.

Days, Jaric basked in the sunlight, warily watching the horizon for sails that never appeared. Nights, he thought of Taen, while the stars wheeled above *Callinde*'s masthead, and the sails flapped gently to the dance of breeze and swell. Slowly the strength sapped by the Thienz venom returned. As league after league passed under the old boat's keel, Jaric's bouts of dizziness subsided; the morning came when navigational sights no longer blurred his vision. His shoulders and back deepened with new tan, except for reddened, angry weals left by Thienz teeth in his flesh. But now the scars itched more than they ached.

When the weather finally broke and rain rolled in from the south, the Firelord's heir had regained most of his health. Though his hands blistered upon the steering oar, he did not complain, but meticulously minded his heading, and checked and rechecked the horizon. No black fleet appeared. The sea heaved gray and foam-flecked, league upon empty league. Shearwaters wove like weavers' shuttles through the warp and weft of the swell, and once a pair of dolphins came to sport in the bow wave. Jaric watched their antics with poignant longing, aware as never before how circumscribed his own freedom had become.

Callinde crossed the latitude of Islamere. Jaric celebrated by eating the last of his dried apples, for the crossing to the Isle of the Vaere was now over halfway complete. No black fleet breasted the horizon to waylay him. Sunset spattered the waters bloody bronze, while a full moon rose like a pearl on gray velvet in the east. Jaric washed his shirts and tied them to the backstay to dry. Then, soothed by the familiar flap of laundry, the slap of loose reef points, and the creak and work of the hull, he settled bare-chested in his accustomed niche at the helm and waited for dark.

At midnight he awakened with the chill uncertainty that all was not well. The moon shone bright as new coin-silver overhead. *Callinde*'s decking gleamed in planes of shadow and light; no weather threatened. Each sail carried its burden of wind in perfect trim. The boat breasted the crest of a swell. The ropes bracing the steering oar creaked taut and slackened, and the yard bumped as *Callinde* dipped toward the trough, all sounds repeated a thousand times, but now their rhythm did not reassure. Jaric swept his eyes across a horizon etched white by moonlight. He saw no silhouettes of dark boats bearing down from the west. Only the sliding crosshatch of ocean waves met his search, yet for some reason that set his teeth on edge.

He rose, and started violently as a damp shirt sleeve slapped his throat. *Callinde* splashed over the crest of another swell. Jaric yanked the offending laundry down and screwed it into a ball, which he wedged beneath the aft thwart. Jumpy as a cat, he paced port and starboard, checking sheet lines as he went. Nothing required adjustment. Finally, in sharpest unease, Jaric hooked the thong at his collar and closed his fingers around the hard basalt edges of the Keys to Elrinfaer. The stone felt cold beneath the leather; and the horizon showed no change.

Demons were there nevertheless, awaiting him. Jaric sensed their presence as surely as he breathed, and that certainty threatened to suffocate him. For this encounter, his peril was tenfold greater, since the weeks he had lain ill of Thienz venom had granted Shadowfane's second fleet time to ply south. Maelgrim Dark-dreamer sailed this time to intercept him. Jaric returned to the steering oar and gripped its solid wood with hands gone slippery with sweat. He owned no sorcerer's training to defend himself. Doomed by his human frailty, he bent his head and apologized for the hilltribes' dead, and old Mathieson, and Anskiere of Elrinfaer trapped in the ice. Then, as if memory were a catalyst, the thought of the Stormwarden gave rise to a desperate expedient. Jaric reached again for the pouch at his neck. With shaking hands, he jerked the thongs open and drew forth the black-and-gold-barred length of the stormfalcon's feather. It gleamed silver-black by moonlight, seed of the most ruinous gale ever bound to a weathermage's bidding. Once that same storm had smashed a war fleet; another time Jaric had battled the edge of its violence on a hell-ridden passage from Mearren Ard to Cliffhaven. *Callinde* yet bore the scars from the batter of rampaging seas. In his hands Jaric cradled all of nature's most killing fury, conjured with the powers of the Vaere-trained he had most sworn to abhor; yet no other option remained. Here, alone, as prey of demons and the target of Maelgrim Dark-dreamer's hate, the feather and its potential for destruction offered the only weapon to hand.

Jaric dared not pause for second thoughts. If he did, cowardice would surely unman him. With a harsh, unsuppressible quiver of apprehension, he lifted the knife-keen stormfalcon's quill between his fingers, waited for a gust, and released it.

The feather skimmed away across the wave crests. Jaric watched its flight with his heart pounding, but no blue-tinged aura of force snapped into being. The weathermage's powers did not manifest to whip wind and wave to violence and storm. Agonized and uncertain, the heir of Ivain stood with his fists glued to the steering oar. Powerless to change the inevitable, he steadied to meet his fate. For Taen, for the dead clansmen of south Elrinfaer, for the sorcerer doomed to the ice, for his own integrity's sake, he must not quit until he had met his measure. *Callinde* would sail until the killing dreams of Maelgrim and his pack of Thienz manifested for the victory. Then Jaric resolved to hurl the Keys to Elrinfaer into the sea; afterward, if luck favored him, he might act swiftly enough to run his rigging knife through his heart, even as his father had before him, to spare the men of Keithland from the Firelord's powers which would assuredly ravage and destroy.

Far downwind from *Callinde's* course, the stormfalcon's feather fluttered and spun, and settled finally upon the breast of the sea. It did not sink, but drifted there, a line silvered like a pen stroke in moonlight. But to a Dreamweaver's perception, the quill appeared as a bar of etched blue, haloed with the fainter lattice of wards that held its violence in check. Only one sorcerer in Keithland could unleash the great tempest from its bonds.

Far off on Imrill Kand, Taen drew a shaking breath. Wind teased her hair from her hood and set it streaming over her cheek. She brushed the strands aside and her hand came away wet with tears. Days she had watched, agonized, while Jaric closed the distance between Elrinfaer and the demon fleet. Though he sailed to certain defeat she had dared not intervene, even to offer the boy the comfort of her awareness. If she tried any contact at all, her brother's twisted talents might sense her probe. With his pack of Thienz to augment his powers, Maelgrim could obliterate her control and, through her, strike Jaric down. But now the stormfalcon's feather and Ivainson's brazen courage offered dangerous and desperate hope.

Taen clenched her hands to still their shaking. Alone on the moon-blanched tors above the harbor, she gathered her powers as Dreamweaver and disturbed the sleep of Anskiere of Elrinfaer. For the continued survival of Keithland, she begged that he unbind the wards which curbed his most terrible gale.

* * *

Dawn failed to brighten the southeast reaches of the Corine Sea. Mantled in clouds and sooty darkness, wind howled and slapped down out of the north. *Callinde*'s spanker banged over into a jibe with such force that her hull keeled and pitched Jaric off his feet. He fetched up against the sail locker, knocked breathless, while the steering oar wrenched loose, and two tons of antique fishing boat wallowed and careened through the spray. The next gust nearly swamped her.

Jaric received a dollop of seawater in the face. Spitting and coughing, he clawed through falling spray to the mast. He dared not think of bailing before he reduced sail. Already the halyards hummed, plucked by the unseen hands of the gusts. Dirty fingers of cloud streaked the sky to the northeast and waves from that quarter raised ragged crests that exploded into spindrift off the stern. Squinting against the burn of blown salt, Jaric hauled the main down in flapping disarray. The forces of Anskiere's storm had assuredly found release, for since dawn the weather had deteriorated with unnatural speed. If *Callinde* were not quickly stripped to bare poles, she would be battered to slivers.

Skinning his fingers in his haste, Jaric bundled the spanker beneath the stern seat. Forward, the jib banged and jerked in rising gusts, slamming fearful vibrations through the hull. The main yard thrashed against the mast, and the waves seethed and hissed, bearded angrily with whitecaps. Jaric wrestled the buck of the deck, and managed to furl the square main. But the jenny fouled with the head stay, and the whipping loops of her sheets had to be cut before they snapped themselves to tassels. Bruised from crashing against stray bits of tackle, Jaric stumbled aft. Water sloshed and sucked at his ankles. The curved sternpost kicked and dipped against sky as *Callinde* careened down a trough. Fighting for balance, Jaric slashed the lashings on the helm and struggled to wrestle his boat on a downwind course. Within an hour his hands were bleeding; still the waves steepened, until the bow dipped low and the surfing slide of *Callinde* threatened to punch her prow headlong into the sheer rise of the sea.

She would have to be slowed lest she pitchpole. After struggling to lash the steering oar, Jaric tore a length off the headsail and rigged a sea anchor. Though the safest course was to hang bow to and ride out the storm, he cleated his line to the sternpost. Then, shaking wet from his eyes, he braced his feet between the binnacle and the chart locker and grimly took the helm once again. If Anskiere's tempest were to founder him, he intended to go down on course for the Isle of the Vaere.

But the hours that followed became an agony of endurance more terrible than anything he could have imagined; the demands of his boat increased to a succession of critical disasters, each one of which threatened survival. The wind increased and buffeted his ears near to deafness. Seas heaped up in green, towering mountains whose heights wore spray like snow blizzards. To leave the helm under such conditions invited disaster. Yet as fittings tore loose, and lines frayed, Jaric had no choice. He lashed the oar, and relied on luck to keep his craft from broaching. Through a maelstrom of boiling foam, *Callinde* corkscrewed and thrashed, trounced like a chip in a millrace. Her mast whipped violently against her stays, stretching stout cable like taffy. Jaric looped belaying pins through and twisted up the slack in a terrified, stop-gap attempt to keep his spars aloft where they belonged. And he bailed, miserably, until his back muscles quivered with the weakness of exhaustion. If he paused, even for a minute, the weight of shipped water might founder his tiny craft.

Still the storm came on. Rain lashed down and lightning ripped the sky. Mathieson's stout planks flexed and sprung, and *Callinde*'s caulking loosened like wisps of dirty hair. Submerged to his elbows in bilge, Jaric labored on his knees to slow the leaks with oakum, then patched with old canvas when his earlier remedies failed. Above him, the compass spun like a drunk. The steering oar banged until the fittings threatened to crack, and to preserve those parts he could not replace, Jaric was forced to draw the pin and lash his rudder inboard. Tillerless now before the might of Anskiere's tempest, *Callinde* reeled her hapless way west.

Once Jaric saw a length of dark timber adrift in a snarl of cord. Through bruises and misery, and weariness that ached him to the bone, he managed a ragged laugh. At least one demon boat fared worse than he; yet if Mathieson's handiwork escaped ruin, the Dark-dreamer also might survive. Taen's brother was a sailor born; on board the pinnace from *Crow*, he had weathered this tempest once before. If Jaric were to reach the Isle of the Vaere to gain his mastery, he would still have to win past Maelgrim.

The eye of the storm passed over on the second morning, bringing a sickly, yellow-tinged sky, and a lull that left the seas sloshing and confused as the tilted contents of a witch's cauldron. Jaric seized the interval to whip *Callinde*'s sloppy stays; then he bailed, endlessly, his torn hands bound with wisps of frayed sail. He ached for sleep as the dying night plead for light. Instead he worked like a madman; by the nature of great gales, he could expect to be hammered with redoubled violence on the west side of the storm. Then the winds would reverse direction, against his desired course. Now, if the watery disc of the sun glimpsed through the clouds at noon could be trusted, the storm had driven him all but aground on the Isle of the Vaere.

A chill roughened Jaric's skin. He looked up, perturbed, and through tangles of his own hair peered at the horizon. There, after days of brute suffering and struggle against the elements, lay a sight to strike him to the heart: a black sloop sailed against a dirty drift of storm cloud. Her course bore directly for *Callinde*. Stripped by the storm of his mists and illusions, Maelgrim Dark-dreamer closed in for his conquest.

Jaric cast down his bailing scoop. Screaming denial, he lunged to unfurl the main. Yet even as his fingers pried the halyards from the cleat, he understood that such effort was hopeless. The winds had already shifted west. With her head-sail in shreds, *Callinde* could make no headway to weather. Cornered now without alternative, Jaric abandoned the sail. Left no time for recriminations, he reached with stinging fingers and jerked off the thong which hung Anskiere's wards from his neck.

The pouch was sodden, the knotted ties swollen impossibly with damp. Jaric cursed. The little air pocketed within might prevent the Keys from sinking if he cast them into the sea still wrapped. Dreading the attack which might rip his mind at any moment, Jaric reached for his rigging knife. Too frantic to agonize over failure, he slashed; and the cube of dark basalt tumbled out into his palm.

The surface of the stone was unnaturally warm to the touch. Jaric turned the Keys over, and light rinsed his face, sudden, blue-white, and blinding. The falcon device set into the face of the cube glowed with a fierce energy that waxed brighter by the second. Terrified such change might be provoked by the meddling of demons, Jaric smothered the brilliance with his hands. Contact blistered his flesh. He fell back with a cry, but the resonance in the ward stone died away, keyed to response by a force entirely separate. A flash like lightning split the air. Mast and yard and rigging jumped out, inked lines against light. The ocean gleamed bright as molten metal, and *Callinde* became consumed by a scintillating explosion of rainbows that spiraled Jaric downward into dark.

Blackness suffused the boy's senses for an unknown interval, then tore asunder as a crackling burst of energy rent the air. Sparks pocked his vision, cold-white as starfields called up by Llondian imaging. Light followed. Jaric opened his eyes to sunshine, bewildered, shaken, and now certain that the sorcery which had transformed storm-torn night into daylight was no invention of Anskiere's. The Keys to Elrinfaer were now cool in his hand. Ivainson tucked them in his shirt and gripped *Callinde*'s thwart. Tackle creaked as he straightened to view his surroundings. No sign remained of the demon fleet. His boat drifted alone upon a sea gone calm as burnished metal. No land relieved the distant edge of the sky; only an odd, silvery haze hung over the horizon. For no reason Jaric could name, the air smelled *wrong,* as if the untimely advent of day had also altered the season. The wind carried a tang of frost.

A glance at the compass showed the needle spinning in lost circles across the cardinal points of direction. Jaric checked in alarm. Denied sure means of navigation, he sought the position of the sun, and that moment discovered he was not alone.

A tiny man sat on *Callinde*'s bow. He perched on the wet wood like a toy, stiffly formal in a fawn tunic and dark brown hose. The laces of his sleeves and boot cuffs were fringed with feathers and bells. Black eyes regarded Jaric from a face nestled amid windblown tangles of hair and beard.

Jaric reached reflexively for the knife at his wrist. His hand slapped an empty sheath. Too late he recalled the dagger dropped in the moment when sorcery had ripped him from reality.

"Violence will not avail you." Bells jingled as the strange man sprang from the rail. *Callinde* failed to rock beneath his weight as he landed, and his shoulder barely topped the rim of the portside locker.

Jaric backed until the hard edge of the sternpost jabbed his spine. "Who are you?"

"Keeper of the Keys, do you not know?" The little man tilted his head, fetched a briar pipe from his pocket, and thrust the stem between his teeth. With no pause to strike a light, he blew a smoke ring in the air and vanished.

Jaric shouted in astonishment. He dashed to the mast, but found no trace of his strange visitor. Only the smoke ring remained, drifting into a smeared oval above the ripped fabric of the headsail.

"I am Tamlin, and you trespass upon the domain of the Vaere," said a sudden voice from behind.

Jaric spun. The creature stood poised on the chart locker, his wrinkled face insouciant. A fresh triplet of smoke rings drifted around his head.

Ivainson steadied shaken nerves, strove to act as if such vanishings and reappearings held no strangeness at all; but his voice betrayed uncertainty. The forces which had plucked him headlong from Maelgrim's path had been Vaerish, and the mystery of them overwhelmed. "Surely you know why I seek the fabled isle."

Tamlin gestured, his movement an indignant flurry of feathers and bells. "Fabled? You presently observe otherwise. And demons tracked you, even over water. That's trouble more grave than you know."

Aware the being he confronted would abide by no human code, Jaric answered with care. "A seeress named me the bane of demonkind."

"And well she may," said the Vaere. "But Kor's Accursed grow bold in their plot to defeat Keithland. Now, after centuries of striving, they have what they sought longest, a man with a sorcerer's potential whose loyalty they command. Maelgrim is their supreme weapon. Dare you oppose the designs of beings many times more powerful than yourself? You could die, and still save nothing."

Poised with his hands against the mast, Jaric felt his palms break into sweat. Had he traveled so far and overcome such odds, had hillfolk died to aid him in reaching this place, only to see him refused through Vaerish caprice? Shaken badly, Jaric fought through diffidence to respond. "I am the Firelord's son," he said grimly. "Gladly would I leave responsibility to another, but Ivain left no better heir than me."

Tamlin tilted his head as though waiting for the boy to qualify. But Jaric added nothing. At length the fey man raised his brows. "Very well. If you prove worthy of your father's heritage, you shall undertake the Cycle of Fire."

That moment, though the sun shone warm on his back, Jaric felt chilled to the heart.

Tamlin raised his chin. "Listen closely and follow my instructions. The weather will change. When it does, you must sail before the wind. Take no heed of your compass. If you delay, even for a fraction of an instant, your life could be forfeit." Beads, bells, and feathers jangled as the Vaere raised his arms. Without warning, he clapped his hands and vanished.

"Wait!" Not at all certain he had understood such instructions, Jaric shouted Tamlin's name.

The little man did not reappear. Almost immediately icy breezes puckered the sea. Caught with his spanker snarled and his jib in ribbons from the storm, Jaric leaped and freed his last functional sail. *Callinde*'s square main unfurled from the yardarm; fortunately the boat required no other canvas for a downwind course. Yet as the boy moved to set the sheets, he frowned in puzzlement, for what weather he received came from no fixed direction; the breeze ruffles on the water seemed contrary and unstable. Even as Jaric sought to decipher their patterns, lightning jagged the sky. The air went dark as ink. Wind howled astern like the roar of an angry giant. Jaric bounded aft and seized the steering oar, just as canvas cracked taut aloft. Deafened by a stupendous peal of thunder, he felt *Callinde* reel forward under the blind fury of the elements.

Jaric wrestled the helm by touch. Waves broke into whitecaps under the stern. Spray splashed his face, and wind stung his back, sharp as a midwinter gale with the scent of snow. But the boy had no chance to contemplate the inexplicable shift of seasons; whirled like a leaf in a maelstrom, he fought to steady his course. Sudden energy slashed the sky. For an instant, the air seemed to scintillate, smashed to a prismatic orchestra of color.

Then the wind died to a breath. *Callinde* rocked upright. Blocks squeaked as her canvas billowed and settled into a gentle curve from the yardarm. Jaric blinked, restored once more to sunlight. Spray-soaked and shaking, he found himself sailing under the mild warmth of spring. The ocean ahead lay empty no longer. An islet rose like an emerald amid the waves. Beaches glittered, trackless and fine as powdered marble beyond the surf, and dunes crowned with grasses lifted against darker stands of cedar. The trees themselves towered spear-shaft straight, unscathed by ocean storm or woodcutter's axe. Confronted by a shoreline so peaceful it seemed bewitched, Jaric forgot to breathe.

Surf nudged the steering oar. *Callinde* surged shoreward on the sparkling crest of a swell. Recalled to his seamanship, Jaric recovered his breath with a jerk. He cast the sheet lines free and swung the yard across the wind just as *Callinde*'s keel grated on sand. The son of Ivain caught a line and leaped the thwart. Barefoot, salt-stained, and weary, he splashed through the shallows and set foot on the Isle of the Vaere.

By its very stillness, the place intimidated; the presence of the boat seemed a blasphemous intrusion. Harried by uneasiness, Jaric immersed himself in the ordinary. With careful hands he landed *Callinde*, lowered the yard, and lashed the torn sails. While he delved among the spare lines for a block and tackle to beach his craft above the surf, Tamlin reappeared.

The little man gestured with an agitated flurry of bells. "No need for that, boy. Can't you see? The weather here never changes."

Jaric set his shoulder against the side of his boat, rope trailing from his fingers. "What about tide?"

The Vaere set his hands on his hips. "Mortal, you jest. Water and weather abide here unchanged, until the day the first riddle is answered, or unless Kor's Accursed learn the heart of Vaerish mystery."

Jaric restored the rope to the locker and reluctantly fastened the latch. *Callinde* had been the proudest possession of an aged fisherman; the boy hesitated to entrust her cherished hull to the vagaries of an enchanted isle.

Bells clashed as Tamlin stamped his foot. "Mortal fool. I am the master of space and time. Are you doubting my ability to safeguard simple timber and cloth?"

"No." Jaric ran his eye over the boat, distressed that wood and rigging should suddenly seem so frail. By the time he recovered the courage to inquire what the first riddle might be, Tamlin vanished. Not even footprints remained to mark the place where the Vaere had stood on the sand.

A mocking tinkle of bells sounded beyond the dunes. "Keeper of the Keys, no man since the founders of Keithland remembers the first riddle. But if you seek a sorcerer's mastery, you must go to the grove at the forest's center."

Jaric loosed an exasperated sigh. When Tamlin did not

reappear, he rummaged through *Callinde*'s gear until he located his boots. Then, with a shrug of resignation, he donned his footgear and hiked inland toward the dark stand of cedars.

The forest was rich with shadows after the reflective brilliance of the beach. In a single step, Jaric plunged from light into trackless tangles of undergrowth. His feet sank soundlessly into moss. The wood sheltered no wildlife; at a glance he saw that deer had never browsed the lower branches of the trees. The ground showed no trace of game trails, and since the moment he landed, the only birdsong Jaric noticed had been the sour call of sand swallows. The sole sound to disturb the stillness was the snap of sticks beneath his boots.

The gloom deepened. At first Jaric attributed the dimness to denser foliage, but as he pressed forward through the matted growth of thicket and gully, sunbeams no longer dappled the moss underfoot. Farther on, the light which filtered through the trees shone eerily silver, as if in this forest time itself stood suspended in the interval between sunset and darkness.

"I am the master of time and space," Tamlin had declared at the seaside. Unable to locate the disc of the sun, denied even the crudest means of guidance, Jaric battled uneasiness. With no visible effort, the Vaere had caused day, night, and seasons to change upon the face of the open sea. Here the boy sensed that he trod soil beyond the borders of any land known by men.

The wood grew darker. Twigs and trunks lay limned against shadow like an etching rendered in moonlight; yet no moon gleamed overhead. Jaric's step faltered. Sweating with apprehension, he thought of Taen, remembered how her eyes looked when she laughed, or badgered Corley about his quick temper. Fear of the brother left free to murder in Keithland drove Jaric forward. He crashed recklessly through the next stand of overgrowth. Light glimmered ahead, soft as summer twilight. Jaric stopped in awe, all terror forgotten. Through the black fringes of the cedars he beheld the grove of the Vaere.

Grasses spread green beneath a towering circle of oaks. Gray trunks rose like pillars in the gloom, supporting leafy crowns which arched into a vaulted ceiling overhead. Jaric stepped to the edge of the clearing. He felt springy turf give under his boots. Constellations of tiny flowers studded the ground, and the strange, silvery light seemed to blur all concept of time. Here lay the magic and the mystery of the Vaere. No man could turn back from this place; to enter the grove was to yield mortal flesh to forces which could alter the progression of nature with impunity.

Jaric crossed the boundary of the oaks with barely a pause to reflect. A stressful, tempestuous year had passed since he had fled Morbrith Keep, clinging helplessly to the mane of a stolen horse. Here for the first time he found peace, and a silence more abiding than the central shrine in Kor's cathedral at Landfast. Jaric settled himself to wait. The perfume of the flowers hung heavy upon the air. Weary from Anskiere's storm, and lulled by the changeless twilight, he sat on the grass and rested.

At first nothing happened. Jaric had time to order his thoughts, to realize at last that his safety from demons was secured. Granted reprieve from the demands of survival, he examined the guilt so recently and painfully inflicted by the seeress, whose clansmen had died for his uncertainty at Landfast. This the grove's stillness touched also. Inside the achievement of Vaerish protection, life and death became framed by a greater truth. Jaric understood that for all her far-seer's wisdom, the Lady of Cael's Falls had accused him wrongly.

Had he chosen his Firelord's inheritance without first finding himself, even had he acted in earnest duty for loved ones he longed to protect, he would have failed Tamlin's initial assessment. The Stormwarden had stated as much from his icy prison on Cliffhaven. No man could be forced to a sorcerer's mastery. A challenge as stringent as the Cycle of Fire required a whole heart and a settled mind.

Drowsy now, Jaric recalled another scene, and a half-forgotten promise of Anskiere's that he would receive his heart's desire if he succeeded in safeguarding the Keys to Elrinfaer. But the memory of the boy he had once been, and what outgrown longings might have shaped his hopes, became obscured by the vision of Taen. The last time he had seen her had been in *Moonless*'s chart room, the lantern tinting her skin with the delicacy of fine porcelain. Hair had cloaked her shoulders like starless night. Aching for the sight of her, but free now to appreciate love as a miracle separate from his happiness, Jaric pondered the words she had spoken then. *"The sanctuary towers contain keys to Kor's Sacred Fires, also answers to the riddles of eternal space and time."*

Now the boy wondered whether Vaerish mystery might be linked to the same knowledge. But weariness overwhelmed him before he could reflect. Ivainson Jaric closed his eyes. Surrendered to the enchantment of the fabled isle, he fell dreamlessly asleep, even as his father had before him.

Epilogue

Anskiere's great storm blew and raged across the southwest reaches, to spend its fury in the empty seas far south of the Free Isles. The sorcery of its binding dissipated finally, leaving swells that churned and rolled green, bearded with flotsam and frothy mats of weed. There, across leagues of empty ocean, Taen threaded her awareness in dream-search. She found no boats, only smashed spars and ripped lengths of planking, rafted together sometimes with shreds of sails and snarled tackle. The Stormwarden's tempest had ravaged the dark fleet from Shadowfane. Scavenger fish now fed on the remains of the Thienz; if Maelgrim Dark-dreamer escaped the same fate, the Dreamweaver's probe detected no trace of his presence.

At last, content, Taen withdrew. As she collapsed the net of her awareness, she sensed isolated points of energy across Keithland's isles and mainlands. Here the seeress of Cael's Falls laid flowers of thanks and offering before the spring which gave rise to her powers. North and east, the King of Pirates penned orders on Cliffhaven, recalling his captains from patrol off Felwaithe and directing them instead to attend the merchant shipping which plied the straits. And in burrows in the wilds well hidden from the eyes of men, Llondelei demons reared dumb, unenlightened cubs with one less of their far-seers' prophecies waiting for fulfillment. The heir of Ivain Firelord had safely reached haven on the Isle of the Vaere, to challenge the Cycle of Fire for his mastery.

Taen roused fully to sunlight and the inquisitive tug of a goat who sampled a taste of her hair. She shouted, laughing, and, with the mercurial energy she had always shown as a child, sprang to her feet and chased the creature back to the flock. Then she turned her face to the wind, which smelled of autumn, and started home. Shadowfane still held demons who hated and plotted, while Jaric must brave the perils of a sorcerer's passage to power. But when the winds blew fair and favorably, the daughter of an Imrill Kand fisherman would not fret upon storms that might bring ruin. Tomorrow could only come after today.

Here ends Book Two of the
Cycle of Fire

From *Shadowfane:*
Book Three of the Cycle of Fire

Available in November from Ace

Light slashed the darkness. Dazzled by an overwhelming discharge of power, the Dreamweaver glimpsed gold-barred feathers. Above her, the light-falcon which once had summoned her to the Isle of the Vaere unfolded wings that spanned the breadth of the heavens. The bird screamed. Its crested head swiveled, eyes of burning yellow surveying the army massed to kill in the valley. Jaric spoke a word. Air hissed between spread pinions; then, with awesome and terrible grace, the focused manifestation of his power sprang aloft. It swooped down upon the ranks of Anskiere's attackers, trailing a wake of crackling flame.

Maelgrim Dark-dreamer sensed the rising flux of power. Pressed by the threat raised by Jaric, his attention shifted; and in that instant, Taen cut through his block and broke free. The crippling despair lifted from her, just as the effects of the Ivainson's conjury reached the valley.

The light-falcon's flight cut the night like a blade heated red from the forge. Scalded by wind off its wings, men looked up, their shouts of alarm transformed to a chorus of terror. No weapon would avail against the unleashed projection of a Firelord's anger. Most men broke formation and fled. But maddened by the appearance of certain doom, others leveled weapons and charged vengefully upon the sorcerer who still stood vulnerable in their midst.

Yet the Stormwarden stayed his hand. Whirlwinds shrieked in check in response to Taen's plea for time to engage her dream-sense. This time Maelgrim's meddling did not cripple her. She magnified fear into a weapon, striking panic into hostile minds, until, in a rush, the last man broke and ran.

Alone in the wash of light from his staff, Anskiere damped the winds of his conjuring. Wrapped in smoke and a drifting fall of ash, he bent his head in sorrow for the dead heaped grotesquely at his feet.

On the hilltop, stillness reigned. Jaric sheathed his sword.
All expression erased from his face as he said, "We'd better
go down."

Taen sensed the emotions he held in check, even under
cover of darkness. She ached to touch him, but sympathy
could not comfort. The survivors of Corlin's army might flee
safely to town walls and their Duke; but the measure of Maelgrim's victory remained. Word of the sorcery which had un-
hinged this war host's manhood would travel the breadth of
Keithland. Folk would believe the malice of Ivain Firelord had
been reborn in his heir. Hereafter, Jaric could expect locked
doors, and welcome at no man's hearth.

Taen shared the chill of that rejection. She averted her
face, as the sacrifices forced upon a man of gentle nature
opened a wound near impossible to bear. But sorrow, even
bitterness, were reactions too costly to indulge. The crisis was
not over. Even now Maelgrim whipped up his Gierj-demons
for a second attack. Too likely this time his targeted victims
would be innocents, the women, children, and elders who
sheltered within Corlin's walls.

"The Dark-dreamer will be stopped," said Jaric, his voice a
reflection of Taen's fear. "If we have to rip down the fortress
of Morbrith to achieve it, your brother will never again wield
Gierj." Hands clenched on his sword hilt, he strode forward to
join Anskiere.

The Dreamweaver followed, bitterly silent. The rending of
Morbrith's battlements could help nothing. Maelgrim and his
demons had grown too powerful to stop by force of arms.
Only sorcery remained, and there the Vaere-trained had run
out of resource. A Dreamweaver's gifts by themselves were
not enough, and with horses the fastest means of travel, distance prevented Stormwarden and Firelord from launching an
assault in time to spare disaster.

Taen was not alone in her assessment. Ivainson reached the
boundary of a farmer's pasture and paused with his hands on
board fence. "What about the relief garrison from Corlin?
After this, we'd be fools to order an army north to Morbrith."

The Dreamweaver tried to match his restraint, and failed.
Her voice shook. "I've warned the Kielmark. The companies
raised at his command already return to their Duke. But the
King of Pirates insisted on coming himself." At Jaric's unspo-
ken protest, she shrugged. "I can ward the man's mind from
Maelgrim's Gierj more easily than I could stop him, I think."

Jaric caught her close. "Little witch," he murmured into her hair. "I'm sorry."

His clothing smelled of cinders and sweat. Pressed against him, Taen felt fine tremors wrack his body. Powerless to ease his distress, or the slightest bit of her own, she made a stilted effort at humor. "I'd rather be here than wait out the conflict at Cliffhaven. Do you suppose Corley's got a blade left that isn't sharpened down to a needle?"

Jaric raised her in his arms and perched her on top of the fence. "I doubt that. The Kielmark has steel enough in his armory to choke the channel through Mainstrait. And look, he's reached Anskiere before us."

Taen twisted around to see a broad-shouldered figure with bloodstained gauntlets striding toward the Stormwarden. The Sovereign Lord of Cliffhaven had taken charge with his usual impetuous propriety; with reins gripped in both fists, he towed four shying horses by main force over the scorched and corpse-strewn field.

"Kor," said the Dreamweaver. Strain broke at last before laughter. "Did he have to anticipate the possibility we wouldn't be mounted? Put me in the saddle again, and I swear by Kor's fires, I'll die of a fall."

"Do that and I'll jump after you." The Firelord vaulted the fence and raised his hands to lift her down. "Some things are more important to me than Keithland. Now will you walk, or because there are horses, must I drag you?"

From *Shadowfane*.
Available in November 1988.

BESTSELLING
Science Fiction
and
Fantasy

☐ 0-441-77924-7	**THE STAINLESS STEEL RAT,** Harry Harrison	$2.95
☐ 0-441-11773-2	**COUNT ZERO,** William Gibson	$3.50
☐ 0-441-16025-5	**DORSAI!,** Gordon R. Dickson	$3.50
☐ 0-441-48499-9	**LITTLE MYTH MARKER,** Robert Asprin	$3.50
☐ 0-441-87332-4	**THE WARLOCK UNLOCKED,** Christopher Stasheff	$3.50
☐ 0-441-05495-1	**BERSERKER,** Fred Saberhagen	$2.95
☐ 0-441-79977-9	**TECKLA,** Steven Brust	$2.95
☐ 0-441-58635-X	**NORBY: ROBOT FOR HIRE** (The Norby Chronicles Book II), Janet and Isaac Asimov	$2.95
☐ 0-425-10059-6	**CALLAHAN'S SECRET,** Spider Robinson	$2.95
☐ 0-441-05636-9	**BEYOND SANCTUARY,** Janet Morris	$3.50
☐ 0-441-02314-2	**A NIGHT IN THE NETHERHELLS,** Craig Shaw Gardner	$2.95